Bliss & Blunder

Victoria Gosling

—

First published in Great Britain in 2023 by
SERPENT'S TAIL
an imprint of Profile Books Ltd
29 Cloth Fair
London EC1A 7JQ
www.serpentstail.com

Copyright © Victoria Gosling, 2023

1 3 5 7 9 10 8 6 4 2

Typeset in Tramuntana Text by MacGuru Ltd
Designed by Nicky Barneby @ Barneby Ltd

Printed and bound in Great Britain by Clays Ltd, Elcograf S.p.A.

A CIP catalogue record for this book is available from the British Library.

ISBN 978 1 78816 501 3
eISBN 978 1 78283 679 7

Bliss & Blunder

——

To Abbie
and in memory of Sophie Raphaeline

... for herein may be seen noble chyvalrye, curtosye, humanytyé, frendlynesse, hardynesse, love, frendshyp, cowardyse, murdre, hate, vertue, and synne.
William Caxton, Preface to *Le Morte d'Arthur*

... know thou this, that men
Are as the time is.
King Lear, Act V, Scene iii

Prologue: Earworm

———

If stories are songs, does Time have a favourite?

... a boy ... a sword ... a stone

Is there one Time likes to drive to, windows down, radio turned up really loud?

... a lake lady ... a magician ... a land united

Which would Time play getting ready for a night on the town? Or at the end of a party when everyone's mashed, slurring their words and staggering, and there's nothing in the cups but dregs and fag ends?

... a young king ... a golden-haired queen ... a castle

What story would Time want at its wedding? At its funeral?

... a round table ... a brotherhood ... an oath

Are there stories that Time can't abide? Is there one in particular that Time can't listen to without welling up, that if played in the supermarket would make Time abandon its shopping and go stand outside in the cold, hands shaking?

... a faithless wife ... a disloyal friend ... a treasonous son

And if stories are songs, are myths earworms?

... a quest ... a grail ... a wounded king

Are myths the songs Time can't get out of its head? Like the theme tunes of cartoons watched in childhood, the ones that play on repeat in fever dreams, that jangle the nerves in the minutes before the maths exam, in the wait for the doctor in the white coat to announce the biopsy results.

> *... a grieving brother ... a flaming pyre ... a broken order*

Are myths the ones Time hears over and over again – for centuries, for millennia – in maddening snatches, making up forgotten words, inventing new ones, the melody wandering in and out of key, the tune cracked, each time different, each time familiar?

> *... a last battle ... a fatal wound ... a prophecy*

What would it take for Time to stop hearing this one?

> *... a chapel*

Is there a cure song that will banish the myth from Time's weary head, that will vanquish the earworm?

> *... an island*

What if this is the cure song? And what if it's not – just this once – about the boy?

> *... an enchantress*

One

—

Right Here, Right Now
March 2019

1

Witch in the Sky

———

The plane screams through the sky at five hundred miles an hour, moving into darkness as the sun falls away. From her window seat, Morgan stares out over the wing. Below, the clouds are grey puffs bowling through pitch-black heavens.

The worst thing that could happen has happened . . .

The worst thing that could happen has happened . . .

Since Rasha died, the line repeats itself in her head – maddeningly, relentlessly – like the marching song of a prisoner pacing back and forth in a tiny cell.

It keeps up as dinner is served from the trolleys, and then as it's cleared away and the cabin lights are dimmed. Finally, Morgan falls into a troubled sleep and when she awakes, the man in the next seat is looming over her, trying to give her a baby.

'My wife—' he says.

Morgan shakes her head. 'Absolutely not.'

'My wife is ill.' Muddled by sleep, she thinks he says something else about a bad chicken. In the gloom, she can't see his face, only the silhouette of a man with his hair on end. 'I ate it too,' he says, voice rising in horror. 'I ate it too!'

And he goes, he goes, leaving her holding the baby.

Morgan's fingers fumble for the reading light. Bathed in its golden beam, the baby winces. It's warm, heavy and surprisingly hairy, pearly of skin with thick eyelashes and downy brown hair, all wrapped up in a blanket.

'Don't worry. I shan't eat you,' Morgan whispers. The baby smiles. It has a single glistening white tooth. 'What's your job and where d'you come from? Oh, the silent type, eh?'

She's not quite sure what comes next. It's trusting of them to leave the baby with her, but then it's not like she can run away with it. Immediately, Morgan imagines carrying the baby over to the emergency exit, opening the door as per the instructions on the safety card, and launching it into the night. Morgan sees the baby falling through the darkness backed by stars, wind whipping at its tufty hair, dark serious eyes wide.

'Sorry,' Morgan whispers. She knows she's not about to throw the baby out the plane. You wouldn't even get a hand to the door before someone would stop you. But who? Her fellow passengers lie dormant beneath their blankets; Morgan hasn't seen a steward since dinner – it's what, fifteen or twenty steps?

For fuck's sake!

But the film keeps rolling: Morgan placing the baby on the floor, then reaching up to release the handle that will allow her to pull the door in, flip it on to its side and then throw it through the doorway into the sucking night, followed by the baby, although in all likelihood it would have already been vacuumed out.

In her mind's eye, she sees the baby falling again, eyes round with wonder. Rasha had wanted them to have babies.

The worst thing that could happen has happened . . .

At the airport, Morgan had lingered among the smokers and vapers, those making a final call before going inside. Just a quick call, just a few words, just in case. *I'll call you on the other side,* someone said and how she envied them. Once through security, she was surprised to find a row of silver payphones against a wall. Without meaning to, she had reached out and lifted a handset from its rest. Mouth pressed to the speaker, hand wrapped in metal coils, shoulders shaking. *I swear it . . . I swear it, Rasha . . . I'm so sorry . . . oh I'm so sorry . . .*

When she'd torn herself away, there was still an hour to go before boarding so she wandered the duty-free and then to a newsagent's where, from among the racks of magazines, Gwen's face stared out at her beneath the headline, TECH BILLIONAIRE'S WIFE IN HACKED VIDEO SCANDAL!

Morgan's business is with Arthur, not Gwen – yet how her heart lurched. She had reached out for the magazine; then, as though it would burn her, turned and hurried away.

'Ow!'

Five tiny fingers have extended themselves and are tugging on a strand of Morgan's hair. The baby gazes up at her.

What does it see? A woman with red hair. Late thirties? Early forties? Freckled hands and face. A big woman threatening to spill out of her economy seat, belt cutting into her middle. Tired, wrung out even, as though in recent weeks she's been under some kind of strain.

'How about a story, then?' Morgan asks. 'Maybe that's the answer. You start. No? Well, if I must.' She clears her throat. 'There was once this baby who fell out of a plane . . . Not that one? Bit close to the bone? Another? Right. OK.'

Morgan runs her tongue over her front teeth thinking of the storytellers she's known and remembers Professor Ragnell, holding her students captivated in the book-lined room where she gave tutorials. *Under Catherine de' Medici, Queen of France, women were not allowed to attend court – effectively excluding them from power – if their waists were greater than sixteen inches in circumference; that's forty centimetres. Think of a skinny seven-year-old child. People were smaller then, but even so it would only have been possible by means of corsetry. All too often, it's women who bind the feet, metaphorically as well as literally. Women who perform the female circumcisions. Patriarchy is a system. Its agents are everywhere. They are just as likely to be female as male . . .*

Maybe not. Her eyes flit over the cabin. Under their blankets, the other passengers look like stones, like people who've been bewitched and turned into odd-shaped stones like the ones that litter Fyfield Down above the town of Abury. She clears her throat.

'Once upon a time, baby, they tried to burn me as a witch on the middle of the school playing field. Imagine that . . .'

The baby's a good listener. Morgan's not sure how long she talks for, but there's the faintest glimmer of light on the horizon when she looks up and sees two silhouettes progressing slowly back down the aisle towards them.

'Time to wrap it up, baby. Of course, you want to know how the story ends. Well, after many, many years have passed, the girl Morgan – a woman now, of course – goes back, back to where she grew up, to Abury. Why?'

Morgan thinks for a moment – she has one card to play, only one – and lowers her voice even further to the barest whisper: 'For a birthday party, baby. For revenge. For destruction. For ruin.'

2

King Stone

———

Out the door, down the long drive, through the security gates, and then along the winding, narrow lanes into town. Abury sleeps as Arthur runs, past the closed shops and cafes, past the Green Knight, the market hall and cenotaph. He takes the steep road up to the church, lungs protesting, as night changes guard with day and the birds start singing.

By rights, he shouldn't be out here alone. Every year there's more pressure to get full-time security, but while he accepts it when he's on the road, he's still holding out against it at home, in Abury. Who'd want to hurt him here?

At the back of the graveyard, a stile leads to a chalk path that ascends across bare hillside, high up on to the downs, right up to the ridge, where the March wind gusts across the open country and tears at his shirt.

Arthur looks down at his watch, at the digital display that should show him his running stats. *Ur wife is a whore*, it reads. And there was him, thinking it was seven o'clock.

If it's not the watch, it's the fridge. *RUblind?* it asked him the other day, on the panel where it should have said 5°C.

Always some mischief or other! He wears the crown so they come at him. Every kid who fancies themselves a hacker the world over. Everything's got a computer in it these days, all of it connected to the web – to send manufacturers performance reports, provide GPS, turn up the heat so it's nice and toasty when you get home. And there's always a way in if you look hard enough. Arthur should know.

A fortnight ago someone hacked the security cameras at the house and uploaded the footage to YouTube. He's warned them: Gwen, Mo, the team, nothing on the phone, nothing on the computer that they don't want shared a million times. But for this, he's got no one to blame but his own inadequate defences.

In the leaked footage, Gwen was in the stables. She led Boxer into one of the stalls. When she came out, she stripped off her shirt and turned on the hose that they used to wash down the floors. Next – and Arthur has watched the clip just as many times as everyone else – she leaned forward and ran the stream of water over her face, then under each arm and, swinging her hair round, down the knots of her spine. She was wearing black jodhpurs, riding boots and a sports bra. As the cold water hit her skin, she narrowed her eyes and pursed her lips.

It was the privacy of the moment that was so erotic. The unguardedness. The sense of trespass. When it got its breath back, Britain had had a good laugh at the founder of its most famous Internet security company. *Zuck keeps a plaster stuck over the camera on his laptop,* Arthur wanted to shout back. *I've seen it!*

The message is still there on the watch. *Ur wife is a whore.* He resists the urge to rip it from his wrist and hurl it off the ridge, to lose it among the tufted grass and sheep tracks. Instead, he takes off again along the undulating path, chalk and flint scattering underfoot. A little further on, it joins the Ridgeway proper and he speeds up, past the Grey Wethers, towards the car park on Hackpen Hill where he'll cut down, following a loop that leads to the valley floor and back to Abury.

Already the day ahead is encroaching – so much to do, as always, and then the party too; so many guests whose names he must remember, who to thank, who to introduce to whom, those with good causes, those with deep pockets. Momentarily, regret threatens to catch and trip him up. *Why not just a piss-up at the Green Knight? Or a load of people invited over to the house? Why so flash?* He outruns it for a bit but ends up winding himself. When Lance comes along, Arthur makes his best times, even though he feels like he's running more slowly than usual. They fall into step so easily, so effortlessly, like they could run the hundred-odd miles down to the coast if they felt like it. But Lance has been MIA for a couple of weeks now.

Arthur slows to a jog, then a walk. Up ahead, there's a standing stone, fifteen feet tall and diamond shaped. It comes up out of the earth like a tooth breaking through a gum. The locals know it as King Stone, so called for the throne-like recess a few feet up.

After a second's hesitation, Arthur hops up and takes a perch. The stone is dry, porous, seeping last winter's cold. On either side of the seat there are protrusions, sort of like armrests. They used to sit in it as kids, or fight over who sat in it, or rather Kay would sit in it and poke Arthur with a stick or his boot when he tried to have his turn.

But he's no one's geeky little brother now ... Below, vast fields of wheat ripple in the wind. Here, at the King Stone, on what is his fortieth birthday, Arthur permits himself a rare and brief accounting: his empire, built from nothing; his wealth, power and influence. With a dispassionate eye, he takes their measure, and then, without really meaning to, he finds himself going over his five-year plan, and then the ten-year plan.

Of course, a small voice informs him, there have been losses – an image of Gwen, sitting on the toilet in her nightdress at the hospital, hugging a hot-water bottle, a burst blood vessel in her left eye from all the sobbing – but the important thing is they survived. The worst is behind them. They have nearly twenty years of marriage under their belts, for better or worse. For better or worse, they have Mo.

A shiver runs through him. A moment's unease, like someone who, lying in bed after checking all the doors and windows are firmly locked, is plagued by the thought that there's something they've forgotten or overlooked ...

Behind him the sound of footsteps. Arthur starts but it's only Kay. His brother doffs an imaginary hat and bows low.

'My Lord.'

Such amusement, such glee! Like he's caught Arthur vaunting himself as he once caught him pretending to shave with their dad's razor or dancing in front of the mirror. The same underlying sentiment: *Who do you think you are, you little shit?*

11

Arthur feels an ascending bubble of love for his brother. What would he do without him?

'No BFF today?' Kay rarely has a good word to say about anyone, but he nurtures a particular animus for Lance.

'What's so important I can't finish my run?'

His brother looks away, down over the sweeping fields.

'Trouble at mill.'

'Can't someone else—'

'It's a worm,' Kay says. 'A real fucker. I had them at it all night. No joy.'

'What about Galahad?'

'On their period.'

'For God's sake, Kay.'

A memory – walking through the lanes with Kay, Gwen and Morgan. When he was still the squirt of a kid brother, thirteen to Kay's seventeen. Kay was trying it on with Gwen. He stripped a sticky green bud from the shoulder of her shirt, his fingers lingering. He gave it its common name, *sweetheart*. A little later, he plucked a flower from the hedgerow and presented it to Morgan who flushed pink, like someone had switched a beacon on inside her. 'Dog rose,' Kay said. Then, 'Emphasis on the dog.'

Another memory – Kay poking his head round Arthur's bedroom door to hiss, *You're adopted!* Kay had done it every night, for years.

'When was Gal last in?'

'A couple of days.' Kay pauses. 'I called but they're not picking up.'

'And you didn't go round? Gal's the best, Kay. Better than me.' Once it would have hurt Arthur to admit it, but all that turned to awe a long time ago. Awe and then, after Gal showed him *Wasteland*, something not unlike fear.

'Their dog tried to eat my daughter.'

Well, there was that. Arthur wavers. What should come first? The worm or Gal?

As if reading his mind, Kay slings an arm around his shoulder. 'The kid will keep, Art. Let's see if you're still king, shall we? Let's see if you can still pull it off, you decrepit old fucker. Happy fortieth birthday, brother.'

And off they go to fight the fearsome worm!

3

The Girl from Crooked Soley

———

In her dressing-gown pocket, Gwen's phone dings and she snatches it free. Perhaps that's the blackmailer now, finally come to put her out of her misery. But no one's slid into her DMs demanding half a million quid (why half a mill? Because that's the amount she could conceivably hide from Arthur?). Instead, there's just a text from one of Arthur's lot, telling her to enjoy the party tonight, that she *really deserves it*.

No relief, though, only a further ratcheting up of her anxiety. Because if it's not blackmail, if it's not money the hacker's after, there's nothing to stop them posting the rest of the video. The bit that shows what happened after she turned off the hose. The bit with Lance.

Riding the surge of panic, Gwen rolls over on the sofa and screeches up the stairs for her son.

'Mo!'

No reply.

'Mo!'

Cavall, Arthur's dog, comes over and presses his muzzle into Gwen's hand.

'Not you, darling.' Gwen kisses the bone-bump on the top of his head beneath the grey fur and waits. But Mo still doesn't answer, so Gwen swings up, stuffs her feet into sheepskin boots and stomps up the stairs, trailed by Cavall whose claws clatter on the golden parquet flooring.

'It's lunchtime, Mo!'

Nothing.

'Happy eighteenth birthday, darling!'

Nothing.

'Your dad's gone into work. Something about a worm. It's just the two of us. Wake up!'

On the threshold of his room, Gwen hesitates. Mo's been known to like a bit of company. A series of horror-possibilities present themselves to her mind's eye: sixteen-year-old twins; his headmaster, the shy and happily married Mr Eddings; a yellow-eyed goat nestling coquettishly among the pillows.

She raps on the door, sighs, opens it. But Mo's bed is empty, the sheets undisturbed. Cavall wanders in to sniff in the various corners. The room is black: black walls, black sheets, black sofa, fridge, desk and speaker system. It had cheered her when Mo picked it out, such a typical teenage choice, something she, Gwen, might also have chosen had a choice been available to her. But in her case, there'd have been posters on the walls, magazines all over the floor, empty CD cases, make-up and clothes strewn everywhere, fug of oestrogen and Elnett. Mo's room is a blank, walls bare, surfaces clean; the black not a statement but the absence of one.

From his wardrobe, Gwen takes out his dinner jacket and hangs it from the curtain rail ready for tonight's party. The trousers are so long. When he came to them, he was four or five. No one knew for certain. How small he'd been. How disinterested in anything they had to offer. But she, Gwen, had won him. In her chest, a warm flicker. Her one good thing. Her one achievement.

'Well, I hope it was a bed and not a ditch, son,' she mutters.

Downstairs, she takes a tube of Pringles from the cupboard and pours them into a bowl to take back to the sofa. 'Lunch is served, milady!'

The old part of the house is nineteenth century, red brick, flint and sarsen stone, a steep-pitched slate roof; the new part, the back half, is glass and underfloor heating, repurposed ship's timbers, exposed brick and pipework. Beyond the glass, the downs spread out, a vast rolling blanket of green stitched with fences and dotted with sheep. Clouds cast shadows that scurry over the fields. Someone else might look at the view and think elevating thoughts about the glory of nature, but Gwen's a farmer's daughter and what she sees is work, never-ending work: hedging, ditching, fencing, ploughing, harrowing, seeding, fertilising, silaging, haymaking, harvesting, lambing, calving . . .

Gwen stretches out her legs. Her feet are bare, the toenails newly polished. She pictures the post it would make. Within seconds they'll want to know the colour and brand she used. Sometimes Gwen imagines Instagramming herself drinking her own urine or smearing herself with her own shit, captioning it with something upbeat about the positive health benefits to system or skin. *Will mine do or do I need yours?* someone would comment, Gwen would bet her eye teeth on it. Someone else would see it as a sign that she needs a good raping. Because what isn't? Sometimes she reads out the things the trolls write to her while Arthur tries to eat his dinner.

You're supposed to block them, not feed them, but sometimes she can't help it and she'll type some variation on the theme of *fuckofffuckofffuckoff*. Besides, they only make new accounts and come back, all the better to fawn and threaten, all the better to send dick pics or deepfake porn videos in which Gwen's face has been superimposed.

For a while there was a really creepy one, who called himself the Invisible Knight and always seemed to know what she was up to.

Arthur would prefer her to delete her account, or at least set it to private. How would he take it, Gwen wonders, if she accepted one of the many offers to start her own line of something? Five million followers. A captive market waiting to be exploited. And why should Arthur and Linnet be the only entrepreneurs in the family?

Gwen imagines herself a scent rubbed between the wrists of British maidens, Gwen wafting on the warm summer air.

Gwen a set of salad forks with one-star reviews on Google, Gwen remaindered in a warehouse . . .

Cavall, tucked in at her side, groans and stretches out a paw, sending the bowl with the last surviving crisps down on to the rug.

'Nice one, mate.'

Gwen leans down to pick them up, shoving the fallen into her mouth as she finds them with her fingertips. All of a sudden, she stops, fingers frozen. What if someone is out there now and this is the next video? What if this is the next footage of her to be streamed to millions: unwashed, covered in crisp crumbs and dog hair, cuddling Cavall in her dressing gown and eating off the floor.

Gwen lets rip a fart. 'Fuck you,' she says. 'Not you, Cavall, not you, my baby. But fuck all the rest of you.'

But underneath the defiance so much fear. *Nothing on the phone, nothing on the computer that they don't want shared a million times the world over.* That's what Arthur told them all and she took it as gospel. They have always been so careful! Not a flirty text message, not a single photograph. If she was going to meet Lance, she left her phone at home.

Yet she had forgotten about the video camera in the stables, forgotten long enough not to object when Lance lifted her up and pressed her against the wall, when he bent his beautiful head to lick the cold water from her throat as Gwen wrapped her legs around his waist.

Suddenly, she feels it keenly, the hacker's malice, knows that somewhere out of sight someone is laughing at her, relishing the thought of her squirming.

Gwen looks down blankly at her phone, at the message there. *Enjoy tonight! You really deserve it!*

Maybe she should do a post? Show the hacker they're not getting to her. Gwen shakes off the crumbs, arranges herself at her best angle, smooths her hair, hauls Cavall up till he's in shot, and snaps a few photos till she gets a good one. Then she opens the app and selects a filter to bang up the colours: yellow hair, green eyes, pink lips, grey sad-eyed hound.

Mo had started the account for her, posting a photo of her on Christmas Day asleep face down on the carpet in a paper party hat while Cavall, then a puppy, polished off her bowl of trifle. By the time she woke up, it had thirty thousand likes. Most of the comments had been from women and most had been nice. The papers always seemed to print pictures of her when she wasn't smiling.

What should the caption be? *Me and my bestie preparing for the big party!*

Gwen deletes both picture and text. Because it's true, she thinks, and he's not even her dog: he's Arthur's.

And all the horrors ambush her at once. The dress laid out on the bed upstairs that she doesn't want to wear. Her husband and son's joint birthday party that she doesn't want to go to. The people she doesn't want to see. The life she didn't choose but which is hers nonetheless. The man she desperately wants to melt herself down and pour herself over.

No word from Lance in over a week. Not a single one, and it's like having a torn nail, one that's split right down to the bed.

If she were wise, she'd go to Linnet's, drive over to Kay's wife's salon and let the girls loose on her. Linnet's always pushing; a conditioning treatment here, a syringe full of botulism there. *Pain is ugliness leaving the body, Gwen!*

Or she could go saddle up Boxer and ride over, take the grey over the downs and then pick up the cycle path, the one that leads across the motorway bridge and round the back of the reservoir.

Lance lives in an old farmworker's cottage. Weeds in the garden. A rotting Land Rover up on bricks on the drive. Gwen imagines herself slipping out of the saddle and tying Boxer up to the fence. Sheets tended to flap on Lance's washing line for days, weeks even. She'd duck between them and then let herself in through the back door. In the real, she'd have to call out his name, because you didn't surprise Lance, not since Helmand, but in the fantasy, she creeps through the house, on mouse feet.

'On your beanbag,' she whispers to Cavall, 'on your bed,' and the dog obediently gets up off the sofa and trots away to the kitchen.

Gwen slips her hand inside her dressing gown. Concentrates. Wonders briefly if there's someone out there on the downs with a long lens. *Oh, let them watch!*

In the fantasy, Lance lies on the bed, eyes closed. He's in his work clothes. No. No. Boxers and boots. Chest bare. She goes across to him, climbs on to the bed, gets a knee either side of his waist. Laces her fingers between his. Feels him start to stir. Looks down, impassive, as his eyes slide open, as his fingers grip hers.

Lance's mouth opens. She sees the pink of his tongue slip out to moisten his bottom lip. That's it. She rewinds the moment. The expression in his depthless blue eyes when he sees her. Just like that first time, that first time on her wedding day underneath the burning hawthorn torches.

His fingers tightening in hers.

       His beautiful mouth.

              His lips. Yes. Look on his lips.

                    Look . . .

                         There—

Bad Motherfucker

———

At the Green Knight, the archaeologist sees the young man talking to the barman and thinks, *a bright candle*. It's a Friday and she's been there all afternoon typing up her notes from the dig. Back to London tomorrow, to Tom and Mattie.

The day dims beyond the lattice windows. The gentle thrum of voices. Idly, she finds herself eavesdropping on the banter at the bar. The barman, whose name is Wayne, and the young man, Mo, are arguing which is bigger, John's bar bill or his belly.

'But you've not seen it, Mo. Not like I have. I caught a glimpse when Vern was doing the books and it was like a black hole. I swear it has its own gravitational field.'

'Nah, Wayne. Must be that bump you took on the head in Afghanistan. I once stood in the shadow of John's paunch and I swear it eclipsed the sun. No living creature should have to endure such darkness.'

In response, John, a white-haired old monster who seems more or less a permanent fixture at the Green Knight, roars that they are knaves, errant knaves, and then calls for another round of pints.

The archaeologist attempts to return her attention to her work.

... early Neolithic long barrow ... earthen tumulus enclosed by kerb stones ... Western variant congruent with West Kennet Long Barrow and

Wayland's Smithy ... two chambers ... human remains ... grave goods indicate a high-status individual, probably a warrior ...

Next time she raises her eyes, Mo's standing by the hearth and smiling at her. A tall young man, dark-skinned, slim as a whip, backed by flames. She smiles back without meaning to and he comes over. Wide shoulders and narrow hips, like he's just had a growth spurt. Does she know, even then?

Black jeans, black hoodie, a blue-black fall of hair. That smile again.

'Doing your homework, is it? Pint?'

She says yes. Not sure to which and he nods to Wayne, who pours out two and brings them over.

'Thanks, cuz.'

The barman – mid-thirties, dark crewcut, tattoos on both fore-arms – retreats.

'Your cousin?' She can't quite keep the note of disbelief from her voice.

Mo helps himself to a chair.

'Everyone's related round here. Just assume cousins. Step-some-things. Half-somethings. It's easier.' He indicates her laptop. 'What's it about, then?' There's a touch of West Country when he speaks. He wears a pearl in his left ear like he's Sir Francis Drake.

She tells him about the dig, about the long barrow. A farmer found it ploughing up a field, a few miles from Abury. Mo listens closely, asks her questions, thinks he might know the spot.

'You staying here?' The way he says it gives her a little jolt. The leaning in. The eye contact.

'I've got a room in the annexe.'

'For how long?'

'I'm leaving tomorrow. We're finished, for now.'

Mo gestures for another pair of pints. As the barman sets them down, she sees the tattoo on his right forearm is of a wyvern, wings spread out. Beneath it, a scroll reads *The Wessex*.

'Thanks, Wayne. Vern not back tonight?'

Wayne hesitates, then nods.

'You'll have your hands full, then.' A note of mischief. Mo's eyes move to the corner of the bar where the landlady, luscious, blonde-beehived, with slightly buck teeth, is checking in a big red-haired woman with a luggage trolley.

The pub's filling up. A couple of girls parade past, turning like swans where Mo can see them. At their age, she'd stayed in. You wouldn't have found her in a pub. Certainly wouldn't have found her with a boy like Mo. She imagines telling Tom, teasing him about her getting chatted up by a young man over pints.

They have another. Mo has snow-white snaggle-teeth. There are yellow stains to the whites of his eyes. When he suggests popping outside for a smoke, she goes along even though she's never smoked.

Beyond the pub's back door is a courtyard that looks on to the annexe, a row of six rooms that would have once been stables. For a while, they stand there in silence. Mo offers her a drag but she doesn't take it.

The Green Knight is how old? Four hundred years? Five? And probably built on the site of an earlier hostelry that would have served the drovers and merchants, the pilgrims and wanderers of England's ancient roads. Water and oats for the horses. Cake, ale and a flea-ridden bed to refresh the weary traveller.

The red-haired woman is moving about in one of the annexe rooms. As they watch, she comes to stand in the lit window and stares out. Suddenly, she lifts both hands to cover her eyes as though the darkness holds something she can't bear to see. The effect is so visceral that the archaeologist draws back, forgetting the step, and Mo has to steady her. When she looks again, the curtains have been pulled closed.

'Which room's yours?' Mo asks.

'That one.'

'You should put your laptop away before someone nicks it.'

So she does and he follows her in. When she turns around, he's sitting on the bed and he's not smiling any more. Between finger and thumb, he rolls the fabric of her nightie. It's silky, bronze-coloured, not the one she wears at home. Mattie's a drooler.

'Nice,' he says, and she knows she'll never tell Tom about him. At Mo's age, there were no boys for her, no romance, no stolen kisses. Once or twice, she'd seen boys like Mo in the street with cool girls, looking worse for wear, going somewhere she wasn't invited, and it had made her ache for days.

When he asks her to take him out to the long barrow, she opens her mouth to say no, but the girl she'd once been – the stutterer, the library-haunter – says she will.

The car is a rental, a four-wheel drive. The next day her knuckles will hurt from how tightly she grips the wheel. There's little on the roads and, once they get on to the rough dirt track that takes them into the downs, no other vehicles at all.

It's a sobering journey, as though everything she could lose is crushed in the car with them, but once they get there – leaving the car parked up by the one building for miles, a derelict-looking brick house at the foot of a small, wooded rise – the other feeling returns. The night is dark with no stars. Going over the fence, the wind comes off the downs in blasts to buffet them and Mo gallantly takes her hand.

The long barrow is in the middle of a huge field that rises to a ridge. The downs are lumpy, full of odd protrusions. It wasn't until the farmer – turning the field over from sheep grazing to barley – hit one of the sarsen megaliths with his plough that the barrow was discovered. They were lucky he hadn't covered it back up and gone on. It happened.

Earth forms clods around their feet. The moon is behind a cloud, but a little silver light falls, marking out the barrow's mouth. Darkness on darkness.

It's different here at night. She finds herself trying to remember the name for the spirit that haunts such places. Barrow wight, that's it.

Mo wants to go inside. Of course he does. Even after she's told him everything of interest – the bones, the artefacts and pottery shards – has been taken away.

'Live a little,' he says.

'I'm not sure . . .'

But when he goes in, past the tape, she follows, into the first chamber crouched over, and then into the second chamber, the one right under the hill, on her hands and knees.

Mo lights the way with the torch on his phone. Then he turns it off. If it was paint, the colour would be Ancient Black.

'Listen,' Mo says. But she can't hear anything. It's creepy, and the stone walls are wet and the air is tainted and cold. Still, when he touches her, when he kisses her, she's fever hot. For precisely as long as it lasts, she wants it more than she's ever wanted anything.

Near the end, she thinks she feels a sigh, not from him, almost as though from the hill itself.

Afterwards, she wants to get away but Mo seems inclined to linger. Outside again, he kneels down on the grass that grows over the tumulus and presses a hand to it.

'Bad motherfucker.' He sounds wry, approving.

'What do you mean?'

'Well, you don't get a monument in this country without fucking someone over, do you?' Mo still has his hand pressed to the earth. For a second, he closes his eyes. 'Bad motherfucker,' he says again.

Going back across the field, her breath's ragged. She keeps stumbling. At the car, she fumbles with the handle, but now Mo's turned his attention to the house.

'Did you see that?'

'See what?'

'A light. Look! There it is again.'

There are boards nailed over the windows, but there must be a crack in one as, from the upper floor, from the window at the front, a yellow light is winking.

Before she can say anything, Mo's disappeared off for a closer look. And he's gone for ages, absolutely ages, until she can bear it no longer and starts shouting his name.

At last, she hears his footsteps coming back.

'All right. All right. Keep your hair on.'

Once inside the car, once they're finally on the way back to Abury, he decides he wants to go to a party.

'Whose party?' She's already thinking: shower, pack up, settle the bill, get going.

'Mine and my dad's.' Mo puts a muddy foot up on the dash and sparks a cigarette. 'Not every day you turn eighteen. Or so they keep telling me.' Seeing her face, he says, 'If it makes you feel any better, I'm adopted. No one's quite sure how old I actually am. Who knows? I could be twenty-five.' A pause. 'Then again, I could be fifteen.' He's laughing at her, radiant with mischief.

'I'll drop you off.'

Mo makes a sad face. 'Callously used and tossed aside. Again.'

She follows his directions until they come to a high pair of gates that glide open as they draw near. At the end of the drive is a massive house. But the windows are darkened. There's no sign of a party.

'Wait here.'

And she does, under the glare of security lights. He seems to take an age. More than once she thinks about going, only she's not sure the gates would open for her. Who the fuck is he?

When Mo comes back, he's wearing a black shirt under a dinner jacket and humming a funny little tune. The weird thing is it's the same tune that's been going round her own head since they left the long barrow. Maybe it was playing in the pub earlier? Although she doesn't remember there being any music playing in the Green Knight.

Mo angles the rear-view mirror to have a look at himself.

'Do you think I'll do?'

'Where are we going now?'

'Alton Castle.'

She's seen the signs, brown and white, at various crossings. It used to belong to one of the families whose name runs through British history like a golden thread: the Seymours, or Howards, Beauforts or Percys. Now it's a high-end wedding and conference venue, the kind of place that holds classical-music festivals on the lawns in summer.

It's nearing ten when they arrive. After a word with Mo, a security guard lifts the barrier so they can drive in. The road leading up to the castle goes on forever. Discreet spotlights lend its towering walls a yellowy moon-glow. From the battlements, pennants are flying. It stirs in her something like a memory, but the memory of something that never happened, perhaps the memory of a dream.

'Gwen and Arthur got married here.' Gwen and Arthur? In her head, the penny begins its roll, heading for the drop. Because hadn't there been something about them adopting a child, ages ago now, some scrap of a kid from a roadside in Jakarta? Calcutta? Lima?

The car park's full and men in black are striding up and down with earpieces in.

'You can stop over there.' Mo indicates the front steps. Every window is lit up. Even with the car doors closed, she can hear the music. 'Sure you don't want to come in?' His voice is gentle again. She shakes her head. 'Well, it was very nice to meet you.'

He leans over and gives her a lingering parting kiss.

When she opens her eyes, there's a woman, a blonde woman in a shimmering silver dress who she can't help but recognise, standing on the stone steps and fixing them both with a nitrogen glare. Mo breaks into a smile and cracks the door.

'Mum!'

'What time do you call this? I said eight. You fucking prick, Mo.'

Gwen's eyes travel between the archaeologist and Mo. She doesn't look happy, but then she doesn't look exactly surprised either.

Mo gets out and bounces up the steps and he doesn't turn back. After a second, she comes to and throws the car into gear, leaping forward so the gravel spits under the wheels. At the exit, waiting for the barrier to rise, she recognises the driver of the car coming the other way; it's her fellow guest from the Green Knight, the red-haired woman.

She goes back to her room, is on the motorway home within the hour. It isn't until she hits Reading that she realises that Mo has, in fact, given her everything she wanted.

The shame, the agony, the awfulness.

He's made her feel exactly like a teenager again.

5

Choral for a Troll

—

The castle remembers being built, remembers the stonemasons, their empty-bellied apprentices, the wolfhounds lolling at the fires, growling over meatless bones.

At seven thirty p.m., the Event Coordinator gives what she hopes is a rousing speech to the floor team, reminds the DJ that – festival headliner or not – the client says he's to play requests, then moves over to where the Head of Security is finishing up his final briefing.

'And remember, absolutely no entry without digital invitation and photo ID. Everyone goes through the scanner. No exceptions. Right. I think that's everything. What do we say, lads?'

'Not on my watch!' the men chorus back.

Still, the Event Coordinator thinks, *it's unlikely there'll be any real trouble.*

The castle remembers its lords and ladies, its retinues of servants, its grooms and kitchen boys, scullery maids and cooks, its fine herb garden.

Arthur's mum Betty wants to know why, when it is now eight o'clock, and when the invite says the party starts at eight o'clock, does no one else turn up till nine?

She flicks lint from her husband's shoulder, accepts two glasses of champagne from a server and hisses, 'It's extravagant, Hector, and I know they can afford it, but we didn't bring either of them up to be wasteful.'

'Of the two of them, Kay's by far the worst,' Hector replies staunchly.

'Well, Kay's Kay and it's not easy for him. You forget that. And not naming names, but she's hardly a steadying influence.' Betty takes a sip from her glass. 'Wonder how many bottles of this will be going home in the staff's bags? Glug-glug-glug.'

She pauses to look around the vast hall, at the vaulted ceiling, the tapestries, the array of flickering candles.

'The castle looks nice, doesn't it? Not like when Arthur and Gwen got married. It was a lovely day, but it was half ruin. Freezing. I had to put my coat on during dinner. I said it at the time, and I'll say it again, the Marriott would have done just as well.'

The castle remembers music. Songs to get you through winter, songs to welcome spring. It remembers the old songs, the ones that always find their way back.

Outside on the stone steps, Kay's wife Linnet stops to admire Gwen's dress.

'Nice Wang, Gwennie. It's not? Who then?'

'Dior,' Gwen admits, 'vintage.'

'How did you get your hands on that? Cheeky bitch.'

Gwen eyes her sister-in-law's corseted black number. 'Yours?'

'This old thing? Versace. I had to lie down flat on the back seat on the way over. Can't sit in it. Kay had to haul me into it while the kids pulled in the other direction.'

Below them, cars are streaming up the long drive. A helicopter makes a landing on the helipad on the castle roof. Linnet steals a glance at Gwen's face. 'Lance coming tonight?'

'How should I know?'

A chill blast of wind blows over the steps and both women shiver. On impulse, Linnet takes Gwen's hand in hers.

'Carly would have loved tonight, wouldn't she? I can't help thinking about her. Last time I saw her was here. At the wedding.

Listen, it's a party, isn't it? Why don't we get pissed, Gwennie? Proper pissed like we used to.'

'Because you always end up fighting with Kay?'

'I don't!'

'You do!'

The castle remembers poachers taken from the dungeons and hanged in the forest. The women too.

From up in the gallery, Arthur watches his guests arriving. He jots down a mental note or two, watches his dad take advantage of Betty's turned back to scoff three mini-steak brioches, sees the crowd ripple when one of the world's richest men makes an entrance. With amusement, he spots an anxious-looking man with a bald spot stepping behind a large potted plant. *Well, we've all felt like that, at one time or other.*

Galahad materialises at his side, face like a wet weekend.

'Still no joy?'

Gal has been hunting the hacker who leaked the video, via VPN and host server, onion service, data packet, exit node.

'They got lucky.' Gal shrugs. 'There's still a chance I'll find them but it's not looking good. I'm so sorry, Arthur.'

'If it could have been done, you'd have done it.'

In the dinner jacket, Gal looks willowy, elegant even. It's a change from the generic oversized hoodies they usually wear.

Gal leans over the stone balustrade, pale hair flopping forwards.

'Is that Elon?'

'Could be. Why?'

Finally a smile.

'Because Linnet's heading straight for him.'

The castle remembers the plague. The corpses giving off the scent of hawthorn blossom.

Corks pop like fireworks. A hum rises up to the rafters. The guests mill about, plucking flutes from silver salvers, knocking back cocktails from the bar. Shoulders unstiffen, tongues loosen, inhibitions evaporating like champagne bubbles. Abury insiders rubbing shoulders with the incomers, with business leaders, founders and influencers, with politicians and celebrities and the representatives of noble endeavours, all of whom want the skinny on their host and his wife, and the Abury lot more than happy to oblige.

'... No, he's still pretty hands-on. He was in today sorting out a worm. Well, you know what a virus is? Very good, well a worm's similar, only it doesn't need a host program to replicate. Nasty bit of malware. Anyway, Arthur fixed it proper in a couple of hours. In the beginning, people said *Black Prince* was a fluke. He was what? Sixteen? People thought he got lucky. But time and time again he pulls it out the bag. Apple wanted him after Jobs kicked the bucket. He was tempted but Gwen wouldn't go. Local girl to her marrow ...'

'... They're both pretty tight-lipped so no one knows. Maybe it's medical. Maybe having Mo put them off. She dotes on him. Nothing was ever his fault. Marching up the school to complain. Quick to drop the R-bomb. He got kicked out of two. And you remember when that crack-smoking rock star came to live in the old vicarage? The one the judge banned from London? Mo was practically living there with him. Fourteen? Fifteen? Very unsavoury ...'

'... Not a pothole from here in any direction for fifty miles. Props up half the local businesses. A billion's not what it was. Running costs. Salaries and what have you. Offices. All that. He has to keep a few years of that in the tank for lean times. I'm just saying, it's not an unimaginable sum. He could have had a lot more if he floated the company, sold off some shares. No, owns it outright. A lot of investors wanted in, and he took the money when he needed it, but only as loans. He wouldn't give out shares – not even to Kay. Not even to his own brother. Because he's nice, Arthur, but he's ruthless. No designated parking spots. Big-time philanthropist. Christmas bonuses for everyone or no one, down to the cleaners. But no doubt about who's boss.'

The castle remembers a visit from the king. Its chambers decked with lavender. The goose-down mattress clothed with linen, samite, miniver.

Meanwhile, Linnet, arm in arm with a certain gentleman – white tux, itchy Twitter-finger – is explaining the lie of the land.

'So right, in that cluster there, at the bar, that's Arthur's lot, the company men. A good half are schoolfriends or players from the team, or both. Serious about football, is Arthur. Did the charity cup at Wembley that time.

'Then over there, that's the techies – programmers, engineers, developers, analysts – former hackers some of them. They say Arthur sets puzzles for them, like hacker challenges, and the really good ones he invites to work for him. Lots of foreign. American, Indonesian, Brazilian, you name it. They don't tend to hang about too long. Abury's not for everyone. No, not many women. Fuss about it.

'And that's Perce, Trist, Lionel and Bors. And that's Garlon. Best buds with my Kay. Those five are all pretty high up in the company, been there since the beginning, always jostling with one another to be top dog. Bors just got made CFO so the others aren't talking to him.

'Oh, and see that one, young one with the white hair, well near as white, that's Galahad, supposed to be the best there is. Good as Arthur, better maybe. No trying to poach them, now!'

Linnet cocks an ear. 'Hang on! Isn't that your song that's playing?' She giggles and tightens her grip on his arm. 'You know, Elon – can I call you Elon? – I just want to say that I for one have never doubted your vibe.'

𝔗𝔥𝔢 𝔠𝔞𝔰𝔱𝔩𝔢 𝔯𝔢𝔪𝔢𝔪𝔟𝔢𝔯𝔰 𝔡𝔢𝔢𝔭 𝔡𝔯𝔦𝔣𝔱𝔰 𝔬𝔣 𝔰𝔫𝔬𝔴, 𝔰𝔥𝔢𝔢𝔭 𝔣𝔯𝔬𝔷𝔢𝔫 𝔱𝔬 𝔱𝔥𝔢 𝔟𝔬𝔫𝔢, 𝔱𝔥𝔢 𝔟𝔦𝔯𝔡𝔰 𝔣𝔞𝔩𝔩𝔦𝔫𝔤 𝔰𝔱𝔞𝔯𝔳𝔦𝔫𝔤 𝔣𝔯𝔬𝔪 𝔱𝔥𝔢 𝔞𝔦𝔯.

Betty shakes her head in disbelief.

'No better than she ought to be. Never has been! And as for that dress ... well, nothing we haven't all seen before, I suppose!'

To her left, she catches a glimpse of Mo sauntering through the castle's great doors and her face brightens.

'Oh look, love, there's Mo! Doesn't he look smart! So handsome. Like a young Omar Sharif.'

'He doesn't look a bit like Omar Sharif!'

'He does! Well, I think he does. Mo! Mo! Come say hello to Granny and Grandpa!'

The castle remembers its lovers, long departed.

In a quiet corner, out of earshot, Lance whispers, 'Don't be like that, Gwen. Don't be like that. You know why. Because of the video. What are we going to do? I can't . . . I can't sleep. Can't think straight. I'm losing it. We haven't been careful enough. Smile, Gwen, smile like we're having a nice chat. People are watching . . .'

The castle remembers fire.

Galahad eyes the two glasses of bubbly Mo's bearing towards them.

'I don't drink, Mo.'

'Oh, don't worry,' Mo says, 'they're both for me. I'm fully legal now, remember.' A pause. 'Just in case you've been waiting for your moment.'

Gal sighs. A thought occurs to them. 'How come you and Arthur share a birthday?'

'Well, owing to mysterious origins and all that, they had to pick me one, so I got to share with Arthur. You know what the real shame is? I'll never know my true star sign. What do you think, Gal? Scorpio? Capricorn, perhaps? I'm fond of goats, although I think I'd have been what I am, Gal, had the maidenliest star twinkled— Hold up, isn't that Jeff Bezos?'

Both turn to the crowd. Everyone is here now. Everyone who was invited . . . and maybe someone who wasn't.

'What's that tune you're humming?' Gal asks after a bit.

'I didn't realise I was humming anything. Not sure. Maybe it was on the radio in the car. I was . . . I was out on the downs earlier. There was this house . . .' Mo falls silent, then he says, 'Tell me, Gal, how much do you know about keypad-operated locks?'

The castle remembers the cold drip of water on stone, a song that lasts centuries.

Of course, some people don't know when to stop, with the drinks, with the talk. Some people, perhaps enjoying the sense of holding court, raise matters best left to rest.

'The castle? They've spent millions. Some consortium or other.

31

Twenty years ago, it was a ruin. Jackdaws living in it. Ivy every-where. Don't know how Gwen and Arthur were ever allowed to hold the reception here. Some of the rooms didn't have roofs and, to get up to the battlements, you had to climb this cracked stone staircase with a sheer drop on one side. But it was a beautiful day, magical. Although the killing cast a shadow for a time.

'Oh, I thought everyone knew about it. It was just a couple of days after the wedding. Gwen and Arthur were still on honey-moon. A girl called Carly from the village. Linnet's cousin. She had this boyfriend, local lad, Dan. But she was seeing someone on the side. At least, she'd gone up Lover's Lane at night. It's a track up on the downs, between two hedgerows, lots of places where you can pull the car in and not be seen. That's how it's been known since forever. My gran said her gran called it that. Couples want to court, simple as that. I wish I hadn't started talking about it now.

'She was found up there the next day in a field. Stabbed to death. Everyone pointed the finger at the boyfriend. But he had a cast-iron alibi. With the football team – on the pitch, then all drinking together, then sleeping it off at Kay's house. No one was ever caught. Rough couple of years for Abury. Police wanting to interview everyone. Suspicion flying about.

'She was a lovely girl, Carly. Different to Linnet, fairer for start-ers, although they have the same voice – same tone, anyway. Can give you a shock sometimes. No, Carly was a bit more like Gwen to look at, but only from a distance. People used to compare them.

'You're not a journalist, are you? Only I've said more than I should and Arthur, well, he wouldn't like it . . .'

The castle remembers feast days and birthdays, tournaments and weddings. It remembers wedding nights, burning words whispered in the dark.

The party approaches its zenith. The company men are making a racket, shouting and jostling, reverting to earlier versions of them-selves. A celebration of Arthur is a celebration of them all.

Ties are loosened. Smart shoes start to pinch. The DJ, in terror of Linnet, plays two Bangles numbers back to back. In the ladies, behind a locked door, a girl tries to weep quietly. She might as well go home. No matter what she does, Lance won't look her way.

A woman in Balenciaga, worse for wear, reapplies her lipstick in the mirror. 'I know people like her Instagram but don't you find it . . . a bit calculated, a bit fake? Aren't I nice? Aren't I unaffected? I heard she had her tits done. And the hair can't be natural. Linnet says it is? Well, it doesn't look it.' In a few short hours, she'll wake in horror. *I didn't, did I? Oh fuck! Oh fuck! I did!*

At the bar, round after round of shots are poured. The booze makes the drinkers cheerful or lonely, full of love or resentment, according to their mood, according to their nature.

Gwen's dad tries to start a fight with one of Barack Obama's security guards.

Kay bowls up to Bezos waving his phone and demanding Jeff show him how to cancel his Prime membership.

And among the throng, someone who occasionally goes by the name the Invisible Knight catches sight of a figure walking with their head down in the direction of the stage and thinks, *Well, he came, then*, and, *This should be interesting*, and, *Let's hope the bitch gets what she deserves!*

The castle remembers might, the divine right of kings to do what they liked.

Arthur, deciding the time is ripe, signals to the Event Coordinator that he's ready for the speeches. He just needs to get Gwen and Mo to the front. He spots Lance passing to his right, looking like he's on his way to shoot a fancy aftershave commercial.

'Mate! You been avoiding me?'

Lance smiles but there are dark circles under his eyes.

'Happy birthday, Arthur,' he says. 'Sorry . . . I've been busy with a few things.'

'I missed you running.'

'Yeah, sorry.' He clears his throat. 'I'll get back to it next week.'

'Listen,' Arthur says, 'have you seen Gwen?'

Lance shifts on his feet. 'No, well, just to say hello to when I got here.'

'Well, can you try and find her? Bring her here for the speeches? Before everyone gets too pissed?'

33

'All right, Arthur. All right, mate. I'll see what I can do.'

The castle remembers every prayer that's ever been offered up inside its walls.

'You'll never guess who I've just seen!' Linnet bursts in among the company men. Her eyes are nearly popping out of her head.

'Wait. Wait. Look! Over there. No, you can't see her now. She's gone behind a pillar. No, I've lost her. Who? Thing is, I could swear I just saw Faye Morgan. Remember her? Someone should tell Gwen. I mean, someone should tell Gwen right this very minute.'

The castle remembers the briars enclosing it.

Lance finds Gwen out on the steps, standing in a patch of darkness against the walls. Her dress glistens and Lance can't stop himself from touching it, from stroking a panel just above her waist.

'He wants you inside,' he says softly. 'He's about to give a speech.' Then, 'I'm going to go, Gwen. It's not right. It's never been right. You'll be better off.' And then, all in a rush, 'Don't. Please don't cry, Gwen. We have to go in now. But we have to talk. The house at Snap? Tomorrow, then . . .'

The castle remembers the ivy's constricting embrace.

Kay shambles on to the stage, relieves the Event Coordinator of the microphone, taps it a couple of times on his thigh and smiles blearily at the expectant assembled faces.

Arthur nods his assent. Let Kay have his moment. He spots Lance delivering Gwen to the left of the stage and gives him a thumbs-up.

'Hang on, everyone, hang on,' Kay begins. 'I know my brother wants to say a few words on his special day. And his son's special day. Mo, where are you? Up to trouble, no doubt. Anyone missing their daughter? Or husband? Or wallet? Only joking!'

He stops to neck what remains in his glass. 'Anyway, so I know Arthur is going to want to thank you all for coming, and thank his friends and his beautiful wife, and blah, blah, blah, and maybe his big brother, his right-hand man and seneschal. What's that? It's an old word – it means . . . Anyway, something very good. Anyway, what I want to say, if you'd all stop bleeding humming for a second –' because the whole crowd are humming, humming an odd yet somehow familiar tune '– what I want to say is—'

The castle wakes for a moment and stops in its remembering because . . .

6

Happy Birthday to You!

———

... because a man leaps up on to the podium, a glinting blade in either hand. It's the anxious baldy Arthur spotted hiding behind a plant. Not a large man, or even that young, but fast and with the element of surprise.

Kay takes a step back. The microphone catches him say, 'And you can fuck off—'

Such Kay-like last words. He puts up his hands. Arthur takes a step forward. Where's security? While he's still looking wildly about, Lance passes in a blur to his left bearing a microphone stand. With his free hand, he scoops up a chair. His face is set, the amiability, the almost-emptiness, entirely dispelled.

The man is shouting over the yells of the crowd. Arthur's close enough to hear. 'Whore,' he's shouting, 'whore of death!'

Kay dodges out the way, trips and sprawls and the attacker darts forward. He's after Gwen, Arthur realises. Get away, Gwen! But Gwen's not moving. Her mouth's ajar, gaze fixed on someone or something in the crowd.

Thank God for Lance! Lance whose charge halts him in his tracks, who holds him off with the chair, while jabbing at him with the stand.

It's breathtaking, the almost-dance of it, the quick, light steps, feinting left and right – all before the professionals can gather their wits.

Then, just for a moment, Lance lets fall the arm holding the stand and the attacker greedily hops forward slashing at Lance's side, which is when Lance drops the chair and punches him in the ear. He tries to steady himself, once, twice, but no, he's going down.

Lance plants a foot on either of the attacker's wrists, who writhes about snarling until he's delivered a smart kick to chin. His head snaps back with a thud and he stills.

Uproar. One of Barack or Jeff's or possibly Elon's security team dashes in with handcuffs. Soon the attacker is encircled by men in black. Phones are flashing. Tomorrow a blurry video will circulate the world over. There will be Tibetan monks in remote Himalayan monasteries who'll watch Lance take down the man the media will shortly reveal to be one of Gwen's more persistent online trolls.

Hurly-burly. Kay struggling to get up. Linnet throwing herself on him, sobbing like a little child.

People are streaming away; they want out in case the attacker wasn't travelling alone, in case there's a bomb. A bomb? A bomb!

Helicopters are taking off outside, blades ripping the air.

Where is Gwen? And Mo? Arthur searches for them among the hurrying guests. Dazed, he descends the steps from the podium towards the centre of the room, then turns back. No sign of Gwen. No sign of Lance. Even the attacker is gone, whisked away by the men in black.

When he turns again, Morgan is standing right in front of him. Arthur jumps, actually starts back.

Her hair is loose, her face unmade-up. Her lips are almost white. When she smiles, her gums are pale and bloodless too.

'Hello, Arthur,' Morgan says. 'Happy birthday. Wonderful party. Thanks so much for the invite. Such a shame it's finishing so early. I've barely had a chance to say hello to anyone.'

Her voice hasn't changed. It always sounded so odd coming out of her, the breathy, squeaky, Marilyn-voice against the heft of her, the weightiness that goes beyond the physical. The gorgon stare.

Then, before he can think of a response, like a viper darting forth, she leans in, brings her lips right to his ear and injects the poison.

'I've got a message from an old friend for you, Arthur. Bobby-Bismillah says hello.'

Two

—

Ancient History

Burn the Witch (1992)

———

The tips of the apple tree tap against the windowpane, keeping Arthur company during the dark hours. The fox moves over the lawn, leaving behind a trail of grey feathers. A November dawn, bloody, short-lived, tells him he's been awake the whole night through. Again. Unrepeatable apprenticeship, feat of his youth.

He turns off the computer. Puts on his uniform. The sleeves of the blazer jacket swamp his skinny twelve-year-old wrists. On the bus, he sits in his usual seat, jammed up against the red-haired girl, drowning in sleep, head jerking as the double-decker rounds the bends.

She draws his head down upon her shoulder. He wakes with his cheek on her breast. Morgan is staring out the window, through the small circle she has cleared in the condensation as though into a crystal ball.

'Crooked Soley,' she says.

The bus boys are quiet. They have a plan.

At lunch break, Perce, Trist, Lionel, Bors, Kay and Garlon catch Morgan between classes. They're wearing elated, hunting faces. She bolts left, but they block her. Kay tries to wrap a dog lead round her wrists. When Morgan sits down on the floor, Garlon stands on her little finger so hard that she yelps and springs back up. They find this encouraging and she resolves to give them no more victories and allows herself to be led down the corridor, across the tennis courts and on to the school field.

The bonfire is for a Guy Fawkes Day fundraiser, the money going to clean-water projects in Sudan and Bosnian orphans. There's going to be a firework display too, and stalls selling hot dogs, candyfloss and toffee apples.

As they tie her to the post intended for the guy, a crowd coalesces of mainly first- and second-years. The boys are cock-a-hoop, the girls quieter, standing close together in small clusters. The air is full of water. It condenses on Morgan's skin as the edges of the field become indistinct.

The wood's soaked in something; there's tar on it, and something else, something heady and reeking.

'Any final words, witch?'

'You got piggy eyes, Garlon. Like there's an actual pig living in your head, looking out. Like you're a pig with a wig on, a bad wig made of pig-pubes.'

Laughter ripples through the watchers.

'Shame my lighter's not working,' Kay says, 'because I think you'd smell like bacon yourself.'

Garlon produces a silver Zippo from out of his pocket. 'Here. Have mine.'

Kay's eyes move from Garlon, to the other boys, to Morgan, to the crowd. Briefly, he looks like an actor who's been fed the wrong line. Into the opening, Morgan hurls a curse.

'You know when they burn people, Kay, I mean when they cremate them, they give people an urn with the ashes in? And this happens all up and down the country, almost every day, the whole year through. Funny thing is, none of those urns have teeth in them. So what do they do with them all? All those hundreds of thousands of teeth? Because they don't burn – teeth, that is. No, you can't burn them. They put them in a pit, Kay, a deep, dark, bottomless pit, where all the walls are lined with teeth and all the teeth point inwards.'

Morgan is shouting now, screaming almost. 'And that's where you're going, Kay! Into the pit! Into the black pit of teeth and once you're inside, you know what it's going to do? It's going to bite!'

And as though slapped hard, Kay jolts and falters forwards, bending down with the lighter to the foot of the woodpile, to the straw and rags that are surely too damp to burn.

What would have happened next is anyone's guess because the Head of Games, Mr Ryan, strides out of the mist in his shorts, whistle swinging round his neck. Kay straightens, jamming the lighter into his pocket. The crowd breaks apart like a snipped bead necklace.

Mr Ryan turns to Morgan. Even with her up on a pyre, he manages to look down his nose at her. 'Faye Morgan! Get yourself down from there. Who do you think you are, girl? Joan of Arc?'

At four o'clock, she has to take the school bus home with them, over the downs, through the villages and back to Abury. Most days, Morgan is the bus boys' sport, what they've earned after a long day of abiding by school rules, of stomaching algebra and sitting through assembly. Sometimes it's someone else's go – Arthur for being a runty little dweeb, or they turn on each other – but they always come back to Morgan.

At fourteen, she's already taller than half the teachers. Hair the colour of a neon highlighter, pale lips and, when she opens her mouth, a tongue the colour of an unripe strawberry. A big girl, a brainy girl, a round girl, red like a fist when the blood rushes to the surface, moving to a backing track of jeers. Large fawn freckles maraud over her skin in hordes.

Now one of the boys is making a terrible pig noise, like a pig screaming, shocking and hog-like and she can tell it's supposed to be her, Morgan, this outraged sound of pig being murdered. The others join in, oinking and grunting and shrieking, impossible to ignore.

And yet Morgan's fellow travellers do ignore them. Sometimes when the bus boys are egging each other on to fresh heights, a mood of condemnation will arise, but directed more against Morgan than the boys. Why must they listen to it? Why won't she put an end to it? Make the right joke or laugh the right way, say the right thing or just be quiet, but the right kind of quiet. Why does she draw it upon herself?

There's something the bus boys want from her – and the silent consensus on the bus is that Morgan should give it to them. Whatever it is. Whatever it costs her.

Many years later, in San Francisco, overlooking the Pacific Ocean, Morgan will get into an argument with Rasha over a tram.

43

They're running late for a party and the streetcar is there, right there, and the taxi hasn't shown. And why, Rasha wants to know, does Morgan always insist on driving or taking taxis or walking? And it's an important party – for a beloved colleague's retirement – and look! The tram's right there! And then Rasha will see something in Morgan's face and she'll take her in her arms and say, *Oh baby, whatever is it?*

On a bench overlooking the bay, Morgan will tell her about what happened on the school bus and she will howl, howl tears she didn't know were in her, because there with Rasha in 2015, six months into the love of her life, she will have started feeling safe in a way that sometimes makes her look, from the outside, like a woman suffering a minor nervous breakdown. What she'll manage to get out between sobs is that the worst thing, the thing that lingers and poisons everything, is that you know people can't be trusted, that people will look the other way, that people are no fucking good—

And then, her face hot and wet in the warmth of Rasha's neck, she'll start laughing as she cries, because the most ridiculous thing of all is that since falling in love with Rasha, since discovering that Rasha loved her right back, everyone seems so good, like Morgan walks down the street and sees the light shining out of people's faces, and the light is love made visible, love streaming in the firmament . . .

Such a future is an unimaginable land to fourteen-year-old Morgan. The bus rounds the familiar bends. The bus boys, sensing they are on to something, step up the obscenely swinish chorus. At the corners of her mouth, in the back of her throat, in her chest, Morgan feels herself giving way – a tumbling feeling; a messy, blurting, shame-filled feeling—

And then, concealed from everyone, Arthur finds her hand in the space between them and holds it in his. His small, pale fingers weave through hers and squeeze gently. Their palms touch, and Morgan steadies, her strength returns, and the bus boys, scenting defeat, fall to fighting among themselves.

8

Best Friends Forever

———

How lonely it is until you have a friend. The things, once they have come, that you will do to keep them.

In the classroom, the English teacher chalks up questions on the blackboard for discussion.

In King Lear *who has power? Who demonstrates it, seeks it, acquiesces to it, resists it? What price does Cordelia pay? What motivates her? What happens to her sisters? Lear seems to want to keep power but hand over responsibility – what do you think Shakespeare wants us to make of this?*

A blonde girl is coming up the path outside the classroom, escorted by one of the admin staff. One by one the heads turn until everyone is looking.

A knock at the door and in she comes, the new student, Gwen. The teacher invites her to find a seat.

'Are your family new to the area?'

The girl shakes her head, slumps down in the nearest empty chair. Soon word will spread that her dad's a farmer, owns half the downs round Abury. But Leo's not forking out for any more posh school, not after Gwen's GCSE results. Why throw good money after bad? Or more to the point, how best enrage the wife who's just left you for another man?

With Gwen among them, the class grows unforthcoming.

'So, Cordelia . . . why doesn't she just give her father what he

45

wants? Anyone . . .? Anyone . . .?' The teacher scans the room. 'Ah, Morgan, what do you think?'

Morgan looks up from her desk. Feels the new girl contemplating her. For an instant their eyes meet.

'Because . . .' Morgan licks her lips, 'because why should she?'

At home time, Morgan's already on the bus with Arthur beside her when Gwen gets on. The bus boys start up straight away, shoving one another into the aisle, loudly competing to offer her a place next to them.

But Gwen ignores them all, stops in front of Arthur and draws him up by his school tie till his lips are an inch from hers.

'Skedaddle,' she says and pushes him off down the bus. Without another word, she sinks down next to Morgan.

The journey home is quiet, the whole bus straining to listen in, because what truck can these two have?

It's a mystery. A mystery that only grows and deepens, on bus rides, in corners and between classes, via notes scribbled in the back of exercise books, during sleepovers in which they will swear they dreamed the same thing.

Who loves most?

Gwen, that stuck-up blonde piece? Or Morgan, Titian's Venus gone rotten, after a week in the weir?

Who holds back even a crumb of their affection?

And what – so Gwen's brother and father wonder as dust floats down from the ceiling of the old farmhouse, as the plaster cracks, the stone trembles – what the hell is it they find so fucking funny?

*

'Well, I'm your penis!
I'm your fire!
At your desire!'
Gwen's singing and dancing round the kitchen. She sloshes a good four fingers of her dad's rum into a half-empty Coke bottle. It's summer now, 1995, they're seventeen and the first year of their A levels is nearly over.

'Come on, Morgan!'

Gwen turns up the radio, shrieks over it.

'Penis on a mountain top!'

'I think it's Venus.'

But Gwen can't hear her. She's wearing denim cut-offs and a Metallica T-shirt, sleeves torn away so you can see the black bra under her arms. She hands Morgan a ladle and a saucepan, then starts slamming a cupboard door in time, eyes on the stairs.

'*Gurning like a silver dame*,' they howl. Morgan hits the sauce-pan. Again! Again! '*The something of beauty and love* ...' From the floor above comes the sound of a door banging open. Thundering footsteps. Morgan's eyes meet Gwen's. Deep breath in for the crescendo: '*AND PENIS WAS HIS NAME!*'

Gwen's brother Aidey barrels down the stairs. He's in his boxers, eyes red as love, face contorted.

'You pair of slags. I'm going to fucking kill you.'

But they're already out the door, running across the farmyard, Gwen clutching the bottle, Morgan desperately trying to keep up.

There's a John Deere parked in front of the barn and Gwen swings up into the seat, offering a hand to Morgan so she can climb in too. They slam the tractor door and throw down the locks. The rum and Coke sprays the windscreen, foams into their mouths.

'He's got a girl up there. Came back at five with her. I had to listen to them at it.'

'Your dad doesn't mind?'

'Leo doesn't give a single shit.'

When it's clear Aidey's not coming after them, Gwen fetches a rug from the stables and they head down to the stream. They take a rutted track, picking their way through cowpats, crusty on the surface, liquid beneath. Morgan's a sweating wreck by the time they reach the bank.

'Right, a paddle.' Gwen drops her shorts and wades in in her pants. 'Come on.'

Morgan shakes her head.

'Fuck's sake, Faye! Don't make me come get you.' When Morgan still doesn't make a move, Gwen drops her voice. 'No one's here. No one's going to see. I promise.'

Morgan swallows and searches her waistband for the zip. She avoids looking at her freckled white legs, at the collapsed black circus tent of her skirt.

The grass is long and blue-green, the water cold and clenching. The clay bed squidges between Morgan's toes. Unsteadily, she makes her way against the current to where Gwen stands, thigh-deep in the water. Sunlight reflects off the surface, moving over her face in golden bars. Her hand is outstretched.

'Better, isn't it?' Gwen says as their fingers meet.

'Oh yes,' says Morgan.

Afterwards, they lie on the blanket. On the other bank, a herd of Friesian heifers come down to drink, lowering the patent leather of their muzzles into the shallows and snorting as it laps at their nostrils, showgirl eyelashes fanning the wet gleam of huge brown eyes.

Gwen rolls on to her side and tickles a blade of grass against Morgan's throat. It's time for her favourite game.

'Remember when . . .' she begins.

*

Remember when . . . *ha ha ha ha* . . . Remember when they were in that cafe and that tweedy-trousered old man came over because maybe they were swearing a bit and upsetting his wife! *Ha ha ha ha!* You've upset my wife! YOU'VE UPSET MY WIFE!

And remember, oh yeah, remember that time in the van with the stag? That white stag! Gwen driving them both back from a rave in her dad's pickup truck, and out on the Roman road going fifty, they closed their eyes and counted to twenty. And then, when they opened them, there was a white stag standing in the middle of the road, staring them down . . .

Remember too, that time, right, that time with Mr Ryan! Oh no, don't start! Please don't start because peeing from laughing is a thing. It's a thing that happens and it's not fair. Mr Ryan! In his shorts with his whistle round his neck, sleazing up to Gwen in an empty classroom, not knowing Morgan was there too. Mr Ryan complimenting Gwen on her *great shape* and suggesting that *maybe it was because of all the riding she did. Because Gwen liked to ride, didn't she?* And Morgan, from the stationery cupboard where she'd been sniffing the wood glue, growling in a voice both demonic and terrifying, *GREAT SHAPE! GREAT SHAPE! GREAT SHAPE!* And Mr Ryan freezing, then turning and slithering away!

And remember when Kay asked Gwen out and she turned him down saying she couldn't because she fancied Arthur, and then catching him, Arthur, by the computer room and making him parade up and down the sixth-form corridor holding Gwen's hand, *ha ha ha* . . .

And the time they had a go on Aidey's bong! *Ha ha ha ha!* And that other time . . .

And the sound of their laughter, drifting up into the clean June air, makes Morgan think of the way that a voice, raised to the right note, can shatter crystal, as though their laughter has something of the same strength to it, the same power.

*

The booze is gone. Gwen's dad's out in the pickup. What next? They could go inside and listen to music in Gwen's room, songs about killing people with axes or losing all your limbs to a bomb, while Gwen lies on the floor, tensing her arms and legs, face screwed up as she thrashes along with the drummer. Only, Aidey's inside and he might not have forgiven them yet.

The bus to Abury goes thrice daily. It's due past at two forty-five. They might as well.

At the farmhouse, Morgan sneaks in to fetch her bag and Gwen's wallet, since Aidey's less likely to enact revenge on her. The wallet's in Gwen's room, next to Aidey's. His door's open and Morgan catches sight of him lying atop the sheets, bong next to the bed, hip bones and treasure trail visible above his boxers. When her gaze returns to his face, Aidey is watching her and she bolts, hammering down the stairs to re-join Gwen outside.

The bus shelter's a couple of hundred yards up the lane, shaded by towering banks and overhung with lilac bushes. There's someone inside, a blurred ghost-like figure moving behind the misted glass.

Carly's in a white dress, bare feet filthy, a pair of heels dangling from one hand. Last night's make-up pandas her eyes.

'Your brother's a bastard. Won't give me a lift back. Made himself a cheese toastie and a huge bong and told me to get the bus.'

Carly, a year above them at school, has been going out with Dan Hinson since they were both twelve. As though reading their minds, she blurts out, 'Everyone's going to see me getting off the bus. Everyone's going to know.' She looks from Morgan to Gwen. 'Will you say I was with you? That I stayed with you?'

Carly's never even spoken to Morgan before, but she warms up considerably after they promise her an alibi, after Morgan lends her the sweatshirt from her bag – even though it hangs on her like a black bin liner.

When the bus comes, late as usual, they pay the driver and then huddle in close at the back even though there's no one else aboard. Gwen licks her thumb and rubs at the rings round Carly's eyes.

'You can say you had too much to drink so we took you back.'

'Oh, I did, I did,' Carly laments. 'Cider always makes me do mental things.' She bursts out, 'Aidey's such a pig! He's a pig but he's so good-looking. I couldn't help it. I didn't even want to.'

'Didn't sound like that to me,' Gwen says, and Carly bites her lip and looks out the window.

In Abury, Carly throws her arms around them both. When it's Morgan's turn, she whispers, 'Come round and get your top and I'll tint your brows and lashes if you like. We can put a rinse on your hair too, tone down the red.'

Once she's gone, they wander the ancient, cobbled streets. They're too old to hang around the pond, and there's nothing doing on the green or the sports field. No shops worth the name. So they end up at the Green Knight, where tradition rules no one with a whisker or a training bra is ever carded unless they're staggering.

They get two pints of shandy and take them out the back. To the right of the courtyard is a car park which backs on to a walled pub garden where they hover looking for somewhere to sit down. Morgan's heart gives an arachnoid skitter when she sees who's sitting at two of the picnic tables.

It's the bus boys: Kay, Perce, Trist, Garlon, Lionel and Bors. A handful of others. They're spotted, and waved over; room for two on a bench is made free.

'I don't think—'

But Gwen strides ahead, plonks herself down.

'Come on, Morgan,' she calls. Then, pointing a warning finger around the table, 'You be nice.'

And they are. Gwen chats away while Morgan sips her drink, inspecting the knots in the wood. In the ladies, Gwen says, 'You can talk to them. You don't have to sit there like a lemon. They're being nice.'

What they're being is careful. For Gwen. Being nice to Morgan is the price they pay for Gwen's company, for the pleasure of a close-up view of her honeyed skin, the glimpse of her black bra, the freckles on her thighs. To have her scoff at their banter and snort at their jokes.

Morgan drinks her pints down, tries hard to make small, appropriate contributions.

At six, Kay's parents turn up with Arthur in tow.

'I've ordered you scampi and chips in a basket. It'll be out in twenty minutes,' Betty says.

'I'll have it here.'

'You'll have it with us, my lad.'

When it's brought out, Kay skulks off to much hilarity. Like it's a stain on him, having a mother who feeds him, when they all have mothers who feed them, apart from Gwen whose mother ran off with a racing trainer and who lives on bananas, chocolate bars, and a nightly ham and pineapple oven pizza. Recently she confessed to Morgan that sometimes she shits once a week.

Or maybe Kay didn't want to go because he knew he'd be the topic of conversation as soon as his back was turned: the fact his dad works in computers, that they have a new car, that while Kay got Cs in his exams, his brother Arthur is a boy wonder.

Morgan's ears prick up. First she's heard of it.

'Clever with computers. Learning all these computer languages. He made his mum and dad take him to Cambridge for this meeting of spods, and thing was they all knew him, because they'd been talking to him via computer, only they thought he was forty or something.'

'Computer language? What, like *Bonjour Madame*?'

'Not a fucking clue, mate.'

More pints. Packets of crisps, ripped open and shared round.

'Have some,' they say to Morgan, 'have some!' So she takes two small ones so no one can accuse her of being a fat, greedy pig.

When Kay returns, Arthur's with him. Nearly fifteen now. Bright-eyed and in need of a haircut. A bit taller. He smiles at her and between them lies the memory of the bus journeys, the memory of Arthur's hand in hers.

As the sun sets, the air begins to bite. The families return home, and the other drinkers go inside, leaving the lawn to them. Carly and Dan arrive, arm in arm, to take up a table in the loneliest corner and gaze into one another's eyes as the garden falls into shadow.

Morgan's pissed. She goes back to the loos to check out how red her face is and, when she comes out, Gwen's not at the table any more. She's sitting on the swing talking to a boy in a grey jumper, his sleeves rolled up to his elbows.

Their eyes are fixed on one another. The tilt of Gwen's face, the openness of her expression, the softness of his gaze upon her, do not make for difficult reading. It is the blue hour. The birds are falling silent, the daisies drawing closed.

Gwen's trainers scrape back and forth on the ground beneath the swing where the grass has rubbed away. The boy, straight-backed and broad-shouldered, says something and Gwen laughs; he takes one of the chains and pulls it, twisting her round.

No one will ever look at me like that. Gwen doesn't even have to try . . .

Back at the picnic tables, the mood has changed.

'Who's that, then?' Garlon wants to know.

'Dunno,' Morgan says.

Bors makes a bit of effort to chat but the rest ignore her, ragging on each other about this and that, the football team.

'Who scored twice?' says Kay.

'Who hangs the goal?' says Perce; then, 'You know Arthur's not bad. He'll do all right if he comes to training.'

Kay scowls and they fall to bickering.

'You got no team spirit, Kay.'

'You can't just wallop it down the other end every time like bloody Eeyore!'

The lamps come on in the garden. The boy has taken off his jumper and given it to Gwen. A motorbike engine buzzes like a fly against a far-off window, then approaches, till its roar cuts off speakers from their listeners. It putt-putts to a standstill in the pub car park. A key turns. The engine dies.

The rider, surely cold in just a T-shirt and jeans, makes straight for them. Aidey pulls off his helmet. Like Gwen's, his hair is a thick and yellowy blonde, sooty at the roots. He picks up Morgan's pint, nine-tenths full, and drains it dry.

'Thanks for the wake-up call this morning.' His eyes are blood-shot and he sits down heavily, crashing against Morgan's side. 'Where's my sister?'

Aidey swings round following someone's gaze. His eyes alight on Carly and Dan, then on Gwen over by the swing. He snorts. Turns back to the table. 'She wants to watch she doesn't turn into one of these local SLUTS!' The last word he shouts out, intended for Carly's ears no doubt. He slams a twenty-quid note down and shoves it towards Kay. 'Let's have some drinks.'

Around Aidey, they're all subdued. Careful not to draw his attention or rile him. There's something pent-up about Aidey and no one's in a hurry to see it loose.

He's at agricultural college, only Gwen says he'll never make a farmer. No discipline and animals don't like him. No aptitude for the paperwork either, the filling-in of herd books, the TB testing data, the ordering of fertiliser and feed, the acquisition of passports, the ever-increasing number of hours of it since Britain joined the Common Market.

Against Morgan's side, Aidey's body burns hot. He smells ripe and she wonders when was the last time he washed. After he knocks back another pint, he thrusts his arm around her, pulls her in tight and puts his mouth to her throat.

'You're a good girl, aren't you? No messing about for our Morgan.' His other hand comes under the table to grip her thigh. 'Any of you lot have a go? No, didn't think so. Well, looks aren't everything.'

It's not like she hasn't imagined being touched by Aidey. He makes you think of sex, not kissing but sex. So it's funny the freeze that comes over her, the stiffness. Why not a playful elbow in the ribs? Why not push him away and wriggle free?

His spit's wet on her neck. Garlon giggles. Kay gives a half smile and looks away.

'Come on, Morgan, let's get on the bike. I know just the place for us, a secret place.'

'Leave her alone, Aidey.' Gwen's standing at the other end of the table. She sounds weary, but there's an edge to her voice.

Aidey's arm slides free from round Morgan's shoulder.

'Where's your lover-boy gone?'

'Fuck off. Come on, Morgan, let's get out of here.'

When she's on her feet, she feels unsteady.

'You going to ride that thing home?' Gwen says to Aidey.

'Why not?'

'One day you'll kill yourself.'

James of the grey jumper gives them a lift back to Morgan's, who gets out and waits a few car-lengths away, staring at the hedge, while he and Gwen enjoy a lengthy goodbye.

Inside, they raid the cupboards for food, bite cheese from the block in lumps, chisel with knives at ice cream from the freezer.

In Morgan's double bed, Gwen squeezes up to her and whispers in her ear about James, how he used to go out with a girl at her old school, how he swims for the county. Next week she'll say *James Who?*

Before they sleep, Gwen tells her to stay away from Aidey, and Morgan promises she will, secretly thrilled that Gwen thinks Aidey would want anything to do with her.

But it doesn't stop her thinking about it. In memory, the discomfort fades. She remembers his lips on her neck, the heat of him, the pressure of his fingers digging into her thigh. Over and over again, she imagines it, imagines what would have happened if she'd gone with him to the secret place he knows.

*

Six months on, Morgan has nothing but contempt for her former self, so dreamy and so alone, who ate breakfast, who ate biscuits, who didn't fit clothes from shops intended for teenage girls. More fool that girl! More fool her! Morgan tints her eyelashes dark brown. She tints her eyebrows mid-brown. Every Sunday night she puts a chestnut-brown rinse on her hair so it's the colour of a wet red setter.

No more afternoons on the sofa with her mum slipping their hands in and out of the biscuit tin, listening to her mum's critique of women on the telly:

. . . feminine, ladylike, common, past her best, mannish, charming, exotic, an English pear, like the back of a bus, up herself, bony, conniving, no oil

painting, neat figure, gorgeous, bossy, not a natural blonde, awful voice, brassy, babyish, catty, sporty, superior, let herself go, starving, shouty, no looker, bloated, out of proportion, rough . . .

When she went round to get her sweatshirt, Carly had taken her in hand. Showed her how to use the diffuser. The benefits of Frizz Ease serum.

'You eat grapefruit and eggs. Drink black coffee. Chicken is OK. Fish is OK. No batter or breadcrumbs, though.' But she has kind hands.

Morgan goes back, to the red-brick row of terraces off the market square, to the warren of rooms under the thatch roof. She doesn't tell her mum. There's something a bit dubious about Carly's family, something not quite respectable. A bit noisy, perhaps. No visible men.

Carly looms over Morgan in the chair. Her face inches away, warm breath on Morgan's skin. Her ten-year-old cousin Netty sits cross-legged on the floor, watching beadily as Carly blots Morgan's lipstick with a tissue.

'Is it her colour?'

'Oh, it isss, it isss,' Netty lisps.

Carly's mum, Shirley, is a dieter. She attends weekly meetings in the town hall where a group of women take part in public weigh-ins, writing down their tally of losses and gains on a little card and then sitting round in a circle to talk about cottage cheese. It's not so much a hobby as a religion.

Losing her puppy fat, her dad calls it. As though the weight has melted away like wax, revealing her true self. In which case, why does she feel so besieged? Why is so much of her energy diverted, her attention forever standing guard, holding the whip, while her appetite cowers in the corner, snapping its teeth, ready to spring.

Odd how many people need to mention it, to reward her with their approval. She's never had anything less than an A, but that's never drawn a tenth of the praise, a fraction of the warmth as stopping eating.

It's not like she's Gwen or anything. In Swindon, in a club, they meet two lads from the RAF camp at Lyneham. After a tussle, Gwen designates one the victor and takes him off to the dance floor. His comrade sourly sips his beer.

'Don't know why I come out with the jammy devil. I always end up with the crumbs off his plate.'

When Gwen comes back, she gives the signal so they excuse themselves to the loos.

'He shaves his chest. I touched it and it was like touching a bristly pig.'

'His mate said I was a crumb!'

So they ditch the pair of them, going over the road to the club that plays metal and grunge and indie hits. The dance floor's the size of a handkerchief but when Metallica comes on Gwen's up there, throwing her hair about, elbows flying. Next to her, Morgan shuffles her feet. Something's trying to get out of her. The music is prising at her body. It wants her to give in. To let go. Her head's bobbing. The music's deafening. She starts to flail, copying Gwen. Tries to strangle and squash the part of her that's always on watch. Succeeds. Fails. Succeeds.

Gwen throws her arms around Morgan. Looks up into her face, eyes shining, arms gripping her tight at they move around in a circle like a drunken couple.

'Crumb! My Crumb! My darling Crumb!'

*

Then there are the things they don't remember, that they try not to remember.

Like when the history teacher, Mrs Grubb, holds Morgan back after class to tell her to stop wasting her time with people who aren't going anywhere, when she, Morgan, has an actual brain in her head, a decent brain that could take her places, out of Abury for starters, unlike some she could mention.

'Promise me blonde is not contagious, Morgan,' Grubb says, creaking in her sensible brogues.

'It's not, miss,' Morgan replies. And Gwen, listening from outside in the corridor, can hear the treacherous smile in her voice.

Like the time a person unknown – but definitely one of the bus boys – painstakingly photocopies Morgan's face from out of the yearbook and goes round and sticks it on to all the *Save the Whale* posters currently adorning the school noticeboards in preparation for the sponsored walk. And Gwen laughing when she sees one. Sniggering and stuffing her hand over her mouth as though to push the laughter back inside. But too late! Too late!

Like all the occasions Gwen borrows stuff from Morgan – small sums of money, class notes, a lipstick Carly gave her – and doesn't say thank you and doesn't return them.

Like Morgan silently disparaging the books Gwen likes, bonk-busters about sex and horses, and the raised eyebrow of disdain encompassing a lot more than the books—

Like Gwen lapping up all the attention she gets, and pretending not to hear it when the same people say snide things about Morgan—

Like Gwen, coming downstairs at a party after a regrettable half-hour with some boy or other to find Morgan laughing fit to die with Kay's kid brother Arthur, her face all red and her eyes streaming with tears, which is how she laughs with Gwen—

—and Morgan disappearing off round Carly's house all the time, and thinking about university all the time, and Morgan's parents talking of moving away—

And! And! And!

*

By spring, with the all-important exams looming, all the kissing has done for Gwen. They go through the accused one by one, Gwen counting them off on her fingers. The glands in her neck are swollen. She's no appetite. Just showering knocks her out, so half the time she doesn't bother, just lies on the sofa all day, listlessly flipping channels on the remote. Can't think of school, can't finish her coursework.

Morgan gets off the bus early to visit, bringing Chocolate Hobnobs, Mars Bars and class notes that Gwen stuffs down the back of the sofa. Today, Gwen can't keep her eyes open and Morgan watches *Neighbours* and *Home and Away*, her gaze flitting between the screen and the clock, thinking about all the revising she has to do. At some point, she blinks and then, when she looks down, a whole chocolate bar is gone, nothing but a couple of crumbs left on the torn open wrapper. Quickly, she shoves it out of sight between the sofa cushions.

'Where are your manners?' Aidey is in the doorway. Morgan flushes and her pulse does the little jump it always does whenever Aidey speaks to her.

He takes a swig from the Coke bottle he's holding, and then pads over and sets it down on the floor where Gwen can reach it. She looks small and sallow, her hair dark with grease. 'Poor Gwennie,' he says.

Underneath the arsehole is more arsehole, Gwen's already warned her. But it's hard not to imagine depths of sweetness. His green eyes have chips of gold in them.

Gwen lifts her lids with what seems like great effort. One arm sticks out and grabs the Coke.

'Give her a lift home, won't you, Aidey?' She unscrews the cap, takes a gulp and puts the bottle back down, eyes sliding closed.

Morgan finds she can't even look at him.

'Ten minutes,' he says. 'Outside.'

Aidey's dropped out of college, much to Leo's fury. Instead, he's taken on shifts behind the bar of the Green Knight, pouring pints and changing barrels, collecting up the empties. When she goes out in the farmyard, he's waiting for her next to a scrambler.

'On that?'

He hands her a helmet. She has to pull up her skirt to get astride it. Her thighs wrap his. She puts her arms about his waist. He drives her home like a madman. So fast, so reckless on the bends, she had to lie down flat on her bed for an hour after.

Still, the next time, when she finds him waiting for her, she takes the helmet when it's held out. Again, he drops her off and disappears without a word, and this time she's disappointed. Instead of dashing inside, she waits on the pavement while he packs her helmet away. Before he roars off, he turns in her direction. She can't see his face, only the black visor. But he is looking at her. No question.

What does he see? She wants him to show her what he sees.

The third time, halfway home he leaves the road and they bounce down a rutted farm track, a bone-shaking ride that brings them to a stand of trees in a dip between the hills. It's a lonely spot, secluded, surrounded by huge fields in which the wheat is rising.

A buzzard sails overhead. Aidey gets off the bike and strides away into the trees.

Among the thicket are piles of stone over which ivy runs wild. A little ahead, in a clearing, a couple of buildings remain standing. Nettles grow in tall ranks around an empty doorway and Morgan gets stung through her tights as she follows Aidey inside the smaller of the two ruins.

The slate roof is only partly intact. Where Morgan is she can look straight up into the blue sky. Weeds grow thick around her ankles between the fallen slates.

In the shadows, beneath the rafters that have held, Aidey takes off his helmet. There's a chewed-up foam mattress, a clutch of beer bottles, broken glass, the remnants of rotted magazines.

'What is this place?'

'Snap. Used to be a hamlet then the spring dried up. They pulled most of it down to stop the gypsies making camp. The one next door was the chapel.'

He takes a cigarette from a packet and sparks it, seemingly inclined to say nothing more. There's purple graffiti spray-painted on to one wall but she can't make out the words.

In her friendship with Gwen, Aidey is *verboten*, like the one room in Bluebeard's castle. Morgan bends down to rub at the spot beneath her tights and sneaks a glance at him, the sourly beautiful young man smoking a cigarette in T-shirt and jeans.

'You get stung?'

'Yeah.'

'I know a cure for that.'

Aidey flicks the cigarette into the undergrowth and bends down to pluck a dock leaf. He smiles a lazy smile and then he spits on it, a gob of glistening white foam that he then spreads along the leaf with his finger.

A short while later, Morgan finds herself thinking, *All that fuss about looks, when in the end you close your eyes.*

*

A week on, Gwen's mother puts in an appearance, scoops Gwen up and vanishes with her to Barbados, amidst a whirlwind of accusations of neglect on Leo's part. After a couple of weeks, Morgan receives a postcard of brilliant-white sands, a turquoise ocean.

'You have upset my wife,' it reads. 'Love Your Wife.' There are thirty-four kisses. So she doesn't know.

No enquiry, Morgan notes, about her own health and well-being. Truth is, she has no power, and whatever power she did have lessens. The coldness afterwards, the way Aidey can barely seem to look at her, the way his face twists in disgust. Can't tell anyone about that, not ever.

It drives her mad. All her thoughts are focused on him.

In the charts, the Spice Girls sing about girl power, about what they really, really want. In the ruined house at Snap, what Morgan wants is to get the performance right. Maybe then he'll be happy.

He wants to do specific things. They don't involve kissing. Quite often they hurt.

Maybe that's the point. Aidey wants to hurt people and to really hurt anyone you have to get close to them. You have to get on the inside.

Why not another girl? There are plenty for Aidey to choose from. Because he likes her and is hiding it? Because other girls would not be so susceptible to silence, would refuse him, would not need so badly what Aidey promises but never delivers.

The last option she can't bring herself to consider: that this isn't about her at all.

*

It's a pleasant surprise when Arthur throws himself down in his old seat and asks Morgan about her imminent exams, as though picking up a conversation just left off.

He takes up a full seat now. Sixteen to her eighteen. Their shoulders rub. No longer quite the little owl. Rain beats against the windows, pouring down the panes so it feels like they're in a watery grotto.

'Which university?'

'Not sure. Durham if I get the results. And you? Will you go study computing somewhere?'

'I might go to Cambridge next year.'

'Next year? You mean skip A levels?'

Arthur nods. Then he says quietly, 'They want me, but I'm not sure they have anything to teach me.'

Not a hint of boasting, not a hint of bravado. Almost fear. Almost an appeal.

'But won't you meet interesting people? People with similar interests?'

It's what people always say about university. Arthur shrugs, unconvinced.

'I know lots of people.' And he lists a load of odd-sounding names with locations: '... Oracle5 in San Francisco, Wertyful in Sydney, BobbyBismillah in Medan.'

A little later she says, 'Hacking, Arthur?'

'Testing. It's systems testing, Morgan. I want ... I want us all to be safe.' Arthur runs a hand through his hair. 'But people don't take me seriously. Because I'm so young.'

'Then make them take you seriously.'

The bus lurches to a stop. Her stop.

'Oops!' She gets up and dashes off before the driver can close the doors. Through the window, she catches a glimpse of Arthur, rigid in his seat, like he's suffered a minor electrocution.

In just over two years' time he will tell her, *That day, it was like being given a sword.*

. They sit together again. Sometimes speaking, sometimes not. How distinct he is in her mind. The fizz she gets from conversation with Arthur, like in science class when they added lithium to water, and it danced and leapt over the surface spitting purple flames.

It's not a boy–girl thing, because she's not a cradle-snatcher, even though Carly teasingly calls her one when she pops in to get her lashes done. Shirley stops her on the way out.

'Have you tried those newfangled rice pots? Two syns each! What about the jelly made with fromage frais? No points!'

Besides, isn't what she has with Aidey what it's supposed to be all about, what she's been primed for? To be dominated and ignored and driven half out of her mind? When Aidey is in a shitty mood, she must mollify and appease him, think of inventive ways to distract him, to flatter him subtly if he's minded to allow it.

How he hates tenderness but especially afterwards. He certainly can't show it. She gives it to him anyway so that anyone watching would be confused at the dissonance, how it would be like watching two people acting together, but in different films. His top-shelf, hers rose-tinted and romantic, in which she calls to the man she wants him to be, even as she kisses the man he is.

Sometimes, she catches an unsteady look about him afterwards, like his centre of balance has been shifted a few degrees.

But today, after sitting next to Arthur on the bus, she says no.

She's walking from the bus stop to her house when she hears the bike. Aidey slows down.

'Get on.'

'No.'

The word dropping from her lips without her ever intending it. But then it occurs to her, what can he do? What can he do really?

Aidey's face sets hard.

'Get on the bike, Morgan.'

'I don't want to any more.'

It's only when he's gone that Morgan's stabbed by the realisation that, in all likelihood, he'll pay her back by telling Gwen. And that Gwen's going to take it really badly.

*

It's worse than she expected. The exams are over, the results are in, and the summer almost out, by the time Gwen reappears. Brown as a nut, hair bleached white-blonde, trailing rumours of an island love affair, a dreadlocked prince who took her sailing at midnight, who caught and roasted lobster for her over hot coals and fetched her down fresh green coconuts from swaying palms.

All this Morgan gleans from Carly because Gwen doesn't call.

The news comes she's won a place at Durham. She's sent the reading list and starts working her way through the few titles she can order via the Central Library. No one calls. On shady days Morgan lies on a blanket in the garden; when it's sunny she reads on her bed, listening to the house around her, the familiar sounds it makes.

Once it was her whole world. Each stain on the carpet, each scribble on the woodchip wallpaper has its legend. Already it feels like a box, one that she is stepping out of, one she may never return to if her parents' talk about a move to Reading comes to anything.

They go out for a farewell dinner, booking a table at Abury's only proper restaurant, an Italian place run by a family who, along with the handful of Poles who came after the war and the Turks who own the takeaway, make up the town's ethnic diversity.

Her father orders a bottle of wine, which Morgan drinks most of as her father is driving and her mother won't have more than half a glass. They avoid the pizza because, as her mum says, they can have that at home. Her parents aren't at home in restaurants, aren't really at home anywhere than at home. How innocent they seem. How she burns to make them proud.

Afterwards, Morgan and her mother wait in the street while her father fetches the car. A hundred yards away, a group of young people spill out of the Green Knight.

'Isn't that your Gwen?' her mum says. 'I thought she was still away. GWEN!'

But Gwen, if it is her, doesn't turn, even though her mother calls loudly enough for anyone to hear. Eventually, she falls silent, shaking her head.

'That little madam. She'll come to nothing. You mark my words!'

*

Everything packed. Everything ready. The map studied and the directions written out, a stop for lunch planned at a service station just north of Birmingham.

Morgan and her dad, tiptoeing round her mum, hoping to avoid the inevitable collapse. She's stoic as a soldier, though, even as they drive away.

'Do you mind stopping at the farm, Dad? Just for five minutes.'

The house is empty and there's no sign of Aidey's bike. Morgan finds Gwen in the barn. She's got a grey horse on a lunge, whip tickling its hooves as it circles her. She clocks Morgan and then turns back to the horse.

'You off, then?'

'Yes.'

'Come to say a fond farewell to Aidey?'

'No. I came to say bye to you.'

'Do you want a go on my dad too? I think he's in the house. You could pop in.'

'Gwen—'

'He said you were like a kebab, Morgan, a good idea after ten pints but – in the cold light of day – slobby and disgusting and much to be regretted.'

'You bitch.'

Gwen casts Morgan a look. The look is of pity (you have nothing) and amusement (you cannot hurt me) and total contempt (you are beneath me), and it unleashes a hatred Morgan didn't know she had, a hatred vigorous and well established and more than ready to put itself into words.

'Daddy buy you a new horsey? Now you're home from Mummy's fancy holiday. What's next? Back to school? Didn't think so. A few boyfriends? Maybe a little job till you marry a bloke with loads of money. Because you haven't got it in you to make anything for yourself, do anything other than what comes easy. You might as well be a table decoration—'

When the words finally run out, she stands there waiting for Gwen to respond. Nothing comes. The grey's hooves thud against the earth. Morgan's blood pounds in her head.

Two years of friendship, only two years. Yet in the years before Morgan sees Gwen again, she'll learn that even plutonium has a shorter half-life.

'Were you in love with her?' Rasha will ask.

It's not a conclusion Morgan will want to reach but by this point she'll pretty much accept any reading of the past that puts it to bed.

But it's not the answer. It doesn't fit. It doesn't help. It remains a puzzle – how much she misses Gwen, how often she finds herself thinking of her. And she knows of no epic poems, no legends, no bardic songs, no *Romeo and Juliet*, that exist to explain it to her. The record is nigh empty, as though women never adored each other, never went into battle, never fought the monster, never wept and bled, killed and died for each other, who separated, didn't feel the other's absence like a missing limb.

'My dad's waiting,' Morgan says. Still nothing. When she turns to go, Gwen doesn't even lift a hand.

The Book of Lance

———

From his mother, Lance gets religion. She tells him God knows each and every blade of grass. That the water running in the brook is a prayer to the Lord. She kisses him goodnight. 'God knows what is in our hearts, Lance,' she says, 'folded up in darkness in the deepest most secret places.'

One evening, not long before it happens, they walk up a farm track to the crest of a hill. They are holding hands and their shadow looks like one spindly, lopsided, two-headed creature. His dad is in one of the fields below, combining or baling, driving a big machine with his tongue stuck out for concentration.

A breeze riffles their clothes. All the living things seem to be dancing.

'"The wind bloweth where it listeth, and thou hearest the sound thereof, but canst not tell whence it cometh, and whither it goeth: so is every one that is born of the Spirit." That's from the Bible, Lance.'

'What does it mean?'

She pauses. 'I think it means that our spirits are like the wind: they go where they like and we cannot tell them what to do. Our spirits are on their own journey and we may not understand it.'

A few weeks later she drowns herself in a lake. Lance is six. Part of him will remain six forever, six years old and waiting for his mother to come back out the water.

From his father, Lance gets hardiness, a knack with machinery, the ability to fix and build and coax and to suffer in silence. The silence is the hardest gift.

They move around from farm to farm. Ireland. Then a few months in the Hebrides. Then the north of England: Northumberland, the Pennines, the Yorkshire moors. When he goes to school, he sits on his own at a desk at the back, kicking his legs. Always behind with no hope of catching up. Only his body can be trusted to do what he asks of it: football, fighting, what have you.

His dad wipes at his bleeding nose with a handkerchief.

'What's the IRA, Dad? Are we in it?'

'No, son. We're not.'

Around the time he reaches his teens, his father's drinking gets bad, so he stays off and does the work for him. Feeds the animals, mucks them out, scrapes the yard, milks the cows. Comes in and makes egg and chips for them both. Turns on the TV so the silence in the caravan isn't quite so deafening.

When he's sixteen, they go south to Wiltshire. He likes the land, how it rolls in waves. Beneath the downs, there's good pasture and pretty villages cut through by chalk streams. The farm they're at is next to a racing yard. At dawn, he watches the horses riding out, stringing the skyline, riders and animals moving as one.

When he's seventeen, Lance is out fencing when he sees a girl on the hillside. Her back is straight and the wind blows her hair before her face. He can only see glimpses of her features as the breeze blows the flaxen strands like a living curtain about her head. She rises steadily up the hillside on a path of white stones.

In the middle of the field she stops. High above her a falcon hovers on the wind. As Lance watches, he sees the falcon fall, plummeting all the way down to the girl's feet. When it rises, it slows a few feet from the ground at the height of the girl's shoulders. In its talons is a small creature, something brown with a tail. The bird seems to look the girl in the face, and on the wind Lance hears her laughing.

A mystery revealed. A picture of his soul before him. The laughing girl. The wild winged creature. Its bleeding prey. Animal and human, suffering and beauty, death and wild laughter. All in balance, and in it the possibility of wholeness.

But he mistakes the epiphany for the girl, whose name is Gwen and whose brother works behind the bar at the pub, along with another new arrival to Abury, a sullen dark-haired boy called Wayne.

He only sees her a handful of times, passing by in the street, in a car, once on a fine grey horse, but it's enough. Soon, he thinks about her all the time, imagines how they might meet, what they might say. Sometimes he wades so deep into the dream of her, he'll look up and hours will have passed. Sometimes it worries him, that he couldn't wade back, even if he wanted to.

Lance does a full-day's work now, earns a grown man's pay. His dad quits the drink, just like that, overnight. He wants to go back to Ireland. There's a job on the west coast on land that belongs to a monastery. It comes with a house. It's somewhere quiet, as if more silence is what they need. It takes every ounce of Lance's strength to tell his dad he's staying.

'Maybe you found something you like here. Maybe you'll come on later.'

He nods and his father's hand falls on his shoulder.

The farmer and his wife promise to look after him. The wife has taken a shine to Lance. Women do.

*

Lance is so beautiful he daren't go clubbing or hang around the pub at kicking out, as each time without fail he gets accused of looking at someone's bird, when of course it is the bird who is looking at him. Lance, who ends up rolling around car parks while the guy's friend fetches a bat from the boot. But never bested, not once, only defenceless when it comes to women, a vacuousness to his bright blue eyes. When teased, he doesn't parry it. Like the Diet Coke man if he was on the spectrum. Helpful. Lonely. But shying away.

Glimpsed on his motorbike, or carrying a pair of tyres with his overalls rolled down to his waist, or holding a puppy or a baby, or washing a car, or welding, Lance has the power to cause traffic accidents. A look from Lance at the right moment can put a teen-ager out of sorts for weeks, his beauty a haunting song sung by Billie Holiday.

Then he goes with Elaine which confirms something's wrong with him. Elaine, of all the girls, with her white tights, and her affected voice, avid member of an evangelical church. Elaine in her Christian coat and Christian shoes; at school when a question's asked, she thrusts her hand so high in the air, like an invisible force is about to suck her out of her chair. An authority pleaser, a teacher-stalker, who tells the whole class Jesus is her best friend.

Afterwards, Elaine says that on the day her parents went to the revival in Birmingham, Lance had been kind enough to help her carry her cello home after she hurt her knee playing netball. Once there, they'd been tempted into sin, first by her parents' drinks cabinet and then upon the soft eiderdown of their bed. Which wouldn't be the way Lance would tell it, only he doesn't say a word.

But there's some truth in it, or why would Lance take to having his tea there? Why does he trail at Elaine's family's heels to church in a shirt and tie? Why is he seen outside the jeweller's with Elaine one Saturday morning while she points out rings oblivious to the misery any watching fool could see?

Rumours after that, unlikely whispers. Something about Lance going round one evening to sit at Elaine's dining-room table and hold hands with her parents while they prayed together to the smell of air freshener and burnt mince, then Elaine putting on a videotape, a preacher from America leaping up and down and shouting about hellfire. So far, so normal.

Lance excusing himself to go to the bathroom, climbing the stairs and then taking all his clothes off and jumping out the window. Lance running off down the back garden and leaping over the fence into the trees. Lance, naked as a baby, out of his mind, seeing things that aren't there, talking to trees in the woods, getting chased by the ambulance crew. Lance shouting something about the wind, too fast to be caught.

Or maybe not, the whisperers go on, maybe he'd just been at the drinks cabinet again. The Irish in him coming out.

It's likely Wayne would know, because the next time Lance pops up it's at the Green Knight, shoulder to shoulder with Wayne, quiet but fully clothed, sipping slowly on a pint of lime soda, while the kid Gareth, the one that works at the chip shop, larks about as usual.

Then Elaine coming in and the smile dying on his lips. Elaine in the pub, feathers all ruffled, fixing him with a beady eye.

'And where have you been, Lance?' Glaring at Wayne and Gareth, so the latter pretends to have been shot in the chest and crumples to the floor making choking noises. Elaine drawing herself up, all five feet and seventeen years of her, lacking only the rolling pin. 'You,' she tells him, 'have some explaining to do.'

So he explains, makes it clear that he's got another woman now.

'And who's that, then? Not that—'

'The Queen,' Lance replies quickly. Then he tells her that he, Wayne and Aidey have signed up, pledged themselves to Queen and Country. They've gone and joined the Wessex.

Black Prince

———

October 1996

Hey Arthur,
You found me. It is really me.

So university, first year, first term, my verdict: you do meet a lot of people, only in my case the people are books. I've been eaten by the library, swallowed up whole. The library has eaten me and I am eating the books. I am relentless. I spare none of them.

The light here is different. You can tell the north was once another kingdom.

Mum and Dad have moved to the suburbs of Reading. They seem to be settling in. So that's where I'll be at Christmas.

How are things in Abury?

Morgan

*

December 1996

Dear Arthur,
Sorry for not writing back for so long. I did get your messages. Thing is, there was a bit of the old trouble. The bus trouble. I'm living in halls this year. Or I was. There were some lads on my floor . . .

Anyway, it's over now. I've moved out. I'm now staying with

Professor Ragnell from the department. She has a room she rents out at her house. Her last tenant was a German PhD student, but Hilde's gone back to Heidelberg, lucky for me. It's in the woods off campus, so I've had to get a bike. Imagine a stone cottage chock-full of books. Some of them are hundreds of years old. I stepped inside and my whole body went TWANG!

What's Ragnell like? Let's see: she could be fifty, she could be five hundred and fifty. She wears a cape. She's got a wide mouth, with thin lips, rather like a toad, and like a toad she's sort of squat but with luminous quartz for eyes. Deep rolling voice. Her hands are covered in rings – and WARTS! And she cuts her hair herself – a kind of tonsure – over the bathroom sink.

Now I think she's rather beautiful. I find myself hanging around the kitchen at suppertime, because that's when she surfaces, usually to heat a can of whatever comes out the larder first and eat it with hunks of bread she tears from the loaf with her hands. If I'm lucky, I get a half-hour monologue about whatever she's working on. Sometimes, when she stops talking, it's like the whole world has shifted a degree or two.

What's new with you?

Morgan

*

February 1997

Arthur!!! I saw you in the fucking newspaper! Newspapers! There was your face on the front page of ALL of them. So I bought the lot. Turns out you (rather insultingly they refer to you as a schoolboy in the main) have SAVED us (your countrymen, but also the world) from a vicious virus!

Computer experts the world over were unable to vanquish the fearsome *Black Prince* virus (great name, who came up with it?) until a young Englishman created a magic code (I must confess that I was getting a bit lost at this point) that defeated it. Last week, there was talk of turning off all the university computers on a certain date. Something about infected 'doss'? Something about the virus being a shape-shifter? Talk of people all over the world losing access to their hard drives. In the library, I heard a PhD student threaten to throw himself in the River Wear if he lost his thesis. The labs were up in arms over their precious data. But now it's all over and everything is OK again – THANKS TO YOU!

However did you do it? Do you think you'll get a medal? Or invited to a garden party with the Queen? Is Kay sick to his guts with jealousy? Is he howling and squirming – do say he is!

What will you do? I guess they'll take you seriously now.

No plans to come back to Abury anytime soon. I've got a job for the summer as a research assistant, so I'll be staying here.

Write to me when you have time. Tell me everything.

Morgan

PS I confess I spent ages looking at the photo of you and the football team. I could name all but three of them! Had no idea you were captain. Are you really as tall as all that?

*

November 1997

Dear Arthur,

Thank you! How did you find out about the prize? It's not a very big one. I don't think anyone outside the department even knows about it. But yes, I am pleased. Usually a third-year gets it, so I must have done something right.

What am I up to? Wandering ever deeper into various thickets. I remember you saying once, 'Isn't history just war and corn laws?' And not really having an answer for you. But now I've learned to talk the talk and can say that conflict and trade are only two of the lenses available to us in our interrogations of the past (if you like, you can imagine me scratching my chin and peering over my spectacles).

Currently my lens is . . . lunacy. The historical perception and treatment of madness, especially in women. And of course, then you end up in medicine, historical cures, the way people used to understand the body.

A flayed pigeon, applied to the privy parts, is the cardinal's cure for the pox!

It's endlessly fascinating, especially midwifery.

Yesterday I came across the description of a suicide in Samuel

Pepys, a young girl with a twisted spine. Before she died, she said she did it *because she did not like herself, nor had not liked herself nor anything she did a great while.*

Often, I look up from my books and I wonder what century it is. Mainly, what I am learning about is power. How power functions, how it shapes reality.

One more thing, since we were talking about war and because it might be useful to you as you build your vast empire. Once I asked Ragnell why historians write about it so much when for most people it's not a defining factor (not like sanitation or taxes), and why books about war – not just in the field of history, but in literature too – are far more likely to win prizes, and wasn't it just another example of the favouring of male narratives and in particular those narratives that glorify a certain kind of constructed masculinity? And she looked at me for what felt like a long time and then she said, 'Perhaps it's because everyone has a war. There are the wars outside, and then there are the wars inside.' And while I was thinking about that, she smiled at me, but it was a sad sort of smile and then she said, 'Oh Morgan, do try to pick one you can win.'

How different our lives are right now, Arthur. I hope the investment comes through like you hope. Write to me now and again if you have time.

Love Morgan

*

December 1997

Hey Arthur,

I'm taking a leaf out of your book and writing this to you in the middle of the night. Tomorrow, if there's anything worth sending, I'll put it on a disk and send it via one of the university computers. Such a modern world we live in!

I had a bad dream, bad enough that I don't want to go back to bed.

You know how at school they used to call me a witch? Well, I don't know if that's what started it but for as long as I can remember, I've had this nightmare about a house, a witch's house, a dark lonely

73

place, touched by evil. In the dream, I know she's looking for me and I'm terrified that she'll find me, but I always wake before she does.

I told Ragnell about it when I was still living with her and she said I should go in, that I should meet the witch, and I've not had a nightmare since – until tonight – only this dream wasn't about the witch, it was about Gwen.

In the dream, she was trapped in an Iron Maiden – you know, one of those torture devices. She was calling out to me from inside, screaming for me to help her . . .

I don't know. I've probably been reading too much Deleuze.

It wasn't about Aidey really, our falling-out. It's hard to put into words. It used to get to me that Gwen took the way people treated her – not just the boys, not just other kids, remember that teacher, Mrs Frank, who was always fawning over her and asking where she bought her clothes? – as something she'd earned. And by extension, what I'd got was also somehow deserved.

And it was about hierarchy, wasn't it? Because in the beginning she had all this capital and I had none and she chose me as her friend. And it was wonderful. Becoming friends with Gwen . . . I used to wake up and leap out of bed because I couldn't wait to see her. But everything was always on her terms: what we did and where we went. How cold she'd go if I was too friendly with Carly or someone else, or if she thought I kept a secret from her, or talked about what I'd got in a test or going to university. And then I'd have to work really hard to win her back. Teenage stuff.

Then I remember how, when she'd stay over, when it was dark, she would ask me whether I really liked her. Whether I really, really liked her. Over and over again. And how she never quite believed me when I said that I did.

And I think about her awful mother and her pig father and fucking Aidey. Do you ever see her?

M

*

February 1998

Arthur – never do that again! I swear you nearly gave me a heart attack, swooping down on me like that. The library will never be the same. I'll always be expecting you to appear out of nowhere and put a hand on my shoulder. You can call that wishful thinking.

It was lovely to see you, Arthur. Just lovely. After you left, I went back to bed – thumping hangover, of course – and I spent the whole day reading the same paragraph over and over and hoping you'd come back so we ... might finish what we started.

Did you like it at the Union? Did it make you wish you'd gone up to Cambridge when they wanted you?

I don't know why Cal was so off with you. Maybe she was jealous of your dance moves. Sorry she gave you such a grilling about *Black Prince* – but then you were being ever so cagey!

I hope that meeting in York went the way you wanted. Or do I? Maybe if it didn't, you'll have to come back.

X

*

March 1998

I can still taste you on my lips. I close my eyes and I see you pulling off your shirt, wrapping my hair around your hand. I want to hear more of that weird computer poetry. Serenade me in 0s and 1s.

You are so beautiful. So tall and so lovely. Happy 18th, Arthur. Happy 18th all over again.

*

March 1998

What? Are you not going to write to me any more?

*

April 1998

Is it because I got fat again?

*

75

I get all that, Arthur, but the thing is – you pursued me. You made it happen. You said all that stuff. And then you disappear for ages. And when you do write, it's to send me a stiff little email in which you try and lie about what happened.

Do you know how it makes a person feel, when someone comes right up close, gets behind the gates and has a good look around, and then FLEES as though from a burning house or a MURDER?

Take your evasions, and your cowardice, and your I-don't-want-to-be-in-a-relationship-right-now, and stick them UP YOUR ARSE, Arthur.

*

September 1998

OK, but what was I supposed to think?

You were confused. That makes two of us. I don't know what it is you want from me, what you've ever wanted. I know we were both a bit unusual by Abury standards. And I know that's lonely sometimes.

Was that it? That you were lonely?

To be honest, Arthur, I think we should just leave it. Apology accepted. A veil drawn over it.

I'm not coming back to Abury anytime soon. No chance. This year, I've got to focus on my finals. Then the MA is a year – King's has already said yes – and after that I'm looking at the US for a PhD, maybe Berkeley. Next summer Cal has invited me to her family's place in Greece, so I'm afraid the answer is no, there's not much chance of us meeting.

*

August 1999

Thank you for the champagne, Arthur. It was very sweet of you. A whole case! We drank it in Ragnell's garden – yes, all of it, I'm afraid. Me, Cal and a few friends from the department, toasting our firsts, drunk on the warm evening air and the birdsong and the future. It was wonderful, although there was this strange moment with Ragnell.

I was down the bottom of the garden, champagne bottle in hand, and I'm leaning with my elbows on the well, staring into its inky depths, thinking about making a wish. Wouldn't you like to know! Anyway, someone comes to stand beside me and, looking down at my reflection, I think I see a young woman. The water's rippling but, still, a young beautiful woman and she asks me what I want.

And I don't have an answer for her.

And then I look up at the person next to me and it's Ragnell. Not a beautiful young woman at all.

Ragnell thinks it's a mistake, the change of focus. She says I'll just end up clearing away men's messes. That women do what they think they ought to do, and men do what they want. She's a bit sniffy about my plans to go to America too.

I'll send you a postcard from the island.

Morgan x

*

August 1999

What should I say? That we'll always have Athens? That I promise to call on you again if I ever need to escape from someone's mad Greek family. The yacht was a nice touch.

X

*

November 1999

A coincidence indeed. My seminar finishes at five. My room's 718.

*

September 2000

Arthur, greetings from the grand old US of A. Howdy-doody-do? Yee-ha! Etc., etc.

It's been ages, I know. Ten months. You wrote me that long, lovely email after the conference and I thought to myself, that email deserves a really well-thought-out response. Not just to all the developments with the company (honestly, Arthur, it's like a fairy tale, you're going to be a magnate, a titan, like the dude in *Citizen Kane*) but the other stuff.

There's been a lot going on. My head's been wrecked. I saw Cal again before I flew out. It was pretty brutal. It triggered . . . I don't know . . . something. I didn't tell you but when we were in Greece, we slept together. Me and Cal. Are you shocked?

I was. I couldn't handle it and I was cold to her afterwards, just like you were to me that time. She was furious and her family thought I must have done something terrible, which is when I called you.

So yes, Arthur, in response to your letter, I love you too and I think I want to be with you, but maybe I'm gay. But I don't know. I am so confused and I am scared as well and, at the same time, I am laughing when I see it written down.

I love you and I'm gay. I want to be with you but in a year, maybe two, or maybe only in my mind. I feel like you're slipping through my fingers and I can't bear it. But last week, I kissed an Italian girl, all biceps and belt buckle. She said her family make ice cream and I swear I could taste it.

Today I saw your face on the cover of a magazine and whoever wrote the piece knows what they're talking about because they called you a GENIUS. And there was a picture of you with Bill Gates! And then there was another picture of you. In a field, I think. And you were smiling and I saw it and had to write to you straight away. Such a lovely photo, Arthur. Who took it?

America is everything. It's like living in a TV series. Yellow cabs and bartenders and Pacific Highways and street cars. I'm gradually finding my feet. It was my twenty-second birthday last week and my housemates took me to a club called the Lex.

Tell me how you are – right now if you can!

X

*

October 2000

Will I come to your and Gwen's wedding? Ha ha ha ha ha ha ha

78

ha ha ha ha ha ha ha ha ha ha ha ha ha ha ha ha ha ha ha ha ha
ha ha ha ha ha ha ha ha ha ha ha ha ha ha ha ha ha ha ha ha ha
ha ha ha ha ha ha ha ha ha ha ha ha ha ha ha ha ha ha ha ha ha
ha ha ha ha ha ha ha ha ha ha ha ha ha ha ha ha ha ha ha ha ha
ha ha ha ha ha ha ha ha ha ha ha ha ha ha ha ha ha ha ha ha ha . . .

11

May Queen

———

Six months into the new millennium – seven months since Arthur last saw Morgan, three months since he gave up waiting for her to answer the email in which he told her he loved her – Arthur gets down on bended knee and asks Gwen to marry him. They're in the stables. Gwen's holding a pitchfork. Her grey, Boxer, blows in Arthur's ear.

Twenty-one years old, he still lives with his parents, still sleeps in the bedroom he slept in as a boy. He owns a company, rents an office, has the beginnings of a team, an accountant who's hired two juniors and gone full-time. He's busy making it, and he wants a wife and a home, someone to share the corners of his life with that aren't work – someone to share gossip and victories with, someone to be at his side, to suggest this jacket not that one, to straighten his collar, to show other men he is a man. What kind of man? Well, the kind who never raises his voice, clear-eyed with a quick smile, almost unbelievably young – and yet one who is married to Gwen, racer of pulses, with a dancer's posture, warm-blooded, speedy on the uptake, steely when necessary, no one's fool.

Arthur is no one's fool either. But they look at one another foolishly.

'Yes,' Gwen says. 'Yes, I will.'

And with that the book of questions bangs shut.

Arthur's unexpected. Arthur's quality. He's in the elevator. He's soft in the right places, unyielding in others. He looks like the handsome young lieutenant in old movies, the one who dies doing something noble. But on their first date, if that's what you could call it – a desolate, rainy Sunday in December, bumping into one another outside the Co-op, why not a drink at the Green Knight? – he'd thrashed Gwen mercilessly at cards at a table next to the fire and then told her mildly that it was her round.

A bit later they'd got talking about Morgan. Arthur said she was doing a Masters in Cambridge but would be leaving in the summer for America. Apparently they were friends of some kind, Morgan and Arthur. Momentarily, she'd felt affronted but this was quickly overtaken by the old pain of missing Morgan. Seeing her feelings reflected in Arthur's glum face, she'd forgiven him and they'd played a couple more hands in companionable silence.

On the way back to the Co-op car park, a surge of panic. She didn't want to let him go, and in the numbing drizzle, by the bottle bank, she surprised herself by barging into Arthur and kissing him.

Sex with Arthur, Gwen decides, is the right temperature. Not too hot, not too cold. If she doesn't call him, he will call her, but when he gets round to it, when he realises he misses her, and he'll be friendly. Not like those other calls she gets, the funny phone calls that always seem to come when her dad's out and she's alone at the farm, calls from a heavy-breather who pants and groans.

Gwen and Arthur are a match. Abury will rejoice. The old folk know a young marriage is a good one, husband and wife will knit together like bone after a break – which overlooks the fact that neither Arthur nor Gwen has any bend in them.

No long engagement, they decide, not like Carly and Dan who've been breaking it off and making it up for as long as anyone can remember.

Arthur kisses her hands. He slides on the ring and then gets up, job done. Soon, the machinery will get going, the machinery in which Gwen will be enmeshed for a good few years – wedding planning and organising, then house buying and renovations, then upscaling, upscaling fucking everything as all falls to Arthur.

For the moment, it's just pleasure: Gwen feels like she's won. So does Arthur. A joint victory, unlike the ones that come later after they wed, when it always feels that one of them getting what they want comes at the other's expense.

From his pocket, Arthur takes a carrot and holds it out to Boxer. It disappears inside the horse to the sound of loud crunching. He's not above bribery.

What now?

In the end they take the champagne Arthur brought but which he'd left in the car just in case and go out on a tractor. Arthur's never driven one before, so Gwen sits on his lap, her feet atop his on the pedals. She turns the key and it roars to life.

'Handbrake off and into first.'

They take off out of the yard and down one of the farm tracks. Inside the cab, it's noisier than he could possibly have imagined and bumpier too. Each time they go over a rut, Gwen bounces on his lap. Soon he's got the hang of it and they're careering through the fields. Gwen tears off the foil from the champagne cork with her teeth and pops it, so it foams up soaking them both. Her hair threatens to blind him. At any moment they'll burst through a hedgerow, down a ditch, into a gatepost. He takes a hand from the wheel and runs it over her body. She presses back against him and his foot slides off the gas. The tractor bucks and stalls.

Gwen slides half round, throws her arms about his neck and kisses him. Arthur's arms are full of her. His mouth is full of her. His heart too.

The bottle, same vintage he sent a case of to Morgan when she graduated, slips free and falls, and the good champagne spills and soaks the cab floor, trickling down the steps and through the tattered seal and falls in fat drops on to the grass, and then slides on further, from blade to meet the ever-thirsty earth.

No doubts for Gwen, not yet. But she does wonder that night in bed as she's drifting off, *Why the bended knee?* Not just Arthur, but in general. What does the bended knee say?

*

They wed on the first of May, 2001. Workers' Days in Europe, Maypole Day in Abury, where tradition demands girls and boys dressed in white are pelted with rain as they ribbon round a towering wooden prick. The windswept attendees are treated to a raffle and a bake sale. There's jumble in the town hall. Tea from the giant urn for twenty pence. But today's turnout is poor; even the mums of the maypole kids are keen to wrap up the ancient rituals and get up to the church for an eyeful of Gwen's dress.

Gwen's dad Leo gives her away. Arthur accepts her from his arm. Kay offers up the rings at the right moment.

When they kneel at the altar, she trembles in her dress and the guests nudge one another. But it's the cold, coming up through the stones.

Leaving the church, they pass under a raggle-taggle sabre arch, the guard of honour composed of Aidey and a handful of his friends from the Wessex in their uniforms. They started drinking last night as soon as they left base and started up again this morning. She recognises Wayne from the Green Knight, but the others she doesn't know from Adam.

A crowd of well-wishers throw confetti and call out for them to kiss. A patch of blue opens up between the clouds. It will be fine, after all.

Later, up at the castle, all Gwen can think is, *It's done. It's done!* The phrase resounding through her like the slamming of an iron door. Relief that she has made it through, relief almost like hysteria, so wild and gay does she feel, like someone very relieved, or someone who has made a mistake of immeasurable proportions.

Morgan hasn't come. *Fuck that bitch*, she thinks. *Just fuck her.* Since getting together with Arthur, she's been all for burying the hatchet, had even gone as far as trying to imagine Morgan in a bridesmaid's dress. But Arthur claims she never replied to his email and best to leave it.

Still, all through the reception a wild happiness spills from her. She wobbles up on a chair clutching a champagne glass to make her own toast, mainly to respond to Kay's barbed best-man's speech, which is funny and fond and teasing, and which also manages to gently insinuate Gwen is a cradle-snatching, gold-digging whore.

'We all love Gwen. Some have even loved her more than once...'

Looking out, there are so many faces she doesn't know. She smiles at all of them. Dances with most. Does shots at the bar with the rest. Hurls her bouquet over her head fit to decapitate someone.

Aidey escorts her up on the battlements, promising Betty he'll make sure she doesn't trip over her dress and plunge to her death. Upon the parapet, the wind blows in from the south-west. They have a nip from his hip flask. He lights two cigs and hands her one.

'Have I done all right, brother?'

If anyone will say what people are secretly thinking, it's Aidey.

But he only nods. 'If you don't fuck it up, little sister.' Then, 'Want me to waterboard that flapping cunt brother of his?'

'Is that what they're teaching you? Hey, don't ash on my fucking dress.'

'Or you'll have me, won't you? And to think they call me Aggro.'

Aidey leans against the stone, flicks his butt in thin air and watches it fall.

'Morgan didn't make it, then?'

'No.'

'You never did like it when I played with your toys.'

But if she didn't know him better, she'd swear there was something in his voice that was almost regret.

'I'm sure you'll find another victim.'

And he does, or at least she assumes he does as no one sees Aidey after nine thirty, not after it gets dark. The dance floor fills, first with girl children and grannies, later with couples, the drunk and the very drunk. Netty, all of fifteen, grinds against young Gareth from the chip shop. Carly and Dan shuffle in a slow circle, their bodies locked from breast to knee, eyes closed. Round and round they go, no matter the song. For most, it is the last time they'll see her. It is how they will remember her. In her pink dress, Carly in love with love as always.

It takes ages to leave. Arthur wants to shake hands with or hug every single person there. Gwen goes from room to room. There is someone she wants to say goodbye to, but she can't remember who. Or is it her shoes she's looking for?

In the castle's ruined chambers, hawthorn torches are burning. Some say hawthorn is right for weddings. It burns long and hot. Others disagree. Hawthorn's for love in the fields, not love in a bed.

A young man in soldier's uniform is sitting alone in a room she can't remember being there before. When she comes in, he stands up.

84

'Why are you at my wedding? Christ, I don't know anyone!'

'I'm Lance,' he says.

'And why do you look so sad and sorry, Lance?'

'A certain lady got married today. And I do not know what to do.' Irish accent. Chest like a door.

She laughs at him and then takes him in her arms and kisses him. She kisses Lance because she's happy and because he looks so sad, and because she wants to, underneath the hawthorn torches. And he trembles in her arms and it is not the cold.

Fuck! She tears herself from him and stumbles away.

Arthur, Arthur, she must get back to Arthur.

When she finally finds him, she throws herself into his arms, half laughing, half crying.

'For fuck's sake, Arthur, take your wife to bed, won't you!'

So he does. They get in the car, a cool silver vintage Jaguar with a driver in a peaked cap and a tangle of cans tied to the back. As they move off, the younger guests run alongside banging on the boot, until the driver puts his foot down and they speed away.

A perfect day. Even if she did kiss someone else. Even if Arthur spends a whole hour on his computer before he comes to bed.

Even if, two days later, while they're still feeling their way into their honeymoon, Carly goes out to meet someone late one night and doesn't come home, though it pelts with rain.

A farmer finds her in a field encircled by his herd of Friesians. They blow on her, touch her with their tongues, but they cannot wake her.

The farmer kneels in the churned ground to turn her over. There is mud in her hair, mud all over her, but it doesn't hide the blood.

The hawthorn is in full blossom, the lambs skip playfully in the fields, and the killer is never caught.

12

The Book of Mo

———

In the early years after his marriage, when Arthur is still in his twenties, he's like the boy who, fishing for minnows in the village pond, hauls a gleaming golden crown up from out of the depths. And it fits! The crown fits! Because Arthur, in addition to his genius for computers, discovers inside himself a further hoard of aptitudes: strategy and cunning, ruthlessness and foresight. Little Arthur – a deal maker; shy, nerdy Arthur – a disruptor, a mover, an earth shaker.

So much happening and so fast, but he can't slow down. He tries to explain to Gwen that it's like Frogger, the arcade game they played on their Atari 5200 back in the day. Great that you got across the road, great that you hopped on to the log, but if you slow down or stop, the crocodiles will get you. She looks back at him blankly, but she's still onside, for now.

So much happening and so fast, he can't do it alone. He couldn't do it without Kay, and Kay couldn't do it without Perce, Trist, Lionel, Bors and Garlon – not to mention the others he hires hand over fist. In Abury, they'll joke that Kay made his barber Head of Logistics. *Jobs for everyone! Jobs for the boys!*

And if, remembering certain bus journeys, Arthur feels a ripple of disquiet, it's dispelled by their keenness to prove themselves, by their hard work and loyalty. The projects they take on. The victories they lay at his feet. When they speak of him, it's with such pride. *Our Arthur*, they say, *our kid*, and they say it with wonder, with respect and, yes, with love.

The love is genuine.

The love of power is genuine.

For the most part, he leaves them to it. He has to because these are years of acquisition: houses, land, offices, a string of rival outfits from Moscow to Buenos Aires, small kingdoms absorbed into the empire Arthur's building.

And then, of course, there's Mo.

Arthur is in Bangalore. It's 2005. Days of meeting after meeting, shuttling through the city in an air-conditioned Mercedes, jet lag like a minor but persistent illness. Arthur and the driver crawling through the rush-hour traffic to and from the five-star hotel near the airport. Arthur tired, his head against the window, eyes moving over the wares on display, the movie posters and rickshaws, the butter-colour dogs who lie scratching and dreaming in the road.

On the last day, heading back to the hotel, cows clog a junction and the horns rise in unison. Arthur opens his eyes, half-dreaming, and sees a child, a small black-eyed boy in filthy rags, standing on the corner. He's wearing a kind of shift and has nothing on his legs. On one shin is an open sore, red and weeping against the dark brown skin.

Their eyes meet: the little boy – four, maybe five? – and the grown man. Neither looks away and something must pass between them, or at least passes from the child to the man, because – cows moved on, road cleared –.while the Mercedes continues on its way, something of Arthur remains behind.

In dreams, in reverie, he returns to the moment. There is the destitute child, there are the peeling Bollywood posters, the refuse, the lifting curtain of red dust. And the child looks at Arthur – cocooned within layer after layer of privilege and wealth – with fathomless eyes. A month passes in which Arthur puts a continent, then two continents, between them, but the boy's gaze finds him, in the deepest depths of his sleep, surprising him in the mirror as he draws a razor over his chin, as he eats and works and tries to rest.

He gives a million to charity. Like a muscle spasm. It does no good.

Then it's time to go back, to finalise the deal that will make the tech industry re-evaluate Arthur yet again now that the scale of his ambition is clear. The same hotel is arranged, the same driver. And again, there is the boy on the corner, and Arthur thinks, *He's just a child* . . .

Still, he orders the driver to stop and gets out. The boy has not yet seen him. It's odd, how he's almost afraid, how in the instant before Mo clocks him, Arthur's instinct is to bolt.

From the car, the driver watches the young man sit down with the boy on the kerb, their knees turned to one another. The man speaks a little. The child makes hand gestures. At one point, the boy smiles and the driver thinks he sees the man flinch as though pierced with a sudden pain.

By the time he returns to the car, no longer alone, Arthur's mind is made up. He'll adopt the boy, save him, take him back to Abury. Gently, he buckles Mo into the seat beside him and makes the first of many phone calls. The boy looks around the car smiling, seemingly entirely at home.

His parents are incensed. 'He's not a dog, Arthur. You can't bring him home because you feel sorry for him!'

Kay says it's because Arthur's mad, that Arthur's always been mad and why does no one ever believe him when he tells them?

Once the news becomes public, a columnist suggests Mo's a salve to Arthur's conscience, atonement for deals done with smartphone manufacturers while kids are hauling rocks in Congolese cobalt mines.

A celebrity therapist speculates whether Arthur was trying to make a deal with suffering, that by transforming the boy's life he intends to buy it off and banish it.

Whatever the truth, he will harness everything he has in service to the cause, will wager the deal, his business, his marriage and reputation. Blackmail, bribery and endless patience, a frenzy of lawyers and, for as long as it takes, his undivided attention.

*

Back home in Abury, and for the second time in his life, Arthur gets down on his knees to Gwen and this time he begs; she realises that until now he's never truly needed anything from her.

They've been trying for a baby for two years, but eighteen months is average and he's so often away.

'I don't understand, Arthur. You want him to be our son?'

'I'm not sure I understand myself,' Arthur says, half laughing but not that far from crying either. 'I might have gone mad. But it feels like it did when you kissed me at the bottle bank.'

'And how was that?'

'Like Fate.'

Gwen blushes to the roots of her hair, and the warm embers of her love for him flare into tall yellow flames.

And maybe it is Fate. Or maybe it's one of Fate's sisters, the one called Nemesis.

Anyway, the madness catches. Gwen says yes to being needed by Arthur. Why not? Why not? Why not? After all, they'll have loads of kids.

'Won't we just!' And Arthur picks her up and carries her halfway up the stairs before it gets a bit much for him and they take the last flight together, chasing one another into the nearest bedroom, giggling as they go.

Afterwards, it's only when they're lying in each other's arms, sated and basking, does Gwen realise how lonely she's been, knows it by loneliness's sudden banishment. Not that she's not got plenty to keep her busy with the house renovation, not that she's actually been alone that much – the company lot always make sure she's included if there's something happening, even if it's just a few drinks at the Green Knight. And if Arthur's away and she needs something, Kay or one of the others will step up. Perce drove her about after she sprained an ankle, Bors comes over to set up the gadgets Arthur's always ordering.

The women are nice to her too: the girlfriends, the fiancées, those who work at the company in admin or customer-support roles. Nice but also a bit nervy – like they probably breathe a sigh of relief when she heads off – seeing as she's the boss's wife.

So, a bit lonely. So much so that when the heavy-breathing phone calls started up again, this time to her mobile, before hanging up on the caller she'd had the wry thought that at least someone hadn't forgotten her . . .

That had been followed, not by a thought but by a memory – a blurred figure moving behind the misted glass of a bus shelter – and then, what can only be described as an aural hallucination.

GWEN!

Carly's voice, she'd swear to it. Carly's voice loudly saying her name.

So she called Kay and babbled at him and, to be fair, Trist and Lionel came straight over to instal the first security cameras. Garlon helped her set up call-screening on her phone.

In one of their fourteen bedrooms, Gwen rolls on top of Arthur, makes a curtain of her hair about his face.

'All right, Arthur, all right, my love,' she says, smiling.

Arthur gets what he wants. He gets what he wants and – heaven and earth moved – Mo comes to them, to Abury, to England's green and pleasant land. Shortly after that, Arthur has to go away again. To San Fran. Singapore. Jakarta. Shanghai. To Silicone Valleys and web summits.

Gwen snapping down the phone. 'Seen any children that take your fancy?'

Because the boy, Mo, isn't doing well.

*

Gwen saddles Boxer. She tightens the girth then puts a foot in the stirrup and swings up. Mo stands on the mounting block where she'd left him, eyes glazed, face blank, still little enough for her to lift him up in front of her.

She has sacked all of them: the play therapist, the English teacher, the jolly Karnatakan chef. She leaves the phone unanswered. It's her and Mo now.

He's been with them two months and he is regressing. That's the official term for it, and the regression is speeding up. In the beginning, he kept asking for Arthur. But now Mo has stopped talking. She's had to put him in nappies. She can't convince him to eat. He grows glassy-eyed, unresponsive for long hours at a time. Sometimes he screams, tears at his clothes, beats himself against the floor.

What could cause such behaviour? Well, cataclysmic loss, cataclysmic trauma.

'And that's us, is it? Is that what you're saying?'

She'd bolted from the therapist's office and tried to get Arthur on the phone but he was in Frankfurt in a meeting.

'You tell him if he wants to stay married, he's to get out of that fucking meeting.' When he came on the line, she was still savage.

'He had no family? No one? Are you sure, Arthur? You weren't lied to? They didn't just tell you what you wanted to hear?'

He swore not. Swore it on all that was holy.

Then, haltingly, Arthur suggested what Mo might need was a residential stay, if Gwen couldn't cope, if it was the best thing for him.

And part of her love, the part that thought Arthur was better than her, that believed she could truly trust him, died right there in Waitrose car park. She stepped over its corpse, hurrying to the car, hurrying to get home to him, to her little boy.

They will not take him from her. Not now. Not ever.

Later, she'll wonder if the fierceness of what she felt for Mo was because the love came in all at once. You're supposed to have nine months to grow it, to get used to it a trickle at a time.

With Mo, it's like being hit by a jet from a fire hose, concentrated all the more by her instinct that she's losing him.

The nights are the worst. Sometimes, he doesn't move a muscle the whole night through, his body stiff under the pristine covers. Then there are nights like tonight when he starts shrieking, a high-pitched animal wailing, heart-rending in its despair.

It is two a.m. Gwen clicks Boxer on, draws Mo in tight against her. They take the track up on to the downs, into the night, the quiet punctuated by the skitter of rabbits and the odd lonely car moving out of sight along one of the lanes.

From the ridge, the world lies beneath them: the purple-orange glow of Swindon, the headlights streaming on the M4 motorway. They leave it behind, head further out, through the beech clumps where no moonlight falls, and then out again, to where the moon is so bright their shadow rides before them, and Boxer's hooves ring out against the chalk and flint.

All this is yours. As much as it will ever be anyone's. As much as it has ever belonged to anyone. That hillock and that hedgerow, that cloud, that stone, that star. Stay, my little love. Stay, it's not so awful.

In the deepest reaches of the night, the boy comes to in her arms, and seems to listen intently as though to something beyond the range of Gwen's hearing. As though the land is speaking to him, as though the downs are reaching for him.

Later, Mo falls so deeply asleep that she can't rouse him when they return, must struggle off the grey with him still in her grip.

So tired now. So tired. Holding Mo, she lies down in the straw, wakes to sunlight streaming over her face. Mo's sitting up, turning her wedding ring between finger and thumb so the light dances off the diamonds on to the stable wall.

After that, it's one thing after another. The boy is a rustler. Shiny things. Keys. Phones. Gwen wanders into the kitchen at midnight to top up her glass and finds him, blue in the light of the open fridge door, eating butter from the dish.

Once, she nicks him a Mars Bar from a garage and they split it in the car. Once, passing the town hall where the brass band is rehearsing, he hears Godfrey Palmer warming up on his flute. He tears his hand from hers and flutters at the door, hopping from foot to foot, eyes wide at the cascade of notes. At her dad's, he only wants to be in the parlour, as the cows amble in, as the milk pours through the pipes into the tank, to be stirred into froth by the great metal blade while the two women who do the milking tap their feet to the radio and sing snatches of song, taking it in turns to adore him.

Music. Animals. Games. Sweets. Nicking. Whatever he wants so long as he stays.

He will not stay. The first time Mo goes off, she doesn't even know he's gone. The milk float brings him back at seven a.m. along with her four pints. Over the years, he'll turn up in Southall, Wembley, Leicester, at Wooky Hole and Scafell Pike. As a teenager, he'll disappear for weeks at a time, but he always comes back.

All lie ahead. For now, Gwen sits up in the straw. Listens to the sound of Boxer shuffling in the neighbouring stall. She has an odd thought. *I have won the boy from Death.* A risky, stupid thing to think. Nonetheless, victory sings in her.

When Arthur finally comes home, they turn to him as one. Two allies with a common enemy.

Three

—

Right Here, Right Now

13

Upon My Oath, Madam

———

Morgan awakes in her room behind the Green Knight. *I have to tell Rasha that*, she thinks. The tiny moment golden and full of hope before she remembers she can't tell Rasha anything any more.

No more pillow talk. No more private jokes. No more whispered longings. No more rows and apologies. No more lies or truths, promises or plans.

No trips to visit Rasha's father Faisal in his self-imposed exile in Alexandria. No glasses of sweet tea served up to them by the professor as he and Rasha argued long into the night. Arguments about the homeland they had fled so long ago, the dictatorship, the civil war. Rasha had accused her father of fatalism, of turning his back. Faisal sniffing at her attachment to a place she had left as a small child, that she only knew through visits.

'Such innocence. She sounds like an American. Don't you think Rasha sounds like an American, Morgan?'

Morgan had been in love with all of it. The dark, rippling Mediterranean; Faisal's polyglot bookshelves; Umm Kulthum or Miles Davis on the record player; the sepia photographs of Rasha's great-grandfather, ambassador to the Ottoman court in Constantinople.

Before they left, Faisal had sought her out. Setting down a glass of tea, he caught Morgan's fingers in his.

'Promise me you'll stop her going there. Syria is not America. It is not even Egypt. Our girly plays with fire.'

The last time she phoned Faisal, she stuttered out what had been obvious. That she had loved Rasha, loved Faisal's daughter.

'I . . . I have no daughter.' And Faisal had put down the phone.

In her room at the Green Knight, Morgan contracts the world to the square of cotton pillowcase in front of her one open eye. Breathes in. Breathes out. Recomposes the mess of blood and flesh and bone-fragments she imagines herself to be. 'I have become a knife,' she whispers. 'I am the knife.'

Up. Shower. She turns on the TV, boils the kettle and takes a teabag from the hospitality tray. The little plastic serving of milk splatters the table as she wrestles it open. Some knife she is.

For the past few days, she's lain low, temporarily emptied of whatever fuel brought her this far. The bin is full of plastic wrappers, all that remains of the snack items she bought at the airport newsagent's: the pork pies and bacon-flavoured crisps, the prawn sandwiches and sausage rolls, the bags of sour sweeties that blistered her tongue. In bed with her phone, curtains drawn, door locked, she'd scrolled through the news while the TV blared in the corner. By mid-morning on the first day after Arthur's birthday party, the press had tracked down the attacker's lair: a semi-detached in Nottingham where he lived – inevitably – with his mother, who stood white-haired and confused on the doorstep to wag a finger at the cameras.

'Brian's a good boy. He's a good boy.'

But Brian had not been a good boy. Brian had spent his days stalking prominent women on the Internet, insulting and threatening them with violence via thousands of messages, until a year ago when all his attentions had become focused on a single target.

There had also been a clip of Kay from the night of the party, wild-eyed and blabbering, a smear of blood on his brow.

'My brother and I . . . I mean, what the fuck? We keep people safe. You want to buy shit from China off eBay, you want to stream your pirate movies and wank over your Russian webcam girls and not get your bank account rinsed, you've us to thank!'

The video of Lance, a viral smash, played again and again. His charge with the metal pole. The jabs. The moment he dropped his arm as though to welcome the troll in, as though to embrace him, and then the felling blow. In school playgrounds, by break time, the negotiations would have already commenced. 'I'll be Lance, you be the troll. You can be Lance next time . . .'

But who was Lance? A former soldier, a close friend of Arthur and Gwen, clearly a man of action. The reporters hoped to learn more although it was understood that Lance himself had declined to be interviewed.

Now, on the screen, a feminist sits under studio lights attempting to *situate the troll's actions into a wider cultural context in which rampant online misogyny—*

The otterish host cuts her off. 'Come on, there'll always be nutters!'

'While mental health undoubtedly plays a part—'

'You've got a man, no job, no friends, no girlfriend, lives with his mum. What we'd all call a loser. In love with a famous woman he can't have—'

The woman grows flustered. 'Is it thwarted love or online radicalisation, when young British Muslims join ISIS or plan terror attacks at home—'

Morgan turns the TV off then disconnects her phone from its charger. No new emails, or rather nothing of note. She's got to get some decent coffee.

The courtyard is nigh empty but, at the sound of her door clicking closed, something moves on the bench by the pub's back door. Two figures, half obscured by a wooden table, lie humped together. There's a powerful smell of beer and possibly piss.

Mo squints and lifts his head from the soft pillow of John's belly. The old man lies with his mouth open, white stubble pricking his baby-pink cheeks.

'Morning,' Mo says.

'To you too.'

Mo springs up, takes a glass from the forest of empties on the table and staggers over to the stone trough in the corner. He dips his head and comes up gasping, water cascading from his hair.

When he sees her watching, he grins.

'Of course, a proper shower, hotel-quality towels, those nice miniature toiletries . . .' Mo nods towards the door of her room.

'Maybe you should ask whoever sold you those drinks.'

He fills the pint pot to the brim and sways back to the bench, gifts Morgan a saucy wink. As she slips into the pub, there comes a splash and then the outraged roar of a boar being speared.

'. . . you boil! You whoreson dog! I'll have your guts . . .'

At the end of the passageway, she pushes open the door to the bar. It's empty but for Lou and the thuggy barman with the tattoos who's polishing glasses, rubbing each one with a cloth and then holding it up to the light.

There's a small table by a window where Morgan sits and peeps out at Abury, ordering coffee and the full English when Lou comes over. Cars thrum over the cobbles, slowing to wait at the traffic lights up ahead.

This is her first visit to Abury in over twenty years, yet Abury has always been with her, at university, in the US, during her years in the field. Narrow, inward-looking, smug, parochial, curtain-twitching – in the beginning, those had been the charges.

Now she sees free education, universal healthcare, working infrastructure, opportunity. Not as good as it could be, but functioning. And who would begrudge any of it? Is this not how things should be everywhere?

If only the country weren't so determined to stay blinded to its shadow – to its hiding of oligarch money, its abetting of foreign tyrants, its role in laundering the proceeds of organised crime, when it's not taking part in disastrous military adventures overseas.

And what about Abury? Should Abury be left to slumber on, oblivious to the source of its riches? Blind to the truth about its favourite son?

She will wake it up. She will make them see.

Breakfast arrives and Morgan eats it with relish, leaving the black pudding till last. It's herby, flecked with fat, granular in texture, unequivocally of the flesh. She makes short work of it, licks her knife. Blood is, after all, what she wants.

When she looks up, Arthur's sitting on a stool at the bar. At the party, he had been dressed for the occasion. Now he's wearing jeans, trainers, a dark green hooded top. He could be anyone. Over the years, she has occasionally imagined bumping into Arthur, in a restaurant or departure lounge, or a pub like this one. She has wondered what they would say to one another, if they would say anything at all. But that was before.

He says something to the barman that she doesn't catch, then he turns and stands, slowly, deliberately, like he's coming over to ask her to dance and she rises to meet him.

'Shall we?' she says.

*

Arthur's parked up on the market square. The car's exquisite, silvery, curving like a fish, with just two seats and a top that he slides down. It's the kind of car her dad would stare at with glittering eyes.

'It's been a long time. How about a tour, Morgan?'

'Why not?'

He guns the engine, looks briefly daunted by all the dials on the dash, and then they're off and the wind whips at Morgan's hair so that it blows across Arthur's face and she sees him smile. Then he puts his foot down, they leap forward and Abury becomes a blur.

Arthur takes her out of town, out to the stone circles and then on to West Kennet, where the long barrow stands against the skyline to the south. From there, they follow the fast Devizes Road with its hungry, deadly corner, past the Cherhill Monument, through a couple of hamlets and then in among the ancient forest that flanks the Roman road. At one point they pass what she thinks is the turning for Snap, where she went with Aidey all those years ago.

Liddington Castle. The biker pub. The barn, once host to a massive rave, where Morgan had danced with Gwen until the sun came up. The traveller camp where the travellers don't come any more. Through villages with ponds and banks of daffodils and signs promising summer fetes.

Kingston Bagpuize, Stanford in the Vale, Goosey, Sparsholt Firs. Somewhere near Compton Beauchamp they leave the road and take an ascending chalk track that scrapes at the car's undercarriage. At the end of the track is a small car park and Morgan realises where she is. Arthur turns off the engine.

'Want to go see it?'

The path up to the White Horse is steep, far steeper than she remembers. Or she's less fit. It takes them across open ground, over a stile and then curls round over the hilltop so that they approach the horse from above. The grass is dun-coloured and in places worn bald, revealing the white rock beneath. There is abundant sky. Behind them the downs roll away in great waves.

Morgan had loved horses as a child, but only in books. In reality, they were alarming, all teeth and hoof and jostle, with enormous arses that were constantly squeezing out huge steaming shit nuggets.

Not this one, though. The White Horse is roped off, but Morgan bends beneath it to pat the chalk trenches cut into the turf. Three hundred feet long, three thousand years old. She'd first come here on a trip with her class in primary school. There had been no rope then and they had queued up to take turns standing on the white circle of stone that was the horse's eye. Because everyone knew the White Horse granted wishes.

What had she wished back then? To be beautiful? To be loved? To be in some way exceptional? If so, had her wish been granted?

In a way, yes. Because to Rasha, Morgan had been all those things.

Morgan slips under the rope and then steps forward on to the eye. Birds fly in the valley below. Beneath her heels the hill seems to hum. She closes her eyes. The new wish is made. When she opens them, Arthur is inspecting her keenly, as though hoping to read her mind.

'So, Morgan?'

'So, Arthur.'

'How did you get into the party?'

'Oh, that. You invited an organisation I consult for to send a representative. I convinced them I would be a good choice. I'm afraid I let them hope I might persuade someone to part with some funding for them.'

'I see. I see. But that's not why you came.'

'No.' She ducks back under the rope and comes to stand at his side. Beyond the horse, the hill drops steeply away. A little to the right is Dragon Hill, its flattened top quite bald from where Saint George spilled the wyvern's blood. 'Quite an empire you've built, Arthur.'

He nods. 'You've been busy too. I read a couple of your papers. Or tried to. Good work. Challenging work. You were on track to become a professor—'

'Still, not quite on your scale. But then you had that push at the start.'

'—but you turned your back on academia and went to work for NGOs. Time in the field. Thailand. Indonesia. Nepal, was it? Guatemala. Iraq.'

'You missed a couple of places.'

'Have I? Still. Early-years education. Microfinance. Mobile clinics. It's impressive.'

'*Black Prince*, Arthur. That virus you cracked in your boy-wonder days. I've been wondering about something. Do you think that without it you'd have got going, without the attention, the investment and approbation it brought you?'

'I've wondered myself. Timing was important. A couple of years later and I would have lacked the edge.'

'I met Bobby, Bobby Bismillah. Although he doesn't call himself Bobby any more.' These days Bobby went by Abdul Marsudi. Back in 2011, he and his wife were newly devout. They ran a refuge for street children in a former canning factory in Jakarta. The white kurta hadn't quite concealed the tattoo of a spider on Abdul's neck.

Morgan glances at Arthur sidelong and sees the side of his mouth twitch.

'You created *Black Prince* together. He uploaded it from Indonesia. You defeated it and saved the day.'

Arthur bites his lip. She can almost hear the cogs turning in his head. Finally, he says, 'Someone told me I should make people take me seriously. So I did.'

'If the world knew, it would ruin you.'

Arthur turns to her; his face is grave. 'Would it? Would it really? Even if it could be proved, even if you were believed, what? I'll get to be bad man for a day or a week. Until it's someone else's turn. I explain and apologise and promise atonement. It blows over. That's hardly ruin. Besides, I'm not a celebrity with my own personal brand, Morgan. I don't depend on sponsors or advertising revenue. I don't need people to like me.'

'They do, though, don't they? You are liked and envied and admired. I think you're more used to it, more invested in it, than you think. All that outrage, all those nasty comments, you think you don't deserve them.'

'And you think I do.'

'Why shouldn't you learn what it's like to have people turn against you? The world has been kind to you and you take it for nothing, you take it as your right.'

'You think I've no sorrows. What is it, Morgan? What is it really? Why do you look so strange? We were friends once, we were—'

There is an invitation in his voice – what kind she is not exactly sure, but she knows she must steel herself against it.

'Besides, I doubt it's everything. It's not all you've done, is it? Not after getting away with it that first time. What will they find, do you think, if they look closely? And there must be lots of people, competitors and the like, who'd love to take a closer look.'

Arthur's face doesn't so much as flicker. 'The paper you wrote about Indonesia was dated 2011. If that's when you met Bobby, you've been sitting on this a long time. Why now, Morgan? What is it you want?'

'What do you think I want?'

'That's not an answer.' A breeze tousles his hair. 'Besides, who knows what women want.' A sour note among the sweetness. His eyes track one of the buzzards as it soars in widening circles. 'If this is a game, if you want me to guess, I can only go by the shape of your life. And in that case, it's not money, or status, or you'd have taken the professorship. Not a wardrobe of expensive clothes. You have no kids, no property as far as I can see. It might be work. That I would understand. Work's always there but I suppose . . . if there's to be any satisfaction in work, there has to be something behind it that keeps you going, keeps you getting up and doing it. Is it justice, Morgan? Is that what you want? It's a big ask.'

She is surprised at how acute he is. As though she had been expecting, not a grown man, but the boy from the bus. Or a monster.

'What's behind your work, Arthur? Security? Keeping people safe? Because if so, you're a failure.' The pain is an egg in her throat. If she speaks, she will choke on it. If she speaks, it will crack open.

'Is it because of Gwen, because I married Gwen?' He's silent for a while. 'It's no bed of roses, Morgan.'

'This isn't about your marriage.' She notes her own resistance to saying Gwen's name. There had been a moment, at the castle, as the troll with the knives stormed the stage, when Gwen had looked straight at her, as though Morgan could do something, as though she could stop him.

Arthur slides his phone from his pocket. On the screen, there's a crush of messages and notifications. She sees the name Galahad before he turns away.

'Sometimes I wonder what would happen if I just stopped responding.'

'More and more, it feels a burden as much as a blessing, doesn't it? Connectivity. But there's no going back. Even you can't undo it.'

'Would you wish it undone?' He waits expectantly for her reply.

'It's so hard to imagine now. We both lived it. The world before. When I asked my father a question that he didn't know the answer to, he used to get down the encyclopedia and try and find an answer for me. Sometimes they would see something on TV and spend the whole evening trying to remember a fact, a name. When you met someone at random, unless you made an effort, you might never meet them again, would never know what happened to them. The infinite knowledge a click away, all the power that comes with that. All the hidden connections brought to light. It's magic. It's a miracle. Yet, at the same time, it's sick and it's terrifying and it's a scourge. All the hate that's been unleashed, all the lies that are spread. All the fake news. All the jobs lost. The amplification of our worst and basest instincts. It is too big to see. Sometimes I open the map on my phone and it shows me where I am and I can zoom out and see the whole world around me. Perhaps another map has been lost. But I can't imagine being without it.' There is a look on his face now. 'Would you wish it, Arthur? You of all people?'

'Wishes are for the powerless.'

'Like prayers.' Rasha's words – not a criticism, only a recognition that for those denied agency, faith was often the only prophylactic against despair. In the days after Rasha disappeared, Morgan had learned their truth first-hand.

She had prayed for Rasha to come back. *Let her come back to me. Please. Please. Let her come back to me.*

And on the third day, Rasha had. A saturation in the air. A thickening. The hairs lifting on Morgan's arm, her scalp prickling. Talking to an empty room and the room not being empty at all.

103

On the fifth day, the call came to confirm what Morgan already knew.

'—dead. They killed her. They killed them both. They got into their phones—'

For a second, Rasha is with her again. What would she have thought of this place? That it was too cold. Too windy and exposed. She liked crowded streets, rooms full of people sitting and talking. She needed noise to think. Noise and coffee and thin smelly cigarettes. The presence fades.

'Rashida Taher.' Morgan says her name as though to call her back.

'What?'

'Rashida Taher! Rashida Taher!' It is impossible he does not know her name. They had four years together, only four. It should have been forty. It should have been forever.

'You've lost me.' He looks at her helplessly and such a black wave takes her it's all she can do not to send him sprawling down the hillside. He has no right to look so lost and innocent. It's his fault Rasha is dead, as much as if he'd pulled the trigger himself. 'Come on, Morgan, tell me. You only have to ask. What can I do for you?'

'Step down, Arthur. Step down from your company. Hand it over. I can't say I care to whom. But be done with it.'

She sees the shock on his face, hears the incredulity in his voice when he says, 'Or what, Morgan?'

'Or else, Arthur.' And then she turns and walks away. Not towards the car park, but in the direction of the Ridgeway, the track that runs the spine of the downs. It is Britain's oldest road and it will take her back to Abury and the Green Knight.

When she's gone thirty paces he calls after her.

'It's twenty miles, Morgan.' When she doesn't respond, he calls out to her again, 'It's not you, is it?'

Morgan falters. 'What's not me?'

'The watch, the fridge, the cameras . . .'

Despite the distance between them, his gaze is scouring. For a second it holds her and then she breaks free and takes off, pebbles of flint and chalk scattering under her feet.

14

Gentle Knyght I

———

After Arthur leaves with Morgan, Wayne finishes up the glasses, goes down to the cellar to change a couple of barrels, fetches in the empties from Mo and John's most recent spree. Gwen phones, wants to know where her boy is.

'Haven't seen him since this morning.' Like Wayne is Gwen and Arthur's watchdog. First Arthur tells him to call when the woman comes out of her room, now Gwen wants him to keep tabs on her reprobate son.

Poisonous thoughts. At lunch, each and every one of the diners presents a valid and unique reason why Wayne should herd them into the cellar and eat the key. They ask for salt when the salt is right in front of them. They want to pay a ten-pound bill with a hundred-pound note. They enquire if the lamb is organic.

'All our meat is sourced locally from small farmers,' Wayne says dutifully.

'But is it organic?'

He nods, not trusting himself to speak, remembering his agreement with Vern.

Ever since Arthur's birthday party, or rather ever since he saw the video of Lance fighting off the nutcase with the knives, Wayne can't settle. He's all stirred up. Next month it will be ten years since Gareth died. Will there never be an end to it?

Wayne's head throbs. Beneath his hair there is a divot, a legacy from Afghanistan. They told him he made a good recovery, no long-term problems. *You're all right, son!*

At the clinic, at his last check-up, he'd summoned his courage.

'Should it affect time?'

'Pardon?'

And Wayne had taken in the doctor's harried expression, the way her gaze had already flitted to the clock on the wall, and told her to forget about it.

But time is different now. Sometimes he'll be mopping the floor and listening to a couple of the regulars, and he knows it's not from *now*. It's from *before*.

What's more, time is supposed to be sequential, right? One thing happening after another. Things further back receding, more recent things feeling, well, more recent.

Not for Wayne. The delivery from the brewery last Monday, rolling out the barrels with Vern in the thin spring sunshine, stopping to mop their faces as the church bells tolled the hour, it feels no fresher than the day Chisholm got shot a decade ago.

Helmand – not only does it feel more recent, somehow it's also more real, more convincing. The waist-high pink and white poppies in the fields around the old British fort at Al-Shabat. The mulberry orchards and pomegranate trees. The dirt tracks leading to squat concrete compounds, riddled by bullets and ripped by explosions.

So close, and then it's no longer past at all, it's present. It's happening again and Wayne is both there, in the bar of the Green Knight, and back in Afghanistan taking part in what was called a ground-dominating area patrol.

The weight of his pack. The heat, even though it's long past midday.

His section proceeds along the field edge and then from compound to compound, making sure each one is clear. It's eerily quiet. The farmers have gone from the fields. The birds have stopped singing.

Half a mile from the fort, they come under fire and take cover in one of the empty compounds which is where it really goes to shit. The interpreter steps on a mine. Bullets ricochet in through gaping holes in the walls and Chisholm, the lieutenant, takes one in the shoulder.

They are pinned down. Cut off. The lance sergeant tries to call in air support but the Bowman radio just coughs up crackle and static.

The mortars at the fort fire again and again, sending up fountains of stone. When it seems like the Taliban are regrouping to the south, Wayne and Gareth are ordered to stretcher Chisholm back to the fort while the others lay down covering fire.

The plan is to use the irrigation ditch as cover, only it's so shallow. Next to Wayne's head, bullets thud into the earthen bank. They drop the stretcher more than once and Chisholm's face slips beneath the green, filthy water. Already he looks more dead than alive.

At the canal, they climb out, back on to the track. The fort lies ahead over a narrow bridge. Before they can pick up the stretcher, a figure darts out from behind the carcass of a rusting tractor and lifts a rifle. Wayne steps in front of Gareth.

Click!

The man in black looks down at the weapon in disbelief as Wayne raises his pistol and shoots him in the head.

They take up the stretcher again. One hundred and fifty yards to the footbridge. Two hundred to the fort. It takes forever. It takes five minutes.

The trees are shaking and shivering, in dread or in delight. Shush, they seem to say, it will be over soon.

At the bridge, Wayne pushes Gareth ahead.

'Fucking go. I'll bring him.'

Darkness is falling, the moon is a shield over the fort. A sniper is more likely to miss the first man.

'Not a chance,' Gareth says.

So they go together, Chisholm a dead weight. Racing with him over the bridge and up the slight incline to the fort's doors and through, dropping as one into the dust. Two men panting, one quiet.

A medic rushes over. The MERT is on its way. More and more men make it back through the gates. But no Lance, no Aidey, no sign of Lance Sergeant Hinks. Ten minutes. Fifteen. Night approaches. Which is good because the Taliban don't have night vision. But it doesn't feel good. It feels bad, the light leaving the men still beyond the walls to darkness. There is talk of going back out, only they've lost contact.

Wayne wrestles with it. If he goes, Gareth will go. But he wants to go, his blood is up. The Wessex's motto is Vindictae Nostrum. He's always been vengeful. 'I won't have spite,' his mother used to say to absolutely no avail.

In a dark corner, Gareth finds Wayne. 'You stepped in front of me. What am I? Your baby? I am your baby, Wayne?'

Wayne opens his arms and Gareth steps in. Wayne gripping him round and pushing his lips hard against his forehead.

'You're my brother,' he finally gets out. 'My brother.' While his wild, traitorous heart leaps in his chest.

They'd made it back in the end, Lance and Aidey. In a cart pulled by a donkey, of all things. If only they hadn't, Wayne thinks. If only Lance had died that day.

Head still throbbing, Wayne lifts his fingers and worries at the spot. He's lucky he's still got his hair to hide it. Or maybe not – maybe it would be easier if he could point to a disfiguring scar, a missing limb. Guilt at the thought. There's plenty that would swap places.

At two, John sidles in for a quick pint or three, his fat arse enveloping the bar stool, bare crack hastening the end of half-eaten lunches.

'Wayne?'

'Yes, John.'

'Do you believe in . . .'

'Believe in what?'

'Doggers.'

'Do I believe in doggers?'

'Yes, because—' and he's off, recounting lurid rumours of what takes place in lonely car parks and quiet lanes at dusk.

'Not in your day, eh?'

More incomprehensible gibberish about witches meeting naked under walnut trees and foul devils disguised as beautiful women who'd lure you into depravity if you only waited for them in certain clearings in the woods at the stroke of midnight upon a full moon.

'You ever see them yourself, John?'

'Not a whisker, Wayne. I kept falling asleep.'

At three, they close and he goes to his room for a rest. It's on the ground floor, reached via a passageway off the kitchen, with thick walls and not much light. Even in summer it's cold. Before electricity, it's where they hung the carcasses. A beam runs across the room for the purpose. Now, there's a rug on the stone floor, a single bed pushed up against the wall, a rail for his clothes, a set of drawers and a bedside table.

Spartan. Neat. Solitary.

Wayne takes off his boots and lies down. Closes his eyes. When he looks up Carly is directly above him, hanging from the beam.

Same pink dress. Same wounds, still bleeding. That awful bubbling noise she makes.

He tries to ignore her. It's not like she ever says anything new.

'Avenge me, gentle knight. Avenge my most cruel murder!'

Wayne tries to turn over but he can't move. Not a muscle. Can't speak either. Blood falls upon him like rain, soaking into the sheets, spattering his face. In his eyes, upon his lips. More blood than a single body can rightfully contain.

'Hush. Wayne. Wayne. Hush.'

He wrests awake. It's Lou. She's sitting on the edge of the bed with a hand on his chest.

'I heard you groaning. Thought you were sick or something.'

'I had a bad dream.' Behind her head the beam is clear. She turns, following his gaze.

'What is it, Wayne?' Lou's beehive leans like the Tower of Pisa. Her lipstick, always the same frosted pink, has wandered into the fine lines around her mouth. Her eyes are luminous, clear and kind, yet he's seen her still men with a look.

'Vern says you might be leaving. Tell me, do you find it so terrible here with us?' The back of her hand touches his cheek and he flinches. 'What harm can a little comfort do?' she says. 'I have to say that sometimes I find you a little bit rude, Wayne.'

And maybe it's because he doesn't want to hurt her feelings, or maybe it's because of the dream or the damn video, but all at once, his resolve to take nothing, ask for nothing, offer nothing, to be done with the world and all its cunning traps, crumbles to . . . nothing.

Wayne's arms reach for her and Lou smiles her imperfect, toothy smile and her heels leave her court shoes behind sitting on the floor. The beehive gives up the ghost and her hair slides free of its grips, blonde in the lengths, salt and pepper at the roots. She kisses him first on either cheek and then on the mouth.

The kiss deepens. His hands slide over her. Part of Wayne's excitement is for her. Lou's girlishness, her maturity. The hotness of her mouth, her flicking tongue.

At the same time, at the back of his mind lurks the knowledge

that part of the excitement – the fizzing in his veins, the feverish-
ness – isn't to do with Lou at all. It's to do with the agreement he
has with Vern.

15

Kill the Pig

Gwen cradles the phone against her cheek. Tonight's dinner, a giant shoulder of pork, sits in the roasting tin, all six pounds of it, pink and sweating.

'—well, because of what he was shouting . . . I'd rather not repeat . . . whore of death, Mum. No, I hadn't done anything to UPSET HIM. I don't know him from FUCKING ADAM.' With her free hand, Gwen takes a knife from the block and pokes experimentally at the meat. 'Sorry. Sorry. Bit on edge.'

Her mum's been rummaging around the Internet and what Tamara wants to know is why don't people like Gwen very much. Her voice down the line is peevish, like she's just seen Gwen's report card and wants to know why her marks are so poor *considering all that your father and I have spent on your education!*

'Can't say I'm exactly sure.' *Poshblondeprettyrichthin.* 'But if you work it out, do tell me.' *Nocareerwhiteprivilegedoesn'tsmileenoughupher selfwearstoomuchwhite.* 'Yes, yes, you do that, Mum.'

Call ended, she puts the phone down on the counter. Lets out a ragged breath. Her hand is trembling!

For some reason she remembers a day when she was perhaps eleven and she and Tamara had gone to Badminton Horse Trials. There had been an argument about clothes which Gwen had won. But in the Jag, sitting there in one of her mother's tops, worn as a minidress and styled up with a belt and then, because the ground would be muddy, her riding boots, the victory turned to ashes as Tamara explained, not in so many words, but still, that there was a price to looking how Gwen had chosen to look that day. And the gist was she should watch herself: men you could handle if you had even a quarter of a brain; it was women you had to look out for.

Her tone was light. Friendly. Confiding. The whole time, Gwen stared out the window at the sodden fields, all pleasure gone, nails digging into her palms.

What was in the message that could account for the way that while she remained sitting there sullenly, showing no response, inside, her spirit had battered itself like a moth against a naked bulb, wanting not only out of the car, but out of her own body?

Gwen takes up the bowl of apricot stuffing and starts ramming it into the pocket she's created next to the bone. It's moments like this she misses Aidey, misses being able to say, 'Then she told me . . .' Misses his contemptuous answering smirk, a small serving from the brimming reservoir kept reserved for their mother. Aidey with his Utah ranch and truck and weapons, his dubious highly paid jobs abroad, his eighteen-year-old surrendered wife and the way he looks at Mo. No, she doesn't want to be complicit in what Aidey thinks of Tamara.

'Fucking Bungle,' she mutters and feels a little better. *Bungle!* Morgan had come up with the nickname and it had been perfect. Bungle was a character from a kids' TV programme played by a man in a hairy bear suit. Bungle was bossy and self-important and a ridiculous pedant towards George, a camp pink hippo, and Zippy, an undefinable annoyance whose mouth was literally a zip. Bungle was nothing like Tamara at all. Yet how they'd laughed at the comparison, laughed and laughed until the tears streamed down their faces.

To be fair, Tamara had loathed Morgan too.

Big, ugly, mouthy. Hammy hands reaching across the table to grab the butter and slather it all over her croissant.

'I think you'll find croissants are made of butter, dear, a ha ha ha!'

Tamara's laugh, a tinkly little bell, sounded different when Morgan was there, tuneless, an aluminium rattle.

Maybe Morgan will come and see her. Why else would she be back?

Gwen tries to imagine it, what they could say to one another, what they might exchange in order to be as they once were, sees instead Morgan in the crowd – the slab of her face, her chin thrust forward – just a glimpse, a tiny glimpse as the would-be murderer hurled himself on to the stage.

Yesterday, she asked Arthur if it was the troll who'd hacked the cameras and leaked the video. He said Gal was looking into it. She didn't know what to hope for. If so, the contents of the second part of the video could come out at the trial. If not, then the hacker was still out there.

Perhaps sensing her fear and misdiagnosing its source, Arthur picked up the conversation they'd begun earlier about Gwen getting a bodyguard. Only now he wanted Lance to do it.

'You want to pay Lance to look after me?'

'Just till things have settled down. Or longer, if you'd like.'

Tears sprang in her eyes and she turned away. Then she made herself stop and went back to where he was sitting at his desk, determined to tell him. To have it over with. But the words would not come.

'You go on up, Gwen. I'll be at this for a bit. I'll see you in the morning.'

And Arthur went back to his screens, his fingers roaming once again over the keys.

What would Morgan say if Gwen could tell her what she had failed to tell Arthur? Once they'd shared everything or at least done a good job of pretending to. On the bus, in the pickup, on the riverbank with Gwen's head resting on Morgan's stomach.

Back then, Morgan had hated her body. It went unsaid between them. Gwen understood. It was not the kind of body they were supposed to aspire to. It was not the kind of body Gwen wanted for herself. But how solid it felt, how reassuring. How plentiful, strong and pillowy.

But how can she tell Morgan anything when in all likelihood Morgan hates her? Hates Gwen for the way she trashed their friend-ship, for the things she said to her – and over what? Over fucking Aidey? – hates Gwen for stealing Arthur away. Over the years,

Gwen had wormed out of Arthur the details of his friendship with Morgan, a friendship more accurately described as a romance, or love story, one brought to an end by the different directions Morgan and Arthur's lives had taken, but which might – Arthur implied, with a shrug, his eyes fixed on the middle distance – have been picked up again if it hadn't been for his falling in love with Gwen.

Once, around the time of her fourth miscarriage, Gwen had asked Arthur to reach out to Morgan, to see where things stood. She didn't care about her pride. There was no limit to the shit she would eat. She needed Morgan so badly. Arthur agreed, but then when she asked him about it again, he'd shaken his head. 'It's not going to work, Gwen. I'm sorry.' He wouldn't elaborate, which she took to mean that Morgan's reply was too hurtful to pass on.

Gwen looks down blankly at the meat.

What comes next? *Make small incisions and insert sprigs of sage.* Right. Right.

She picks up a knife and stabs the joint as hard as she can. It takes an unexpected amount of force to really get it in there through the skin. The flesh closes around the blade. She yanks it free, so the shoulder lifts and then drops back into the tin. The knife's not quite right. She takes another, narrower but sharper in the point. The flesh parts more easily this time. She draws it out and inspects the oozing entry mark, then retreats to the other side of the kitchen to recreate Brian's charge.

'Whore of death!' she cries. When she reaches the joint of pork, she throws the arm with the knife forward and stabs once, twice, and then a whole volley of times. With the last thrust she hits the bone and loses her grip, so her hand slips down to meet the blade as it springs back.

Gwen lets the knife fall and snatches her hand to her lips. Mo is suddenly at her side. Blood pours into her mouth, slides through her closed fingers.

'Come on,' he says and leads her to the tap, runs it warm and makes her uncurl her palm into the stream.

'It stings. It stings.' But it's not quite as bad as she feared, a clean slice across the heart-line of her palm.

Mo brings her a stool, makes her a sugary cup of tea. When the bleeding slows, he leans in to take a look. 'Stitches.'

'No.' No hospitals, no doctors, no grist for the machine.

'It'll keep opening.' Seeing her face set he says, 'Mum. Come on.'

'No.' Blood keeps seeping up, like lava from a fissure.

'Well, I suppose we could glue it?'

Which is how Arthur finds them when he gets in, both bent over her hand with a fresh tube of superglue and a home-surgery YouTube video narrated by a man from Kentucky whose friend Curtis has had an altercation with some barbed wire.

'You stink,' Arthur hears Gwen say, 'like a rat that choked to death in an ashtray.'

'Careful or I'll glue it to your head.'

He notices Gwen's got blood all round her mouth. There's an enormous hunk of meat on the side that looks like it's been torn at by wolves.

Cavall pads over. 'Hello, love,' Arthur says. Neither head at the table lifts in greeting. 'Everything all right?'

'... *any superglue will do. Pass over it once and then use the head to make a thicker bead. It's going to burn like a whore. You want to do about three coats. Always keep a supply in your prepper pack* ...'

'Well, I've got a couple more things to get on with. Call me if you need anything.'

He's almost out the door when Mo says, 'Who's the woman with red hair staying at the Green Knight? The one you went off with in the car?'

Arthur doesn't turn, doesn't want to see Gwen's face. *Fucking Mo.*

'I'll try and be back for dinner.'

16

Love Object

——

The girls come in pairs, walking the path through the woods that skirts Lancelot's house. Sometimes a bold girl passes by alone, slowing as she approaches the gate. Sometimes Lance goes out and there are flowers wilting in a jam jar by the front door.

In summer they stop at the petrol station, buy ice creams and lick them on the forecourt steps.

'He wasn't there!'

'He was. I saw him.'

'You didn't!'

Heat rises from the concrete, warming their thighs. The ice creams melt in the sun.

'I swear it. Peeping out his kitchen window!'

Sometimes they come as the sun sets, the damosels, in pairs or boldly alone, past the flickering fluorescent strip lighting of the petrol station, into the woods as the air grows damp and cool. Shoulders bare. Hair loose. Lingering on dew-soaked grass to listen to the sound of a tap, the TV going on, cutlery on plate as Lance eats his lonely tea.

At night, nightingales sing in the woods by the reservoir. The girls imagine the warmth of Lancelot's skin. Imagine him reaching for them, that first moment when his skin touches theirs. They imagine being in his arms. Imagine being in his bed. The first star is for Lancelot and all the stars afterwards.

He is what they've been promised, for a long time, for perhaps as long as they can remember. Lance is what they've earned, what they deserve. To be in Lancelot's arms, in Lancelot's heart, it will all have been worth it, all the restraint, all the parts cut away, or buried, all the work done, all the work that will continue long after they know they'll never be a Lancelot, long after they learn there is no Lancelot.

Sometimes the girls see a woman out by the reservoir, crouching down at the edge muttering at the water. Something not quite right about the way she's dressed, a winter coat but bare legs, a glittering dress with a dirty hem. Moonstruck, with starving eyes. And when she staggers to her feet and rushes at them, teeth bared, ragged nails outstretched, they tear off, take to their heels and pelt headlong back down the path and out of the woods to where they'll clutch one another, hysterical and panting beneath the lights of the forecourt.

'Did you see her eyes? Did you fucking see them?'

So they never find out what she has for them – gift or threat or warning.

*

Today it's Arthur on the step. He needs to talk to Lance, would have come in person even if Lance hadn't turned his phone off days ago. Nothing Lance could do to stop the letters arriving. Some, in business envelopes, hail a natural synergy between Lance and their brand. Marketing teams invite him to discuss endorsements, campaigns, photoshoots, partnerships, a starring role in an ad for shaving cream. Others flap through the letterbox like butterflies, each with its own colour and markings, often with its own particular scent.

When Lance opens the door, there are two pink ones lying on the mat, one in the shape of a heart. He hurriedly picks them up and shoves them in a drawer like a guilty child.

'You won't tell Kay, will you?'

'Kay got hair plugs last year when he and Linnet went to Turkey,' Arthur says, surprising himself. 'Billed it to the company.'

They're still laughing as the kettle boils. The milk's out, so they

117

have it black at the kitchen window, looking out over the back at the knee-high tangle of grass. The bin's overflowing and the fridge makes a racket. Disorder bothers Arthur like a rankling tooth but he bears it. No sudden moves. In the past, when he's tried to help Lance, by creating a role for him at the company, or putting something else his way, Lance has always turned him down.

'Was anyone out front?'

'No camera crews if that's what you mean.'

In profile, Lance is as straight and still as a pillar. Then, when he turns, Arthur sees a ripple of movement at the corner of his eye, like the lid is being pulled upwards by an invisible thread. Lance rubs at it with his hand.

'How's the sleep?' Arthur says.

'I kept thinking I could hear them out there, crawling about.'

'The TV crews?'

'Yeah . . . No . . . I don't know. I was thinking about going away. Going to Ireland, at least for a bit.'

'To your dad?'

Lance nods.

'What's it like there?'

'There's a lough where the eels hatch. The monastery's up on the cliff. The monks don't speak but you can hear the sea all the time. It rains a lot.'

'It sounds . . . lovely.'

'If I go there, I don't think I'll ever leave.'

'I was hoping you'd stay, Lance. I haven't even properly thanked you for what you did. We owe you. I owe you so much—'

'No, you don't, Arthur. You don't—' Lance sounds pained. A flush steals up the skin of his throat.

'—and I'm afraid I'm going to ask for more.' He does his best to explain. 'How did he get the knives through security? How did he get in in the first place? He must have had help. Maybe they'll have another go.'

'At Gwen?'

'It's possible. We'll find out who they are. But in the meantime, someone's got to . . . watch over her.'

'Get a professional, Arthur. Get a few of them, for the love of God.'

'She won't have it. Says she won't be followed about by a stranger.'

'She's got to, Arthur.' Lance slaps a hand down on the counter-top and a pile of dirty dishes topples with a crash into the sink.

'I can't tell her anything, Lance. You know what she's like.' A cautious silence blossoms. 'I was thinking you could do it. I think she'll accept it, if it's you. It shouldn't be for long, like I said.'

Lance takes a step away from the window and then turns back. 'What does Gwen say?'

'She says she doesn't need anyone, but when I said I'd talk to you, I had the feeling she'd consider it. She knows you. She likes you. You're a good friend to the both of us.'

'Where's she now?'

'Home, I think. Said she was going out riding this afternoon. Said she'd take Boxer out and think about it. Come over tomorrow, say seven thirty? We'll have a bite and talk it through. You'd get the going rate.'

'You'd not need to pay me, Arthur.'

'The going rate, not a penny less.' He puts the ice into his voice but his heart gives a little warm leap. A top personal protection officer gets twenty times what Lance makes doing relief milking or driving forage harvesters. It could be a new start for Lance, the beginning of something better.

One of the fence panels, rotted through, swings in the breeze. One sharp gust will tear it free, will probably bring the whole side down with it. In his mind's eye, Arthur replaces the fence, turfs over the weeds with a neat lawn. The kitchen is refitted, new doors hung, the floor retiled.

As Lance sees him out, he replaces the tatty carpet with oak flooring, repaints the walls, adds new lighting, furniture, a skylight; he landscapes the front lawn, repaves the drive. With a wave of his hand, it could be done tomorrow.

*

After Arthur leaves, Lance thinks about having a lie-down. He gets as far as the end of his bed and stands there staring at the mattress. It looks so innocent, like one of those peaceful grassy fields in

France where a hundred years ago a hundred thousand men bled to death in the mud. Only, here, in Lance's bed, the battle begins afresh each night.

One thing he knows: you don't die from lack of sleep, but in the end you'll want to. Instead, he grabs his jacket from the peg and goes out, taking the path round the reservoir. More and more, he's drawn to water, to the flooded gravel pits at South Cerney, the dew ponds on the downs. A spreading ripple on a puddle around his boots has the power to stop him in his tracks.

At the far end, the swimmers are out. Not the families who come in summer for a splash; it's too early for them, the water too cold. It's the triathlon trainers and winter-swimming fanatics in their wet-suits who plough the pewter lake.

There, at the lakeside, Lance contemplates the mess of his life.

In the army things had been simpler. Not better, and sometimes much, much worse. But simpler.

Out at the old fort in Helmand the two factors had converged. Worst. Simplest. The enemy attacked every day: small-arms fire, rockets, usually around teatime as the light was fading. The others slept inside, behind Hesco barriers, but Lance preferred one of the turrets, slept on the stone floor among bat droppings and rubble, the violet Afghan sky overhead.

Around him were his kit, his bedroll, the blanket acquired in the bazaar at Lashkar Gah for the cold desert nights.

His father sent parcels – tins of custard, Mars Bars, scribbled notes with news of horses, dogs, his work for the brothers. *There's always a job for you here, son.*

The letters from Elaine he burned without opening. In his pack, hidden away, was a photograph of Gwen.

Why do you look so sad?

Because a certain lady got married today . . .

It was eight years since she kissed him, since her wedding. Eight years of army life, including two tours of Iraq.

In 2009, Helmand was as deadly as it got. Yet, Lance had been accompanied by a sense of belonging.

The bats belonged to the tower. The March moon belonged above the badlands to the south. At dawn, the sun belonged to the east, at sunset to the west.

The fort belonged to the Dasht-e Margo, to the Silk Road, to Helmand Province between the desert and the Green Zone.

The Reaper drones, Chinooks, Black Hawks, A-10s and F-18s belonged to the sky.

The soldiers belonged to 8 Company, to the Wessex Rifles, to the British Army, to Battle Group South, to NATO's ISAF forces, to each other. Lance belonged to Wayne, Gareth and Aidey and they belonged to him.

His boots belonged on his feet. Lance's assault rifle belonged in his arms. His finger belonged on the trigger. The bullets belonged to the air. To the dirt, blood, bone in which they buried themselves.

IEDs belonged in the dirt, on footbridges, in compound doorways. Insurgents belonged hidden in the compounds, in firing positions among the wheat and poppies and ditches.

Here, he sometimes feels that nothing is where it ought to be, nothing belongs – least of all Lance – and it fills him with dread. If he tried to put it into words, no one would understand. The only person who could will not speak to him at all.

Lance remembers visiting Wayne at the hospital at Camp Bastion. After the bomb. After Gareth died. Gareth, who was everyone's best boy. Gareth, who they had all loved.

Wayne had been in restraints and not one word was exchanged. After a few minutes, Lance had hauled himself to his feet and blundered away, as though through the sockets of Wayne's eyes, through the crack in his head, an unbearable heat was escaping.

Lance is tired. Lance is so very tired. On the bench, he sinks into a kind of fugue, his eyes tracking the swimmers' slicing arms. Past forty now. No wife, or kids or property to speak of. No plans. At the unit, the psychiatrist told him to avoid stress – to keep things simple. Not, for example, to fall in love with the wife of the man who is your best friend, who you admire above all others, and certainly not this kind of love.

He has been trying to leave, or rather trying to return, return to when he laid his love at her feet and was rewarded with touches on the arm and smiles and what seemed a special pleasure in her voice when she greeted him. And then, perhaps after a few drinks, if their eyes met and lingered, or turning he found Gwen watching him, it could keep him for a week, a warm current running through the days and all the long nights.

This is the place which he would row back to, so Lance tells himself, yet after the business at Arthur's birthday party, after the men in black rushed the stage with their handcuffs and their shouts to secure the area, Lance had glided away, taken Gwen by her arm and marched her out a side door and then up two flights of stairs, fingers digging into her biceps, down the long corridor, away, away, until they had somehow found themselves in the room where they first met, where they first kissed, on Gwen and Arthur's wedding day.

No fire burning in the hearth this time, but they brought their own. He locked the door as she pulled the zip down on her dress. He knocked the light out with his elbow, his mind alive with that final image of her before the darkness. Next, a quiet conflagration, but white-hot, immolating, the kind that makes you wonder how much left of you there'll be afterwards.

He's not seen her since, not with the press on his doorstep, not with the pair of them all over the news.

But Gwen is going out riding this afternoon.

'Speak to me,' he tells the lake, 'just speak to me.' But the water holds its tongue. So after a bit, he goes back to the house, fetches his mountain bike and takes off for Snap.

*

Boxer and Gwen crest the hill. Lance waits, concealed by the ragged grove of trees that grows around the ruins, as the grey picks its way down the track. The gnawing feeling of wrongnesss, of mistake, of misstep abates. After all, she's only Gwen.

Her eyes scan for him but he stays where he is, eight feet up in the crook of an oak among the ivy. Enjoying the moment of being looked for. Anticipating the moment of being found.

Then the horse pricks up its ears and she knows. They enter the copse at a trot. Lance clicks his tongue to announce himself to Boxer, then drops down to the earth, so soft beneath his boots, sweet with the smell of spring.

Lance takes the horse's bridle and brings his cheek to Boxer's damp neck.

'Hello, boy,' he says. When he lifts his eyes, he sees there's something close to breaking in her. She frees her legs from the stirrups, swings forward and slides down from the horse into his waiting arms.

Beneath the broken rafters of the ruined house at Snap, Lance brings her his not-enoughness, his long-held pain and loneliness, his unslept nights.

These are the minutes stolen from death.

A thrush sings.

Stone wall scrapes bare skin.

How can they have each other and still be so hungry?

Further and then a little further still.

Mouths locked, drenched in sweat. His heart knocks against his ribs.

It's the kind of fuck that makes you want a lie-down, a blood transfusion, a heart transplant, to go to a quiet white room where no one bothers you and a cool hand delivers the pills and strokes your hair. But Lance knows better than most that's a fantasy; what there is, what you'll get, is a unit where they're desperate for beds, and a man called Norris begs God to have mercy all day, every day, and all of the long, deadly nights.

Finally, Lance had snapped. 'Good lord, man! If God was going to have it – the mercy, that is – don't you think he would have by now?'

It hadn't helped. He'd found himself wondering how God's mercy would manifest itself to Norris. A hand held? A forehead kissed?

Eventually Lance had tottered to his feet and shuffled across the room in his pyjamas, settling for standing at the foot of Norris's bed.

'God has mercy on you, Norris. God loves you.'

After which Norris was quiet for a bit.

Afterwards he watches her dress. Grazes on her back and knees, an armlet of bruises from the other night, yellowing now.

'Fear not,' she says, 'no one will see.' By which she means Arthur will not see. A small, unexpected kindness.

Lance lifts a beetle from his jeans and then slides them back on. He wants to hold her, but she's past that now.

'He came over. He wants me to be your bodyguard or something.'

Before the party, he had made his decision. He would go to Ireland, with or without her. But she needs him now, and the thought of anyone hurting her is a pure hell.

Gwen sighs, runs a hand through her hair, dislodging a twig. 'And you want to be on his payroll?'

'Let me help.'

She stands still for him while he combs her yellow hair with his fingers. He plucks free a leaf, then a ladybird.

'He's frightened someone's out to get you. He's not a man to overstate a case.'

'He wants you in his pocket, he wants to own you, but that's not enough. He wants you to like it and be grateful!'

'I could see you. It'll be easier for us to see each other.'

Her face twists and he knows what she's thinking. How do you make a betrayal worse? How do you really twist the knife?

'It might still come out. The rest of the video. You want to be here when it does?'

'If they were going to do it, they'd have done it, Gwen. Look, we'll stop this. I'll be your bodyguard. Nothing more. I won't touch you if that's what it takes.'

'Ah, but Lance,' she says sadly, 'how will I not touch you?'

Before she goes, he gives her an acorn that's found its way into his boot. Astride Boxer, she balances it on her bandaged palm. A kitchen accident, she says. They both look at it, the acorn, the burnished brown nut held in its perfect cup. Lance wants to say something, but he doesn't know what. It'll only occur to him on the ride home.

There was a moment, in the journey of my life, when I gave a woman an acorn.

A nameless man, a nameless woman underneath an oak tree. A worthless, perfect gift. A moment that could be a thousand years old, or from a thousand years in the future. And summed up so, stripped of identity, of temporality, blameless . . .

At home, Lance goes about his business, trying to trick the coming night, a perfectly normal man enjoying a quiet evening before turning in, a weary man looking forward to a deep and satisfying rest.

No chance.

Out the horrors come, one by one and then in droves, till he flees his bed and sits in the armchair in the living room.

Gwen is the torch he wields to hold them off. He remembers their meeting only as fragments, flotsam and jetsam, splinters of wreckage.

Gwen's arms around his neck as she slipped from the horse, the arch of her spine, her open mouth, the ladybird plucked from the silk of her hair, the acorn on her outstretched palm.

One by one he takes them out, one by one he pores over them in the dark, a man wrapped in flames.

17

Wasteland I

———

Outside Gal's house, Arthur sits in his car in the dark reviewing the day. Once he'd watched a film in which an assassin referred to his job as *wet work*. Ever since, secretly and only to himself, Arthur thinks of the parts of his life in which he must navigate the unruly lands of people and their desires as *wet work*.

Today had been dripping with it. Morgan looking like she wanted to murder him there on the hillside. Lance twitching at phantoms. Gwen smeared with blood. Mo's barbs – the way he sees things, the way he always twists things!

Still, it will be fine. It'll all be fine. Lance will keep an eye on Gwen till Arthur and Gal can sort out whoever's causing the mischief. Morgan might take a bit of handling but not much. Not really.

He'd wanted to say, 'What do you think will happen to your story after a word from me in the ear of a press baron or two? I encrypt the minutes of Cobra meetings. I prevented the Russians from hacking our nuclear submarines. The only place you're going to publish is on a blog alongside conspiracy theorists, next to illuminati freaks who think I'm a shape-shifting lizard creature!'

Much better to let her chase down dead ends. To let her tire herself out. By then he'll have found out whatever lies at the heart of it and he'll fix it for her and then she won't be angry with him any more.

Handling Morgan . . . it brings back certain memories. Sense memories: the smell of Morgan's hair, the dewy warmth of her skin. And then there were the visuals: the billion freckles, the huge ghostly nipples, his fingers sunk deep into the pink and white flesh of her hips. It had been a bit much then. He'd been what? Eighteen? Keenly aware that his desire was a bit off-centre, anxious what it meant about him. Callow and unproven.

Well, he thinks, firmly shutting the car door behind him, not any more.

Gal doesn't respond to the bell, so Arthur lets himself in with his key. The high fences, sunk five feet deep, the reinforced security gate, are – despite appearances to the contrary – measures designed to keep someone in rather than out. Superfluous now that Hercules has departed to prance among the stars; Hercules the monster dog, love incarnate but for one fatal weakness, not counting the heart attack that took him three summers ago. Tonight, Arthur finds himself glad of them. There's something on the wind, a bug in the code . . .

The house is an ecohome, wooden clad with solar panels on the roof, a composting toilet, water pumped and filtered from its own well. Designed and built on Arthur's tab despite Kay's howls of protest, a measure to keep Gal sweet, keep them on task, to prove Arthur's heart is in the right place.

No answer at the front door either, but a light is on so Arthur follows the path around the back, to the long windows that look out towards the forest. Inside, Galahad sits at a table in front of three monitors. In the white light, with their hood up, they look like the ghost of a medieval monk. He raps with a knuckle on the glass and Galahad makes a face Arthur knows well: *I'm working! I'm trying to concentrate!* But seeing who it is, the expression softens and Gal gets up to let him in.

'How's it going?' And then, because Galahad has that surfacing look about them, Arthur sets off to the kitchen – Gal forgets to eat – and puts together a snack from what's in the fridge and cupboards, a selection of vegan pastes and vegetable crisps, thinking guiltily of the pork at home.

'Here. Have a bite.' Arthur puts the plate down on the table and even though Gal says they're not hungry, they make short work of it. Arthur had been the same. How often had Betty slid a piece of cake under his elbow while he ignored her? And the next time he looked down, there'd be nothing but crumbs.

An odd sort of music plays low from the speaker in the corner. High voices like flutes. A language that isn't English as Arthur knows it. An instrument he struggles to place.

'What is this?'

'The other night, at the party, I heard a tune. It's been going round and round my head and I thought it would help if I could find it, could listen to all of it. Only I can't find it. I even tried to hum it into a song-finder app, but it didn't know what it was. It suggested this, though. Early music, they call it. I've had it on all day.'

'Catchy.'

'Each time I look up, it's like the woods have come closer to listen.'

Arthur looks up quickly, but to his eyes the trees are where they've always been, massed at the end of the lawn, although in the darkness, it is quite possible to imagine them pressing in, to lend them an attentive quality.

'Was it him, Gal? The troll?'

'No.'

Arthur sighs, disappointed. How tidy it would have been if it had all been Brian: the fridge, his watch, the footage of Gwen in the stables.

'I did what you suggested. Phone. Home computer. No sign of any talent. No ability. Spent his time playing *Crusader Barons*, or on social media, YouTube and Reddit. Alt-right shit. *Hail Odin*, all of that. He had a dating app too but didn't use it much. His email was a Hotmail account.'

'How did he get into the party, then? It's not like we invited him.'

'Are you sure?' There's something in Gal's voice.

'Why?'

'Well, I did find something. He had a high-encryption app on his phone. Didn't even have WhatsApp, but he had today's drug-dealer app *du jour*. So he was talking to someone.'

'You got into it.'

'I did.' For a moment, Gal looks rather wolfy for a vegan. 'No contacts. No conversations. I think the sender deleted them.'

'But?'

'He'd worked out how to take a screenshot. Seems Brian wanted a little insurance. I found something in his photos.'

'Show me.'

Arthur pulls up a seat and sits down next to Galahad. A ripple of excitement tracks up his back as he calls to mind previous adventures. An early foray: Gwen's friend Babs had had her card cloned and Gwen was livid, had demanded action. So, over vegan pizza, he and Gal tracked down and hacked the outfit's server, had a look around and then introduced a virus into their network that overwrote all their files. Oh, and they'd rinsed the bank accounts, transferring half a million euros to Greenpeace. On the sofa, Hercules had snored and farted, occasionally hauling himself up to come and drool on Arthur's knee. It was fun. He'd wished it was how things could be with Mo.

Already he feels nostalgic for it. AI is coming. AI will hack. AI will defend. No human can compete with machine speed and he and Gal, for all their God-given talent, will be shown up for what they are, children playing with pebbles on a beach.

Gal opens a file and Arthur finds himself looking at . . . some kind of glistening Martian life form? A split second later he realises it's a cock pic.

'Sorry. Not that one.' Quickly Gal brings up the next image from the troll's photo reel. This time, it's a screen capture of a chat. Just a few lines.

– *She's not the virtuous woman she pretends to be. She's a whore. Takes all-comers. I've proof. She laughs about it, laughs at me as she lies and lies.*

– *Can you not do it yourself? She deserves for it to be you!*

– *I wish the pleasure could be mine, but for that I must find a champion.*

Arthur feels queasy. They're talking about Gwen.

There's a further screen shot of another text in which the messenger carefully explains where two knives will be concealed at his birthday party.

'Who are they from?' Arthur asks.

Galahad looks awkward. 'Don't you see? They're supposed to be from you, Arthur.'

When Gal exits full screen, Arthur glimpses another photo, a selfie of a face last seen hurtling in Gwen's direction brandishing knives. Without even asking, he knows it's from the dating app. From the artful composition, from the pathetic attempt at winningness. He wishes he hadn't seen it, even more than the photo of the troll's dick.

'So if it's not him doing the hacking, who is it?'

'They stay invisible. They're not talented, Arthur. But they are careful, very careful. I had a look into how Brian got his invite. I went through all the systems. No signs of a break-in. It's like . . . he was added manually. His name was already on the list by the time it was sent to the events team.'

'Is it . . . ?'

'Someone from inside the company? Yes, Arthur. I think so.'

Night approaches. The forest is in shadow, and yes, the trees do seem a little closer, truth be told. After Steve Jobs died, they offered Arthur the throne. He could have taken it, could have gone to San Francisco, laurels in his hair. But he didn't. And this is his repayment.

An enemy inside the company? A traitor. One of the contractors, perhaps. A new hire with a grudge. He imagines a maggot, a wriggling dark spot burying into pristine flesh. They will be rooted out. They will be excised.

Arthur picks up his car keys from the side.

'You off to football tonight?' Gal asks.

'No. I have to talk to Gwen.' It's Lance or the London operation, the outfit that does the security for retired prime ministers. She can take her pick but it's one or the other. In his mind's eye, he sees the troll charge again, only this time Lance isn't there to stop him. The knives had been huge, practically swords. 'Another thing. You know the woman I asked you to—'

'Faye Morgan? It was all public record, no hacking, as requested.'

'I know. I saw her today. She's making noises about *Black Prince*. Turns out she knows Bobby.'

'BobbyBismillah?' Gal's face lights up. Bobby was quite something in his day. 'Do you think she has something to do with what happened at the party?'

'No. I asked her. She didn't have a clue what I was talking about. I never really thought . . . we were all at school together. She was . . . a bit different. Kay hated her, of course. I was rather—'

130

Arthur stops, feeling the heat rising to his cheeks. 'She said a name today. Rashida Tear. Tayer. Something like that. Can you see what you can find out?'

'Sure, Arthur.' Galahad looks at him with the pure eyes of absolute truth. 'You know, you can ask me anything.'

At the door, Arthur turns. He'd like to hug Gal, but there's something untouchable about them so he settles for a pat on the shoulder. 'Don't forget to eat, now. I'll see you soon. The other thing. *Wasteland* . . .'

'Yes?'

'Just so you know, I've upped security. There's no remote access. No way in. It's on a hard drive on an unnetworked computer in a private location. You're sure you didn't make a copy?'

'There is no copy, Arthur.'

*

After Arthur's gone, Gal closes the door and puts the alarm on, although they know any intruder is unlikely to come in person. They turn off all of the lights but one. There is no need for waste.

Last time they were at the office, Kay called them a fanatic because they'd asked if the hand wash in the bathrooms could be replaced with a vegan alternative that cost the exact same amount. A fanatic? The accusation was troubling and Gal had dwelled on it for longer than it deserved. If you were against elder abuse or child pornography, you were against it and you did everything in your power to make sure you weren't complicit in it. No one called you a fanatic.

A fanatic would not have kept their promise to Arthur, would not have created *Wasteland* and then allowed the virus to be hidden away where no one could ever get their hands on it: not the NSA or the FSB, GCHQ or the People's Republic; not Anonymous, Lazarus or Black Axe.

'It can do what humans are unwilling to do! It can save us!'

The argument took place shortly after Gal and Arthur had met in the real. Back in 2013, a few weeks after Hercules crashed the christening party. The summer had been glorious. Arthur had cancelled everything to spend each day alone with Gal. The companionship, the kinship, the wordless understanding!

Only when it came to *Wasteland* were they in conflict.

'If you had a button, Arthur, and you could push it and stop it, everything that's going wrong, wouldn't it be your duty to push it? What's coming – the fires, droughts, famines, mass extinctions – if you had any way of stopping it, shouldn't you try, even if it came at great cost?'

Release *Wasteland* and the power plants that burned fossil fuels would be stilled. Industry would cease. The skies and seas and roads would empty. Anything with a computer in it that was part of a network would inevitably be infected, and in the case of *Wasteland* infection was fatal. *Black Prince, ZeuS, Stuxnet, Triton* – even *NotPetya*: they were mosquito bites in comparison.

'What about the hospitals, Gal? What about the people who need to heat their homes? Food would rot, people wouldn't be able to feed their kids.' Arthur's voice had been mild.

In the end, Gal backed down because Arthur asked them to trust him, asked them not to do this irreversible thing. Secretly, they'd been desperately, desperately relieved. Somewhere inside, Gal knew that *Wasteland* was a response, not only to the world, but to the darkness, pain and bewilderment of their life before Arthur. The pain they had numbed with endless bongfuls of skunk, not realising they were losing their mind in the process.

Gal thinks again about the invitation implicit in the last Easter egg Arthur had left for them: a photograph of Arthur aged about eight sitting in front of a gigantic old monitor, turning to smile at the lens, his arm around the back of the empty seat beside him.

When the moment is right, Gal will find a way to tell Arthur about the stuff at the office. Some of the team using *it* rather than *they*. The jokes and jibes that never go too far since Arthur's made clear how important Gal is, but which make them dread going in to work.

Arthur will be supportive, Gal is sure of it. It's only Arthur's rarely there and when he is, he's not keen to be drawn into what he refers to as *personality clashes* or *office politics*.

Gal returns to the screens. The moon is peering over the forest when they next lift their head. Something or someone moves among the trees.

The buzzer goes again. This time whoever's out there keeps their finger on the button until they thrust back their chair and skip over to the intercom.

'Who is it?'

But whoever is out there doesn't respond. Gal starts to head back to the desk, but then the buzzer goes off again and this time they release the gate and wait. Footsteps up the path, a light rapping on the wood.

Gal draws back the bolt and opens the door.

'Oh,' they say, 'it's you.'

18

Gentle Knyght II

———

Wednesday nights is football and after practice the team come in. Wayne ferries pint after pint over to the usual table. Assembled in the firelight, the golden cups cast amber prisms upon the scarred wooden top.

Tonight they're bellowing. A few of the regulars, reveries shattered, slope off scowling, either home or into the pub's furthest reaches away from the noise. It's because of what happened at Arthur's party. It's the same with soldiers when they go on R&R after battle, although in this case it was only Lance who'd done anything.

Lance isn't with them. He doesn't come to the Green Knight, although occasionally in summer he'll be seen in the beer garden. Someone will let Wayne know – just drop it in in passing – and he'll stay inside. It's the same with the football. Wayne will go along if he's not working and Lance won't be there. But on the nights he's behind the bar, he'll overhear Lance's name mentioned in relation to the form he's shown on the pitch. When Wayne shops, he drives to the Lidl at Devizes. Lance gets the supermarkets in Swindon. And so on.

Back and forth to deliver more drinks and fetch away the empties, keeping John topped up, beer swirling into the glasses from the taps. The air's warm – from the fire and the men's bodies and breath. After his fourth, Kay climbs on a chair.

'To Brian the troll, may he rot!'

Trist, Lionel, Percy, Garlon, all the rest, roar their approval and lift their drinks. Bravado, Wayne thinks. The scab's hardly dry on the cut Kay took when the troll rushed him. A thought that's occurred to more than a few of them from their faces. Easy to judge, Wayne thinks, even the best falter when taken by surprise.

Not Lance, though, but then there never was a soldier like Lance. All those bodies in the tower. All that death. Gareth smiling over his shoulder—

A cold finger of night air.

'Ooh, shut that door,' someone shouts.

Wayne lifts his head. The red-haired woman is in the open doorway, backed by darkness. Her feet are caked in mud, her hair a wild frizz. She bends down to work on her laces.

'Shut that bloody—' Kay turns towards her.

'Hold your tongue,' Morgan snaps. Briefly, she straightens and points a finger at him, cheeks burning, and Wayne knows he has seen her before. Not recently, not here. Not anywhere good. Like an anemone, the memory closes around itself as he grasps for it.

Kay recovers himself and his face twists with spite. He's not going to be told off in public, not after half the planet has just watched him go arse over tit, eyes bulging in terror. He draws himself up and the men around him quieten.

'Look who it isn't?' Kay begins. 'You remember Morgan, lads.'

Bors and Perce are looking down at their feet. Garlon is smiling. Some of the newer recruits look from face to face in puzzlement.

Wayne grabs a plastic bag from the drawer and heads over, blocking their view.

'You can put them in this.'

'Ta.' She bends again and wrenches off first one shoe, then the other. Her legs are muddy halfway to the knees.

'Where did you walk from?'

'Uffington back across the Ridgeway.'

'Might want to consider different footwear next time.'

'I wasn't planning on it,' she bursts out. 'Look, I'm bloody starving and I want a drink.'

'Kitchen's closed.'

Her face falls then she sets her chin. 'Just a whisky, then.'

He indicates an empty stool at the bar. 'Sit there.'

In the kitchen, Lou's packing everything away but he manages to rustle up some cold sausages and chuck them inside a bap. He takes it out with a bottle of brown sauce, pours her a double and then deals with the backlog of orders.

The footballers give her a wide berth and talk in undertones. She keeps her head down, bulk hunched over the roll. Her socks are filthy. There's sauce in the corners of her mouth. She is an uglyish woman, odd even. He wonders what Arthur wants with her, whether he kicked her out the car or she walked back by choice. Hard to imagine the former.

Next time she looks up, it's to give him a transforming smile. Oddness to charm, ugliness to something else.

'I'd almost forgotten about brown sauce. Thanks for that.'

'How can someone forget brown sauce?'

'I was abroad.'

'But you're from round here?'

'I am. I was.'

'What year did you leave?'

They work out he arrived not long after she left. It's on the tip of his tongue to ask her where he might have seen her, because he's sure it wasn't here, but then someone wants to order, and by the time he's done she's been taken prisoner by one of John's tall tales.

Mountains have crevasses. Forests are home to wild beasts. The Green Knight has a portly white-haired siren who lures the unwary into conversations from which they quickly feel they'll never struggle free.

Then Wayne loses track of her because the door is thrown open again, the fire takes a deep breath, and in strides the towering figure of Vern, landlord of the Green Knight.

*

Later, when they've all gone home and Lou's gone up, Wayne lingers while Vern does the till. He empties and refills the dishwasher, wipes down the tables, brings in more wood for tomorrow's fire.

Vern licks a finger and riffles through a pile of twenties, counting under his breath. His hair is black with white stripes at the temples.

It sweeps back from his craggy brow and curls over his collar. A lot of big men are slow, but Wayne's seen Vern catch a knocked glass before it hits the floor. Sometimes he's wondered if Vern might have served Her Majesty – either in her services or at her pleasure – but if so, he's not telling. 'Good trip?' he'll ask, and Vern will reply that it was, or shrug or grimace. He comes and goes and in between he keeps his own counsel.

Finally, Vern finishes counting, enters the figures into an app, and thrusts his chair back from the table.

'Not bad. Wait here.'

As he goes off to put the takings in the safe, Vern flips out the light over the bar, leaving Wayne in the red gloom of the dying fire.

He listens to Vern's footsteps retreat and a stillness falls over him. One of the streetlamps in the marketplace is cutting in and out.

There's one more settling-up to do.

Wayne's agreement with Vern has several facets. One is atonement, because a year ago, Wayne – less than twenty-fours hours back in Abury – had done the Green Knight over.

Before that, there had been months of free fall. Everyone he knew had had enough. Spain with his dad. Cardiff. Newport. London. Burning through family ties, the affections of friends. Watching sympathy turn to frustration to dislike. The sense of himself as leaking, full of holes from which not blood nor tears but hate was escaping.

Hatred dripping on everything he touched like tar. Down. Down. Down. A couple of nights on a step near Paddington Station in London. A bad bender. Big black craters in his memory. Snippets of a journey, first by train, then a bus.

What had drawn him back to Abury? Because it was where he met Gareth? Or because, on leave from the army all those years before – the day of the football match, the day of the comet – there was, within the drunken haze, a memory of kindness: a pillow placed beneath his head, a kiss, a glass of water set down within reach.

But once back in the Green Knight, Wayne had not behaved like a man looking for kindness. Instead, he had drunk himself insensible. At some point, Lou and Vern cut him off. He'd gone to the gents, passed out in a stall and at locking-up he'd somehow been overlooked. Wayne had come to in the middle of the night, surrounded by broken furniture and smashed bottles, Vern half-dressed, roaring and shaking him like a kitten.

Wayne had cried like an engine tearing itself to pieces, saturated with shame. Not supposed to ask for help. Not supposed to need anything.

'Nobody speaks of it, the war, what happened, what it did ... Nobody speaks ...'

Vern had locked him in the store cupboard with a blanket. The next morning Wayne woke up covered in the bag of flour he'd knocked over, wanting to die, expecting the police.

Instead, the job and an agreement: a portion of his wages against the debt, a portion for his keep, a portion kept by for when Wayne needs it. No drinking. No losing his temper. No unpleasantness with the clientele. There was one more thing.

'I have to go away sometimes. I don't like leaving Lou by herself.'

Wayne's clothes were in the wash. He was standing there in his pants, flour in his eyebrows. It was not a good negotiating position.

'When I'm not here, anything you gain you give to me.'

'You mean like my tips?'

The landlord of the Green Knight gave him a wry smile. 'I'll tell you what, I'll do the same. Let's call it ... an exchange of winnings.'

Wayne could barely put a sentence together or form a coherent thought. Horror possessed him. In the end, he'd just nodded. It was to become apparent, if not clear. There's nothing clear about it.

The debt was paid off months ago, and while Wayne's been making noises about leaving – sometimes it's like there's an alarm going off inside him, like something's waiting for him out there in the world, something he must go in search of – he's frightened of what he'll encounter, of the dangers that lie beyond the thick stone walls of the Green Knight. And at the heart of it, the fear he can't trust himself, can't live properly without the army or Vern to tell him what to do.

Wayne hears Vern's footsteps returning over the ancient flagstones.

'Slim pickings, Wayne, I'm afraid. I found a band for you. A good one, but they won't be down for a couple of weeks. And you? What did you gain this time?'

From his pocket, Wayne extracts thirty-odd quid of tips and presses it into Vern's palm.

'And what else?'

'The Hughes boy called me a prick when I kicked him out and then nearly puked on my shoes.'

'Anything else?'

A silvery sensation. A creeping shudder. He could lie. Vern won't know unless she tells him. 'Maybe you won't want it,' he gets out. His breath catches for a moment and he has to stifle a laugh.

'I think I made it clear at the beginning, Wayne. We exchange all our winnings. Now, will you honour our agreement or not?'

It's hard to read the expression in Vern's eyes, but Wayne thinks a smile is playing on his lips. But then he stops thinking, takes a step forward and delivers a kiss to each of Vern's cheeks, and then one more upon the landlord of the Green Knight's mouth.

19

Lullabies

———

Night falls, night deepens, but not all of Abury are in their beds. Not all are asleep.

Five minutes ago, Mo was sitting at the other end of the sofa, decorously sipping the herbal tea Gal made him. Now, he's slithered himself down and round, plucking a cushion and placing it, then his head, on Gal's knee.

'Tell me,' Mo says, 'do you have any hobbies? Because as far as I can see, literally all you do is work for my dad. You must love it. The company.' When Gal doesn't respond, Mo says, 'Well, do you?'

'Not the company itself—'

'Because it's full of arseholes?'

'I love the work,' Gal says firmly, 'and I . . . I'm . . . I get on with Arthur. He understands.'

'Understands what?'

Gal swallows, looks out again at the dark forest. The music is still playing. Perhaps without realising, Mo flutters his fingers along with the melody.

'To me, code is like music. Like something living. I came to Abury because of code Arthur had written. I was sixteen but I'd hacked into the DVLA and the Home Office and sent myself fake ID saying I was eighteen. I rented a house out on the estate. I didn't want people asking questions so I hid away. It was just me and then, after a bit, it was me and Hercules. In the middle of the night, I used to take him for walks. We'd always end up at your house. I would just stand outside. Arthur was looking for me but I didn't let him find me. His code was ... I think you can tell a lot about someone by their code and his was so fine.'

Mo nods. 'Go on.'

'Then there were the comments. When you write code, you can leave comments in it, to help with refactoring, or to make finding bugs faster. People can be snooty about them, like it's a sign of bad code if it needs comments. Arthur's a genius, but his comments were always so generous, so helpful. I wanted so badly to meet him, but if he wasn't like I hoped, I didn't know what I would do.'

'Perhaps it's where he puts the best of himself.'

Gal bridles at the unfairness. 'You're always so down on him. You're lucky. Don't you know how lucky you are?'

Mo's body tenses as though Gal has hit a nerve. 'I wonder if he's as loyal to you as you are to him.' Then he sighs, relaxes again. 'What about your family, Gal?'

'Have you ever left the cinema part way through a film because you really, really didn't want to see the end? That was my family.'

'Genre?'

'Horror-comedy. Although the comedy part is much easier to see in retrospect and from a distance.'

It's quite nice having Mo's head on their lap, Gal realises. As a puppy, after Gal adopted him from the animal rescue centre, Hercules was always climbing up; when he got older, he didn't understand why he still couldn't spend his evenings nestled on Gal's knees. So each night Gal found himself buried under sixteen stone of Neapolitan mastiff.

'Wasn't there a fuss about some comments in code? To do with that developer, the American with the piercings? Lisa Something.'

'Lisa Gomez.' Gal shifts uneasily.

'What happened?'

'She was brilliant. Absolutely brilliant but not everyone thought so. She wanted to change things and it didn't make her very popular. And Lisa, she wasn't going to tiptoe. Arthur wasn't around a lot and some of the others, they rewrote bits of her code.'

'And?'

'No, Mo. They rewrote bits of her code! And there were comments added, questioning her ability. So she left.'

'And that was all there was to it?'

'As far as I know. I was in Japan when she walked. Arthur sent me out for a few weeks to work on a project.' Gal remembers how disappointed they'd been. How they'd wished Arthur had done more to make her stay. 'It was a shame. But, you know, Arthur can't be responsible for everything. It's a mistake when a person tries to take on too much responsibility.'

Gal thinks again of *Wasteland*. Mozart composed his first symphony at five, his first opera at fourteen, but 'Jupiter', his greatest completed work, at least in Gal's opinion, didn't come along until Wolfgang was in his early thirties and he was still working on his Requiem when he died. What if he'd known his greatest work was behind him at fifteen? How would he have reacted if faced with destroying it?

But *Wasteland* should be destroyed. When Gal made it, they believed they were being courageous when in fact they'd been high as a kite and sick with sadness, with loneliness. It's a dangerous thing, perhaps even a wicked thing, and it's only pride that's stopped them erasing it already. They'll speak to Arthur about it first thing tomorrow, they'll obliterate it from the face of the earth . . .

Why is Mo smiling like that? When Gal looks down, they realise their fingers have found their way into Mo's hair.

'God. You think you're irresistible.'

'I do. I do.'

'Well, I don't fancy becoming another feather in your cap so you may as well give up.'

'You think I have a feathery cap?' Mo bursts out laughing and Gal has to resist the impulse to shrug him on to the floor.

'Are you ever serious about anything?'

'Once you stop laughing and start crying, Gal, where do you stop?' And now Mo's not laughing at all and his eyes are serious. 'I understand people can't be responsible for everything, but if you can do some good, if you can help someone, then you should, shouldn't you?'

'Of course.'

'Well,' Mo says, and Gal has the sense they've wandered straight into a trap. 'I'm so glad you think so because I need your help. And you could definitely call it something serious.'

*

Outside in the darkness, the Invisible Knight curses his luck and slips back into the forest. It's too risky with two of them there. Although if anyone poses a danger to him, it's the albino freak. He wanted to see that eco-shithole burn!

Cast down. Regret a taste in the mouth. No fun. No fun. No fun.

What a disappointment Brian turned out to be. Still, he's not done yet.

Underfoot a branch snaps like a bone. The trees are madmen waving their arms.

If he goes home now, he'll only end up watching the video on a loop. Working himself up into a state over Lance and Gwen. Jacking himself up into a frothing frenzy with no one to take it out on. Lust and rage. Rage and lust.

He couldn't believe it when he saw the footage for the first time. He'd nearly missed it. It's not like he's got the time to review every second of video from every single camera. The majority of the cameras at Gwen and Arthur's were focused on the perimeter so there was rarely anything of interest. Mostly, he watched it on fast forward. Skimmed it. Then, he snatched a glimpse of Gwen stripping her top off, pressed pause and went and fetched himself a glass of wine, a good glass, to mark the occasion.

'Come on, Gwennie,' he muttered to himself as she ran the hose over her sports bra. But then Lance had stepped into frame, and then Lance had kissed her, and she'd done nothing to stop him. On the contrary, she was all too willing.

It was like Carly all over again. The betrayal. The insult. Happening right under his nose.

Back at the car, he puts the can of petrol away in the boot. The long night stretches ahead. And at some point, he'll start remembering.

Lover's Lane. Lover's Lane. Lover's Lane . . .

Funny how one night can define your whole life.

143

He's already halfway home when an alternative occurs to him. For a moment he prevaricates and then, at the bypass roundabout, he spins the wheel and heads back into Abury.

*

In the annexe at the Green Knight, Morgan roams the inhospitable border between wake and sleep. The sheets ensnare her. The foot that's escaped the covers blackens with frostbite, her forehead burns.

A chill from the walk, or the whisky, or the moment in the pub before Wayne handed her the bag. The blossoming antipathy in the air, her body prompting her to cringe or run away. It had come back, those mornings of horror, at the end of her road, Monday to Friday, rain or shine, waiting for the school bus and what it would bring.

The bus is out there somewhere and Rasha is aboard. The bus is taking Rasha to her death. Rasha may ring the bell, but the bus will not let her off. Perhaps somewhere near the end she calls for Morgan.

Waking and sleeping, dreaming and waking. Morgan presses on, over the border, into dreamland where marshy scrub gives way to forest, to towering beeches, bracken and copper leaf mulch.

Sounds reach her from far away. Someone is outside the annexe, moving around. Someone or something is scratching at the door, slowly twisting the handle.

In response, Morgan goes deeper into the dream, deeper among the trees, plunging down a steep bank into ankle-deep black water. The stream is another border she must find her way across, over slippery piebald boulders to the far side, and then onwards into a dark thicket.

The sounds pursue her: a laugh, half giggle, half gasp, and then the voice at first wheedling . . .

'Let me in.'

. . . and then guttural. Half human and hungry and far from sane.

'Let me in!'

The door handle jerking.

And in her dream, Morgan is running now, unable to see the

144

way ahead. Clawed at by thorns, struck by branches. She knows she must not open her eyes, even here, because then it will be real.

'Little pig, little pig, let me in . . .'

The creak of hinges as though a heavy weight is bearing against them. The door handle rattling.

And finally, Morgan can resist the urge no longer and she wrenches her eyes open . . .

. . . and sees ahead, in a small clearing, derelict mouth ajar . . .

. . . the witch's house.

Four

Gather Ye Rosebuds
2009

20

Comet

———

The day of the comet, the whole of Abury turns out to watch the team play on Arthur's new pitch.

Aidey, Lance, Wayne and Gareth have a fortnight's leave. Yesterday, they were on a plane to RAF Fairford, three days ago they were at the fort, today they're guest-starring in the match against Marlborough, leading to accusations of unfairness, of ringers, of foul play. Marlborough get thrashed five–nil and won't come for post-match drinks at the Green Knight much to everyone's relief. Because Aidey's nothing if not predictable.

The pub's under new management, a husband-and-wife team, Vern and Lou. No one's sure where they're from but they keep the beer flowing, bring in live music, win over John with complimentary plates of bacon sandwiches, a few crisps on the side.

News comes of a major DDoS attack in South Korea so Arthur excuses himself after a single half of lemonade, leaving an open tab at the bar. The footballers mill about making a din. The wives and girlfriends are there too. A couple have jobs outside the company, while the rest work for Arthur in some capacity – sales or admin or customer support – or care for the small people, who won't be taken away till bedtime, who are crawling and squalling, smacking one another, demanding stuff.

Everyone tries to buy drinks for the conquering heroes.

'It's taken care of,' Vern tells them smiling, but they still press tenners on him. Want a stake, an anecdote, a penny down the well.

Oh, poor Wayne, Wayne imagines them saying in a couple of months, *I bought him a pint only a few weeks ago! Is it both legs or just the one?*

Gwen misses the game because she's having a miscarriage, her fifth, but she makes it to the pub later on. Dress by Roland Mouret, smile by double the recommended dose of co-codamol.

Arthur doesn't know. She didn't even tell him she was pregnant. She tells herself it's because it was too early, but really she doesn't want to have to watch him fail her again. Watch him bury himself in work, watch him distance himself and turn away. It's an odd way to try and save a marriage but there you go.

Later she'll refer to it as her bling phase. Everything expensive. Trips to London to get her hair done. Sitting in the front row at Fashion Week. Corseted and cantilevered. Spike heels. A full face of make-up each morning. Handbags that grow bigger and bigger as her body gets smaller. A twisting dissatisfaction, almost a horror, of everything she looks on.

'Mum, you look like a lollipop!' Mo tells her. He's eight now. Eightish. She's tried to protect him as best she can, but the last four years have been a battery of loss: miscarriages at two months, three months, ten weeks, eleven weeks. Test after test after test. Poking and prodding her. Injections. She tells no one. Arthur has to swear to tell no one. A single drop of pity and she's done for.

Aidey spies her coming through the doors and pushes Garlon off his bar stool.

'Look! I've saved you a seat, Gwen. G&T for Gwen, make it a double!'

Her brother seems to be in the middle of a long tale, which sounds very much like a tall tale. His section surrounded by the enemy. A wounded comrade. Fighting their way out. Low on ammunition.

'—he was gone. Just me and Hinks left. For a second, I thought he'd fucking left us there. And I am thinking we have had it. Fucking had it. But then, I hear this noise over the firing and then I look out over the back, and there he is, driving a horse and cart, only it's a donkey not a horse, with massive ears. Some farmer had left it tied up and done a runner when the bombs started. It's berserk with fear, but somehow Donkey Boy's got it doing what he wants—'

'Donkey Boy?' She lifts an eyebrow.

'Get your mind out the gutter, Gwen.'

Gwen imagines some hulking ninny. Two brain cells to rub together, pointing and grunting.

'Oh, and he's got a photo of you. Keeps it secret.'

'Has he indeed?'

She loses track of the next part of the story, struck by a memory of Aidey aged six, charging at her with a stick, shouting, 'Nazi swine!' There was always too much energy in his body. If you hugged him, he was hot. He was never still unless he was sleeping, forever spraying them all with imaginary bullets, insisting she was dead, that he had killed her. Leaping out from behind doors or down from trees. Chinese-burning her or throttling her or tying her up with their mother's dressing-gown cord and kicking her down the stairs.

In the school holidays, if he had a friend over, he'd beg her to join in. They needed an enemy or they'd fall to squabbling. A common enemy to bond them, so they could be close. It's what the army's for – finding men to kill, so other men can feel close to one another.

Through the pills, through the gin, she feels a clenching in her lower belly, a fist tightening. In her bag, she's got more pads, thick ones to catch the clots. Six weeks, not even worth a trip to the doctor.

'You listening?'

Everyone's listening, but it's Gwen Aidey wants to make sure of. Her brother loves her, and she's almost certain she loves him, if only she could like him, if only he could be trusted, if only he didn't appal and frighten her. If only he hadn't terrorised her, and said such awful things, and believed such awful things, and fucked Morgan, the best friend she'd ever had.

They keep falling out of me, my babies keep dying, seeping out from between my legs, I can't hold them in, one had a face ... it's sending me fucking mad, Morgan.

'Sounds dangerous,' Gwen murmurs.

'Makes Iraq look like the teddy bears' picnic.' In Aidey's puffed-out chest, she sees the six-year-old. When he was ten, he fell out of the barn and broke his leg. She'd run to fetch help, her feet flying beneath her as she imagined the life ebbing from him.

Aidey could die, she realises afresh. In some corner of a foreign field that will become forever awful.

'Where he is then, your donkey-loving friend?' Gwen asks. She puts an arm round her brother's shoulders, suddenly eager to touch him. 'I'd like to buy him a drink.'

Aidey waves a hand at the crowd.

'Around somewhere.' But it turns out no one's seen him since the game.

Then it comes. The sea change. His eyes roam her face. He looks down at the shoes, takes in the handbag and the dress, grimaces as though he's tasted something rancid.

'Sister of mine, what the fuck do you look like?'

*

Linnet's never been sweet. Not even when she was sixteen. One of the red-tops did a countdown to her birthday. Photos of her in her bikini, promising the big reveal. On the big day, there they were on Page Three. Undeniably legendary tits. Real. Big. Large pink-brown areoles and infinitely suckable nipples. Although harder to wank over than you might expect. She'd managed the smile, but the eyes were unnerving. Like jerking yourself off over a starving tiger. Best to fold the picture over, to be honest.

At the game, she didn't turn up till half-time, then spent the second half stalking the sidelines barracking Gareth, can of cider in her talons. Making an absolute exhibition of herself and not for the first time. The mouth on her. C-words, F-words, T-words, S-words. Easier to list the letters Linnet doesn't have an obscenity for.

'Fucking useless.'

'Tackle him, you tosser.'

'Could you move any sodding slower?'

'Move your arse and pass it.'

'Stop shitting goal-hanging!'

'Get back to the bloody chippy!'

This last a reference to the job Gareth had held before joining up, ferrying out baskets of chips at the Golden Fryer.

Gareth first half was unspectacular, but in response to Linnet's presence he stuck it in the goal twice in a row, turning to wave at her and smile.

In the Green Knight, she dresses him down. Loudly boasts of photographers with convertibles. The letters she gets sent from maximum-security wings. A London publicist who wants to make her a star—

Then, just like that, she's kissing him, mouth open, the blade-tongue pink as a raspberry.

Everywhere Wayne looks, there's Gareth and Linnet, sucking on each other's faces.

Chasing each other round the pool table.

Disappearing into the gents and barricading the doors.

Everywhere he turns, Gareth's got his hands up Linnet's skirt.

Linnet's holding a cider in one hand, the other pumping under the table while Gareth's eyes roll back in his head.

Linnet's boobs are squashed against the windowpane as Gareth dry-humps her from behind.

Young and panting. Hot for each other. Yelping and grunting and squealing. Shameless as sap in spring.

Wayne wonders how much he'll have to drink before he dies. Stops wondering, keeps on drinking. Feels the landlord's eyes on him. His wife, Lou, has blonde hair in some kind of puff and flicky eyeliner. It's not like Wayne doesn't like women too. It's just less.

One of the old boys is asking him about the war, asks him how the crusade is going.

'They're trying to kill us. Every day.' To his own ears his voice sounds shocked and boyish.

Aidey comes and puts an arm round him, starts telling the bar about Wayne and Gareth stretchering Chisholm back to the fort. Always the same with Aidey. Always vainglory or provocation, always boasting or bellyaching, or asking someone what they're looking at.

Wayne throws off Aidey's arm, stumbles out into the pub garden and slumps down, sloshing half his drink over the table. He sucks it up, splintering his tongue. Laughs to himself. Knocks over the rest. Tears springing to his eyes. He tries to get to his feet. Too dangerous. Too dangerous. IEDs everywhere. If he puts a foot wrong, that's it for his legs. His legs . . .

He'd never given them any thought before. Now it's like he has them both on loan, can't help but picture them sailing through the air, or draped over a hedge.

His head falls, his cheek meets the sopping wood. At some point, he realises someone is talking to him.

'Bit worse for wear, aren't you, mate? Bit shit-faced. Someone's going to have a headache in the morning . . . unable to speak, is it? Dear, oh dear. Quite understandable, mate. Must be a bit stressful like, all that shooting and getting shot at.'

Wayne can't place the voice, although he thinks he might have heard it before. He'd like to lift his head from the table to see who it is, but even the thought of it makes the bile rise in his throat.

The voice gets quieter, closer, insinuates itself into his ear.

'And killing's stressful too. Jangles the nerves. You don't sleep right after, jumping at shadows. Thinking about it all the time. Replaying it. Least you don't have to worry about the coppers . . .

'But you've got to do what you've got to do and get on with it, right? You know . . . Dan was bad enough. After Carly and I got it on, I told her to chuck him so we could be together. She kept putting it off, saying she didn't want to hurt his feelings. And I said, well, his feelings are going to be pretty hurt when I tell about what you and I got up to. It went on like that for ages.

'But then I found out about the others. Just kissing is what she said. But if a man kisses a woman, why wouldn't he take advantage of her afterwards? You can't believe someone kissed her without doing more. One thing leads to another: if a man kisses a woman and nothing more when they are alone together, there's something wrong with him.'

'Something wrong . . . something wrong with me?' Wayne mutters.

'A woman who lets herself be kissed gives the rest if someone insists on it; at least, that's how it was with Carly. She'd said yes to everyone, why should she say no to me?' A pause. 'Anyway, whichever way you choose to look at it, Carly was asking for it. One way or another. And she got it.'

A moment passes – a minute, an hour? Wayne starts, looks about, but finds himself alone.

Lance is in the car park, sitting on the wall behind a van out of sight, eating chips in the dark. In Afghanistan, he dreamed of chips soaked in vinegar, hot and salty and steaming. The little ones crunchy, brown at the edges. The big ones like melting fingers. He closes his eyes, tries to focus on his mouth, to create a sense-memory he can return to when he's back at the fort, or wherever they send him next, when all he's got to look forward to is chicken sausages, beans from a ration pack and tins of his dad's custard. But his stomach's a contracted knot.

He'd expected to see Gwen at the game. Before kick-off someone had asked Arthur where she was. 'She'll be along later,' he said. Each time someone said her name, Lance took it like a jolt from a taser.

He'd played hard, scored twice, imagining her watching. Hugged by the other players, he'd scanned the crowd for her face, her perfect face, but nothing.

Afterwards, he'd hung back and then ducked down a narrow, cobbled lane. Not fit for company. Not fit for carousing. Not really fit for life, not a normal life, a man who kept himself apart by means of a fantasy, by making use of some other man's wife, creating an image of her, making it holy, cleaving to it, in order to hide, to conceal the holes in him. So he stalked the streets, stared into shop windows, read the small ads in the mini-supermarket:

Golf clubs, never used . . . Child's bed, outgrown . . . Average-size dog with lead . . .

Every single one of them struck him as a barely disguised suicide note, the whole noticeboard a blaring announcement that the things you thought you wanted – because wanting things made life bearable – did not help.

Here, where Gwen lived, where she walked and bought stamps and possibly nipped into the butcher's for a pound of sausages, he couldn't hold the dream of her in his head, and without it he knew how alone he was, how alone he'd always been, ever since his mum—

Lance slipping down the spiral. Then as night fell, buying himself a double helping of chips wrapped in newspaper, holding them to his body, warm and steaming, and hiding behind a van in the car park of the Green Knight.

*

The gins, the pills. It's thinning, the layer between Gwen's exterior and what's inside; it's breaking down.

If she stays, she doesn't know what she'll do. Poke a child in the eye. Mug a stranger.

That's what it's all been about: the clothes, the make-up, the hair, all the fucking shit she's mired in – policing the exterior lest it crack, lest the molten-horror, the woman-shaped thing, comes spilling out, naked and shrieking.

Gwen needs to be out of sight. Like a wounded beast that crawls under a car to bleed to death, instinct telling it that if it lies very still, keeps very silent, it will be spared.

'Just nipping to the ladies,' she whispers. No one pays any attention as she walks with measured steps to the corridor leading to the loos, then flees, staggering through the fire exit into the car park.

She has not thought of darkness as kind before. *Accept me like an offering*, she thinks. *Let no one ever look on me again.*

Gwen makes for the darkest corner, on the far side, behind a large van, where she finds ... Lance, the soldier she kissed on her wedding day. Bigger. Older. More handsome if that's possible.

'Give us a chip, then,' Gwen says.

Lance holds out the newspaper solemnly and she jabs in and grabs a couple. Then she bursts out laughing.

It's not a very nice laugh. Almost like there's glass in it.

'Oh, you're Donkey Boy. Everyone's looking for you. Aidey's been telling me all about you. Can I see the photo? The one you have of me?'

Whatever she's expecting, it's not for Lance to screw up the newspaper, dump the chips down on the wall and slide his wallet free from his back pocket. Mutely, he draws out the tattered image and offers it to her.

In the picture, Gwen is about eighteen. She turns towards the camera, mouth half open, eyes alight. Behind her a window is open to darkness. Her skin is bleached by the flash, her hair a glowing sheaf.

Morgan had taken the picture with Gwen's camera. They were getting ready to go out somewhere. There is a tiny hole in the corner from where it was pinned to a board of photographs of Gwen and Arthur at their wedding.

Gwen would love the girl in the photograph too. To be like that again. To get back there.

'So you're in love with me, then? Is that it?'

'Not what you'd call love. Not like the songs on the radio, or on the TV. But yes, I had a feeling. I didn't ask for it.' His voice creaks like a door from want of use. 'I thought I could serve it. That I could love the girl I saw on the hillside, even if we never spoke. To love without asking for anything. I thought that would be the test of it . . .'

So sanctimonious, so po-faced.

'Is that so?' She goes to give him the picture back but he shakes his head. He doesn't want it.

'I thought you were someone else. You're not . . . you're not . . .'

How it hurts. The disappointment in his voice. How it chimes with something she hears on the wind. Children's voices. That she's not worth staying for.

'You don't know me.'

'No.' But he is agreeing with her, shaking his head at the dress and heels, the make-up and jewellery. Judging her and failing her, like everyone else.

'I didn't enter your Miss World competition.'

How bereft he looks. How beautiful and bereft. She'll leave it there. She will go now, with dignity: one step, two step . . . total loss of control—

'I lost a baby today. And you think you . . . you think you get to talk to me . . . you think you've something to say to me? You don't like the way I dress? The way I talk—'

The comet burns; Gwen's rage is hotter. She sticks a finger in his chest and at her touch Lance drops to his knees. Literally, drops down on to the hard concrete, eyes lowered.

'Forgive me. Oh God, forgive me, Gwen.'

She takes his head between her hands like she could twist it off. He wants her to. He would let her.

His hands slip around her calves, encircling them. He groans and falls forward, his face thudding into the bottom of her ribcage, where the bones swoop round like the wings of a bird.

Gwen teeters there on her high heels. There is a moment when she might turn away, turn back. But then, forward she falls, like a sack of rocks dropped off a cliff into a river.

The comet passes. It looks down and it says, *Oh no, not again, not you two . . .*

And the heavenly bodies meet.

*

The comet goes over a little after ten and the bar empties to go watch it in the garden. The wandering star. The portent. The flaming traveller spuming gas and ice, dust and solar light.

John declines to come. 'It's a disastrous star, a longing wanderer. It makes you feel its loneliness. You'll not catch me under it again.'

On the sopping grass, they stand there looking up – a couple of footballers, some of the company men – gripping one another's shoulders to stay vertical, trying to ignore Gareth and Linnet under one of the picnic tables.

The little white jizz trail flames into sight and then out again. They watch, waiting for it to reveal itself once more, and in the quiet, gazing into the vault, each heart finds itself troubled, silently pours out its lament . . .

How can she kiss that boy when I love her so?

I never said, because who was I to say? That night, I woke up and I think . . . I think that one of them was gone. But I can't be sure, so I stay silent and forget about it and then sometimes I see Carly's mother and it stabs me—

This place! Like being stuck in school forever! Where would I ever find a job that pays like this one? And doing what? I'm no good at anything, not really . . .

Nodding and smiling and laughing at the jokes. Not leaping over my desk and killing Kay, not burying him deep in a hole and pissing on it, not returning every midnight full moon to cavort upon it, heart bursting with joy.

If I told them what I saw on his computer, the pictures, he'd make a joke of it.
He could have deleted them by now. Or he'd say they were from a film. I'd
have no proof. It'd be me who'd end up on the outside . . .

'Are the stars the same in Afghanistan?' someone asks.

'How should I know?' Aidey says. Wayne's past speaking.
Gareth's mouth is full of Linnet. Lance holds Gwen in the dark of
the car park behind the van, thinking,

> *How can she be so light when she feels so heavy?*

*

Later, Wayne kisses someone's mouth. Is it the landlord, is it his
wife?

'You're all right, son.'

Kind hands in any case. Helping him up some stairs that he takes
on his hands and knees, and then to a sofa. Putting a cushion under
his head. A pint glass of water within reach but where he won't
kick it over.

Stroking his cheek. The landlord, Vern. Or the wife, Lou.

Darkness follows and then a dream, surely only a dream, of a
blonde girl in a puffy pink dress, bare feet sinking into carpet, a
plaster on one heel. A girl he served up drinks to a couple of times
over a decade ago but never really spoke to.

'Avenge me, gentle knight. Avenge my most cruel murder!'

A great rent at her throat which bubbles crimson as she speaks.

'Who did this to you?' Wayne says. 'Carly, who—'

'You know who. You know, Wayne.'

And the girl vanishes.

21

Helmandshire

———

The journey back is bad. Delays, diversions, thirty hours in Cyprus, another ten in Qatar. In the ether between what they've left behind and what's to come; in the uncertainty, nerves fraying, liverish and red-eyed. Even Gareth is snappy. He turns his back on them, on Wayne too, and begins a letter to Linnet.

My Lionesse...

At the airbase in Al Udeid another delay is announced. The flight won't leave till the morning, possibly the afternoon. They sleep on the floor, face down or with an arm shielding their eyes from the fluorescent strip lighting, surrounded by Third Country nationals, civilian staff and NGO workers.

Wayne opens his eyes in the small hours, throat parched. Beneath the hellish lights, everything is off, weirded. Gareth lies rag-dolled beside him. Lance sits with his back against the wall, his head folded on his knees, like a child desolate for being told off.

Some way off, Aidey is having an altercation with a woman, biggish, with red hair. A Westerner in drab civilian clothes. She is pointing at him, two fingers – index and middle – outstretched. Wayne thinks he hears her say, 'Old times' sake? For old times' sake?'

At Bastion they're left kicking their heels inside the fence for a week. Compared to the fort, there are all the comforts of home

– Internet, fast food, shooting ranges, games of cricket and volley-ball outside the dead, killing heat of day. The base is huge, a desert city of thirty thousand soldiers and workers, most of whom will never leave the relative safety of the camp.

Beyond the fence, the Danes at Gereshk are getting it. The Estonians at Pimon. Their lads at Sangin are taking a hammering. Each time there's a casualty, the Internet's cut off until the next of kin can be informed. No one's wife, no one's mother, should learn of their death on Facebook. It's getting cut off daily.

'What's the fucking point of having it?' Aidey rages.

A man with a wart in his ear. Around him, people melt away. The jokes are nastier, the complaints more relentless. No one escapes his ire.

Why's he even here? It's a mystery to Wayne. Aidey went to the right school, he comes from money. He could have done Sandhurst, could have been an officer. With his dad's backing, Aidey could have been anything he wanted. Instead, he enlisted. Whenever he's given anything, any titbit or step-up, he does something that means they have to take it away. Gareth's dad is a smackhead. His own works the bars of the Costa del Sol. As far as he can figure it out, Lance grew up in a series of caravans, his dad some kind of itinerant labourer.

The wind drops. The helicopters go out and come back, go out and come back. Dust devils rise a hundred yards into the air, whirling, whirling.

Finally, it's time to go. The elections are coming and a series of operations have been planned with the objective of securing large swathes of territory. Create a safe zone, then extend its limits. It worked in Iraq. It's like they're always fighting the war before, rectifying past mistakes in a new place where the rules have changed.

Someone tells Wayne that this is Britain's fourth war in Afghanistan. It's the first he's heard of it. For some reason, no one's eager to talk about the other three.

At first, they're stationed at Lashkar Gah and given light patrol duties. Kids follow them in the streets, but the danger is minimal. Then they're put on convoy duty, escorting supplies out to the patrol bases. The dirt roads are seeded with mines and the Viking armoured vehicles offer little protection. The Barma-men go out front with Vallon detectors, but now the Taliban are using graphite components, which the detectors don't pick up.

Inside the Viking, the air-con doesn't work and the temperature gets up to forty-five, sometimes fifty, degrees. They move forward in inches, taking it in turns to ride top-cover and in the death seat up front. And while, in the field, there's no soldier you'd prefer to have at your side than Lance, here he just can't cope with it. Sits there sweating and trembling, has to be prised free whenever they get where they're going.

Just before the blast, Wayne hears Lance muttering to himself. Something about belonging. Over the sound of the engine, Wayne thinks he hears him whimper.

Then a noise so deafening, it's like no noise at all. The mine detonating. Tearing metal. Not them, though. The Viking behind them. Either they missed the plate or it was on a control wire.

Immediately, the ambush, the RPGs, the bullets.

Aidey's on top-cover and starts firing the machine gun.

The radio operator in the Viking behind isn't responding and the CO orders them out.

Lance goes first, then Wayne, then Gareth, into the blinding sunlight, on to the stony dirt road. On either side are fields in which maize stands taller than a man's head. The ears yellow and ripe. Above, swallows dip and bank like fighter jets in the powder-blue sky.

The Viking behind is a heap of smoking, mangled metal. Two soldiers are performing CPR on someone. Another man lies in bits.

The CO is shouting for no one to leave the track. The bullets are coming out of the fields and from somewhere above.

'Over there!'

Wayne turns. There's a building on the far side of the field, mottled grey-brown and squat with some kind of tower. A man pops up, there on top of the tower; he's carrying something over his shoulder, and then Wayne sees it, sees the rocket firing, the puff of smoke.

'Incoming! Take cover!'

The shockwave knocks Gareth down on top of him. A shower of stones pelts them, followed by a suffocating cloud of dust. Wayne helps Gareth to his feet, pulling him further behind the armoured vehicle.

162

There's a hole in the road, a crater where the two soldiers and the wounded man were moments before.

Lance stands exactly where he was before the rocket hit. Someone is screaming. The CO is shouting into his radio, calling for airstrikes. But Lance is just standing there, the dust swirling in a cloud about his legs. Slowly, he turns to Wayne and Gareth.

'I saw a woman,' he says. 'There's a woman in the tower. I saw her at the window.'

'What the fuck, Lance? Get down!'

But Lance turns back towards the tower. There is a window, or rather a huge hole in the upper floor of the tower, but there's no woman in it. It's what? Two hundred yards away? How can he be sure it was a woman?

'They're about to bomb that place to shit.'

Lance nods. Then he steps off the road into the maize. Within a few paces he's gone, leaving only the swaying stalks to show in which direction he went.

Gareth goes next before Wayne can stop him.

Aidey jumps down from the Viking.

'Where they hell are they going? Has he gone mad?'

'He thinks he saw a woman.'

Aidey raises a hand to point at the field. 'It's full of fucking Taliban. I seen them. It's moving, like there's currents in it.'

'Fuck,' Wayne says. And then he goes after them, into the maize, running. His breath and the crackle of the maize in his ears. His rifle in his arms, finger on the trigger. Can't shoot, though, in case he hits Lance or Gareth.

He's aware of Aidey some way behind him. His CO screaming in his earpiece to come back. Which way? Which way?

He follows the trampled corn. A hundred yards in, in a circle of flattened stalks, he blunders on to a young man, lying curled up like a kitten. Thin wrists. Very young. Bleeding from the head. Dead or dying.

Wayne steps over him.

A cold feeling has taken hold of him. Which way's the building?

A few steps on, he surprises a brown snake which whips away. His body armour and pack are trying to drag him down. The thought flashes up that he could lie down too. Like the boy back there. Just lie down. For a bit.

He stumbles on. Then, without warning, he reaches the far edge of the field and steps out from the maize on to a track outside the building. It's another fort, smaller than the one at Al-Shabat, perhaps even older. There's a wall round it, entered via a huge gate that lies wide open, a few feet to his left.

There could be mines anywhere. In his head, from out of nowhere, he starts to hear a tune.

You put your left leg in. Your left leg out.

From inside the wall, there comes the sound of shots being fired, a shout cut off.

In out.

In out.

You shake it all about.

Wayne shakes his head.

'Gareth! Lance! Where the fuck are you?'

A burst of energy. He darts across the track and through the open gateway. If there are mines, he misses them.

You do the hokey cokey and you turn around. That's what it's all about!

Inside the courtyard, there's no one in sight. Ahead, three uneven steps lead up to a door into the building. It's open; beyond, a staircase is just visible in the gloom.

'Aren't you listening, Wayne? They're going to drop the lot on this place. Comms are down. There's no stopping it.' It's Aidey, face dripping with sweat. 'This place is a fucking nest. Don't go in there, Wayne. Don't—'

But Gareth's inside, Gareth and Lance and maybe the woman Lance saw at the window and Christ knows who else. They've got to get out, get out before they drop the bomb.

So Wayne goes in to fetch them, into the dark building, and then, since the lower rooms are choked with rubble and broken beams – bombs have fallen here before – up the stone stairs.

Oh, the hokey cokey—

Oh, the hokey cokey—

As children, at the school Christmas party, they had held hands in a circle and rushed into the centre of the room, excited children screaming and grabbing at one another's slippery hands.

Oh, the hokey cokey—
That's what it's all about.
There's blood, a lot of it, dripping down the steps.
You put your whole self in.
A man splayed out on his back still gripping his gun.
Your whole self out.
Wayne bursts into the tower, gun cocked. Gareth is standing at the hole in the wall. He turns. There are what – three, four, five men – all dead – lying where they've fallen. One has a knife sticking out of his chest.

'You should have seen him,' Gareth says. 'You should have seen Lance. Fucking hell, Wayne.'

A ladder leads to the roof. Legs appear and then Lance drops down into the room.

'She's not here. I can't find her.'

''Cos she was never here. You imagined it, you mentalist.' All at once Wayne knows with an icy, absolute clarity that all this is his fault. He should have told the army about Lance, way back, right at the beginning. My friend, he should have said, is potentially the finest soldier you'll ever enlist. But he's also been known to see and hear things that aren't there.

All those years ago, back in Abury, Wayne had found him in the woods, covered him up with a blanket from the car then coaxed him home. Sat up with him while he rambled, made him a Pot Noodle and kept the tea coming, until at last he'd slept.

'She was here,' Lance says, but he's confused now. Uncertain. 'I saw her. I saw her standing here. She wanted me to come—'

Wayne crosses the floor to Lance. Hits him. Hits him hard in the shoulder and pushes him back towards the stairs. Thumping at him with a clenched fist. 'Get the fuck out of here before they bomb us to bits.'

Lance goes first, then Gareth.

'You could have been killed,' Wayne says, voice lowered for Gareth's ears only. 'You stupid tosser, running off like that. You could have—'

'What is it, Wayne? Am I your baby?' Laughing, Gareth dances down the steps on light feet.

Above them the MQ-9 Reaper drone, piloted by a controller

in a trailer a few miles outside of Las Vegas, arrives in position. No countermand arrives and seventy thousand dollars of Hellfire missile falls from the sky.

Gareth turns to smile over his shoulder at Wayne.

That's what it's all about!

And then darkness. Total and utter darkness.

22

Grete Dole

―

On Friday 1 May 2009, the Internet at Bastion is shut down. News reaches Tidworth. Casualty notification officers are sent out to inform the next of kin. Once they've done their job, the welfare office will arrive to take over.

'Are you Linnet Savage?' they are supposed to say. 'May we come in?' Then, 'Gareth was killed by a bomb blast this morning, just before midday.'

They are supposed to make the tea. Check in with the officers sent to find Gareth's dad, to rouse him from his smacked-out slumber on some flophouse floor in Swindon. As soon as this is done, they'll let base know they've completed their task and the Internet can go back on. They're supposed to ask Linnet who they should call. Who she wants to be with her through this. Gareth's CO will send her the letter he wrote for her to read in the event of his death and a box of his personal effects.

The welfare officer will keep her informed, update her on the progress of Gareth's body – from Bastion to RAF Lyneham, through Wootton Bassett to the John Radcliffe Hospital for post-mortem. They will arrange the funeral in accordance with her and the family's wishes.

They are not supposed to have to chase her through Abury's streets, Linnet in her nightie, barefoot, shrieking to wake the dead.

The nightie is one of Gareth's old T-shirts. Pale blue from Sports Direct. When he was packing up to go and she wasn't talking to him, Linnet snuck back upstairs and kicked it under the bed so he'd miss it. As she runs, feet slapping on Abury's cobbles, she can still smell him on it. Gareth smells of love. When they make love, it comes out of his pores. Linnet tastes it on his tongue and on his skin. When he sinks into her body and sighs, his breath is the breath of love, holy, sainted, living, human.

Gareth is love, Gareth is Venus as a boy, Venus behind the chip-shop counter loading her chips with the little crispy bits of batter she likes, Gareth shooting his deadly smile at her like an arrow between the ribs, Gareth swooping her up into a fireman's lift and plunging into the stream intent on carrying her to the other side, only losing his footing and sending them tumbling into the shallow babbling waters; Gareth grinning, droplets sparkling on his brow like diamonds as he caught her foot and drew her squealing body into his arms, lapped by the freezing chalk stream, her sopping clothes floating on the surface as she met his joyous embrace.

Gareth is love and the men chasing her in their dark suits are death, so Linnet runs to keep him alive, slender legs pumping, the T-shirt riding up to show her neon-pink thong, the famous tits hammering against her ribs.

When Linnet was sixteen a photographer had asked her if she wanted three hundred pounds for topless pics and she had said that yes, she thought she would, and when they were published everyone looked at her differently, except for Gareth who looked at her just the same. And when she got home and unwrapped her chips, head held high, having ignored the snickers and stares, she found he had wrapped them in Page Three. Her Page Three.

Smoothing out the paper, Linnet saw he had defaced her photo-graph, only rather than a cock sticking out of her mouth or a Hitler moustache or a huge furry bush sprouting between her legs, he had drawn a crown upon her head and a red heart upon her breast, and rather than writing *whore* or *slag*, he had written in uneven capital letters – some of them back to front – MY LIONESSE!

In 2009, Linnet is twenty-three. No spring chicken by glamour-girl standards. Recently, she's wondered about leaking a sex tape. It doesn't seem to have done Paris or Kim any harm. But then, after she and Gareth had made one – much harder than you'd think, more exhausting, they'd had to stop halfway for a kebab – she'd watched it back and realised she'd never show it to anyone, not only because of the stupid, delirious look on her face, but because once other girls saw Gareth in action, they'd make it their lives' work to steal him away.

The men are gaining on her so she screams louder. People stick their head out their windows or come and stand on their front steps, older women wearing aprons with floury hands, younger women holding toddlers. Inside her house, Carly's mum, ripped from her daytime-TV hypnosis, rifles the kitchen drawer for a carving knife – her daughter is screaming, is still alive, and this time Shirley will save her, like in the dreams she wakes from sobbing – then wrenches open the door and takes up the chase in her slippers.

At the cenotaph, Linnet slams into John as he makes his way to the Green Knight for his first pint of the day, knocks over Mrs Tearsheet's shopping trolley, sending new potatoes and carrots rolling on to the road.

Gwen's in the Tesco Express, aimlessly wandering the aisles, lifting items into her shopping basket and then taking them out again. It's her and Arthur's anniversary but he's in Washington and won't be back for days. She doesn't know what she's looking for, doesn't know what to do with herself truth be told, pauses to stare vacantly at the small ads.

Golf clubs, never used . . . Child's bed, outgrown . . . Average-size dog with lead . . .

The automatic doors slide open and Linnet skids in. Christ, she looks terrified! And the noise she's making, the shrieking, it touches a nerve. Or rather it wakes something, something Gwen's been numbing, keeping in a drugged slumber with gin and vodka and pain pills, shopping and TV and not eating. Or perhaps it's been dormant even longer than that, something she lost touch with in her girlhood, something she sent to sleep with a prick from a spinning wheel.

Gwen puts the shopping basket down.

Linnet is huddled crouching in the middle aisle, eyes wide, boxes of cereal on one side and tins on the other.

'Don't let them find me. Don't let them, Gwen!'

'Who is it? Who's after you—'

Then she sees them in the curving mirror above the till, two burly men in dark suits, coming through the doors. Linnet throws her arms around Gwen's neck.

'Don't let them,' she says. 'Please.'

The first man puts his head around the end of the aisle. He has short hair, a thick neck. He ducks back as Gwen launches a tin of peaches at his face. Next, it's a can of evap, hurled over the tall shelves to explode over his shiny black shoes. More, and harder. A can of Spam shatters the shop window. Pears in syrup splatter the floor, creating a slick which brings down the second man hard on to his back.

'Come on,' Gwen says to Linnet. She shakes her by the shoulder. Someone must have called the police. They'll be here soon and whoever these men are, they only have to hold them off a bit longer . . .

But Linnet won't help; she slams her hands over her ears, screws her eyes tight shut.

The man on his back covered in pear juice has had enough.

'Linnet Savage,' he shouts.

'No,' Linnet whispers. She opens her eyes and looks at Gwen naked-souled. 'Don't let them, Gwennie.'

Too late.

'Oh no,' Gwen says. 'Oh Netty. Oh no.'

And Carly's mum, crossing the threshold with her carving knife, is in time to hear it too. And the blade falls from her hand.

*

The first time I met her, I met her in white.
All in white, all in white,
She led me through the night,
Down in the valley where nobody goes.

The next time I met her, I met her in red.
All in red, all in red,
I nearly lost my head,
Down in the valley where nobody goes.

The last time I met her, I met her in black.
All in black, all in black,
She nearly broke my back,
Down in the valley where nobody goes.

Kay doesn't know where the words come from. But he hears them, set to an old tune, as they line the streets to watch Gareth's body brought through Wootton Bassett, and then again weeks later at his funeral.

He doesn't take in the coffin bearing Gareth's sword, cap, belt, medals and a Union Jack. Kay doesn't hear the words spoken to Linnet by the man in uniform with all the medals: 'How lucky we are that this country is still blessed by wonderful men such as Gareth who choose a path of service and sacrifice.' Only the small hiss that escapes Linnet's lips, the flinch of her shoulders as the firing party fires three shots into the air.

All in black, all in black . . .

With a lace veil and six-inch spike heels, standing ramrod straight, Linnet radiates grief like a black sun. Kay wants to throw himself down, allow her to walk over him in the stilettos, to soften the ground she treads on, to bear her up.

All in black, all in black . . .

A madness following him round the wake, half-listening to the mourners' chatter.

'Twenty-five? Or twenty-six? He had that job at the chippy but the army took him at seventeen.'

'The building was rigged with explosives, came down on top of them.'

'Wayne's in the hospital, but he'll be all right. Lance got out in time.'

'I heard it was friendly fire. There's going to be an investigation, an inquiry or something.'

Linnet doesn't notice Kay, doesn't seem to see him. Like he's invisible.

So, later that evening, when he's alone in front of the TV and the doorbell rings, he expects it to be anyone but her. He's in his track-suit bottoms, half pissed, gnawed rind of a pizza in the box on his lap. Whoever it is holds the bell down, so he struggles up swearing, intent on giving them a mouthful. Just before he opens it, he has a moment's fear, because it's a big house and lonely, and sometimes he's imagined being murdered in it with no one to hear his screams.

But it's Linnet on the doorstep, still all in black with the veil covering her face, backed by night, by the bone-white moonlight on the empty drive.

'Kay.'

'Linnet, what—'

But she brushes past him into the dark hallway.

'What is it, Linnet? Has your . . . has your car broken down or something? Would you like –' to his own ears his voice sounds unnatural, higher than usual and overly polite '– a cup of tea?'

'Do you want it, Kay?'

He'd ask her what she means but his mouth has gone dry. At the same time, in his pants, he's hard as wood.

'You know what I'm talking about. Do you want it?'

'I . . . I . . . Yes, I—'

'All of it, or some of it?'

Once, Kay saw Linnet and Gareth with a carrier bag of cans on the green, staggering drunk. Cawing like crows. Linnet tucked under Gareth's arm. Laughing . . . laughing . . . like the world was a marvellous joke.

He had gone home, taken himself to the guest ensuite bathroom, the smallest room right at the top of the house, locked the door and wept into his hands, unable to speak, unable to understand himself.

'All of it, Linnet—' He wants to tell her everything but, before he can speak, she tells him to get on his knees.

'On my . . .?'

'You heard me. On your knees, Kay.' Imperious, implacable, undeniable.

Then she asks him if he will serve. He looks up at her from the new carpet he had laid last week. He can't see her eyes, only her mouth beneath the veil.

'I will,' he says. 'I will serve. I swear it.'

With one finger to his chest, Linnet pushes him down till he's on his back, and then she herself kneels down over him and stops his mouth, thighs clamped either side of his ears, so he can't hear her sobbing, only feels it, the shaking, the rattle of a woman coming apart.

Five

—

Right Here, Right Now

23

The Comment in the Code

___

```
private Engine_Action EvalIteration_Evaluate (Evaluator
    evaluator)
{
/* Once I thought the world of Gwen/Endlessly orbiting her
    matchless grace/In comparison all others were tiny distant
    stars*/
    m_Log.Dump("Iteration = " + evaluator.Problem.Engine.Stat.
        Iterations +
        ", Objective = " + evaluator.Problem.FcnObjective.
            Value[0]);
}
/* But she chose Arthur/Desolate, I found a speck of
    consolation/In another's arms*/
Set EvalIteration = New SolverPlatform.Evaluator
prob.Evaluators.Item(Eval_Type_Iteration) = EvalIteration

problem.Evaluators[Eval_Type.Iteration].OnEvaluate +=
    new EvaluateEventHandler(MyEvaluator); try
{
/* Until I found, beneath her fairness/Putrefaction. Carly died
    choking on roses/Embracing the lover she earned, Death*/
    Problem problem = new Problem(Solver_Type.Minimize,
        nvars, ncons);
```

```
        problem.FcnConstraint.UpperBound.Array = rhs;
        problem.Model.FcnQuadratic[Function_Type.Objective, o] =
            new DoubleMatrix(Array_Order.ByCol, nvars, nvars,
                qmatval);
}
```
/* Now I spy, with all my little eyes/No queen, but a faithless,
   loveless/Suppurating whore*/
```
catch (SolverException ex)
{
    m_Log.Dump("Exception " + ex.ExceptionType);
        m_Log.Dump("Exception " + ex.Message);
}
```
/* Gwen dies before the week is out*/

24

The Belle Savage

———

Tonight there's a band playing at the Green Knight, some live music for the people.

'Just so you know,' Wayne tells Morgan at breakfast, 'it'll be fairly loud.'

After clearing her plate, she heads out. What a nice place Abury is, what a nice place to live. The clean cobbled streets, the green hills that surround it, soft and curving as pillows. The church is left unlocked. Inside, you can sit on an ancient pew as sunlight streams through stained windows where saints in chain mail brandish swords and shields. In what was once the workhouse, there's now a playschool – Little Dragons – with cheerful gaudy finger paintings on the walls. Abury has a local newspaper, a post office, a bank with actual cashiers. There are boutiques selling organic soap and organic groceries and organic linens and organic meat. In the hardware store, a kindly old gent will patiently talk you through what you need for that tricky little repair. Next to that, there's a well-stocked library and, if that happens to be closed, an old red phone box where residents leave their cast-off books.

Morgan steps inside and runs a curious finger along the shelves. Which stories does Abury choose to tell itself in the hour before sleep?

Romance. Crime. History books about WWII. The lovers will be united. The baddies will be defeated. The plucky little nation will triumph over fascism. In none of them will the baddy be the lover or the policeman or the island. Morgan hesitates for a moment, and then, one by one, knocks the books from the shelf to the floor.

None of the journalists Morgan contacted showed any interest in her story about Arthur. She was met by incredulity, then when she persisted, caution and suspicion. Only when she let slip to one of them that she'd grown up with Arthur and Gwen had he licked his lips. What had Gwen been like? Was she popular with the boys? And did Morgan have any photos?

It's been almost two weeks. April showers soak hidden roots, April blossoms deck the hedgerows. Morgan's faltering. Her purpose blunting.

More and more, she lies on the bed in her room staring at her phone, scrolling back through the different threads of correspondence with Rasha, reliving their relationship from the beginning.

Four years they'd had together and for the three before that they had wandered in and out of one another's orbit.

The first time she laid eyes on Rasha – some conference or other – Morgan had taken in the hijab, winced at Rasha's speech coruscating the ineptitude and short-sightedness of various Western-led NGOs operating in the Middle East, noted the elegance of Rasha's posture as she stood at the lectern, her eyes roaming over the seated delegates – and that was all.

Later, her ears pricked up when she heard that a former rival, a woman who'd accepted the professorship Morgan had walked away from, had thrown a bucket of paint over Rasha's car after they broke up.

'Queer, then?'

'Undoubtedly!' And Gaby, the friend she was talking to, went on to spill everything she knew about Rasha: her father's fame, her own meteoric rise through academia, rumours of an affair between Rasha and an Emirate princess that led to the woman being placed under house arrest. And then, following the Arab Spring, an increased seriousness, a deepening involvement with various activist groups.

On the radar, then. Their paths crossing a handful of times. Exchanged pleasantries. A bruising encounter where Rasha disparaged a report Morgan had written. A meeting six months later when they had found themselves shoulder to shoulder outside a bar watching fourth of July fireworks. Inside, a mutual acquaintance was celebrating her birthday. After the fireworks were over, they lingered, Rasha's cigarette long since gone out.

Finally, Morgan had accepted an invitation to a weekend house party, a get-together at the home of a wealthy married couple, two women who, once at the forefront of the gay liberation movement, now cultivated low-intervention wine on a vineyard overlooking the ocean.

Rasha had been there too, sitting in the garden room in a red sweater with a hole in one elbow reading a book. When Morgan came in, she put the book down, and that had been it; they started talking and did not stop until late in the evening when Morgan helped clear the wine glasses and returned to find Rasha gone.

Going up the stairs, Morgan saw the door to Rasha's room was standing open. But she passed on. Perhaps, she reasoned, Rasha had gone to fetch something or wanted to air the room – while at the same time knowing this was not true.

The next night too, the door stood open, and this time Morgan paused on the threshold, feeling her life's path splitting, but again she passed by, went on to her own bed, where she lay awake the whole night stewing in self-hatred. *You don't want anyone who could actually love you back... You only want the shallows because you are frightened of the depths... You pretend you love independence when actually you're a coward...*

The next morning, Rasha was not at breakfast, nor was she seen all day, to the point Morgan became convinced that she had left. Panic crept over her, regret, a sense of having made an appalling error. She went back to bed choking on her own stupidity.

And then she heard Rasha's voice, unmistakably Rasha's voice, coming from below, and had thrown herself off the bed and down the stairs and marched into Rasha's room, only to find another woman there, the one Rasha had spent the day walking with and who wanted to borrow a book that Rasha had recommended, only now they couldn't find it.

Rasha stood by the window silently as the woman ferreted about. Could it be in the bedside table, or had it fallen under the bed? Maybe it was by the window seat, or had Rasha perhaps taken it to another room? Could it be downstairs or even in Rasha's car?

Eventually Rasha had thrust a set of keys at her. 'Yes, now that I think about it, it's probably in the car.'

The woman left.

'Is it in the car?'

'No,' Rasha said.

'Then she will be back.'

'So lock the door.'

And Morgan had locked it, laughing, and turned to find Rasha an arm's length away, and then closer, and then closer still.

So much time wasted. And now no more time.

Morgan's waiting for something, only she doesn't know what it is. Perhaps if she can get someone from inside the company to talk.

Outside the estate agent's, she stops to look at the properties for sale and chokes over the prices. Even London is cheaper. Morgan scents Arthur's money and hears Ragnell's voice in her head: *Pick a fight you can win, Morgan!* Well, slim chance of that.

A little further on is a toy shop. In the window is a child-sized mannequin dressed in a Cinderella costume, all spangles and glitter and branding. A cardboard cut-out of a pumpkin-coach completes the display. The mannequin, sinister even by mannequin stand-ards, has a curly plastic wig slipping down over one eye. Morgan becomes aware of a small presence around waist height.

'It won't fit you. You're too fat,' a voice says. 'My mummy's going to get it for me.'

'In *Cinderella*, you'll notice the only good women are dead, like Cinders's mother, or magic fairies with wands. The real women are rivalrous and cruel, they want to keep her down, they're competi-tors for the prince. He's got all the wealth and power, you see.'

The girl bites the end of a mousy plait and scowls. 'I'm going to *be* her.'

'You seem like more of a sister to me. You've got that vibe.'

The girl looks up at Morgan blinking and then, from the outer corners of her eyes, fat tears emerge, sliding down her cheeks, to make way for others. She opens her mouth: 'Ohhaho . . . ahuhuhuhuaa . . .!'

180

Behind her, perhaps twenty yards off, a woman with a pram is bearing down on them and, oh, she does not look happy. Whoever is in the pram is howling like a siren. Morgan considers her options, notices the shop next door has a few steps up to it, mounts them quickly and pushes open the heavy door, allowing it to swing closed behind her.

Her first impression is of a luxurious dentist's. White walls, burnished floors, a fur rug in palest apricot in front of an old fireplace filled with cut flowers.

A woman sits behind a desk in a clinician's outfit, only upon closer inspection, it's candyfloss pink rather than white, and on the swelling breast pocket the name *Chantelle* is embroidered.

'Do you have an appointment?'

'Not yet,' Morgan says brightly, trying not to stare at Chantelle's teeth which glow blue-white against a vibrant layer of tan foundation.

'What is it you want?'

'People keep asking me that.'

Chantelle blinks slowly under the weight of her false eyelashes. Next to the fireplace is a comfy-looking armchair. Outside is one angry mother.

'Show me the menu!'

Chantelle hesitates and then offers her a glowing tablet. 'You'll find most of what we offer here, although Linnet prefers the Belle Savage to custom-tailor services for our clients.'

'Good to know.'

Linnet. Linnet. The name rings a bell.

Customers arrive, all of them women, each fetched when her time comes from the waiting area by another woman in a sexy pastel lab coat. Morgan's eyes travel down the list, swiping from page to page. Who would have thought women needed so much shaping, filling and draining, painting and stripping, waxing, freezing and burning? That there was so much in need of removal, or that they would benefit from so many additions. Who would have thought a woman was like a house? At the same moment, Morgan realises she has in fact always thought of herself rather like a house, like one of those first drawings you did as a kid, with the door-like mouth and the eye-like windows and the roof like a hat. And she has always understood that people looked at the house, but the real you lived in it and looked out.

'Your therapist will see you now.'

'I didn't make an appoint—'

But there's a girl in lemon with an auburn bouffant smiling down at her, a lovely girl, despite the drag, and seeing Morgan's hesitancy she outstretches her hand and Morgan finds herself taking it and allowing herself to be led away down a corridor and past a series of closed doors.

After all, why not? Isn't this how other women chose to console and reward themselves? The temptation being to give yourself over to someone and not be hurt, or to be hurt a little but not too much, and with your consent, and to be able to say *stop* anytime you want and be improved and restored by it.

A pedicure, a head massage, a light boiling in oil followed by an acid peel. Make me into pâté, Morgan thinks, feed me to the beggars.

The embroidery on the girl's uniform says *April*. The room she takes Morgan to is twilit. A giant white candle burns among an arrangement of flowers. The warm air smells of cedar and blossom. There's a massage table and a chair, a cabinet full of glass bottles.

'Linnet says you should start with a massage. It's the Belle Savage's speciality. Leave your clothes on the chair and then hop up on to the table under these towels. I'll be back in a few minutes.'

Well, if it's a speciality. And why not compliance? Why not, just for an hour, when you've tried everything else? Morgan strips, arranging her clothes on the chair to hide her disgraceful underwear, then clambers up and under the fluffy cotton towels.

The door reopens. April is back. She gets to work and her hands are warm and firm. When was the last time Morgan was touched deliberately? Beyond the handing over of money and the receipt of goods and change. Arthur had not touched her. Perhaps it was the baby on the plane, the baby that had reached out and grasped her hair. And before that? Rasha's cousin, Farah, a paediatrician who worked at UCSF.

Farah's fingers digging into her arm, voice strangled with horror: *You could have stopped her. She wouldn't listen to us, but you – how could you let her go there . . .*

April is placing hot stones on her back and legs and shoulders, the stones dry and heavy, their heat sinking into her body. Then, once again, she leaves promising to return.

Her thoughts grow fleeting and diaphanous. In the next room, Morgan swears she hears a woman weeping. Perhaps her treatment is not working. How sad she sounds. How sad it is to live in a world where women are supposed to be lovely, but you aren't one of the lovely ones. Not yet anyway. Or only briefly. Or that you were, but not for much longer. Or you had been once, if only you'd known.

Morgan remembers how, when she and Gwen were young, when they'd celebrated their bond by hating on another woman, a teacher perhaps, or another girl, the feeling seemed to fixate on their hair, or clothes, their way of speaking, or their weight; their contempt would often circle some feminine detail – frosted blue eyeliner, a scrunchy, court shoes. In the swimming-pool changing rooms, how they'd had to mask their horror of older women's bodies, at the occasional bristly chin, the wrinkles that pursed their mouths, the dimpled, hanging flesh.

Hags. Lost souls, irredeemable, gone beyond hope. And under the horror and hatred, fear. Because who could love you then?

And outside, just now, hadn't the little girl cried, cried like Morgan had stabbed her in the heart, because what she heard Morgan say was not that she wasn't Cinderella, but that she wouldn't be loved.

The door reopens and closes. The stones are removed. Strong fingers begin to work at the knots around Morgan's shoulder blades. It's not April, Morgan realises, the quality of touch is different.

Strange, how you could recognise people by touch, by something as little as a tap on your shoulder when you were hunched over your desk, part of you knowing who it was before you turned, almost as though one day we will all enter a great silent churning dark and have to find out each other by the touch of hands alone.

And Rasha will never touch Morgan again, not ever, not a squeeze of the hand, or a caress, not a playful slap to the wrist because Morgan is looking at her phone rather than paying attention to their game of backgammon. There will be no more of it. Not on this earth.

The last text message from Rasha:

Love something has gone wrong—

She was in Damascus. Her third trip. This time she'd gone to meet a source, a low-ranking civil servant who had evidence that would prove the regime was responsible for the gas attacks, documents that would hold up in court. Rasha had become fixated on the possibility of a trial at the International Criminal Court in The Hague, of holding the regime accountable for even a fraction of its crimes.

'It could be a trap. He could be a plant.'

'No one can fake his level of fear. Not for so long.'

For each of Morgan's objections, she had a reply.

'They'll be watching you. It's not like you keep a low profile.'

'I won't use my passport. I'll go on Hayat's.'

But she had taken her phone, the phone with spyware on it. Spyware sold to a rogue state, a regime everyone knew was responsible for mass surveillance of its people, for hacking and tracking, for disappearing, torturing and murdering anyone who opposed it.

Spyware that had been created by Arthur's company, and then sold on by one of its subsidiaries in a deal that would never be made public.

Morgan's lungs are devoid of air, and the reflex that controls the in-breath has given up, and all her blood seems to be in her face and the view through the hole in the massage table becomes a squirming dot matrix. She pushes herself up off the table, the towels sliding off her and down on to the floor, air sawing over the back of her throat.

The masseuse steps away.

'Grief?'

Morgan nods.

'I thought so. I could feel it in my hands.'

'Linnet?'

'Yes.'

'I don't know you.'

'Are you sure?'

Perhaps it's the light. Morgan allows herself to be encouraged to lie back down, this time face up. The towels are drawn back over her.

If Morgan's great-grandmother walked into the room, she wonders if she would recognise Linnet as a human woman. Improbable – the enormous tits and tiny waist, the puffer lips and pile of hair. The lips, teeth, lashes and brows give her a family resemblance to Chantelle and April.

'What brings you to town, Morgan?' Linnet asks as her fingers knead around Morgan's collarbone. There's something familiar about her voice.

'I would say business more than pleasure.'

A pause. 'You were friends with Gwen. Always together you were. Is your business with her or with Arthur?'

'What's it to you?'

'They're family to me. Through marriage. So you could say I have an interest.'

'Kay?'

'Twelve years.'

'You'd have got less than that if you murdered him. Tell me, Linnet, what would you do if a person was responsible for the death of someone you loved?'

Linnet's fingers are moving down her arms towards her hands. 'A difficult thing,' she says finally, 'to apportion blame.'

'That hurts a bit just there.'

'Pain is ugliness leaving the body,' Linnet mutters.

'I have an ugly heart. What can you do for it?'

'I know a good surgeon.'

'Not good enough, I fear.'

Linnet moves round and takes first one hand and then the other in hers, pulling Morgan's fingers, popping the knuckles.

'Well, I've done what I can do!'

And the penny drops, the memory bursts like a thundercloud. The makeovers all those years ago, the smell of strawberry shampoo as Carly leaned over her, the little goblin cousin.

'Is that you, Netty? Is that you in there? Little Netty, Carly's cousin? How is she? How is Carly? How is that sunny girl?'

And all the ugliness in the world visits itself on Linnet's face.

25

Friday Night is Pizza Night

———

'Now, before we wrap this up, can we first address an old rumour? Is it true, Arthur, about the Iranian nuclear reactors? Was it you?'

Arthur closes his eyes and shakes his head as if to say, *Get outta here!* and the audience break into whoops.

The interviewer turns to camera. 'For those who don't know, about a decade ago, certain government agencies here in the US and in Israel arranged for a computer virus to be smuggled on to an Iranian scientist's memory stick, from where it was uploaded on to the computers at a nuclear facility, setting the Iranian nuclear programme back years. Now, Arthur, would you like to comment on the identity of the person or persons who wrote that virus?'

Arthur shifts in his seat and opens his hands, and in response the crowd roar. When they quieten down, he clears his throat and just like that the room is silent.

'No. Not one of mine, I'm afraid. Sorry to disappoint you all. Besides, if a person had done something like that, they'd be pretty foolish to boast about it. I don't know if you all heard, but I had a little bit of trouble at my birthday party recently. As assassination attempts go, I'm good. I'm good.'

When they stop laughing, he opens his mouth to speak and then hesitates. His brow furrows.

'Arthur?'

'Joking aside, security is what I do. It's what my company does. All of us here know there's a war going on. It's not just fraudsters after money. We're talking state-sponsored teams of cybercriminals. We're talking digital warfare on an unprecedented scale.

'The average person, what are they worried about? That a private photo gets stolen or their Facebook page hacked? Maybe they get locked out of their computer by ransomware?

'People need to wake up to what's really at stake: critical infrastructure – the ability to power, feed and defend our nations; the economy – how to protect research from foreign spies who'll steal it and produce a rival product, only cheaper as they haven't had to spend billions on developing it; and if we're being honest, democracy itself. Democracy. Our way of life.'

Around Arthur, the room holds its breath.

'The war is digital and it's here. And as a good friend of mine recently showed, sometimes attack is the best form of defence.'

For a moment, he seems to lose his thread, looks momentarily adrift.

'And in any war, there are casualties. Mistakes get made. I mean, the inventor of . . . I don't know . . . the sword? Was he responsible every time someone—' Arthur stops, gathers himself. 'It's not only what we do. It's what we allow. I'm saying this to Mark. To Sergey. To Sundar. To Jack. To everyone. We have to do better. Or we deserve . . .'

But whatever he goes on to say is muffled as Arthur pulls the mic from his collar, stands and, after quickly acknowledging the crowd's applause, strides from the stage.

At company HQ in Abury, Kay clicks the mouse and pauses the video. He turns to Gal.

'You know, I've been wracking my brain but I cannot remember the last time I saw my brother look that rattled. Can you shed any light on what the fuck he's going on about?'

'Did you speak to him?'

'He was about to get on the jet. Off to see his mentor, his magic man. I thought he said something. A name, perhaps. Rashida something. Sounded like an ointment. Fuck. You know what he means?'

'He'll be back tomorrow. You can ask him then.'

Kay's expression sours further. 'So what you're saying is fuck off.

All right. All right. Leave me in the dark like a total knob. That's fine. I'll see you for pizza night and be sure I bring along some twigs and dung for your supper. It'll be vegan dung, though. I'll put a non-binary bow on it. Don't you worry about that, now.'

Gal manages to duck out the door so that the pot of pens and pencils that Kay has launched in their direction smashes into the frame. Everyone in the room beyond looks up from their screen. Someone sniggers.

Rashida Taber, Gal wants to say. The name is on their lips.

What would it mean to them if they knew what Gal knew?

*

Pizza night. The last Friday of the month. Ever since the early days, ever since it was just a handful of them, and Murat used to pop out a dozen meat feasts from Bodrum Nights on the back of his moped.

Now a team of caterers in white monogrammed polo shirts swarm around a number of portable wood-fired ovens. At a table, Murat shapes the dough with expert fingers. When he sees Kay come out on to the terrace, he shakes off his hands and collars his eldest son to take over, keen to show Kay the photos of the villa he's having built for his parents back in the old country.

Smoke curls from the ovens, vanishing quickly into thin air. No marquees tonight. No heaters. A touch of sun. Birdsong from among the trees that shield the car park and buildings from the approach road. Ahead, a clear view of hills and sky that reflects on the building's glass facade.

'Linnet coming?' Murat asks.

'Not a clue. But she was in a foul stew about something last night. Asking me questions about Morgan – you know, the ginger bint staying at the Green Knight.'

Mo is suddenly at his elbow.

'Do you know "bint" is Arabic for "daughter"?'

'Is it? Funny that. Same word meaning two different things in two different languages.'

'Not quite. British soldiers brought it home from Egypt in the 1800s.'

'Really? Wonder what they were doing out there.'

'Repurposing the word for "daughter" among other things, I imagine, uncle.'

By seven it's thronged. Everyone is talking of Arthur's performance at the VivaTech event.

Murat promises Gal a cheese-less pizza. When it doesn't appear, they take out a Tupperware container full of carrot batons and hummus and sit down at a picnic table up near the trees. A pair of finches chase one another from twig to twig. In the woods, a cuckoo calls. Birds, of course, sing the oldest songs of all.

A bit later, Gal watches Gwen arrive in a car driven by Lance, watches people's heads draw together, the amused glances.

When Gal told Arthur what they'd found out about Rashida Taher – or to be more specific, when they told Arthur that it was their software, software Arthur had written himself, that had been used to spy on the communications of a group of Syrian dissidents of whom Rashida was a part, after which a number had disappeared, their bodies turning up at rubbish dumps in subsequent weeks – Arthur had wept, fat tears splashing off his chin on to his jeans, and when he stood up to go, it was like he was a different man to the one who walked in, and his hand had been heavy, oh so heavy, on Gal's shoulder.

Gal wonders if Gwen knows and a small voice tells them that she does not, tells them that Arthur has not told anyone.

Rashida Taher: born in Syria, raised and educated in the US, an only child, mother died young, father a prominent academic and author who left America for Egypt following the 2001 invasion of Iraq. Rashida herself cutting a swathe via Harvard, Oxford and Lahore, accumulating accolades, clashing publicly with establishment figures – a whiff of scandal too, gossip columnists reporting her rapid departure from Pakistan causing 'great sadness' to the wife of a rising political star in the midst of a messy divorce – and then, following the Arab Spring, academic papers giving way to journalism, to reports of what was happening on the ground in Erbil, Gaza, Raqqa . . .

From her Twitter profile pic, Rashida looked back at Gal coolly, as though amused by their efforts to pin her down.

'All right, Gal?'

It's Mo. Unusual for him to come. More unusual still, he's out of his customary black and wearing a faded lilac T-shirt. The colour looks so well on him – the shade is perfect – Gal wonders if it wasn't chosen by a computer.

Mo takes in the carrots and raises an eyebrow. Gal feels their face gets hot.

'Is it all right with you that I don't want a part in animals being herded up and taken to abattoirs where they are frightened and slaughtered and chopped up? Is it all right with you that I don't want a part in day-old male chicks being thrown into blenders? Did you see the photo of all the buffalo calves in a skip so you get mozzarella on your pizza? I want no part in it. I want no part in any of it. Is it OK with you?'

'I'm not sure,' Mo says. 'I'll think about it and get back to you.'

'Sorry,' Gal says after a moment.

Mo nods. 'I'm glad Arthur wasn't involved in the Iranian thing. I'm not sure you could trust Arthur not to write a virus that would set off all the reactors rather than close them down. Sit Arthur in a doom-bunker eating gruel and he'd be merry as a cricket. I don't fancy it myself.'

Gal looks up. 'Arthur loves people. He doesn't wish anyone ill.'

'Arthur likes order, Gal. He likes black and white. Good and bad. Two and two making four. Incremental progress towards specified goals. Patient, yes. Accepting, no. I'm not sure how compatible that is with loving humankind.'

Gal doesn't respond. When they told Arthur they wanted *Wasteland* destroyed, Arthur said that he would think about it.

'I wrote it, Arthur. It belongs to me.'

'It does, Gal. And you trusted me with it and I'm just asking you to go on trusting me. Just for a bit. You can do that, can't you?'

Another worry. Work and worrying: sometimes they're all Gal seems to do.

Mo leans forward, rests his cheek on the table and looks up in a way that reminds Gal of Hercules when he wanted something. Or at least it gives Gal the same feeling.

'I went back to the house with the code. The default one, the one you gave me, it wouldn't open it.'

'Mo, I told you. It's probably just full of tractor parts. You shouldn't be snooping.'

Mo shakes his head. 'Someone's in there, Gal. I don't think they can get out. Like they're being kept prisoner.'

Gal raises an eyebrow. 'And you spoke to them, did you, to the Count of Monte Cristo?'

'I did. Through a crack in the wall.'

'What did they say?'

'Well, the thing is, Gal, I'm not exactly sure.'

'And why's that, then?'

'Because I don't speak Vietnamese.'

*

'I'll come with you.'

'I think I can change a tampon without you, Lance. If that's all right.' Gwen doesn't wait for a response. It's getting on her tits having him there the whole time. She needs him not to be there to want him; she needs to want him so that when she gets him, she can obliterate every pain she's ever felt, if only for a little while.

Inside, it's quiet. Everyone's gone home or been lured outside to stuff their face with pizza. She's wearing nasty little Italian boots and the heels click on the polished concrete floors.

A grey shadow looms behind one of the glass partitions like a shark in a tank, but then a door opens and it's only Garlon.

'Still at it? Have you been a bad boy?'

'Oh, you know me.' Garlon looks up and down the hallway; when he sees there's no one in sight, he beckons her in with a finger.

'I was just popping to the loo.'

'It'll only take a minute.'

A tiny wave of resistance before she submits, steps inside and the door falls closed behind her. Gentle flirting or mothering? A flash of tooth or a pat on the head? Which does Garlon want?

'Have a look at this.'

On the screen before him is a page of code. Gwen can't read it, but she knows enough to know what it is.

'I didn't know you were a coder.'

'Oh, I'm not. But you can't work around your husband for two decades and not learn a thing or two.'

'What is it?'

'Something I've been working on for Arthur. It's a little work-around for a problem he's got. It's taken me ages. I'm hoping to show it to him soon.'

'He'll be back by tomorrow.'

'I'll have to pick my moment.'

'I'm sure he'll be really pleased and grateful.'

Garlon is looking at her a bit closely for her liking. So Gwen starts babbling about how much Arthur needs and relies on his crew. Apart from her voice, it's quiet. Her tampon's about to give out, she can feel it, a sodden dam sliding southwards. What colour pants is she wearing?

At the same time, she remembers – a quarter-century ago? – going home with Garlon fully intending to sleep with him. She'd been pissed. It'd been after her falling-out with Morgan, when she was all eaten up inside. Before Arthur.

She'd got herself a bit of a job doing admin and working on the reception of a farming supplies company alongside a woman called Babs, mainly to prove Morgan wrong in her assertion she'd never earn herself a penny.

Babs was already in her sixties with a white elfin haircut and thick 1960s eye make-up. Hardly anyone came in, but if they did and if they were a man, Babs would inevitably nudge Gwen in the ribs and say, 'He'll do for me, dear,' or, 'I saw him first.' Till they took to competing outrageously to flirt with every delivery man needing a signature, with the salesmen and account managers, sucking on pens and dropping papers then bending over to pick them up, while the other shook with silent laughter behind the desk.

Babs had been married to Ron until he keeled over from a coronary. Ron, when young, had looked like Tony Curtis and driven a red MG. But he didn't want to do it. That was the gist, much repeated by Babs. Wined and dined, marriage, trips to the Costas in the summer, following the Grand Prix from Le Mans to Monaco. Nice hotels. A modern detached.

'But he didn't want to do it.'

'Not once?'

'Four times.' Four times in a forty-year marriage.

'And you didn't . . . you know . . . with anyone else?'

Babs hesitated. 'Only once, dear.' She shook her head. 'But that was just a kindness.'

Babs's eyesight wasn't very good, but she was too vain for glasses. Sometimes she drew her eyebrows on all wonky. It was alarming; it threw Gwen's hip out to look at her.

'They fell out at the menopause along with half my pubes. It's cos we're blondes.'

Gwen took her to have them tattooed on. They had a glass of fizz beforehand. 'He'll do for me, dear,' Babs said, spotting the tattooist's giant arse crack. Along with Babs's eyebrows, they'd got matching hearts on their hips. Although Gwen hated tattoos and could never have imagined herself with anything as tacky as a heart. Sometimes they bumped them together.

Babs has been gone five years now. *Friend of my heart,* Gwen thinks. Gone but not forgotten. More than once, talking about Ron who didn't want to do it, Babs had said, 'There's no worse feeling than knowing, Gwen, that there's something you have to give and you haven't given it.'

What have you given?

The question nags at her. She is the envy of world, has everything her heart desires – wealth, beauty, a husband, a lover, a wayward son, a stable full of horses, millions of followers – but what has she given? What is it that she hasn't given and that pricks her from the inside like a thorn?

'Gwen?'

'Sorry, Garlon. I was miles away.' A ripple passes over his face, almost like he's got a tic. It draws his top lip up, showing tooth and gum, and she drops her eyes politely.

What had happened that night she went home with him? Where was everyone else? No idea. All she can remember is sitting on a chair, while Garlon sat opposite her on the bed looking at her, rather like he's looking at her now, and instantly becoming very sober indeed and incredibly certain that however awful she was feeling, it wasn't going to be in any way improved by letting Garlon anywhere near her, that she was only there to have something to talk about with Babs on Monday. So, she'd given him some old guff about how she was waiting for true love . . .

'Put your finger here.'

'I beg your pardon?'

Garlon indicates the forward-slash key. 'Go on. That's right. And now the underscore.'

'I really must—'

'Let's just do this last line. Then we can say we wrote it together.'

So she does, she complies, aware suddenly of how tired she is. Tired of smiling. Tired of compliance. Tired of evading whatever the compliance is meant to evade.

'Now press execute.'

'Execute?'

'That one there. That's right. All done.'

She presses the key and the room gives up its tensions. Garlon accompanies her back down the hallway and then outside, making breezy chit-chat.

'Not too deathly being driven around by Double-O-Dullard?'

'It's all right.'

'You not scared, then?'

Gwen shrugs. If she was, how would she know? In her family, you didn't show fear – along with most other emotions, really – which led to a situation where identifying what you felt was a challenge.

'Glad to hear it. What have you got on for the rest of your week?'

So she prattles on about her plans – her new mare that needs schooling, an Easter family get-together the following weekend, that tomorrow she's off to Stroud to pick up some curtains for the house – realising as she steps out into the cool evening and takes a deep breath, a huge gulp in fact, of the fresh evening air, that she forgot to go to the loo in the end.

In the dimming light, the ovens look like hives. Half the crowd have departed and Murat's crew are packing up. Mo and Gal are sitting together talking, or rather Mo is talking and Gal is listening. He has that persuasive look about him. *Arthur won't like that*, she thinks.

A knot of the men are clustered by the beers. She thinks she overhears Kay say, '—it's got to have something to do with her. Winding people up. Upsetting people. Not seen Arthur like it since he was a kid. Poisonous witch.'

A hand on her arm. Lance. 'You were ages. I went searching for you—'

She shakes him free and then looks about to see if anyone saw her do it. But they've all drifted over to where two minibuses have pulled up by the front entrance. Kay holds the door while everyone piles in.

'You coming, Gwen?'

'Where are you off to?' she calls back.

'Live music at the Green Knight.'

Morgan is staying at the Green Knight. Morgan, who has not been to see Gwen once. *What do you expect?* she thinks. *You compared her to a kebab.* At other times, she's breathless at the thought of Morgan and Arthur having private business together, zooming off in Arthur's car all cosy like, as if Gwen's of no importance at all.

Suddenly the answer comes to her: if the mountain won't come to Muhammad, then Muhammad must say fuck the consequences and go to the mountain! And all at once, she feels dizzyingly alive.

'Why not? Sounds fabulous. You can count me in.'

'Gwen. No.' Lance speaks in an undertone. 'I really don't—'

'Then go home, Lance. Go home.'

And she gives him a little pat and trots over to the minibus and gets in beside Kay, who swings shut the door, leaving Lance wringing his hands because of Wayne.

Wayne. Wayne. Wayne. Wayne. Wayne. Wayne.

26

Live Music

———

The world is full of spirits, some benign, some mischievous. In the Green Knight, they flitter down from the old beams, battering against the inverted glass bottles, congregating around the till, drawn by the sound of the drawer sliding open and closed, by the promise of a big night.

Slips of lustre, half-thoughts, one parades the length of Wayne's tattoo, another sips the ale from John's lips. In the dim light, Wayne glimpses a toppling wisp, a glimmer, spiralling down towards the scuffed boards, rubs his eyes and goes through his list:

Barrels. Float. Glasses. Ice. Snacks. Little lemon half-moons. Toilet paper and hand towels in the bogs. Soap in the dispensers, condoms and tampons in the vending machines. Fresh ashtrays outside.

The band arrived just after lunch in an old Bedford van – Vern's half of the bargain, Wayne's winnings, which somehow, he notes, seem to have resulted in quite a lot of extra work for Wayne. Inside, his frustration bubbles away. When Vern comes back, he wants to have another kiss to give him, more than a kiss if he's honest, but he senses Lou's not playing.

Maybe . . . one of the band?

When the van doors opened, out spilled more humans, more kit, than Wayne would have thought possible. Guitars, a violin, a drum kit, a double bass. Amps and cables. A set of decks. Two girls: one black with braids in cut-offs; the other white, tall and fulsome in a tie-dye dress. Four, or possibly five lads. An assortment of accents. A mutt on a string with a handkerchief tied round its neck.

He'd shown them the makeshift stage by the dartboard and they'd sniffed it over, cheering up when Lou brought them out a mountain of bacon rolls, which they fell upon like starving wolves. Even the dog got one. Now they're out in the pub garden, the black girl sunning her midriff on a picnic table, the others sat about smoking something suspicious. Nonetheless, they have a keyed-up look Wayne recognises.

The tie-dye girl comes in to use the loo.

'Which one of you's the singer?' He tries to give her a twinkly smile; then, as she nears, he realises she's younger than he thought and quickly resumes scowling. God, he's hopeless.

'Ig. But we all sing.' Ig is the foreign-seeming one. A bit older than the others. Tangled black hair and beard.

'He ... French?'

Her laugh is a rippling scale. 'Ignacio's from the Basque Country. He's a true Celt.' Her own accent is Scottish. Grimy nails. Bright eyes. Dyed red hair with a fringe she must have cut herself.

'And what do you play?'

That laugh again. 'Oh, I can play anything.' And she picks up a pair of spoons from the cutlery tray and runs them down her arm to produce a flourish of clickety-clacks.

A feeling, just an inkling, and he could be wrong. Still, Wayne goes down to the cellar again and rolls a few more barrels into position.

When he comes back up, Morgan is waiting on a bar stool, a look on her face that can only spell trouble.

*

By six, the pub is filling with the after-work crowd, the regulars and a bunch of teenagers who colonise the garden, sending in their most mature-looking representatives to nervously order rounds of snakebite and black, vodka–lemon or blue WKD.

The band's dog makes friends with the youngsters who marvel over his appetite for salt and vinegar crisps. The way he curls back his lips at the sting while wagging his stumpy tail.

'What's his name?'

'Why don't you ask him?' Mary-with-the-braids says. From the pocket of her shorts, she pulls out a harmonica and runs it across her mouth and the notes are like a finger drawn down the spine.

They eye the various band members assessingly. Fit or not? And who is with whom? And the one in the flowery shirt with the green nail varnish, is that lad a girl or vice versa? And who might be up for it? And which of them would they be up for it with, given the chance?

Messages get sent, photos posted – the dog, the drinks on the table, a shot of Mary and Ignacio laughing in front of the van's open door, tie-dye girl holding a guitar by its strap. *Live music tonight!* *#Abury #TheGreenKnight*

And then the car park's full and Lou has to close the kitchen early as the thicket of customers at the bar grows three people deep.

All the while Morgan hunches over her drink, oblivious to everything except the level of whisky in her glass.

Carly rinsing the dye out of Morgan's hair over the bath, singing along to the Backstreet Boys.

Carly regaling Morgan with blow-by-blow descriptions of what she and Dan got up to.

Carly throwing Netty out of her room and then standing with her back braced against the door, eyes wide, as Netty hurled herself against it.

Then, as though it were a memory, not an imagining, someone hurting Carly and not stopping, leaving her dead in a soaking field on the downs.

Morgan's mother must have known. She kept in touch with people in Abury. She read the newspapers. Why hadn't she told her?

A protective instinct, perhaps. After all, mothers have often hoped that ignorance will keep their daughters safe.

She can't stop thinking about them, Carly and Rasha. Since yesterday, since the Belle Savage. She's been losing her grip, going down, down, down. And now, clasping her glass fit to shatter it, not knowing how she got there, she arrives at chivalry.

As a child, it had been her most beautiful word. Chivalry. It filled Morgan with pictures so sharp, so beloved to her, she almost believed they were memories. Pennants flapping. A towering stone castle. The sounds of hoof beats and ringing swords. Ranks of knights, kneeling before their king, sworn to chivalry, to the quest, to the rescued maidens and slain dragons.

Perfect in its beauty, chivalry. The highest praise, the greatest good. A word whispered at night when the light was off. To be held fast in the small heart thudding under the covers. Toothpaste taste on her lips. But where was her place in it all? How could she serve chivalry?

Morgan sinks what's left in her glass and remembers the pain of the exclusion, remembers sitting on a five-bar gate looking out over a boggy field – at the dun winter grass, the bald hedgerows – wind biting through her bodywarmer, heart bleeding over chivalry.

In the stories women didn't get to be chivalrous. They couldn't reach the bar.

She taps her glass.

'Another?' Wayne says, thinking, *is it her eighth or her ninth?* Thinking, *at least her room's only a stone's throw away.* Calculating whether he and Lou can cart her there if necessary, if one takes her arms and the other her legs.

When he sets down the glass, Morgan doesn't lift her eyes. She just stares at it, stares into it, considering that if chivalry has a modern equivalent, it's honour – although even honour has begun to feel like an archaic concept. In recent years, it's disappeared from the public discourse along with such sentiments as the public good, but there's still the rough comprehension that a man of honour is someone who tells the truth, who keeps their word, who is reliable, decent. Someone who might make a difficult choice because it was right. There is still the understanding of what this might mean.

Woman of honour doesn't have the same ring to it. When men talked about women's honour, it meant something quite different.

Morgan summons the women she has known, keeping the word 'chivalry', the word she had loved so much as a child, in her mind. Mrs Dickinson the reception teacher comes first, leading the four-year-olds in a flowing stream down to the pond, her arms free, cardigan buttoned at the neck like a cape. They're off to find creatures, to draw and name them and stick them up on the classroom wall.

Then she remembers Gwen, remembers the time she rescued a starving pony from a field, rustling it away bareback under cover of darkness despite everyone knowing the owner took potshots at trespassers.

Next, she recalls a trip to Nepal in the early 2000s, the miles of women breaking rocks at the side of the road. She'd asked the guide who they were, and he said they were mainly widows, but the truth was they were often women who had been abandoned by their men or pushed out of their villages. They broke rocks all day with hammers and were paid in rice. They lived at the roadside under tarps, caring for their children as best they could.

Last comes Kwang, the girl in Phuket, the sex worker. Fourteen? Fifteen? The girl lived in a fanless concrete room she decorated with pictures of animals. What pittance she could save, she sent to her family up north. Morgan was there to advise an anti-trafficking project. Kwang had been one of the interviewees. They had communicated via interpreter but Morgan had, patiently, by cunning, extracted a smile from her. No easy task. Kwang – her name meant deer – had given it. But it was like a gift in a fairy tale, one that has got heavier in all the years since.

To all of them, Morgan gives the word 'chivalry'. The highest praise, the greatest good.

You are my knights. You are my women of honour.

She raises her glass, knocks back the contents.

'Another.'

When Wayne brings it, she chokes it down.

And Rasha, the bravest person Morgan had ever known, who'd decided young that she would live as though she were free as a point of honour whatever it cost.

But in the end, what good had it done?

'What use is honour?'

She doesn't realise she's spoken aloud, until the old man – John, isn't it? – at the stool next to her leans in and says, 'Can honour set a leg?'

'No.'

'Or an arm?'

'No.'

'Or take away the grief of a wound?'

Morgan shakes her head.

'What is honour?'

Morgan looks up from her drink into John's face, takes in the ruddy complexion, the greasy shock of white hair.

'Tell me,' she says.

'A word,' he says at last. 'And what is in the word? Air.'

'Air,' Morgan says. 'Just air?'

A buckling feeling. Despair like a vice. But then, as Morgan closes her eyes, she sees a red-haired child in bed. Piled around her are cuddly toys. A book lies spread-backed on the floor. The girl is looking at her expectantly.

'You're on a quest,' she says. 'You will not fail them.'

Morgan becomes aware of the crowd, of the press of people at her back. An elbow digs into her side. She feels someone's breath on her neck and turns around on the stool. But they're all looking the other way; she can't see at what because they're blocking her view. They're waiting for something, but for what?

*

By the time Gwen gets there, music pours out of the Green Knight in a great lapping wave. The drinkers having a fag on the step have a dazed look about them. They tap their feet and nod their heads, stamping out the butts before they're finished and charging back inside.

She's not half out the mini-bus before it takes her. She forgets Arthur's lot, forgets Arthur in fact, Lance too, even as he pulls up alongside. For a moment, she even forgets Morgan, forgets she's here to have it out with her once and for all.

'Hang on to this,' she says to Kay, thrusts her handbag at him, and makes a beeline for the door.

Inside the Green Knight, it's warm and dim, the air dense with breath and bodies.

The music is deafening. The music is a command.

It says, *Let's fucking have it.*

It says, *Your life is petty. You care about the wrong things. You waste your time. You worship tiny gods.*

Gwen pushes through the crowd to the bar. There's an empty

stool next to John and she takes it and shouts, 'I want vodka. Give me vodka!' at Wayne. When it comes, she drains the glass dry, and then gets up and heads towards the source of the music, weaving around clusters of people clutching pints, to the edge of the dancers where she can get a look at the band.

The stage is so low and there are so many flailing limbs in the way, she can only catch glimpses. A bearded man drenched in sweat howling into the mic. Bows sawing at the air. A silver flash of flute. A ferocious hail of drumsticks. A girl bent over her guitar, her braids brushing the floor.

How lit up they look! How unified and filled up and emptied out! How she envies them and at the same time loves them for what they are doing.

And the music says, *Here is the flood. Here is the deluge.*

And the music says, *Make merry. Make merry. For the time is too short.*

And Gwen finds herself laughing and pushing in among the dancers because someone wants her dead but the music wants her alive. And while, cold sober in daylight, Gwen would put her dancing about on the same par as her cooking, now she knows in her bones that she is an excellent, excellent dancer. It's not enough, with music like this, to step from side to side, swinging your elbows. It requires leg kicks. It asks for jumping and spinning and crashing against your neighbour, beating the floor with your heels.

'Have you had enough?' the singer roars.

And the music demands that they roar back, *No! No! No!* Howling in outrage.

Over at the bar, pouring drinks like a dervish, Wayne sees, or thinks he sees, among the dancers, a girl in a pink puffy dress, throwing her arms in the air and twirling. The lights cast a red wash over her face and throat.

For a moment, her eyes meet his and Wayne hears a voice in his ear whispering, 'He's here. He's here.'

Too old to dance. Too dignified. Too ungraceful. Too weak in the pelvic floor. Too stiff, too ugly, too unrhythmic, too unwanted. The music swallows them all. *What you believe about yourself is a lie . . .*

Among the dancers, Gwen executes a particularly exuberant leap and feels something slide free, and then yes, it's confirmed, she's given birth to her tampon – *fucketyfuckingfuck!* – and all she can do is scurry away, thrusting past the revellers, away from the throng to the empty corridor and then to the ladies, where – thank the merciful Christ – one of the three cubicles is unlocked.

Gwen drops her trousers and pants, sits down and inspects the damage. How lovely it is to be a woman sometimes. How delightful to be so fragrant and angelic. She pulls free a handful of tissue from the Kimberly-Clark and sets to work. From the neighbouring stall comes the sound of vomiting.

'You all right in there?'

Whoever it is draws a couple of panting breaths, and then another surge of liquid hits the porcelain. A waft of whisky.

'Mixed your drinks? You got a friend out there I can get for you? I'd offer you a mint but they're in my bag and I left it with Kay, which also means I don't have any tampons. I don't suppose you . . .?'

No reply, nothing in fact. A shadow moving on the floor, as though the person on the other side of the partition has straightened up.

It's Morgan next door. Morgan.

Involuntarily, Gwen's hand presses itself against the thin wall between them. When she lifts it, there's half a red palm print left behind.

What is the silence saying? Is it angry or hateful? Conciliatory or . . .?

Another jet of vomit.

'Charming,' Gwen whispers. Then, 'You shouldn't overdo it, Crumb.'

She tidies herself up as best she can, fashions a wodge of loo paper into a makeshift pad and sticks it in her knickers, while desperately trying to think of what to say next.

In the third cubicle, a toilet flushes, a bolt's drawn back and the door opens. Soap dispenser. Taps.

A voice says, 'Fucking rad band, my loves. That singer's gorgeous. Hot. Hot. Hot. I'll see you both back out on the floor.'

Footsteps. The door opens and closes and then Gwen is pulling up her jeans and blundering out of the cubicle, her eyes full of tears, because that was Carly's voice. That was surely Carly. But the corridor's empty and there's no Carly in the room beyond, unless . . .

Gwen spies Linnet at the edge of the crowd.

'Linnet, were you in the loos? Was that you just now?'

'What?'

So Gwen shouts it in her ear.

'No. I just got here. Singer's hot. Looks like he needs a wash but still.' She raises herself on tiptoe and peers in the direction of the band.

What was it with women and singers? Gwen points in the direction of the exit. 'I need air.'

Linnet shrugs and follows her. The song is ending anyway. The singer promises they'll be back after a short break.

Outside in the courtyard, the sky is clean and paling.

'What's with the hands, Lady Macbeth?'

Gwen grimaces and walks over to the trough where she dunks them in up to the wrists.

'Morgan's here. She was in the loos.'

'And what? You killed her?' When Gwen doesn't reply, Linnet says, 'I saw her yesterday. She came in the shop. You know, it might not be a bad idea if you— Shit!'

'What?'

But Linnet is already moving because there is Lance striding towards them. His eyes on Gwen, relief written all over him. And there is Wayne, empty pint pots pinched between his fingers, clocking Lance.

Wayne puts the glasses down. He lifts a hand to his head, fingers a spot on one side of his scalp.

'Wayne,' Linnet says. 'Wayne.'

But Wayne doesn't hear her because what Wayne hears is a voice saying, 'Am I your baby, Wayne? Am I your baby?'

And it hits him all in a rush, the lust for vengeance, like the most dizzying moment of desire, and he's almost upon Lance, blood thudding in his ears, when Lance spins on one heel and drops him with a punch to the cheek.

Like he was expecting it. Like he's always expecting it.

Wayne's on his arse. He presses a hand to his face. Watches the people disappear as his left eye swells shut. He struggles to get up, but Linnet's there now. Linnet on her knees beside him with a talon sticking into his chest.

'Get him out of here,' she shouts at Gwen. 'Get that idiot out of here right now.'

Then before he can collect himself, she's got her talons into Wayne's arm and she's hauling him away.

In the kitchens, she finds a bit of steak and slaps it over Wayne's eye and cheek. The band have started up again, the racket making the pots of kitchen utensils tremble on the steel countertops. After a few minutes, she lifts the meat and peeks beneath.

'Quite the shiner,' she says.

Wayne reaches out his fingers and touches Linnet's face. He wonders if Gareth would recognise her now.

'It was Lance's fault. It was his fault Gareth died.'

'It wasn't your fault, Wayne.'

'I didn't say it was. I said it was Lance's fault—'

'It wasn't your fault.' And Linnet puts her arms around him and presses her face into his chest. She says something else, but it comes out muffled. It sounds like, *It wasn't my fault.*

When she finally draws back, she takes his fingers and folds them into his palm, holds his fist in hers. Paper covers stone.

'You look after yourself Wayne,' Linnet says.

Later, when Vern gets back, he'll say in the face of Wayne's blank refusal to pass on Lance's punch, 'You give what you get, Wayne. That's where it starts. It's the agreement.'

For now, he watches Linnet go with his one good eye, her reflection moving in panels over the kitchen's stainless-steel surfaces.

*

When Morgan comes out, it's quiet and dark, mercifully dark. The bar's closed and the band are packing up the van. A group – men, judging from their voices – are clustered around the picnic tables.

'Excuse me.'

Morgan stands aside and a girl squeezes past, a girl in a short tie-dye dress with a huge drum in her arms. By the van, she bends over to set it down, revealing a flash of knicker.

Morgan doesn't hear the comment. Or she hears it but can't make out the words. Only the tone and the communal laugh that follows.

The girl in the dress straightens up. She takes her time before turning round. She's making the choice, Morgan realises. The choice Morgan used to make every day on the bus, the choice between silence, pretending it wasn't happening, or responding, sinking to their level, saying vile things back, enraging and delighting them, making them worse. The third option, of course, was to accommodate them, try on a small smile, submit and win them over.

The girl makes her decision. She plumps for silence and dignity, walking past them with chin held high but eyes lowered.

Once she's back inside, Morgan goes over. It is the bus boys. Or some of them. Plus a few new faces.

'Which one of you was it? I know it was one of you.'

'What are you talking about?' Is it Trist or Bors, Perce, Lionel or . . .

Kay turns to face her. 'It's a free country. People can say whatever they want, Morgan.'

'I'm not talking about that. I'm talking about Carly.' She doesn't know why she says it. Because she's drunk? Because she's mad with loss? Because of a whisper emanating from somewhere deep within, from a hag's hut in the woods?

Whatever the cause, it properly rattles them. It makes them hum.

'Look at the state of you. No one wants you here. I doubt they want you anywhere.' Now there's a voice she remembers. Once she'd wondered whatever she could have done to make Garlon hate her so.

'One of you knows something. More, maybe. Why don't you speak?'

But now they turn from her; they make a wall of their backs and say nothing.

'You are such cowards. In your hearts, you must know it.'

Morgan totters to her room, shoving the key in the lock with an unsteady hand and then slamming the door behind her.

Fuming in the dark, her bed a pyre, Morgan lies there squirming, sleep an impossibility, until she's unable to take it any more and gets back up, rifling through her suitcase until her fingers find what she's looking for.

It's two, maybe three a.m. The car park's nearly empty. The pub windows are unlit, the security lights switched off.

As Morgan comes out on to the high street, she thinks she hears a noise behind her and speeds up. Under a streetlamp, she stops and turns but there's nothing visible in the darkness. Only the closed shops, the parked cars and the empty marketplace.

At the far end is the cenotaph. The tall stone cross and beneath it the names of the dead Abury chooses to remember: 1914–1918; 1939–1945.

They used to be marched round as kids on the eleventh of the eleventh, for the laying of the wreaths, for the silver band and then the minute's silence. Morgan's eyes had always lingered on the names of the Hawkins boys, all four of them dead in 1917.

They laid down their lives. That had been the message and it made it sound so very peaceful. Like the placing of silver cutlery on a starched white tablecloth.

Half of them would have been conscripts. Most of the first lot wouldn't even have had the vote. Some of them wouldn't have wanted to go, would have cried bitterly in the dark, would have, before they died, cursed King and Country and whatever meant it became an acceptable choice to march young men into machine-gun fire for four years running.

Country. Empire. Monarchy. Christianity. Manliness.

There, on the steps, Morgan feels history like an iron hand on her shoulder pushing her down, an insupportable weight. On her knees, at the foot of the cenotaph, she takes out the marker pen and in unsteady script writes two names on the stonework.

Lest we forget.

When it's done, she lies back on the cold stone. Closes her eyes. Opens them. The stars are tiny puncture marks. A waft of some rotting thing passes by her.

The rage is out now, so it's grief's turn again. *It would have come as a relief*, she thinks, *when the gorgon looked into the polished shield and met her own reflection.*

The smell again, more intense now. And a sound of something moving over the cobbles, stopping and starting, creeping closer . . .

Then suddenly a hand on her shoulder and a bright voice saying, 'Wake up. Wake up, Ms Faye Morgan. Rise and shine.'

27

Top and Toe

———

'Well, this is cosy, isn't it?' Mo says. 'I love a bit of top and toe.'

'Shut up,' Morgan says. 'Shut your awful face.'

At the other end of the bed, Mo has the covers pulled up around his throat, so that his head on the pillow – he has taken all the pillows! – looks oddly disembodied. Christ, she hopes he has his clothes on.

She does. All her clothes clammy on her skin, and in her mouth the ghost of a small putrefying rodent. Her stomach? Acid. Her bowels? Liquid. Morgan closes her eyes and listens to the dark song of her body. Betrayal. Pollution. Poison. Guilt. Paranoia. Fear.

When she opens them, Mo has her phone in his hand. He makes a face.

'Don't suppose you fancy sharing your passcode?' Then, 'Who's the chick?'

He's looking at the wallpaper, an image of Rasha taken on one of the Egypt trips, bending to stroke a chorus of alley cats, her hair swinging in a bobbed curtain, the tattoo of an eye visible between her thumb and forefinger.

'Your wifey?'

Morgan nods.

'Sexy.'

'Dead.' Morgan swings herself out of bed and goes to the window, pulling back the curtain a fraction.

'Rashida Taher.' Seeing her face, Mo says quickly, 'You wrote it on the cenotaph last night. Her name. Carly Savage. She was that girl who got killed. Linnet's cousin, right?'

He's sat up now. His chest is bare, the sheet's round his waist. A little light falls between the crack in the curtains to gild his torso.

'Your mother would have a fucking fit,' Morgan says.

'My mother acts weird when anyone says your name. I always thought it was a dude that broke her heart. But it was you, wasn't it? Why haven't you been to see her?'

Because what's she going to say? *Hi Gwen, fancy some rum and Cokes for old times' sake? By the way, I'm here to ruin your husband and tear down your perfect life. Not that I'm making much progress.*

A befuddled memory of throwing up in the Green Knight's loos. Had Gwen been there? She had . . . and then she hadn't. A wave of nausea.

No one is in the car park. The pub's still closed up. If Morgan can get Mo out now, no one will ever be the wiser.

'Why did you come back? Word is you've a bone to pick with Arthur.'

The look they exchange is measuring.

'You don't get on with your dad? I thought Arthur got on with everyone.'

'Once I heard Arthur talking about an acquisition he made. It was performing unexpectedly well. Quite the bargain, he said. His eyes wandered my way and he frowned.'

'Some might say you should be grateful.'

'Yes. They would like to show me a book of accounts in which next to my name a great debt is outstanding. But I don't see my signature. Those aren't my sums.'

'Spoken like a true princeling.' Mo's shoulder is within arm's reach and she can feel her fingers wanting to creep out and touch it. As if reading her mind, a smile tugs at Mo's lips. *A dangerous boy,* she thinks. *Bad at boundaries. Far too easy to love. Definitely Gwen's son.*

'I'm not getting anywhere,' Morgan admits.

'With your bone?'

'Uh huh.'

'Tell me about it.'

And although it makes her feel even worse, she does. It's

unscrupulous, underhand even, stirring a teenager's resentment towards his father – but she's out of options.

'How did you find out about the spyware on her phone?'

'After she died, someone in the regime leaked it. Maybe someone who knew her father. Faisal was well known, well respected. A very likeable man, like his daughter. The regime bought the spyware from an Israeli company. You cannot imagine how I felt when I found out that it was a subsidiary of Arthur's operation, that it was Arthur who wrote the software used to hack Rasha's phone.' Morgan stops. 'You know, you don't seem unduly surprised.'

'Arthur's attitude towards his responsibilities has always been a bit . . . patchy. And you can't just go public with it?'

'He'll say they sold it without his say-so, a few heads will roll and then it'll be business as usual again.'

Morgan turns back to the window. She can almost hear the cogs whirring in Mo's head.

'Lisa Gomez,' Mo says after a while.

'Who's that?'

'A woman, a developer. She used to work for Dad. You might want to talk to her. Just a thought.'

A noise outside the room. When Morgan pulls back the curtain, it's to see Wayne bursting forth from the Green Knight's back door. One half of his face is a liverish purple. Later, she'll see Vern and do a double-take.

Wayne strides over to the door of Morgan's room and bangs on it. Mo's shoes are on the step, she sees, tossed off as though in passionate haste.

'What is it?'

'Mo, you in there?'

'What's it to you who's in my room?' Morgan gets out.

'Mo, it's your mum. There's been an accident. You need to come now.'

28

Brake Failure

––––

She wants to die in his arms.

Smoke. Heat. Pain.

Choking now. Held in her seat. Plucking at something – strap? strap? – with the arm that still works.

So much pain.

'Lance. Lance.' Beseechingly, but no reply. No response. The smoke is dense, black. Tears pour from her eyes.

'What the . . . What? Gwen, Gwen, the brakes are gone. They're gone.' They were sailing down Birdlip Hill on the way to Stroud, going seventy. Lance pumping the pedal but nothing, nothing. At the bottom of the hill was the roundabout, the queue of traffic, the Air Balloon pub on the left – never stopped there, always meant to – on the display the words DIE BITCH DIE.

A handful of seconds, the fragment of a moment when she met Lance's eyes. *Can I step into your blue eyes, Lance? Can I not live this?*

'Do something. Do something,' she said.

On the left, the drop. On the right, a guardrail, and behind it a steep bank thick with trees. Ahead a white lorry, getting bigger, bigger, bigger.

Then a chance and in a split second Lance took it, spinning the wheel right and cutting across two lanes of traffic towards a spot where the rail had dropped away and there was a bit of bank without trees, just those plastic reflector posts. A blare of horns, nearly across, nearly across, and then an impact at the back, a crunching noise that sent them spinning. They hit something else, maybe the kerb, and the car was flipping, rolling. Her handbag tumbling upwards, raining down pens and lipsticks and keys. The airbag punched her in the face, then deflated.

A hail of shattered glass and the passenger door buckling in.

Shaking and hammering as they slid over the ground, soil showering over her. And then, finally, finally, they stopped.

The windscreen is gone. There's blood all over the dash. Her feet are hot, hot-hot, burning. And she screams, Gwen screams and tears herself free of the seatbelt and there's no way out her side, the door caved, the window a mouth of jagged teeth.

She climbs over Lance, calling his name. Flames now. Somehow, she gets the door open and tries to pull him out. Has to go back in to undo the belt.

He is so heavy, so heavy but she is a strong girl, she has always been a strong girl, and she hauls him free, pulls him down on to the grass and bracken.

The car is burning and they are too close.

Buzzing in the sky. Buzzing in her ears.

But she wants to die in his arms. Her Lance, who she loves, loves, loves. Only here, on the precipice, can she admit it.

'Baby,' she says. 'I love you. I love you. Don't die.'

And she leans over his face, weeping and choking.

Her clothes are slick with blood. His? No, hers.

Lie down now. Lie down beside Lance. Put her face against his, her arm over his chest. She takes his hand and holds it in hers.

Oh Lance. Lance . . .

All the while the drone hovers overhead.

Six

—

Banger
2013

29

Baby Meat

———

On the morning of Lily's christening, a fine August day in 2013, Gwen gets up at dawn to start on the food.

It's the year Obama gets a second term. The year the regime in Syria attacks its own people with sarin gas. The year the NSA is forced to admit to illegally snooping on tens of thousands of personal emails between private citizens.

In the quiet kitchen, as the sun rises over the downs, Gwen fetches the mixing bowls from the cupboards, sets out the ingredients, turns the oven on.

Six months after Gareth died, Kay and Linnet had got married. As she weighs flour, butter, sugar, Gwen remembers the wedding.

For October, the day had been mild. In the churchyard, a breath of wind loosened the petals from the September roses and they blew in a crimson drift to the door. Arthur was best man, Gwen matron of honour; Mo bore the rings, even handed them over at the right moment, albeit reluctantly.

A magazine paid for photos of the reception and the following week there was a glossy twelve-page spread complete with pictures of the bride and groom on his and hers thrones, raising glasses of champagne to the camera, shoving cake into one another's mouths. Kay with the footballers and company guys. Linnet with the women. In one, she lifted her dress to show off her frilly garter. In another, taken later on as the music got going, Linnet whipped off the lower part of her dress à la Bucks Fizz so she could strut her stuff. If you looked carefully, in the background you could just make out Arthur and Kay's mum, Betty, hands raised to her face in horror.

Only Gwen knew about Linnet's slippers, pristine when she went to bed, filthy the morning of the wedding. In the churchyard, the newly seeded grass on Gareth's grave had been torn and flattened, as though visited by a small tornado in the night.

Carly-Dee was born the following spring. Twelve months later Rio arrived. Then came Angelo. Lily was the last along, a baby so sweet, such a poppet, Gwen finds herself turning up at Linnet and Kay's almost every day, just to have a hold.

In her arms, Lily smiles bashfully and clenches her toes and Gwen feels as though a tiny invisible hand is pinching her windpipe.

Afterwards, she'll offer to take the older two for an hour, down to the reservoir to feed the ducks, or to one of the local farms to pet the calves. Often they'll bump into Lance.

'Shit. Shit.' Did she just use plain flour or self-raising? They're both out on the marble countertop. If it was the former, she'll have to add baking powder or the cakes won't rise.

Not for the first time, Gwen chides herself for not bringing in caterers. They've become so rich that there is no reason or need why Gwen should ever have to lift a finger again, at anything, for the rest of her life. Put another way, why doesn't she just die now? So, she keeps the help to a minimum, cooks and mucks out her horses, takes care of Mo and Cavall. She is so frightened of her hope for a child, of the waste it can lay to her, that she fortifies herself against it.

No more IVF, no more drugs, or updating Arthur's calendar with Xs. Sometimes, aided by a couple of stiff ones, she'll pounce on him or give him the look. But it's harder. She'll be touching him and remember the time she lost the baby at eleven weeks, the one she'd been sure was a girl, the one she was sure would stay. Arthur had gone to the hospital with her, but afterwards he'd left on a plane to Miami. Unavoidable, he'd said. An urgent meeting following the Belgacom scandal. And perhaps it was, but he came back with a light tan and Trist, who'd also gone along, had posted a picture of Arthur poolside, raising a mojito and smiling.

Sod it! She'll add some baking powder anyway and hope for the best.

Once the cupcakes are in the oven, Gwen moves on. She preps the apple-crunchy coleslaw and mini-jacket potatoes, assembles platters of cold meats and cheeses, dips and little quiches. The meat she'll leave to the men.

Mo comes down in his pyjamas, hair on end. He is twelve now – or thereabouts – but still a child to look at. Puberty won't get its hands on him for another eighteen months. He takes up her hand and kisses it, and then, when she goes over to the fridge to fetch the milk, she hears him swipe something from the countertop, then the sound of Cavall clattering over and happily receiving a morsel.

A year ago, Arthur bought him as a pup out the back of a Land Rover, a scrap of velvet grey sorrow. He and Mo bore him home wrapped in Arthur's jumper, their eyes solemn with love.

'Will Uncle Aidey be there today?'

'I think so.'

Aidey's over from the States and staying at the farm with Leo. He and Lance came out of the army as soon as their contracts were up. Wayne sped matters along by buying a load of coke, snorting the lot and making an exhibition of himself. One drug test later, he was out on his ear. Linnet saw him once.

'How was he?'

Linnet winced.

'People cope differently.' She was hungrily flicking through the brochure from a Harley Street clinic. Once Lily's weaned, she swears she's getting the lot done. *And they don't cope differently,* Gwen thought.

These days Aidey gets himself a fat pay cheque providing security for oil-drilling operations in Angola. A few weeks on, a few weeks off. When he's not there, he's mainly in the US with new friends, uploads photos of himself on to Facebook drinking beer in the company of bearded men holding assault rifles.

Lance was off the radar for a bit, then he took his old job back on the farm. The first thing Gwen knew about it was when Arthur brought him home for dinner.

'You've met Lance, haven't you? He was with Aidey in the army, with Gareth and Wayne.'

She'd been washing a head of lettuce at the sink, water splashing all over the green leaves, running down in torrents to soak the white and secret heart. Finally, she silenced the tap and turned.

The oven timer goes. Gwen puts the gloves on and draws out the tray of cupcakes, risen but slightly singed. The doorbell rings. That'll be Lance now.

*

In a scrubby garden on the edge of Abury, Hercules – Neopolitan mastiff, four feet at the shoulder, descendant of the famed Molossus, whose ancestors fought gladiators in the Colosseum in Rome and whose presence causes the local postmen to run a weekly lottery with a black ticket – scratches his rump against a fence post and the whole fence creaks.

Inside the house, Gal reaches for the bong. A thin layer of dust lies upon the keyboard of their computer. *There is no point. There's no point to any of it.*

More and more they spend their days catatonic in bed, rising only to fill Hercules's bowl and to open a can of food that more often than not they give to Hercules, moved to pity by the monster's slavering expression of starvation. They spend most of their time thinking about *Wasteland*, and the more they think about *Wasteland*, the more paralysed they become.

A warm breeze is blowing down from the hills. Hercules paces the fence perimeter, nose twitching against the gaps. A turquoise butterfly lands for a moment on the jet-black coat and then takes off, dancing upwards into the blue.

That itch again! Hercules positions himself against the post and gives it his all, and this time the post shifts in its hole and the panel buckles ever so slightly.

In bed, wrapped in weed-funky sheets, Gal fires the lighter, the bong bubbles, and smoke streams up through the water and into their lungs.

Outside, in the garden, Hercules starts to dig.

*

218

Kay and Linnet are having an extension built so the barbecue will be at Gwen and Arthur's. Lance sets up the tables outside, takes out the crockery and glasses. Arthur's gone to the office. He'll meet them at the church. Gwen goes to fetch some sticky labels from his study so she can mark out what's got nuts in it, and there, lying on the desk, is a freshly printed article by one Faye Morgan.

Prick goes the thorn.

'Prick,' Gwen mutters. Not sure which of them she's referring to. Slams her way out the door and bangs straight into Lance, who's got a box of wine glasses in his arms.

'Whoah there, Gwen.'

She steadies herself against his shoulder, sneaks a deep consoling breath of him.

Two years ago, when Lance first came back, when Arthur brought him over, she'd been nice, she'd laid an extra place for him and asked him polite questions that he answered so quietly she struggled to make out what he was saying. He had a look about him, like if she tapped him with a finger, he'd ring hollow.

She took Mo up and read him his story. When she came down, Lance was sitting alone at the table. Arthur had stepped out to take a call on the terrace.

A burning whisper, 'Where've you been?'

'Here and there.' Then, 'I was in hospital for a bit, Gwen. For my head. I didn't want to add to your troubles.' And then, 'How are they? Your troubles?'

The hawthorn torches at the castle. The scorched circle in the car park of the Green Knight. Arthur out there in the dark while over the great oak dining table the pendant lamps grew incandescent.

Lance cleared his throat. 'Can we be friends, Gwen? Do you think?'

Before she could answer, Arthur was back.

'Whatever's up?'

He had a wild look about the eyes and when he slumped into his chair, he ran both hands over his face. 'Is it your parents? What—?'

But it turned out it was all about some hacker he was on the trail of.

'They breezed through all the usual challenges. Left no trace. They all use VPNs. Usually I've a way round that, but not this time. So I made them something special. It took me . . . well, quite some time. I was certain it would take them at least a week to reach the end of it. But they got through in a matter of hours.' Arthur shook his head, eyes focused on his plate. 'I wondered if it was maybe a team. Bogachev's people, perhaps. But the last gate, it was a trick. There wasn't a way through but they . . . they hacked into my system and created a door. Perce just called to let me know.' By now his voice was barely audible. 'It's one person. I know it. And they are better than me. I've left messages for them, inside Easter eggs. I want them to trust me, but I don't think they trust anyone.'

Gwen could not remember the last time she had seen Arthur so upset. *Your life takes place elsewhere*, she thought, *not here with us.*

'Easter eggs?' Lance said.

When he had finally risen to go, she was stacking the dishwasher so Arthur walked Lance to the door.

'Come again,' she called after him at the last moment.

They're all friends, so much so it's remarked on; Arthur and Lance haring across the downs at dawn; Lance and Gwen leaning on a fence in companionable silence at the fete, or bucket-feeding the calves at the farm with an assortment of kids.

They touch only by accident. Instead, as though to make up for it, they tell each other things, confidences slipping out, like creatures emerging at dusk to stand cautiously in the half-light.

His mum. The truth about what happened with Elaine all those years ago. Afghanistan. Gareth. The six weeks he spent at a mental health unit last year. Pushing back the silences one word at a time.

In return, Gwen finds herself saving things up to tell Lance, panning her days for their gold dust: something Mo said, the hares she saw boxing out on her ride, their black-tipped ears, the way the wind silvered the grass as it chased them up the hill.

What harm does it do? Who's not the richer for it? There are fewer fights with Arthur; the undercurrent of resentment since he turned down the Jobs job dissipates. People start telling Gwen how well she looks, their eyes lingering. The thing that bothers them about Lance – the soundless car alarm that makes them back away – diminishes.

One Saturday afternoon, with Lance over to watch a game,

she made cookies. At half-time they all wandered in – Mo, Arthur, Lance, Cavall wagging his tail – and she took up four from the tray. Cavall put his paws up on the counter and she put a cookie in his mouth. Then one for Mo, then for Arthur.

'. . . and one for you.'

Her fingertips touched Lance's lips. No one reacted. Not a ripple.

She went in for the second half, sat on a beanbag next to Mo. One shoulder against Arthur's leg, one approaching Lance's knee. Cavall padded over and rested his head in her lap, lifting it tragically when they cheered or shouted or made disgusted noises.

There was a moment of enoughness.

The clock on the wall says ten fifteen. They have to be at the church at eleven. On the lawn, Lance holds a tablecloth by two corners, snapping out the creases in the breeze before drawing it down and anchoring it with a pair of tumblers.

His hair falls forward on his forehead. He bends to lift a box on to the table and starts setting out a forest of glasses. His shirt has come free of his jeans. Time performs a glissando. Five minutes later, she's still standing there, mouth slightly ajar.

When the doorbell rings again, she jumps. She's not expecting anyone else.

*

A fountain of dirt rises and falls. In the hole, Hercules's huge, square head butts against the fence so the boards quiver. The sun caresses the furrows of muscle that track his haunches and his coat ripples like oil.

The sound of his breath. The sound of dirt spattering the ground. The sound of splintering . . .

*

A woman in a beige coat, with thick straight hair and a determined chin, stands quivering on the front steps. Thirty-something dressed as sixty-something but with bulging, childish eyes.

Pallid martyr, wronged woman, Elaine not waiting when Gwen opens the door but coming straight in. She looks Gwen up and down, turns her head to take in the place, nodding as if what she sees is what she expected.

Starts in with the God-bothering. Says she woke this morning and God told her today was the day to put an end to the nonsense between Lance and Gwen. He belongs with her, with Elaine.

'He had my maidenhead and what the Lord has joined, let no man separate.'

'That's not the way I heard it.'

'I am an earthly woman and I have loved him out of measure. You're married. You've got Arthur, Gwen. It's greedy is what it is.'

She sounds so infantile. Any moment now, she'll hit Gwen round the head with a Barbie. *Give it back, it's mine!*

'Lance and I are friends—'

'Liar! You fool no one. Everyone sees it, apart from your husband.'

Since he came back to Abury, Lance and Gwen have done nothing they might be reproached for, yet the words slash at her, there's a roaring in her ears. *Everyone sees it?*

'Now,' says Elaine, 'I'll have a word with him, if you don't mind.'

Gwen goes upstairs and sits on her bed, very still, very quiet. Gwen knows. Gwen knows the truth because Lance told her.

All those years ago, when they were still teenagers, when Elaine had asked Lance to carry her cello home, she had given him a drink as a thank you, a sweet, tangy drink, not sour like beer or fiery like the whisky his father drank. The first had made him giddy, the second elated. After the third, all the silences in him dissolved and everything had poured out, years of it – his mother's suicide, his father's drinking, that he was in love, in love with a girl – and then after the fourth drink, he had vomited, all at once, over his own shirt. Elaine had taken it from him, led him to a bed and closed the curtains. After that, he didn't remember much. Just pieces. A hand fumbling at his jeans. A whisper of the girl he loved's name . . .

Everything is a weapon: a pencil, the nail scissors on the bedside table, the sash from her bathrobe. Gwen clenches and unclenches her hands, the blood beating in her ears. She sees herself sticking a fork in Elaine's eye. Or throat. Or eye. *This is how people feel when they kill people*, she thinks. *This is how they end up doing the terrible things you read about in the newspapers.*

'Everything all right, Mum?' Mo is watching her from the

222

doorway. Each of the hairs on his head seems to grow at a ninety-degree angle to his scalp. She took him to the barber what feels like yesterday and still he looks like a midnight dandelion.

'I want her out of here.'

And without asking any questions, Mo makes it happen. Arthur couldn't have done it. Nor Kay. Nor any of the others. Elaine with her invincible propriety, her death-grip on virtue and righteousness. Like being female is an unmentionable wound, an invalidity men have to compensate for.

Not Mo.

Gwen follows her son, perches out of sight at the top of the stairs as he trots down to the hall and then wanders over to where Elaine and Lance are sitting opposite one another on the big sofa.

Elaine looks annoyed at the interruption. She's clearly in mid-flow.

And Lance? He looks exposed. He looks the way a rabbit looks when it's chosen to freeze rather than run and its hiding place is uncovered.

'—you have a responsibility to me. All these years, I've been patient, but we'll have enough of this nonsense now—'

Gwen's fingers clench around the banister. She will cut off Elaine's head if she doesn't go. She will cut off her head and lift it by the hair ...

Mo comes to stand at Elaine's side and bends down, almost like he's going to kiss her on her cheek. Instead, he whispers something in her ear. Small for his age – not that anyone can be certain of Mo's age – a fine-boned child with long fingers and narrow feet, the dentist already impatient to get braces on his snaggle-teeth.

He speaks for less than a minute before Elaine picks her handbag up off the floor, stands and, without a word, walks straight out of the house, down the drive and away, away, away.

Gently Mo touches Lance on the shoulder, then he turns and, over the thirty feet that separate them, throws Gwen a look of such adult understanding that it pierces her to her heart.

Liar! You fool no one. With Elaine's words ringing in her ears, she flees back to her room, closes the door and rips off her clothes, her breath short and shallow.

Maybe it's because she grew up around Aidey, or maybe it's

the years she spent at boarding school – all those girls packed in together, nowhere to hide, each vulnerability someone's opportunity – but the thought of people having access to her private thoughts is more than she can bear.

Snarling, her anger turns upon Lance. It's Lance's fault Elaine came. His fault that *everyone sees*. Sees what? She's not fucking him! Not laid a hand on him! Not kissed the paradise of his mouth, not since the night of the comet, not in four long years.

Sunlight filters through the dress hanging from the curtain rail, casting a rosy pane on the wall behind the bed. She snatches it down and tears it off the hanger. It's a simple thing, with a flippy skirt and tight bodice. She's had it two years but the tags are still on. She always finds a reason not to wear it.

Now, with it on, she understands why. It's the same colour as the dress Carly wore at her wedding.

Quarter to eleven. Too late. Too late to change now.

She shoves her feet into sandals, coils up her hair, then lets it fall again, applies lipstick and blusher, stabs her earlobes through with pearl drops that tremble as she stands before the mirror. She gives her reflection a wide, convincing smile. Dabs a tear in the corner of her eye with the end of her little finger.

When she goes down, Lance is still on the sofa, head in hands.

'Mo! Get in the car!'

'Gwen, I—'

But she cuts him off, snatches up her phone and keys, herds Mo out in front of her.

'Your love life is none of my business, Lance.'

She knows the cruelty is unforgivable, even as the words leave her mouth. And still, she slams the door behind her.

*

And Hercules is out, bursting free in an eruption of soil and splinters!

A clatter of his prehensile claws on the cul-de-sac pavement as he bounds into the road, eyes rolling, tongue lolling to taste the breeze.

Freedom for Hercules! Freedom at last . . .

Arthur misses the christening, misses Lily smiling and gurgling over the font, kicking her chubby legs and blinking as the vicar drips water into her peepers. In his place, Garlon promises to reject Satan and all his works, struggling – so it seems – to keep a straight face.

Afterwards, the congregation drift down to Gwen and Arthur's. Various teenage nephews and nieces have been promised folding money to put on a white shirt and keep the corks popping. In penance for missing the ceremony, Arthur applies himself to the barbecue. A thicket of men forms around him. Through them, he can see Gwen in a pink dress snapping open boxes of Tupperware and dumping the contents into bowls, ripping the cellophane off various platters. Garlon brings her a drink but she waves it away, stone-faced, and turns her back on him. Oh well, perhaps she'll snap out of it.

The sun pours down. Heels come off and lie abandoned on the lawn. Arthur stands red-eyed in the smoke. Some of the small people effect a raid on the buffet, licking the icing from the cup-cakes before returning them to the stand. A pool of empty silver cans grows beneath a greengage tree.

Women milling on the terrace with wine glasses. Women sunning their legs on picnic blankets crawled over by infants, the sky above a forever blue. Women complimenting Gwen on the food, on her dress, on the house. Wonderful. Beautiful. Lovely. She nods rapidly. *Yes, yes. Thank you. Thank you.* There's no hint of insincerity but still it feels like being sandpapered.

Men you can handle if you've even a quarter of a brain; it's the women you have to look out for . . .

Arthur burns a batch of sausages but they're smeared in ketchup and eaten up before Cavall can get a look-in. At the end of the garden, a group of the men strip off their shirts and start a kick-about against the backdrop of the downs.

Lance is in his best shirt and making careful small talk by a barrel of melting ice and bobbing cans. There's not a single non-alcoholic drink to be found, so he fishes out first one beer and then another.

'And what do you do?' he asks. 'Cryptography? Sounds interesting. Is that . . . something to do with rocks?'

Something's happening on the lawn behind him, some thundering commotion. As he turns, Aidey spies him and calls out, 'Oi, Donkey Boy, what's this remind you of?'

Aidey has Mo in a wheelbarrow. He has the boy in a wheelbarrow and is racing him round the lawn. Smiling brown boy, alive-alive-oh. Aidey's smiling too, but a different smile.

What Aidey is recalling is the occasion, the day after Chisholm was shot, when two local men had pushed a wheelbarrow up to the fort. In the wheelbarrow, underneath a blanket, was the body of a boy killed in the previous day's bombing. The corpse had been in four parts . . .

Lance leaves the cryptographer standing. At first, he walks, but then after a couple of steps, there's a gear change and it becomes a hurtling run.

A moment of regret in Aidey's eyes? Or is it relief?

Two hands flat to Aidey's chest send him flying, but he's up again in a flash, although only for a second as the weight of Lance's body brings him down hard. If Wayne was there, he'd know what to do. But Wayne's done with the pair of them, so they roll over and over grunting and panting on the grass, not a word exchanged between them as a crowd gathers round.

Who hasn't wanted to see Aidey given a kicking at one point or other? But it's not the same feeling as when you watch it happen in a film; it's not a good feeling when Lance forces Aidey down. Aidey's heels dig into the earth trying to gain purchase; he flails at Lance with his fists to no avail. Lance gets a knee on his chest. Punches him in the face. Gets a hand to his throat.

A couple of the women watch with statue faces. One gives a curdled laugh.

Where will this end? Is it going to take Linnet pulling off her heels and battering them round the head? Gwen turning the hose on them? But neither woman makes a move.

Arthur pushes through to the centre of the circle.

'Enough. Stop it. Stop it. Lance.'

And at Arthur's voice, Lance does. He turns his face to Arthur and whatever he sees makes him stop. Then he gets up and walks away.

Aidey wrests himself to his feet, hopping mad, fat lip popping out, blood dripping from his nose.

'I think you should go home, Aidey,' Arthur says.

'I should go home? He started it.'

'I know exactly who started it. Stop trying to drag us down into the muck with you!'

Aidey's face twists, in pain or disgust or contempt.

'You're already in the muck. But you don't want to see it. Why should you live in blissful ignorance?'

Who is he referring to? Arthur? Gwen? All of them?

Aidey bares his teeth and taps a canine with a finger. 'What do you think these are for? Cows don't have them. Rabbits don't have them. Dogs have them. Wolves have them. Lions and whatnot. You want to pretend you're lambs. While people like me do the tough stuff for you. Isn't it terrible what they're doing to those poor brown people over there? You wring your hands. You even went out and got your own one.' He looks down at Mo. 'I pity you, mate, I really do.'

In the wheelbarrow, Mo's head is cocked to one side, his eyes alert.

'Get out, Aidey. Don't come back. I can't stop Gwen seeing you if she wants. But never darken my door again.'

'That's it. That's my boy. Show them what you're really made of!'

Arthur doesn't flinch or lift his hands as Aidey steps in, but the men around him press closer. The air thickens and Aidey thinks better of it. His shoulders fall and he looks at Gwen. 'You know, he killed more of them out there than any of us. He's a madman, a murderer. But as long as he stays quiet that's all right with you lot.'

But Gwen's looking at Mo, at her little boy, sitting in the wheel-barrow surrounded by all these tall people, crowding round, all these tall white people. A shape emerges. Not from the darkness. It's more of a shift. Something that's always been there.

'Fuck off, Aidey,' Gwen says.

Her brother barks. At least, it doesn't sound like any laugh Gwen's ever heard. She turns her back on him, takes Mo's hand. 'Let's get you an ice lolly, huh?'

In the house, rooting around in the freezer, her hand finds the bottle of vodka she keeps there. She de-sheaths Mo's lolly for him and pats him off and then, obscured by the open door, lets the freezing air blast her as she twists off the cap and knocks back first one deep gulp, and then another.

227

Hercules released, Hercules stretching his paws at last, bounding through forest and field, then up and on to the downs. The deer scatter, the rabbits go to ground, the ewes draw together and flow up the hillside, a living, bleating carpet of wool.

Up on the ridge, he stops. The sun falls over the edge of the world. Warm summer air rises up from the town below. From the town below, he catches a whiff of smoke, sizzling fat, of roasting meat on the wind.

Down again, through a hedge, and on to a lane, following the smell, the delicious smell, until it brings him to a place he knows well. A house, a big house, the one they visit so often at night on their midnight walks . . .

*

No one's going anywhere. Not after the fight, not after Aidey's casting out. After the sun sets, after the stars come out, they're all still there. The night's hot, the breeze warm as a tongue. Gwen goes upstairs to fix her face and finds two teenage girls in wine-stained white shirts collapsed on the floor of her walk-in wardrobe.

'Out! Out!'

One makes a wobbly dash for it, the other crawls after her on her hands and knees, choking with laughter. In the living room, children lie strewn across the furniture and floor. Linnet's put Lily down in her travel cot upstairs. Out on the terrace, she holds a bottle of pink bubbles by the neck, waving it at her audience as she talks about the salon she's opening.

'—I'll do the lot of you. First time's on the house—'

Kay's under the table, face planted in the grass, Lance nursing a can trying not to look at Gwen, Arthur carving a huge flank of steak that's just come off the coals.

No one sees the beast lurking in the darkness beyond the firelight, and then – since the humans are so many and so noisy – slipping in through the double doors, dripping saliva up the stairs, as Hercules follows his nose in the direction of the other delightful smell, the milky, meaty scent of the slumbering guest of honour.

But they hear the howling when it starts, the snarling, the sound of furniture tipping over, and Lily's sudden cries, until – abruptly – they stop.

Arthur is first up the stairs, still clutching the carving knife.

Straight from a nightmare, the scene. Cot turned over. Double wardrobe smashed through the window. Clothes everywhere. Mattress half off the bed. Blood spray up the wall. Already the footsteps behind him on the stairs.

Deepening the nightmare, darkening, Cavall, his hound limping towards him, blood dripping from his jaws, teeth red with blood as he totters towards Arthur, fur a matted crimson.

Arthur lifts the knife. He lifts the knife and steps towards his dog, and in that moment he has a vision, a vision of a red-haired girl turning to the bullies at school and saying, 'Keep going and I'll tell you a story about a man and his dog so sad you'll never smile again . . .'

Who had it been that time? Kay and his cronies? Other boys?

Morgan. Morgan, who he hasn't seen in years.

A sob catches in his throat. A sideswiping, smashing blow from out of nowhere: *They were my babies too . . .*

Cavall would have submitted to the knife. He'd have been a good boy to the end. But in the moment of Arthur's hesitation, Lily starts crying again. Linnet streaks past him and snatches the baby out from under her cot.

'What the fuck?' Linnet turns to Cavall, voice growing shrill. 'What did that fucking dog—'

Arthur blinks the tears from his eyes and spies a pair of burning coals beneath the mattress. Then a dog, the biggest he's ever seen, greater than the greatest of Danes, more wolfish than any Irish wolfhound, leaps out, knocking him flying, thundering down the stairs, now trailing not drool but blood.

Cavall in pursuit. Arthur in pursuit of Cavall, and quickly all the others too, haring under the streetlamps, a wild hunt coursing into Abury, half of them barefoot, Kay still clutching his can, as they chase the monster down to its lair. Past the Green Knight, down the market square and then left at the roundabout into the council estate until they reach a tatty yellow-brick bungalow at the end of a cul-de-sac.

Hercules thrusts his way back through the hole and then shoots through his beast-flap into the house, down the hall, and then, with a flying leap, into his owner's bed.

Arthur orders Cavall to stay outside. One by one the men climb over the fence, silently making their way across the scrubby grass – skirting the elephantine piles of dog shit – to the back door, which is unlocked.

They find the dog in the arms of a pale, thin youth, who blinks when the light is thrown on, like a sea creature accustomed only to the darkness of the depths. Hair almost white. Dry lips a wan pink, like the inside of a shell. Not much more than a child.

Gal's eyes fall on Hercules's torn ear, his bleeding front paw.

'What have they done to you, puppy?'

'He tried to eat our baby,' Kay says. 'My baby!'

They watch as Gal tries to shift Hercules's rump so they can sit up. With one hand they start to fumble for the giant bong standing next to the bed.

Hercules whimpers, rests his huge head on his paws and starts licking a wound on his leg.

'State of this fucking place,' Kay says.

The filthy, hairy sheets; the smell of dog. The thinness of Gal's arms, the dark circles under their eyes. The cheap bed, stained carpet and rickety nightstand. Layered over it all, the sweet-rotten smell of skunk, the smell of youth gone sour, the grey kingdom of despair. Seeing it so, the fight drains out of them.

'He's been a very naughty lad,' Perce says.

'Not his fault if he's not trained,' Bors adds. Soon they will want to know how much Hercules eats, if anyone had ever tried to ride him.

One by one, they reach down and stroke the massive velvet head.

Arthur picks up the notebook next to the computer and flips through it. His eyes widen.

'You're Galahad?' he says. 'The Galahad? I looked and looked. For months. You disappeared.'

'I've given all that up,' Gal replies. 'There's no point. Humans are a disease. The earth's dying. We have to be got rid of—'

Their eyes fill with tears. Gently, Arthur takes the bong from out of their hands and puts it down. He sits on the edge of the bed.

'There, there,' Arthur says. 'It'll all be all right now.'

A lie, of course, but truth has its limits.

Besides, sometimes the miracle happens. Sometimes strangers burst into your life. They take you in and take you to their hearts. They give you a place among them.

May it happen for you. May it happen for you. May it happen for you.

*

Gwen has sent everyone home. She checks on Mo. She doesn't touch him, doesn't want to communicate to him what she's feeling, to seek reassurance from his drowsy warmth. In the glow of his night light, she kneels and closes her eyes.

The man hiding in the darkened hallway sees her kneeling at the child's bedside.

The pink dress . . . The way she turned her back on him . . .

But it looks like she's praying, hands clasped, head bowed. Humbled and penitent. Mercy springs in his breast. After all, she's been through a lot.

Gwen listens to the small bellows of Mo's lungs drawing in and out. Tomorrow, she'll ask him what he said to Elaine.

'I said that God had told my mummy to shoot her with my daddy's pistol, only you couldn't remember the safe combination. Then I told her that I could and did she think God wanted me to tell you.'

Behind her, the sound of footsteps on the stairs, then the front door clicking shut. One of the teenagers, perhaps, sneaking out after coming round still pissed in a stranger's bedroom.

She wanders through the other rooms in case there are any more stragglers. In her bedroom, the walk-in's empty but the drawers where she keeps her underwear are askew. On her bed, a pile of knickers lie in a jumble. She lifts a pair and sees it's been ripped apart, the crotch torn out. It's the same with the rest of them.

Those spiteful little bitches!

In the kitchen, she finds herself back at the vodka bottle, pours out a sloppy measure over ice. Two fingers then a third for luck.

The ice cracks. Gwen twirls the vodka in the glass and takes a gulp. Beyond the window, in the living room, the sky is darkest blue. In the penumbra of the lamps, the blue becomes violet, mysterious and full of portent.

'I am a madwoman,' she whispers, 'and a murderer.' She says it again. The words are satisfying. They feel true, or perhaps she only wishes them true. Better to be mad and bad than heartsick, than sad to your rotten core.

Gwen raises a hand and presses her palm to the wall of glass.

Outside, a security light comes on. A movement on the terrace, and then Lance steps out of the darkness. There are grass stains on his knees and blood on his shirt.

He comes forward to bring his hand up and outline her palm with his. She spreads her fingers and he mirrors her. Through the glass, Gwen fancies she can feel his pulse throbbing, or maybe it's her own. There's a flow, a warmth, as though they share a single circulatory system.

She brings her body against the pane, then her lips and, after a moment, so does Lance. Tomorrow, Arthur will – bleary-eyed and throbbing of head – rub at the smear with his sleeve, briefly annoyed when he realises one smudge is on the other side.

In her drink, the ice cracks again, like a bone in the neck after a rough night's sleep. Their lips against the glass, their eyes closed, like Christians at a saint's tomb.

Something about the distance is perfect. For a certain kind of love, this is its apotheosis. From here on in, it's ruin.

And they know it. They both know it.

Seven

Right Here, Right Now

30

The Regulars

———

What do they want, the regulars? Cold lager, temperate ale, a clean glass, sometimes a salty snack, a bit of welcome, perhaps a titbit of local gossip. Not too much noise, or the right kind of noise. No wet tables or soggy beer mats. A game on hand – darts, perhaps, or billiards. Toilets that, if not pleasant, can be faced.

A clap on the shoulder, the sighting of an old friend, the glad eye, one on the house, a moment when, through the liquid in the glass, the world seems to possess its measure of harmony as well as chaos, and the bartender offers the usual and sets it down squarely where you like to sit.

A public house, a house for everyone. A house that must stay on its toes because it's close to five quid for a pint and at Tesco you can get eighteen cans for a tenner and not have to bother yourself about getting home, not say a word to anyone and pass out in the chair as the next episode loads.

At the Green Knight, John can taste the poison between Wayne and Vern in his pint, yeasty and sour. He can feel his guts curdling, pestilent gases brewing, and there's not a dog about to blame it on.

Lou's taken herself off to her sister's for a few days. Wayne's cheek is green now, fading to yellow. Vern's socket the colour of liver.

'Tiff not, boys.'

'I've prepared your quarterly, John,' Vern says coldly and sets down a white envelope.

235

Nothing but gossip, gossip, gossip. The accident. The arrest. *And, did you see the video? Well . . .*

The phone rings and Wayne picks up. It's a woman asking for Mo's number. Probably another journalist.

'We don't give out private numbers to strangers.'

'I'm not a stranger. It's important. I . . . I need to speak to him.'

'About what?'

The voice on the other end of the line falls silent.

'It's a private matter. Listen—'

But before she can go on, Wayne hangs up.

At the Green Knight, the regulars come and go, in body or in spirit. For a thousand years upon this spot, minstrels have sung that death cannot vanquish true love. The Green Knight is a great pub, a legendary pub, some argue the best pub in the British Isles. No such trifling matter as mortality will prevent her favourites coming in for their afternoon tipple.

Billy trotting through the door. Roll-up balancing on his bottom lip, clutching a carrier bag that's dripping blood on the flagstones. Cow man. Serial tax evader. Back from Cirencester Market bearing meat from a beast that's never known serial number or passport.

Albert, former potboy, at seven weeping over his ripped trews – *They be I's only 'uns!* – at nineteen dead in Flanders, a boy who, before the war, had never been further than ten miles from home.

Nance, the shepherdess, slipping her arm through his: *I'll be company for 'ee, and 'ee'll be company for I.*

Ken opening his greatcoat to reveal his week-old daughter, no bigger than a rabbit. Showing her off – so tiny in his huge blacksmith's hands – and then, when she starts mewling, pulling a bottle from his pocket, giving a hearty suck on the teat, then plugging it into her rosebud mouth.

Fred whispering that today, doing the haymaking, he thinks he mowed up Mrs Wilkes's cat, and if she finds out, if she finds out . . .

Don the poacher, waiting for night to fall to go check his snares. Got to get something for the pot, for the nippers, gamekeepers be damned.

Peggy and Lucy eyeing up airmen from the RAF camp till they're chased home by their fierce Aunty Enid.

Keith telling a tale about putting out his hand for the strap – for missing school to follow the hunt on foot – and at the last moment drawing it back so the headmaster belted his own leg.

And John, Sir John Falstaff, to give him his full name – not that he claims it since that bloody playwright Will What's-His-Name stole all his best lines and paraded them all over the London stage – stares at the bill Vern gave him like it's his own death warrant. *There's nothing for it. He'll have to go along on Mo's mad escapade . . .*

Regulars present, regulars past, at two in the afternoon, Vern kicks them all out.

'We're closing early. Out with the lot of you!'

And out they go – grumbling and grousing – leaving Vern and Wayne alone in the empty bar.

'We have an agreement,' Vern says, 'do we not?'

Wayne nods.

'Why do you think?'

'It is an absolute mystery to me, Vern.'

'When you came here a year ago, what were your winnings?'

Wayne keeps his eyes off the bruises on Vern's face. Vern had made him do it three times because, on the first two goes, Wayne had pulled his punches. The last time, though, something had snapped and he'd struck a blow fit to take Vern's head off.

An immediate torrent of shame, like a flash flood, sweeping his legs out from under him and bearing him along. Back when he was drinking, it was how he lived. It is not how he wants to live now or ever again.

Once Vern had got back to his feet, Wayne gave him a month's notice.

'You know what my winnings were, Vern.' Since he was eight, Wayne can count the times he's cried on the fingers of one hand. Instead, a stone comes to sit at the base of his throat, cold and heavy and pressing downwards upon his heart. He raises his eyes. 'A broken heart, empty pockets, bottomless rage. Total failure.'

A muscle works in Vern's jaw. When he speaks, his voice is tight, like he's struggling not to lose his patience.

'You still don't get it, do you, Wayne? You give what you get. You give what you get.'

31

Fleysshly Lustes

———

In the morphine dream, Gwen is in the Savernake, in the forest with her friend Babs reliving the day they found the rabbit. It's in a glade, unmoving but alive. Its flanks rapidly expanding and contracting.

Myxomatosis, Babs declares. It's a goner!

'Excuse me! Excuse me!'

She stops a man with a terrier and explains about the rabbit. 'I think it should be put out of its misery, don't you?'

He blinks. 'Well, yes . . .'

'Only it has to be done right. I mean, a woman's just not strong enough. It needs to be a single blow.' Babs is holding a thick branch. The man is wearing nice clean chinos. 'A strong whack. A good strong whack. Here, let me hold the dog.'

It's probably not the way the man envisioned his morning going, undertaking a mercy killing in the forest, goaded on by an elderly woman wearing false eyelashes.

After it's done, he gives Babs back the branch, now smeared with rabbit brains, like it belongs to her, like it's her godly trident.

Another time, she made one of the delivery drivers catch a toad that was living at the bottom of a drainpipe outside the office kitchen.

'Rescue it and pop it over the fence, poor thing.'

They had watched from the windows as Tony covered himself in leaf mould, slipping and sliding among the mush, while a small smile played on Babs's lips.

Not for the first time, Gwen had wondered about Ron who didn't want to do it. Whether he had been frightened of Babs, whether there wasn't something malicious in the way she obliged men to perform masculinity, vengeful even.

Now, in the dream, Babs turns to Gwen and offers her the branch.

'What does the rabbit in the woods say, Gwen? What about the toad at the bottom of the drainpipe?' She looks extremely sprightly for someone five years dead.

'I've not given it much thought—'

'The tumour is in our own body, Gwen. Who among us is brave enough to take the sword and cut it out?'

Her hand closes around metal. A clap of thunder overhead. *What have you given?*

'Gwen.'

'Arthur?' She cracks an eye.

'How are you feeling?'

'I was dreaming. Dreaming about Babs. Remember when I made you go find out why her Internet wasn't working, and it was just the router needing to be switched off then back on again, and you missed that call with Tim Cook?'

'We caught him, Gwen. I want you to know. We caught him.'

The room, on the first floor of the hospital's private wing, swims into focus. There are no soft furnishings and it still smells like hospital.

'Is it Monday?'

'Tuesday.'

Inside the morphine bubble, nothing can hurt her. Still, it takes her a while to ask.

'Who, then?'

'Bors.'

'Bors? As in Lionel's brother!'

'Gal managed to track the purchase of the drone. When the police went round to arrest him, he was completely deranged, shouting out the window about a white swan and a black bird, and a lady and her twelve gentlewomen who threw themselves off a high tower because he wouldn't sleep with them, and who'd turned into fiends and were all about him!'

'I always liked Bors. He was always a bit awkward but, you know, nice. You always said he was so dependable. Rock solid, you said. That's why you made him Chief Financial Officer.'

'I know. I did. But when they broke down the door and took him away, they found a laptop that proves he did the hacking and a whole heap of collages under the stairs.'

'Collages?'

'He'd cut out pictures of you and mixed them up with porn and stuck them on to animal bodies.'

'What drone?' Gwen says after a minute.

'There was a drone filming the crash but it hit a tree so we got hold of it.'

A drone so it could be filmed so Bors could ... watch her die?

'Where's Lance? They told me he was all right but I've not seen him.'

'Lance is fine.' But there's something curt about the way Arthur says it, and the nurses aren't any help and it's not till Mo comes and shows her the drone footage on his phone she understands why.

It had gone straight on to the Internet, live-streamed. The bit with her dragging Lance out the car is bad enough, but the stroking, the leaning over him, is arguably the desperation of a wounded woman, not necessarily that of a lover. No sound, thank God.

What comes next is less open to interpretation: Gwen passes into unconsciousness; the car burns, great swathes of black smoke enveloping the two supine bodies. And then, Lance; Lance emerging from the smoke with Gwen's body in his arms, staggering clear before collapsing, among the tangled grass.

No mistaking the sentiment as Lance cradles her and weeps, rocking back and forth, smoothing her brow and kissing her lips. When she does not stir, he brings her face in to his neck and holds her to him like she is everything on earth that has ever mattered, while falling tears cut channels through the soot that coats his cheeks.

Gwen hands the phone back to Mo. Her voice comes out as a hiss.

'Where is he?'

'Not sure. Word is, he's out of a job and out of a house.'

'Arthur?'

Mo nods.

'They're letting me out tomorrow.'

'And you'll come home?'

Gwen makes a noise that could mean yes.

Outside, someone is pushing a trolley down the corridor. It has a squeaky wheel.

'Not on my account, Mum,' Mo says quietly. He looks up from his feet. 'You know I'm not always going to be there.' When her eyes fill with tears, he changes tack and asks her what's the new mare like.

'Why?'

'I was thinking of taking her out.'

'Nell? She's flighty. Be careful on her.' Even with a mild concussion, she has a sense for when he's up to something. 'What mischief now?'

'Nothing I can't handle.'

'Is it something to do with Gal? Don't play with them if it's just to annoy your dad.'

'I just think they need to get out more.'

She knows she's in no position to give advice, but she wouldn't be his mum if she didn't try. 'Don't be careless with the people who count, Mo. In the end, there's fewer of them than you think.' Another thought. 'I've been meaning to ask you, who was that woman? The one who gave you a lift to the party?'

'Oh, her?' Mo says airily. 'A professor of archaeology.' But he seems keen to get off the subject. Before he goes, she kisses his hand.

'My beautiful boy.'

'Quiet, you.'

After he leaves, the nurses come and change her dressings. Burns to her shins. A deep gash to her inner arm that caused all the blood loss. Minor cuts and bruises.

Once they've gone, under the cocooning influence of her pain-killers, she looks at the situation dispassionately.

They are going to make her choose.

Gwen loves Arthur, truly she does. Still. Despite. Even though.

Maybe it's her farming blood, the generations of ancestors who worked the land whatever the weather, come drought, come flood, come pestilence. Who worked till they dropped, till their bodies were too busted to work any more.

Maybe it's a similar tenacity that's kept her in her marriage. But it wouldn't have been possible without Lance.

Lance who gave her what Arthur had neither time nor inclination to supply. Lance who saw her, who held her sorrow for her when she could no longer bear it . . .

Mo's right. He's a grown-up now. Sooner or later, he'll go and then it'll be her and Arthur. And how will that be?

Hollow. It will be hollow.

What about Lance? How would a life with him be like?

All their passion, all their pain, all the time.

Before the nurses change shift, she gets a last shot of morphine. From tomorrow on, it'll be tablets.

Back into the golden bubble she goes as night falls, into another dream in which Bors, wearing the England football strip, chases her over a pitch. Only her body's not her own. She's got a tail and claws and wings. She flaps them, but she's too heavy, she can't quite get off the ground. The spectators are roaring and Bors keeps tapping at her. Tapping, tapping, tapping with his sword, only it's not a sword at all, it's a great meaty phallus and she doesn't like it, doesn't like it one little bit.

'Get off of me! Gerrofo'meeeee!'

Gwen wrenches free of the bubble and grasps for the glass of water next to her bed. The tapping continues. Something at the window. Someone. Blood pours down her spine in a cold stream.

She swings her feet out of bed and totters over. Outside the golden bubble, the pain is circling.

An extendable ladder, of the kind used by window cleaners, has been placed up against the wall and a man is climbing up it. She struggles with the catch and thrusts open the window as far as it will open, which is six inches. A face, white in the moonlight, tilts upwards, and then Lance is racing up the last few rungs.

His hand snakes through to find hers and she grips it like it's freedom itself. Freedom from a hated prison.

Whispers in the dark. Burning words.

'I wish you could come in,' Gwen says.

'With your heart, do you want me with you?'

'Truly.'

And Lance wrenches the window free from its lock, tearing his hand to the bone in the process, and then hauls himself through and into her arms.

In the morning, the ward sister finds what looks like a crime scene – handprints and footprints in blood, the outline of two bodies on the floor – and screams bloody murder.

Arthur is called, the police alerted and a helicopter scrambled.

Morgan, arriving at the hospital with a wilting posy and a packet of Chocolate Hobnobs in her sweating palms, encounters a pack of reporters assembled out front complete with bloodhounds.

Abduction! Ransom! Speculation of the most gruesome kind . . .

. . . until it all stops, just like that, when, in grainy black and white, the hospital car park CCTV reveals two figures, one barefoot and limping in a hospital gown, the other all in black, running hand in hand across the tarmac towards Lance's beaten-up Land Rover.

32

Friendly

—

After a warm-up, they divide into two teams for a friendly. A small crowd has come along to practice, cheering Arthur every time he gets a touch of the ball. Seeing his brother's face, Kay goes over, thanks them for the sentiment but strongly suggests they jog on.

Everyone's keen to show their support for Arthur, keener still to share what they think of Gwen and Lance.

Bors is in the nut-bin and – after an initial week or so in which a surprising number of people claimed they'd always suspected there was something funny about him – everyone's lost interest, apart from when that funny meme went round over the Easter weekend showing him and the troll doing one of the dances from *Grease*, their faces superimposed on the bodies of John Travolta and Olivia Newton-John.

Online, a vocal contingent is claiming Arthur put Bors up to it, and moreover that Gwen deserved everything she got. *Burn her*, they cry, *burn the witch!*

A cold dropping rain falls as they flow over the pitch. Shouting and grunting. Boot smacking on ball. At nine the floodlights come on. There's water in Kay's eyes; he senses more than sees the other players spread out around him.

'Did everyone know?' Arthur had asked.

'No. Well. No. I mean, he had a thing for her. We all knew that. You knew that. A blind man could see that.'

And Arthur nodding, nodding.

'Everyone fancied Gwen. It's kind of the point of Gwen, isn't it? It's not like anyone saw them at it. You know, you all seemed very cosy. I wondered, well, cuckolding is a thing, isn't it? All the rage. So each man to his own.'

Meanwhile, Arthur looked like a man who has mistaken a whale for an island, pulled his boat up and made camp, only for the demon beast to wait for him to go to sleep before diving to the depths of its watery kingdom.

Kay gets a touch of the ball but immediately loses it to Perce, chides himself: *Useless fucking wanker.* Still, it's good, it's good, even when the other side scores, the sense of shared purpose, of ranks closing.

Wayne's playing, and normally there's a bit of distance with Wayne for reasons Kay doesn't care to put his finger on, but everyone knows about his beef with Lance, so tonight he's everyone's best friend. Unusually for Wayne, the feeling's reciprocated. Throwing his arms around the other players, thrusting into the centre of a group post-goal hug. And when a tackle sends one of the young players sprawling, and the kid leaps up bent on starting something, Wayne apologises, talks to the lad till he accepts a hair ruffle and runs off.

Lionel's not there. He won't believe Bors did it, keeps insisting his brother's been framed and demanding tox-screening.

'. . . said he did what he always did, made himself a full English, coffee, toast, juice. Popped on *Saturday Breakfast Kitchen*, next thing he knows the sofa's attacking him and the walls are screaming.'

A pass comes Kay's way, but he's not quick enough and the kid that wanted to wallop Wayne gets there first. He's not got the speed any more, the quickness. He's tempted by the idea of a course of testosterone. Women get the HRT, don't they? Only he's afraid his balls will shrivel up and the plugs fall out.

The rain's stopped falling and glistens gold on green under the floodlights.

A long ball down the middle. Trist sends in a soaring cross. Perce goes in for a header but it's off-target so he lopes over to take the corner.

245

Sometimes the pitch is an unearthly place, as close to an idea of heaven as Kay can allow. They spread out over the hallowed ground, each man trying to stick to or evade his opponent, to make or close the space around them. In all of it, the gesture towards the past, when the only thing between you and the woolly mammoth, between you and the marauders with clubs, between you and your family's starvation, were your band of men.

A scrum around the keeper's box, and everyone's hacking at it and then . . . GOAL!

Garlon! Garlon! Garlon!

Which is a surprise as Garlon's not usually up to much. Still, fair dibs. It reminds him he wants to talk to Garlon later. Get his advice. On the quiet. About what Arthur told him. About the calculations Kay's been making.

The game ends in a draw, which feels right somehow.

The changing room fills with steam and chat. Limbs and voices emerging from the mist to the sound of falling water. In the shower, Kay zones out.

He'd asked Arthur what they were going to do about Gwen and Lance and Morgan. It's not like he'd been imagining a mob with flaming torches.

'Morgan? Why Morgan?'

So he'd told Arthur what she'd done to the cenotaph. What she said to them about Carly.

'All this started when she came back. She's a bad penny. And she had no right to go pointing the finger about ancient history. She wasn't here. She doesn't know what it did to everyone.'

'I don't want you to ever do anything about Morgan, do you understand me?' Kay can't remember Arthur ever sounding like that. His mild brother. The voice of reason. But it's understandable, after what he's been through, understandable for him to let off steam and lash out. So Kay had let him simmer down after which Arthur told him what else they found at Bors's house.

By the time he's towelled off, packed up and is suited and booted, he's one of the last. Arthur's still sat on the bench, seemingly frozen in the act of unlacing his boots, one pale ankle on display.

It comes to Kay like a song, the ancient refrain, *Help your brother, help Arthur . . . you're a big boy and he's only little.* How it used to make him see red, like a literal veil of red before his eyes, because their mother and everyone else favoured, petted and indulged the little shit. Cuddled him and sang to him while Kay gnawed impotently on the bars of his cot.

Now, Kay crouches down and slides off one boot and then unlaces and removes the other.

Arthur looks up. 'Big change is coming, brother.'

Kay nods. One thing he is sure of is that no one knows Arthur like he does. How could you say you truly knew someone, unless you had spent your childhoods together, unless you had shared baths, and listened to the same creaking stair at night, and sincerely tried to kill one another over a biscuit?

For some reason, he finds himself remembering an occasion when Arthur was about nine and, pecking away at the computer as usual, he'd suddenly stopped. Then, making a terrible keening noise, Arthur lifted up the monitor, ripping loose the cables, struggled over to the open bedroom window, and tipped it out on to the concrete drive twenty feet below.

'You murdered the computer, Art.'

'It wouldn't do what I told it to do.'

Side by side, they'd stood looking down at the wreckage below, at the glinting fragments of glass and scattered components.

Of course, Kay took the blame. He got the blame for everything anyway and his parents wouldn't buy a new one unless he said it was him. Of course, they believed his confession because Arthur was such a good boy – such a good boy and so sensible – until he absolutely fucking wasn't.

A pang of unease. Kay puts the boots down on the bench and stands.

'I'll take care of everything, Art. You just do what you do best and focus on the old blue-sky thinking.'

*

In the car park, Kay catches up with Garlon as he's stowing his bag in the boot of his black Merc. The darkness has collected itself about them. No stars. Hardly a breath of wind. Headlights switching on as the other players drive away. Wayne's already on the corner at the crossing, bag over his shoulder, a spring in his step.

'What's new?' Garlon says.

So Kay gives him the update.

'. . . he's holding up. I think. Gwen and Lance are at his place. He's had his notice so they've only got till the end of the month. I keep telling Arthur to get the lawyers in because, after twenty years, she's going to be pretty fucking entitled. Thing is, and this can't go any further, mate, the police told Arthur that when they searched Bors's house they found something.'

'Like what?'

'Like a box with a knife in it, a knife and an old rag.'

But Garlon doesn't make the connection, looks blankly non-plussed, so Kay has to spell it out. 'Carly. They're testing it for Carly's blood.'

'Jesus.' Garlon's brow furrows like he's doing a complicated sum. 'They think Bors killed her?'

'Maybe. But he can't have. And you know, maybe it's just a rag and an old blade in a box. Least, I fucking hope so. I haven't said anything yet because of Dan. He's in Belfast. He's got his Siobhan. The twins. He's doing all right. At last. Finally. And once I open my mouth, it's going to rip the whole thing open again.'

He's got Garlon's attention now.

'Go on.'

'That night, we had practice. Arthur was on honeymoon, so while the cat was away . . . we got pissed at the pub and went back to mine. You know all this. Had a tournament on the PlayStation. You made us those slammers. Total carnage. Me and Dan and Bors out for the count on the sofa. And as I told the police, Dan was there all night, snoring in my ear fit to burst the drum—'

'Yeah. Yeah. Everyone vouched for everyone, I remember. But, you know, maybe Bors could have sneaked out.'

'No.'

'No?'

'And I can prove it. I got up for a slash. State I was in, I could hardly stand. Anyway, there in the bog with the door open is Bors with his trousers round his ankles, fast asleep with his mouth gaping. And I had that camera that printed the time and date on every photo. It was on the side and he looked so funny, I picked it up and took a snap, forgot about it. Two a.m. Which is when they said she died.'

'You didn't say at the time.'

'Listen. I didn't know about it. Or I'd forgotten about it. I mean, memories of that night were anything but clear. A couple of years ago I developed a load of films that were kicking about. That's when I found it.'

'You still got the pic?'

'I do.'

'But you've not said anything?'

'I don't know what to do! It's what I wanted to ask you. What the fuck should I do, Garlon? Carly was Linnet's cousin. To say it's going to upset her is the understatement of the century, you know. Maybe it's nothing. The tests come back negative, we can forget about it.'

There's a sheen on Garlon's skin. He wipes the sweat from his lip with the back of his hand. After the runabout and the shower, the cool night air draws it out of the body.

'But if it is, you know, Carly's blood, it's going to be all dug up again,' Kay continues. 'I'll show them the photo. They'll know he couldn't have killed her, which means, how did he come by the knife? Does he know more than he's saying? Or was it planted on him? The police will be all over Abury again. Everyone will get interviewed again.'

Garlon bows his head, kicks a heel back against the tyre.

'You could just let sleeping dogs lie, Kay. I mean . . . burn the fucking photo.'

'I have thought about it, Garlon. I have. But if there's a maniac still out there . . . I have to say, I'm pretty spooked. The thing with Bors. I mean, we all go back forever. How did we miss it? What else did we miss? It makes your skin crawl, doesn't it?'

'Absolutely, mate. Absolutely.'

'Anyway,' Kay continues, 'I've got to get on, but one last thing.' When he's practised it in his head, the speech begins, *As a father of daughters* . . . What he gets out is, 'That thing you said to the lass at the Green Knight. Can you just not?'

'You losing your sense of humour in your old age?' Garlon says, like a man who's just lost his sense of humour.

Briefly, Kay feels the stab of it, the implication that some plentiful, invisible reserve has dried up to nothing. That he's been robbed in the night.

Where were you if you didn't find the same things funny, if you weren't up for sharing a laugh? Who were you then?

Just two men alone in a dark car park turning away from one another.

33

Coven

———

The women come one by one, into the clearing, where Morgan is already waiting, sitting on one of the logs that have been drawn into a rough circle. It's just after six in the morning. Last autumn's beechnuts litter the ground. Under Morgan's fingers, the tree bark runs in deep, crenelated wrinkles.

Last night, she dreamed again of the witch's house, in a clearing not unlike this one, surrounded by trees. It was night in the dream and Morgan was afraid. Yet she had gone on; she had gone inside.

A single candle burned. The walls of the hut seemed to be breathing in and out. Someone was there, obscured, outside the circle of light.

Groping her way forward, she found, not the witch, but a mirror.

And in the mirror, her own face.

And in the mirror, Morgan's lips moving.

Her own voice whispering. *The hag is you. The witch is you. Turn the key. Unbar the door. Undo all the locks. Let her in, in all her evil, in all her power . . .*

She looks around the clearing. All she needs now, Morgan thinks, is a big cauldron over a fire in the centre.

The first woman arrives in jogging gear, red-faced and panting. The next, in wellies, is pulled along by an excitable cockapoo on a lead. The last is office-ready, having parked up in the nearest lay-by and taken the path through the copse in her smart shoes. She twists her car keys in her hand.

'I can't stay long. I really can't.'

These are the women Lisa Gomez suggested Morgan talk to. When she contacted them – via LinkedIn, Twitter in the case of the woman with the dog – there had been no response at all, and then someone had slipped a note under the door to Morgan's room. A time. A date. A place. And the instruction to leave her phone behind.

'So,' she begins, 'Lisa says hi.'

It was not all Lisa had to say, not by a long shot. Not after she'd had a good look at Morgan and decided she was trustworthy.

The video connection was so crisp, it'd felt as though Lisa was in the next room rather than Arizona. She was about thirty-five with straight black hair and enviably toned arms. An olive singlet revealed a tattoo of what looked like circuitry over one shoulder.

'Are you there now? In Abury?'

'Yes.'

Lisa shivered. 'I mean. Ugh. Fuck. That. Place. Am I right?'

Right now, Lisa was taking part in some kind of residency in the desert. Behind her, there was a chunk of sky like a big blue tile.

'When Arthur offered me the job, I liked the idea of a change. I'd had my fill of California. I thought I'd eat some scones. Maybe learn to restore antiques. Call me weird, but I like rain.' Lisa laughed and her rose-gold tongue-piercing caught the light.

'In the beginning it was OK, at the company. It went south slowly, by degrees. I didn't get some of the jokes, but that was fine. They didn't get all of mine. But then I didn't like some of the jokes and that was more of a problem, because that meant I was uptight.'

From then on, a growing resistance to her input. 'If it was my idea, it was a bad idea.' Professional discourtesies relating to coding Morgan didn't understand. An atmosphere. Entrenched management who couldn't or wouldn't see there was a problem. 'They've been there since the beginning, it's all worked out for them, why should anything change ever again?'

Then Lisa had been ill. An asthma flare-up. 'God, the damp!' So she stopped socialising, turned down invites. 'Which in Abury is unforgivable. I was labelled stuck-up.' Things got worse, more openly hostile. Lisa went back to management. This time she was met with sympathy, which was a huge relief, only the sympathy was followed by a request for a dinner date, and when she said no . . . well, the sympathy dried up.

Pranks, deleted files. 'Just high-school shit.' And then they found a soft spot and went to work on it. 'They started calling me by a nickname my dad gave me. Our relationship was . . . troubled. It sounded innocuous but it drove me mad. It wasn't that big a leap from Lisa. They could have stumbled upon it by coincidence. But I was having meetings with my therapist back home over Skype, and we'd been talking about it in a session, and it made me feel so paranoid, like someone was listening in. But I was on a team of people hired for their hacking skills, maybe it wasn't that paranoid.'

Lisa had complained to Arthur and something did filter down – at least they shut up for a bit. And the other departments seemed fine, or at least better. And it wasn't like Arthur's company was the only one. 'Tech is notorious. You just expect a certain amount of it.'

But then things got creepy. Phone calls from a caller who withheld their number. Someone ringing her doorbell at night. A couple of times, she'd had the sense she was being followed and then, out running, having gone further than she meant to and coming back in the dark, a car drove straight at her.

'I took a head-dive into a ditch. If I hadn't, I'd have been run down. It was a big car, blue or maybe black. Didn't have its lights on so I couldn't have got the number plate even if I'd had the presence of mind to try. After that, I considered myself told and I did not need to be told twice. I got my ass out of there.'

A pay-off, no admission of wrongdoing on the company's part, an NDA.

'It was a shame. I didn't get to do the work I went there to do. I thought I could do something there. And then there was Gal, this genius kid Arthur had found, absolutely the sweetest. I hoped we could work on a few projects together.'

Lisa looked away and Morgan thought she could see a crack in her sunny composure, as though what happened in Abury had left a lasting mark.

'Did you ever meet Gwen?' Morgan asked.

'A couple of times. At company events. Not like we hung out or anything.'

'How did she seem?'

'I liked her. She was funny, not what I expected. I don't know. She struck me as kind of sad. Is she going to be all right? I saw the car crash. Hell, I think everyone did.'

'They're saying the car was hacked by one of the guys from the company.'

'Which one?'

'Bors.'

Lisa chewed it over. 'Not the one I'd have put my money on, but OK.'

'And who would that have been? The one you put your money on?'

A long moment. 'Thinking about it, I'm not sure. That was the worst thing, maybe. Going into work every day and knowing it could have been any of them.'

Before she ended the call, Lisa wanted to know why Morgan was going after Arthur. 'I googled you. You're not a journalist.'

In as few words as possible, Morgan told her. When she was done, they sat in silence.

'I am sorry to hear that,' Lisa said finally. 'I really am.'

'Sorry enough to go on the record?'

'You get some women together and my NDA won't be worth the paper it's written on. So yes, sure.'

She gave Morgan three names and wished her luck.

Above the clearing, the leaves are fluttering; layers and layers of leaves, tessellating, overlapping, creating washes of colour, in every shade of yellow and green. Each woman takes up a place on a log. The cockapoo greets them all as though they are the best of friends.

These three are long-serving employees at Arthur's company, each high up in their respective departments. They will know where the bodies are buried. Looked at one way, they have a lot to lose. But if the company were to be restructured, perhaps a lot to gain.

Besides, their Chief Financial Officer has been accused of attempted murder; maybe they scent a change in wind direction.

Now they want Morgan to show her hand, to know what it is she wants from them.

Morgan lays it all out: *Black Prince*, Rasha, the attacks on Gwen, Lisa Gomez. Could it be there are systemic problems at the company, a lack of accountability, even a certain lawlessness?

'What Lisa describes sounds like a problem with the culture . . .'

The women look at the ground.

'Lisa came in all like, this is who I am and this is how good I am, and if you don't like it, that's your problem,' the dog walker says.

'She was confident,' Morgan says.

'Arrogant, maybe. Like she had nothing to learn. I liked her, but you have to read the room.'

'So it was just Lisa. The company doesn't have a problem hiring and retaining women in tech roles?'

The woman in the suit – the one with the senior HR role – shrugs.

'Not many want to come. I mean Abury's dull. They could be somewhere sunny, somewhere cool by the ocean with nightlife. If they do come, they move on quickly.'

'Which is easier than speaking out and having people thinking you're difficult to work with?'

Before she can respond, the jogger cuts in. 'Let's not waste time mincing words. The tech team is toxic. Everyone knows it. But they're the talent. They have the skills. Customer support, finance, HR, admin, what-have-you, we're all replaceable. They're not.'

'Do you think the company prefers to hire women for roles in which they can easily be replaced?'

The jogger's face reddens further. 'You can make it about gender but it's really hierarchy. There's always a hierarchy and if you're not at the top, you have to bend the knee. Honestly,' she bursts out, 'they're nice. The vast majority of them are nice.'

Morgan nods. 'They're nice to you.'

'Yes, they're nice to me.'

'The thing is,' Morgan says, 'you're not really the targets, are you? You're from Abury or you've been here a long time. I'm guessing your kids play with their kids. Maybe your partner plays football on the team. What if I spoke to . . . I don't know, the incomers, the young women, the ones who stick out—'

The woman in the suit butts in. 'Look, we tell them which ones they need to be careful around!'

'So there's a whisper network.'

'If you're smart,' she continues, 'it really isn't that hard. I always tell them to look around, see who you most need onside, and then ask for their advice on something and take it, demonstrably. Then tell them how well it worked out. Daughterly is what you're going for. Not too heavy, just a hint.' She nods a couple of times. 'Light banter with your peers and a bit of daughter with the higher-ups. Sometimes a bit of mothering. Bake a cake on their birthday. You know. Use your judgement. You're not a threat, but you're not prey either. You're an ally.'

The woman with the dog looks depressed. 'Don't tell me in a company full of women, the same shit doesn't apply. It's the same everywhere. Stick it out long enough and it'll be someone else's turn.'

'OK,' Morgan says, 'so as long as you're careful with what you say, and how you behave, and how you dress and what you laugh at, you're fine. Or maybe you just need to believe that. Then if something happens to someone, it's their fault.'

'Well, maybe it is!' The jogger rips the band from her ponytail and starts retying it. 'In every organisation there are malcontents. Naysayers. The ones who whinge, who don't get on, and it's never their fault so they need someone to blame.'

'What happened to Kelly wasn't her fault,' the woman with the dog says. The other two freeze. Then they all start talking at once. Something about a team-building weekend. Someone claiming they were drugged.

'Whenever there was a party, she was pissed.'

'Exactly. She was used to drinking which is how she knew she was drugged!'

'She sent him a load of nudes before it happened. Not just nudes. Worse than just nudes. You don't send someone pics like that unless you're up for it. God, you don't take pics like that unless—'

'She said she didn't send them. She said they were stolen.'

'Was it Bors?' Morgan asks.

All three shake their heads. But they won't say who it was.

'Where's Arthur in all this?'

'We're not sure how much Arthur knows.' The woman has called the dog to her and is ruffling its fur. 'He doesn't have much to do with the detail. There's sort of a ring around him, if you know what I mean. If you saw his calendar, you'd understand. I don't know how he does it.'

'So HR doesn't tell him when—'

The woman in the suit gets to her feet. 'I'm going to be late. I'm off.'

'Can you find me some evidence?' Morgan tries to keep the note of desperation from her voice. 'With evidence, a handful of witness testimonies, more people will come forward—'

The jogger snorts. 'You don't get it. We didn't come here to help you, Morgan.'

'Then why did you come?' Morgan frowns. 'Oh. You just wanted to find out what I knew, didn't you? So you could cover your arses.'

'You haven't really got to grips with the reality of the situation. The company does good work. You've no idea how bad it is out there. You think the stuff about *Black Prince* would be news to the people that matter?' The jogger puts a foot on the log and stretches out a calf muscle.

'I'm missing something,' Morgan says. 'What do you mean?'

'Oh, we've said more than enough,' the jogger says, eyeing the other two.

Since talking to Lisa Gomez, since getting the women's note, a suspicion has been forming in Morgan's mind.

'Why did you ask me to leave my phone at home?' None of the women has looked at a phone since they arrived.

'As a precaution,' says the woman in the suit. 'Anti-virus software – it exists to keep threats out, protect against malware, against hacking, but to do that the software is on the inside, it's behind the firewalls. Once an app or a bit of software is on a device, whoever wrote it or has developer privileges, or just knows the exploits, can easily—'

'Shut up, Michelle!' The jogger turns on her and the woman quails.

'Your girlfriend,' the dog walker says. 'It was a mistake. If you've told Arthur, it won't happen again.'

'An oversight? I see. What about the other ones? How many are there really?'

257

'But against how many successes, Morgan?' The jogger has moved on to her hamstrings. She stands on one leg, gripping her heel, the other arm outstretched.

'So, success excuses Arthur from his errors. How many more errors would he need to be held accountable? Or is it how much less success?'

'A lot,' the jogger says. 'An awful lot.'

The other two women, not meeting Morgan's eye, turn and go. Only the jogger remains.

'I don't think this is about your girlfriend. You've got an axe to grind. I remember you, Morgan. I remember you from on the bus.'

She gives an oink – a little, piggy oink – and smiles, and then jogs slowly from the clearing.

34

Sex Bomb

———

The first time, after they've spent the afternoon making love at his house, in his bed, Lance is on his way to the kitchen to make her a cup of tea, when he falls to his knees, right there in the hall, head bowed down to the scruffy carpet. There's a pain in his chest. An opening feeling.

Outside there are men with cameras. Sometimes they shout things.

He takes the tea and a saucer of biscuits back to bed. After re-bandaging his palm, he bathes and dresses her wounds like they taught him in the army. Feels his cock swelling as he holds her feet in his hands. Lance puts a safety pin in the bandage and looks up to meet Gwen's ravenous eye, the pupil like a hole.

A terrible gravity. He is on top of her, her arms and legs wrapped around him, tongue in his mouth. She looks ugly sometimes, as they make love; he thinks this as his bones liquefy, as sparks collide in his head.

He braces a forearm against the wall, grits his teeth. Their every-day selves burn off, become heat shimmer, vapour on the wind.

And fall to earth.

In the kitchen, Gwen puts bread in the toaster and heats up a pan of water while Lance stands in the doorway. His gaze holds her up, buoys her like a float in the churning sea. She flips the radio on, casts him a surprised look. The Radio Three announcer introduces Prokofiev's Symphony No. 5.

The toast leaps up. The eggs dance in the trembling water. The clock tells four in the afternoon. Lance looks at her and her eyes fill with tears as the music pours over the kitchen, over the immortal cracks and scuffs, the chipped paintwork, the calcified taps and rusting hob.

The eternal mop stands, grey with filth, upended in the bucket. Such terrible gravity.

They watch TV together, curled up on the sofa. Whatever's on, so long as it's not the news. Sometimes she falls asleep there. Lance always seems to sleep there in front of the flickering screen. When she forces him up to come to bed with her, he lies next to her, arms folded over his chest. Whenever she wakes, she finds him awake.

'Don't you ever sleep?' she asks, half in and half out a dream, like a person climbing through a window. 'Don't you ever sleep?'

So it goes the first week.

*

Week Two, Lance goes to the shops and comes back panting. Once inside, he leans against the door, sides heaving in and out.

The photographers diminish in number but there's always one or two, standing out there like stalkers or parked up in a car, lenses trained on the house. But fuck it, they go out for a walk, taking the path round the lake where no car can follow. Two men get out of a Prius and come after them. Beside her, Lance tenses but she plucks at his arm, hurrying them along.

The things the photographers shout to get a reaction. Obscene things. The same men who would have begged her for a smile on the red carpet, to give them a twirl and show off her dress.

'No, Lance. Ignore them.'

They plunge onwards, down to the lake edge where the Coke cans and crisp packets surge against the shore, where the path is only wide enough for them to hurry along single file.

Then, somehow, one of the men is coming the other way, coming towards them, clicking with his camera, snapping, snapping, snapping, and the next thing Gwen knows, Lance has him in the water, has him off the path and down the steep slope and falling over backwards, still holding his camera, into the reservoir.

Lance, in up to his knees, bends over the photographer. Pale green leaves lie on the surface, rocking with the swell.

'Lance,' she says. He turns, a stubborn look on his face. 'It's a bit early for murder, isn't it?'

The photographer bobs to the surface, spluttering, and Lance draws him to shore.

'You were lucky we were here to pull you out after you fell,' Gwen says. 'Send Arthur the bill for the camera.'

Back at the house, back behind the locked door and curtained windows, Lance prowls from room to room. By evening, she's stopped expecting the police to turn up.

Lance wants to know if they shouldn't go to Ireland. He looks at her pleadingly. 'We can't stay here.'

She nods but turns from him so that he comes to her and draws his lips along her collarbone, and they fall as easily as before, the bodies hungry, the souls only slightly jaded. A slip of shadow hangs over them, peering down over Gwen's shoulder as she rides him. Behind her eyelids the photographer sinks under the pale green leaves.

She opens her eyes to look into Lance's wild blue eyes. Over they go, rolling and turning. Sometimes when they make love, he looks so ugly; she thinks this as the small of her back lifts from the mattress, as her toes flex for the big jump.

The shadow slips away as she lies in his arms, drenched with sweat like she's just run the National. They eat beans and toast with grated cheese and watch a documentary about whales. Later, she finds him peering out between the curtains of the back bedroom, the muscles in his neck and shoulders clenched to iron.

'Come to bed, come to bed.' And he does, he lets her lead him to the bed like a lamb and for once he sleeps, and Gwen sleeps too.

Deep in the night, something of Lance's dream slips into hers.

They stand on a vast and barren plain. Around them the night is a living thing, a great, dark, billowing tent. Something is happening to it, to the fabric of night. Its skin is swelling like a balloon. A sense of puncturing, of tearing, and then through the rent slides bloody horror, violent death and murder.

261

Gwen tears herself awake, but even awake there is the overwhelming sense that something evil is in the room with them.

Lance groans, a sort of terrible croaking that rises to a wail. All the hairs on Gwen's arms stand on end and she leaps up from the bed and throws on the light.

Lance is on the floor in the corner, back to the wall. He groans once more and it's a sound she hopes never to hear again in her life.

'Lance. Lance, my love.'

But his eyes stare unseeing, or rather seeing something beyond her vision, the thing she felt in the dark dream. Something tells her not to touch him so she remains on the other side of the room saying his name, calling him back, out of the night terror, and eventually he comes.

In the white dawn, she throws back the curtains, opens every window, whoever's outside be damned. At six, he joins her in the garden, by a nettle patch that grows along the rear fence.

Gwen turns to him fiercely.

'How often does it happen?'

Lance smiles sadly. 'Only when I go to sleep.'

'How have you managed on your own? How have you coped?'

And then she opens up her arms and he walks straight in. Her arms around his neck. The whole misery and beauty of him tight against her.

How hard it is to keep her balance.

How much she loves him, finally understands the severity of it, its grievous nature.

And Gwen hears, in her head, a song from a children's programme from her infancy, a stop-motion show about an old saggy cloth cat.

How sweetly the mice sing, how sweetly they sing to a tune a thousand years old:

We will fix it, we will mend it, we will stick it with glue, glue, glue . . .

35

Let It Be War, Then

———

Arthur's up earlier than ever, so early you can barely call it morning. Running gear on, he goes downstairs in the dark, fumbles for a glass of water at the sink.

There's a light on outside over by the stables. His first thought is that Gwen's back.

In the yard, three horses with riders are milling about. Arthur creeps out, over the silvery soaking lawn, ready to take to his heels if the need arises. But it's only Mo. Mo, Gal, John and a Vietnamese youth, who sits behind Mo on Boxer with his arms round Mo's waist. He's wearing a pair of shorts, a grubby vest, and a dazed expression. A single flip-flop dangles from one foot.

Gal slides down from Gwen's new mare, slips a sports bag free from their shoulder and places it warily on the ground. The Arab is sweat-drenched, foam-flecked but quiet, standing with her head down like she's run her heart out. Gal looks happy, happy and more than a bit shifty, and Arthur realises he has never seen Gal truly happy, or even a touch guilty, ever before. And what's that smell coming off them? It's weed. They all stink of weed!

'A bit peckish,' John says, 'a basket of eels, half a dozen capons, a ham, a wheel of Cheddar. Sauce, a great deal of it. At least a gallon …'

'I didn't know you rode,' Arthur says to Gal. Then, 'I'll see you in the office at nine.' Annoyed by his own petulance, he heads off. He takes his usual route, runs through the lanes, through Abury, to the church and then up on to the top.

The good thinking that often comes when he runs stays away. No vision. No insights. No solutions or resolutions. Only the feeling of betrayal. Lance, his friend. Gwen, his wife. Only the observation that, along with the sympathy, along with the offers of consolation, many accompanied by bikini pics, people think less of him for what Gwen and Lance have done.

Did you know? is the unspoken question. *Surely you can't have been so blinkered? You poor idiot . . .*

He pulls up hard and rubs his temples, gasping. Had he known? No. No. They all got on well. Gwen loved him and Lance loved him – he was in the middle.

Simultaneously, he recalls a day when he watched Lance and Gwen chasing Nedward around the paddock when the sly, wicked pony didn't want to be caught. Gwen's laughter. Lance's admiring eyes. The relief he'd felt that she wasn't sad any more, a stirring of desire to see her so revered. Everyone fancied Gwen. But not everyone was Lance.

More than ever, he's aware of the uncommon weight of their friendship. Why? Because Lance possessed all the skills that he lacked, but nonetheless was full of respect and liking for Arthur. Because with Lance there was none of the jockeying or watchfulness of the company men. Because Lance was not interested in what Arthur could do for him, because of his subtle humour and quiet integrity . . .

Arthur bends double, close to puking. The pair of traitors. The venomous, back-stabbing traitors!

What had Morgan said? *You are liked and envied and admired. I think you're more used to it, more invested in it, than you think.*

When he comes back down into Abury, his feet find their own way to the Green Knight, into the car park round the back and then over to the courtyard and the row of annexe rooms. Which one's her door? While he's wondering, the church bells chime eight and he realises it's too early to pay a call.

He turns round to go and there she is, Morgan, sitting on a bench with her shoes and coat on, like she's just got back from somewhere.

'You heard about what happened? The car . . . Gwen and Lance?'

Morgan nods. People keep saying sorry. We've got your back, Arthur, and so on. She doesn't seem so inclined. When she speaks, it's to ask a question.

'How was the car hacked?'

'Via the entertainment system.'

'Was it your software?'

Arthur hesitates then nods. 'Modified but, yes, based on code I'd written. Sometimes coders leave comments behind to help out anyone who tries to adapt it later. Only Bors had left this awful murderous poem . . .'

He wavers. Can he tell her about what the detectives found at Bors's house? About the knife and the rag? About the possibility that for all these years Carly's murderer has been living among them?

'Strange,' Morgan says. 'I wanted you to suffer what I've suffered. Then this happened. It threw me. You make a wish and it comes true but in a way you would never have wanted. A cursed wish, you know? Like I'd willed it.'

'That's what you wished for, Morgan, up at the White Horse? For me to suffer?'

'I wished to be a knife.' In the morning light, she looks formidably plain, colourless and lumpen, like a potato-eating Russian grandmother.

'This is about that woman, about Rashida Taher, the activist who died.'

'Who was murdered.'

'Tell me about her.'

'No.'

'You upset people, graffitiing the cenotaph. Don't you think it was a bit childish? Did you think about how Carly's family might feel?'

'Who do you think killed her? Who was she meeting up there on Lover's Lane?'

'I don't know.' But he says it too fast, can feel the colour rising in his cheeks. 'Could have been anyone. Carly was a friendly girl.'

'Did you sleep with her?'

'Half of Abury slept with her.'

265

'Not an answer, Arthur.' Morgan looks down at her hands. She spreads her fingers and makes a movement like she's playing a chord. 'After I left, after I went away and after things went well for me, and I became happy, or at least happier, I re-evaluated what it was like growing up here. I remembered some of the things I said back to boys like your brother.

'I wondered if it was as bad as I remembered, if I wasn't over-sensitive, hadn't brought it on myself. People do that when they're bullied or otherwise victimised. It's a protective mechanism. If it was your fault, then it's within your power to stop it happening again. Now I don't wonder if it wasn't worse than I remember. Something's rotten in Abury, Arthur. Something stinks to high heaven. And you're part of it.'

'Me? I never—'

'But you employed them. You gave them jobs and money and power. You set the limits of what was tolerated.'

'I'm getting tired of this, Morgan. I know why you came. I know—'

'Do you? Rasha and her friends were not terrorists. Not even extremists. They were dissidents. They opposed, I don't know, cor-ruption, oppression, tyranny. They communicated via an app. It was supposed to be uncrackable. She was only supposed to be there ten days. But they were taken from their beds at night, driven away in the darkness to prisons without name that everyone knows exist.

'You made the software, Arthur, and you sold it. In the wrong hands it was a weapon. You knew it, but what? You didn't care? You had other things on your mind? Rasha and her friends were disappeared. Rasha is dead. They found her body on a rubbish dump. She had been shot, but that came last. Do you understand? That was only the last thing.'

'I'm so sorry, Morgan.' His voice in his own ears sounds boyish. What will he say next? That he didn't mean to?

'Do you think I loved her so little? Do you think you can say sorry and that can ever be enough? I waited my whole life to meet her. She was the bravest person I've ever known. The bravest and the best. She died because she wanted justice, risked her life for even the tiniest measure of it. And you think I'll walk away? You have to pay, Arthur, and not on your terms. Not a donation to my

266

favourite charity and a kiss where it hurts. You asked what I want. In truth, I want you to be Rasha and for Rasha to be you. But I'm not going to get that so instead I want everything. Everything you have that gives you joy.'

A stabbing pain. Only now does Arthur realise that he came here hoping for comfort. From the old Morgan, the one who had once loved him. He wants to laugh at his own stupidity.

'If it makes any difference, Morgan, the subsidiary has been dissolved, the people who ran it, fired. The software was not sold with my say-so. I have lived an unusual life. There were opportunities, unbelievable opportunities. I wonder sometimes if the world will ever see anything like it again. I have done my best and I have made mistakes. No question. I went to see my mentor. After VivaTech. We talked and talked. You know, I'm not going to roll over for you. You can't make an omelette without breaking eggs. I know you've had no luck with the newspapers. *Black Prince*, it goes nowhere. Bobby's not going to back you up.'

'A donation to his favourite charity?'

'Something like that.'

'The oil company regrets the spill, all those dead birds. The police regret the actions of a few bad apples. The government regrets—'

'We loved one another once.'

She shakes her head, tight-lipped.

'Mistakes get—'

'So you keep saying.'

'So it's war, then? You think you'll win? It only ever really goes one way, doesn't it? The one against the many.'

'Traditionally, perhaps.'

'With the best will in the world, Morgan, you're a small fish.'

'Rasha an egg and me a fish. Fancy that.'

'Kay still thinks you're a witch.'

'You know why people are frightened of witches? Because they have power and they are alone. It's not power that comes from the group.'

'Shame they don't exist, then. Have you seen Gwen?' He's staring at her like he's afraid of the answer.

'No. Saw Mo once or twice. You've got a nice lad, Arthur.'

'Nice?'

Both pause, looking for a word that's more apt for Mo. Arthur gives up first.

'You know what? Stay the fuck away from my family. Your bill here is paid. The room's booked from the end of the week.'

'Then I'll take another.'

'You'll find all the rooms in Abury booked, Morgan.'

'You're running me out of town?'

'Yes, I rather think I am.'

Morgan puts her head on one side and looks at him. It sends a shiver through him, starting in his neck and tripping off each vertebra as it descends to his balls.

'No. You hear me. No, Arthur. Now fuck off.'

36

Is There a Doctor in the House?

———

Mo, back from the chemist, hops into the car.

'This what you need?'

Gwen takes the paper bag from him and peers inside. They're in the multistorey car park overlooking Swindon town centre. Hung's in the back, along with the stuff Mo brought her from the house. In her lap is a new phone and SIM to replace the one burned up in the accident.

'You sure you don't need to see a doctor?'

'I'll have a go with this first.' Gwen tears open the sachet of sodium citrate, dumps the cranberry-flavoured powder into her bottle of water and gulps it back. She'll have to wait till she gets home to insert the pessary and apply the thrush cream, even though the pain is relentless. The thrush gnaws and the cystitis burns, and she can feel the evil creeping up from her bladder to her kidneys, which will mean antibiotics.

'Things going well with Lance, then?'

'Fuck off.'

Lance is an angry and scared little boy. Lance is sleepless and suffocating and silent. Now he's shown himself to her, he can't believe she'll stay so he follows her from room to room, scenting her unhappiness, unable to master his own panic.

Next thing she knows, she's throwing her arms about Mo. The

trucker cap and sunglasses she's wearing for want of a better disguise butt against his neck.

'Oh Christ, I'm sorry, Mo. Sorry for everything.'

Bad person. Bad woman. Bad wife. Bad lover. Bad friend. Bad mother to her little boy. What kind of mother asks her son to buy vag-meds from Boots for her? But who else did she have to ask?

I'd have died rather than give you back, she wants to say, *but I'm sorry, sorry you were dragged into our catastrophe, sorry I . . .*

Instead, she sniffs and sits back in her seat. 'Who's the lad? He doesn't say much.' On the way into Swindon, Hung had gazed out the window, exclaiming at everything they came across, as though seeing England for the first time.

'Hung's a friend. He's staying at the house for a bit.'

'How is it? At the house? How is he?'

'I'm not sure.'

Mo starts the car and they drive through the gloom down the spiralling concrete ramp to the barriers where he slots the ticket into the machine. As the mechanical arm raises, he says, 'I mean, what would it look like if Arthur lost it?'

Immediately, she thinks of Lance. Lance crouched in the corner during a night terror, groaning and shaking.

Gwen sighs. 'In all honesty, I can't imagine Arthur cares enough to lose a wink of sleep, let alone lose the plot. He'll manage this like everything else.'

They stop at traffic lights to let a stream of pedestrians cross. A woman with a buggy does a double-take and nudges the man walking beside her. She shouts something at the car, but the windows are closed and then the light turns amber and Mo's pulling away.

'Maybe it's not just you. Your friend Morgan had some bad news for him.'

'It's been a long time since I could call Morgan a friend,' Gwen says in a small voice.

'There was a woman . . .' Mo begins. After he's done telling her what Morgan told him, they drive on in silence.

Morgan had a girlfriend! Morgan is a lesbian! When all these years, Gwen had assumed Morgan hated her for stealing off with Arthur.

As the car speeds up on the dual carriageway, her stomach tightens.

Morgan had a girlfriend and her girlfriend is dead and she blames Arthur for it. Arthur, who has always believed himself to be a good man. No whoring or bullying. Nice to old ladies. Gives a lot to charity. Well behaved even when pushed, even when goaded. Everyone likes Arthur!

Over the years, there was not one argument Gwen'd had with him, where he'd not managed to convince her that he was right and she was wrong, that his grasp of reality was not superior to hers, a feat achieved through a combination of certainty and Gwen's own appreciation of Arthur's intellectual gifts. In the battles she had won, she had simply set her teeth, refusing to argue or concede.

A chill creeps over her, a seeping apprehension, like in the moments before you realise you're coming down with something nasty. The car is an airless metal box, hurtling among other metal boxes, one instant from becoming a flaming death trap.

With great effort, Gwen steadies her breath.

If the world picked a fight with Arthur, what would the outcome be? What would happen to his certainty? To the certainty that had brought him so far, that had never failed him, only elevated and enriched him beyond the wildest dreams of ancient kings?

'You can stop here.'

The spot she's picked is half a mile from Lance's, close to the cycle track.

'Did you ever hear Dad mention something called *Wasteland*?'

'No. Why?'

'One of Gal's . . . projects. It's probably nothing to worry about,' Mo says. Then, 'Gal's not happy, you know. Bors bought the drone, no question. And they found a laptop hidden under the floorboards and Gal said it was the one used to do the hacking. Only Gal says Bors was always the decent one. They say it doesn't add up.'

'People aren't always what they seem.'

Mo nods, then points at the box with her new phone in it. 'I'd think twice about going on the Internet, Mum.'

Before she gets out, she kisses him on the cheek and then, for no other reason than he leans forward, she kisses Hung too, surprising them both.

271

She hurries along the cycle track and then cuts through the trees to the back of the house in case anyone is lying in wait out the front.

Lance opens the back door as she reaches for the handle and she screams. Her nerves are in ribbons.

'Did you talk to him?'

'No. I told you. I was seeing Mo.'

Is it a flicker of disappointment she sees on his face?

In the bathroom, packets torn open, balm applied, she wonders if Lance misses Arthur as much as she does. If he loves and resents him as much as she does.

Or is it just confirmation of what she has always suspected – that men long for one another, for the companionship of other men, long for their comradeship, approval and support, never imagining that women long for it as well.

37

Wasteland II

The lawyer spoke plainly about what Gwen could be entitled to. Even if they put her on the bonfire, *longstanding betrayal with close friend of the family, sexual infidelity, big spender of her husband's money,* she could still come away with something close to half.

'Half of what? Liquid? Assets? The house?'

'Half of everything.' The lawyer shuffled some papers. 'Including the company.'

It was laughable. Gwen, who couldn't tell Python from Java. Gwen, who was currently squatting with a penniless tinker in a rotting hovel!

Arthur'd found himself calling a panicky meeting where he'd endeavoured to reassure everyone, instead sending ripples of panic over the boardroom. If you're at the top, it flows from you. He might as well have set fire to their socks.

To clarify, the lawyer wanted to know, was there anything on Arthur's side? Specifically, was there anything that Gwen could bring along as a counter-accusation? On the whole, the public didn't like his wife but it was surprising how easily these things could change. Seeing his mouth fall open, the lawyer stood up, smoothed down her skirt and extended a hand for him to shake.

'Have a think before we speak again.'

She might well have been good enough for Paul McCartney, but how could you leave a man alone with a question like that? With those calculations?

Hung hands him a plate.

'Thanks, mate.'

The lad nods and hovers while he takes a bite. Earlier, with nothing in the cupboards, Arthur had given him a roll of notes and the keys to the Vespa. *Maybe get some food?* he'd typed into the translation engine.

Hung had gone off and a couple of hours later come back with shopping. Where had Mo found him? Why is he staying with them? Arthur puts the forkful in his mouth and ceases to care. Pork belly. Lime. Peanut. Coriander. More flavours he can't identify. The rice is sticky. He takes another bite, then one more.

An undeniable truth announces itself in his head to the sound of trumpets: Gwen is a mediocre cook, very, very mediocre!

In the imaginary witness box, she turns to the jury – they don't have juries in divorce cases – nonetheless, she turns to the jury, pale of face with great suffering eyes, her dark gown long-sleeved, demure, and she lifts a hand to point at him and says . . .

What? What is it she will say to justify herself?

Hung pats him gently on the shoulder. When Arthur's cleaned the plate, he takes it away and returns with some chicken skewers, a small tangy salad of grated carrot and . . . radish?

The TV's on and together they watch the news, all of it grim, until Arthur can take no more. Out on the lawn, he feels briefly better and strolls the perimeter of the property with Cavall moping at his heels like an Italian widow.

In the witness box, she's in a different mood now, fierier than before.

What about Camille? she shouts. *What about that French operations manager?*

You don't know about that, he retorts. *You never found out. It was only once!*

What about when you adopted a homeless beggar child without consulting me?

You worship him. He's the light of your life!

He's almost enjoying himself until he remembers it's all in his head, that he's alone, and whatever Gwen's doing right now, it probably doesn't involve having imaginary arguments with him. Sensing an opportunity, the pornographic image – Gwen and Lance, at it like knives – swims up from the depths.

Arthur ducks it, only for witness-box Gwen to say calmly:

When I lost our babies, you hid from me. You hid from my grief because it frightened you. You wouldn't feel your own or share it. It was a loss and you only do winning. You pretended the company needed you so you could avoid me, and when you were there, you said the right things, made the right noises, but you were dead behind the eyes.

It doesn't even sound like her any more, the witness-box Gwen, and he lets her sock-puppet crumple in the dock.

If you admit it, a little voice says, *you can be even and then you can ask her to come back.*

Arthur rubs at his nose with the heel of his hand and sets a course for the stables, feeling an urge to be close to Boxer, the old grey. He takes a handful of oats from the bin and puts out his palm with the thumb tucked in like she taught him. With the other hand, he strokes Boxer's nose, warm and velvety, feels breath and whiskers tickle his wrist.

In one of the stalls a couple of doors down, he can make out low voices. Mo and someone.

'The musician? I suppose I wanted to get up close and see what it was like when someone ruined themself. If there was anything in it. And he played well, of course.' For once, Mo's tone is neither bored nor mischievous. 'If I'd stayed, it . . . well, it might not have ended well. But Gwen wouldn't have it. Kept coming up. We used to hide from her, laughing behind the door. One day, I'd been out and when I got back, he told me she'd been up there in her best dress to bargain for my soul. He wanted to laugh about that too. But I gave in there and then and went home the same day. For all his talent, he had nothing as fierce as Gwen's love. I don't know if Arthur ever knew what to do with it.'

'What about . . .' Gal hesitates. 'I mean, your birth mum?'

The seconds draw out before Mo speaks again. 'I have nothing of hers. Although . . . I was in Brighton once. I was in a shop and this song was playing. I knew it. It stopped me in my tracks. There was an old Indian guy behind the till. I asked him who the singer was. Only after I'd said it, I realised I hadn't spoken English.' When he speaks again, the words come out in a tumble. 'I thought it was my mother's voice.'

After a long pause, Arthur hears Gal say, 'I read somewhere that in parts of India, they once believed there were six genders, not two. I've never . . . I mean, I've never . . .'

Arthur takes off at a clip. When he gets back to the house, he notices Cavall has chosen not to follow. In the kitchen the plates are neatly washed and stacked, although Hung is nowhere to be seen.

On the side is the bag they gave him at the hospital. In it are the few things he'd taken in for Gwen and the clothes they'd cut from her body when the ambulance brought her in. The bag's made of paper. It crackles in his hand. When he dips his face to it, he can smell her overlaid with the odour of smoke.

Sometimes he feels like he was in the car too. Only they left him inside.

In his pocket, his phone shudders and he gets it out and sees a message has arrived from Gwen – as though, by thinking of her, he's somehow conjured her.

All those years ago, when I asked you to talk to Morgan for me, did you? Did you even try?

Fuck off, Gwen. Delete.

I'm fine! Thanks for asking. How could you do this to me? Delete.

Morgan hates you and you know what? She's right to. She was right all along about you. Send.

In his study, Arthur logs on, knowing so little of self-destructiveness he doesn't recognise it now it's arrived.

He types the name Rashida Taher into the search engine. Morgan refused to tell him about her so he will find out for himself.

When Garlon arrives an hour later, Arthur is deep down the rabbit hole, hunched over a wobbly YouTube video of a birthday party. Chatter in a language that might or might not be Arabic. A cake borne aloft by a black-haired girl with pigtails and set down at a crowded table in front of a woman with enormous eyes. She kisses the girl's cheek as the table, young and old, bursts into song. *Happy birthday, dear Rasha*, they sing in English, *happy birthday to you!*

The candles on the cake cast moving light over Rasha's face. Her smile seems to flicker. In the final frame, she looks up and straight into Arthur's heart and makes a wish.

Garlon coughs.

'Just thought I'd pop by,' he says.

Once the tea's brewing, Arthur asks him how he got in through the gates. 'Someone buzz you in?'

'Kay left his doodah in my car so they just swung open.'

'He said he'd lost it a while back. I think he and Linnet have taken the kids to Thorpe Park.'

Chat. Chat. Chat. In truth, he wishes Garlon would go away so he could get back to watching the video on repeat. Still, he supposes, it's times like these you find out who your friends are.

Garlon wants to know if there's any word on how Bors is doing.

'I mean, it's awful, Arthur, just awful what he did, but he must be sick in the head. Any word from the coppers about ... the situation?'

'No, they seem to have stopped talking to me. But I've a feeling we are going to be seeing quite a bit more of them.'

'So it was her blood, then. On the knife, like?'

Of course, Kay would have told Garlon. 'It seems so.'

'Have you told Kay?'

'Why would I tell Kay? What's it to him?'

'Oh, you know,' Garlon says quickly, 'what with Linnet being Carly's cousin.' He clears his throat. 'I have to say I was surprised when you made Bors CFO. When you look back, he was always, like, a bit stuck-up. Even on the bus. Always doing his homework, looking like he smelled a fart. Holier than thou, you know. You were a bit younger, you probably don't remember.'

'I remember the bus.'

You find out who your friends are and ... it's fucking Garlon? When Arthur zones back in, Garlon seems to be talking about Gwen.

'We all thought the world of her.'

'I want a clean slate! I want to start again!' Although Arthur's not thinking of Gwen now, but rather of the woman in the video, of the luminous face of Rashida Taher.

'I won't let you down,' Garlon is saying, 'I'm hearing you loud and clear.'

Eventually, Arthur gets him to the door. On the step, Garlon turns.

277

'I've been thinking, England are playing Germany on Saturday. May first. Could be a chance to get everyone together. What do you think? Shall I spread the word?'

Arthur makes affirmative noises, stands there grinning like an idiot as he waves to Garlon's retreating car, remembering Gal saying:

If you had a button and you could push it and stop it, everything that's going wrong, wouldn't it be your duty to push it?

The line ricochets round his head like a squash ball. Arthur shakes himself to dislodge it. It's persistent, though:

Everything going wrong. Button. Push it.

As he walks through the empty rooms, the rooms which contain everything of his wife, except his wife, it breaks down into elements, and the elements form a rhythm.

Duty. Stop it. Push it.

And the rhythm buries into his brain like a worm.

Wrong.

Stop it.

Duty.

Arthur rubs at his face with both hands. No one's been able to make a firewall for the mind yet.

Button.

Stop it.

Pussssshhhhhhh it!!!

Eight

—

Night-Tripping
A Week or So Ago

38

Our Growing House

––––

'Why did you bring him?' Gal asks.

Mo's given John the pony, a piebald Welsh cob, all feathers and fat arse. John's eyes are closed. He slumps in the saddle, beard rocking forward to almost touch the cob's mane. Nedward, the cob, rests his whiskery chops on Boxer's haunches, breathing deeply. Gnats swarm beneath the streetlamp, like pelting silver rain. In the lamplight, the insides of the cob's nostrils are baby pink.

The third horse, a fine coal-black mare with a white star on its forehead, is for Gal. Mo holds the mare's reins in one hand and offers Gal the other. 'Put your foot in the stirrup.'

Gal looks doubtful but raises up one green Adidas Gazelle and wedges it into the steel hoop, hopping on the other leg to keep balance. Mo leans over, clasps a hand and hauls Gal up.

'How did you get John on? Was there a crane handy?'

Mo smirks and touches his knees to Boxer's sides and the grey starts forward, pursued by the pony. 'Hold the reins,' he calls over his shoulder. 'Not too tight. Nell's lively. She won't like it. And don't fall off.'

They're on the edge of Abury, on the estate where Gal once lived with Hercules. The windows of the boxy pebble-dashed houses are dark, the night sky veiled with cloud. At the back of the playing field, past the swings, they take a cut-through into a meadow. A little further on, Mo leads them on to one of the bridleways out of town.

The only sound is hooves on track as they pick their way up on to the downs. On either side, tall blackthorn hedges loom up like waves.

Gal reaches down to pat the mare's neck, feels the fever of her, the blood coursing beneath the satin coat. On Lover's Lane, she takes a step sideways, a dancer's step, shying at the invisible. Mo's arm shoots out and catches her bridle. 'None of that now, Nell,' he says and the mare quietens.

On they go, following the track higher still and then taking a narrower path between a fold in the hills that descends into the coombe. The cob jostles the mare, and in retaliation Nell nips its arse so it bolts, cantering over the tufty uneven grass, its rider bouncing wildly like a ball attached to a bat by a string.

'How does he ever stay on?' Gal asks.

'Oh, death has lost interest in John Falstaff.'

A steel trough fed by a spring sits in the basin and Mo gets off to let Boxer drink. Gal slides down from the mare. The sky is clearing. Above, moon rays make a halo around a bank of cloud. As they watch, the cloud breaks into frills and the moon, naked and fierce, unleashes a flood over the valley. Boxer lifts his head as though the moonlight is a sound.

The water in the trough is black; over Gal's shoulder the moon asserts herself upon the rippling surface. Their fingers dip into the water and touch the reflection.

'"My gal, talkin' to my gal . . ."' Mo sings. He hums the next few bars. In the trough, his fingers slide up against Gal's like curious fish.

Gal draws back and the moon breaks into fragments.

'Do you know my earliest memories are of riding the downs at night with Gwen?' Abruptly, Mo turns his back and strolls over to where the cob is cropping the grass. A wine bottle protrudes from the long pocket of John's coat, but before Mo can pluck it free, a hand snakes out and grabs his wrist.

'You would not thieve poor John's last sip, would you?'

'All booty is to be shared.'

John takes a draught and hands the bottle over to Mo. 'This nag is for the knacker.'

'I wouldn't let Nedward hear you say so. He can be vengeful.' Mo rattles the bottle. Empty. He tuts.

'What are we doing here?' Gal asks. 'Where are we going? You said—'

'We are gentlemen of the shade, Gal! Diana's foresters, minions of the moon.' John lifts a hand and gestures towards the heavens. 'See our fair chaste mistress, under whose countenance we steal—'

'Steal? Mo said we'd be helping someone.'

'There are people who are going to be helped,' Mo begins patiently, 'and people who will—'

'John will be helped! John's unbearable reckoning at the Green Knight will be alleviated. The knave Vern has threatened me with scalping!'

'I'm going home,' Gal says. 'If this is a scheme, I want no part in it. I've got better things to be doing.' And they do: going over all the evidence against Bors again, for example. They're not sure what they're looking for but they'll know it when they find it.

Mo smiles. 'Unlike you, Gal, we can't all just transfer ourselves a bit of cash every time we feel the urge.'

In answer, Gal stalks over to Nell and takes her by the bridle. At the trough, they attempt to balance on the side while holding the mare steady.

'Wait.' Mo fetches Boxer, thrusts a boot into the stirrup and springs up on to his back. He brings the grey alongside Nell and offers Gal his hand. 'Arthur once told me that when he met you, you were like a prisoner in a tower. Was he right?'

'Yes.' Gal allows himself to be pulled into the saddle.

'The person at the house. His name is Hung. I got a phone in to him. We've been messaging using a translator app. He came here in the back of a lorry six months ago. He was promised restaurant work, wages he could send home. Instead, he got trafficked and locked up in that house. It's a growing house, a weed farm. He tends the plants, all alone, as much a prisoner as you ever were. We're going to get him out.'

'And John is keeping you company from the goodness of his heart?'

'John's goodness is John's business. And if we come away the richer, you can give your portion to Hung.'

'—drawn and quartered!' John cries. 'Now let's go fleece the rascals before we wither.' And he claps his heels to Nedward's sides, the cob lets out a thunderous clap of wind and all three horses take off at a trot.

With the valley at their backs, they rise again, following the chain of hills. The stars move in shoals. Further on, they cross a gallops and then pass down through a copse where the ground is soft and the air damp and mossy.

Where the ground begins to level, Mo slides off Boxer, takes the reins over his head and loops them around a branch, followed by Nell's.

John lands with a thump and immediately sinks to his knees. 'My legs are dead. Sweet boy, rub them back to life and resurrect me.'

Mo makes a face. 'On no account!'

Nedward lets forth a powerful jet of foamy piss and John struggles up. When the cob is finally finished, the wood falls silent. Mo pulls back his hood and stands, head cocked, in a patch of silver. And then, as though reassured, he leads them from out among the trees, to open ground.

Ahead is the house, all alone, surrounded on every side by hills. Plywood sheets are nailed across the windows, and those lower down have rusted grilles fixed over the wood. Weeds grow between cracks in the path, twigs and shattered roof tiles litter the ground. A track, passable only by tractor or 4x4, veers within a few yards of the front door.

'This is the place?' Gal asks.

In response, Mo points to the wires that reach from one of the eaves to a pylon.

'They're clever. There are no helicopters here, no spies with infrared goggles overhead. The power usage can be put down to farming.'

It seems unlikely, but the door is reinforced with steel bars and concealed inside a wooden box is a newly installed keypad.

'How did you get a phone in to him?'

'I climbed up on the roof and lowered it down the chimney.'

'Like Father Christmas?'

'I prefer to think of myself as a big bad wolf. Or at least a medium-sized morally flexible wolf.'

'You could just call the cops, Mo.'

'He's got no passport, no English. They'll what? Knock down the door and find him surrounded by thousands of pounds' worth of ganja. He'd be swapping one prison for another.' It's a good point. 'Now, can you hack the lock, or no?'

Gal draws closer. From inside, there comes a faint ticking. Switching on their phone torch, they bend their head to the keypad, and catch it, like perfume rising from a warm body, a scent both cloying and sweet. It's been years since Gal gave up cannabis, but instantly their mouth begins to water.

If this doesn't work, they can try using a Bluetooth sniffer or hacking the network . . .

Gal types in a five-digit code, there's a beep, an LED flashes green, and then the sound of unlocking.

'But the default code you gave me didn't work!'

'I hacked the manufacturer and created an update which set a new override code for all their smart locks.'

Seeing the admiration in Mo's eyes, Gal's body releases a chemical that sends a pleasurable tide flooding through them.

In the next moment, the door is pushed open, and a boy tumbles out in a blaze of light to throw himself into Mo's arms.

'Mo! Mo!'

When Hung lifts his head and steps back, Gal sees that he is not quite a boy. He could be Mo's age. Only he is small, little over five feet in height. He wears a grubby singlet, shorts and flip-flops, and has straight black hair that he pushes back from swollen, red-rimmed eyes.

From his pocket, Hung pulls a mobile phone and thrusts it at Mo, with the other hand plucking at his sleeve and drawing him into the house. All the while, he talks rapidly in a language that see-saws between tones.

After the darkness, the light comes as an assault, although it's nothing compared to the smell. It makes Gal's head reel. The plants are everywhere, an army of hairy, green triffids, standing in pots, or sprouting in trays, or cut and hanging from lines.

Throughout, blackout material covers each wall and lamps glare down from above. A staircase leads to an upper storey. Beyond the main room, in the first of two small rooms at the back, a mattress lies on the floor. Next to it sits a microwave alongside a cup, a bowl, a fork and a spoon. A couple of T-shirts are folded over a plastic chair. These are the only visible concessions to human occupancy; everything else is given over to the plants: bags of fertiliser and soil, buckets, pots and watering cans. In the third and final room, packed into clear plastic bin liners is a vast harvest of green.

Sweat pricks Gal's scalp and they rub the back of their hand over their mouth. 'How long has he been in here?'

'Half a year or so, he thinks.'

Hung is tapping on the phone now. He holds the screen up for Mo to see, and then shows it to Gal. The text in the translation app reads: *They will be here soon. Very soon. They will kill us.*

Mo takes the phone from him, types something back and shows it to Hung, who stills and looks from Mo to Galahad with frightened eyes.

'What did you tell him? Who will be here soon? Who's going to kill us?'

'The growers. I said we'd get him his passport back and take all their money.'

'And just how are we going to pull that off?'

Mo's plan, such as it is, is simple. It's also weak, even Gal can see that.

The growers are coming to sell the house and everything inside it, including Hung. They will bring the buyers, who will bring the money. Naturally the buyers will want to inspect their purchase, to look around. When Hung takes them upstairs, Mo and Gal will make their exit with the loot.

'It's not like they'll carry it upstairs with them.'

'They might not bring it at all. They might pay in Bitcoin or via an offshore account.'

'Hung has heard them say it would be cash. John will stay outside. After we're out, he'll create a distraction that'll allow Hung to get away. They can't follow us through the woods in any vehicle. Even if John hasn't slashed their tyres.'

'And where will we hide?'

Mo looks about, as though the thought is just occurring to him. 'Behind some bags? They'll hardly be looking for us.'

Outside, under the lunatic moon, beyond the fog of weed, the plan seems no better. John sits on a pile of bricks. He balances a pie on his knees and hacks at it with a large knife.

'And you're up for this, are you?' Gal asks.

John takes a bite, rubs the crumbs from his beard. 'A man must eat, not that you bony pair would know it. Fear not, John will not let you down! Pie?'

'Is it vegan?'

John snorts. 'Tell me, do you think the boy loves me? I think his father loves him not, though nowhere will you find a more English knave. There is not a drop of Scots in him, nor Welsh or Irish. Free of Frenchiness, thank God. Body, heart and soul – a true Englishman. Drinks his ale and shirks his duties, riots when called upon, cheats and swaggers. The boy can corrupt a saint. If the villain hasn't given me medicines to make me love him, I'll be hanged.'

'What are you two talking about?' It's Mo, although neither have heard his footsteps.

'Your Englishness, among other matters.'

'Flourishing.' Mo reaches down to take a slice of pie from John's proffering hand. 'Some argue they have priority through ancestry. But the land recognises no ancestry. It has the dead, your dusty kings and queens. It doesn't care for them. It wants the living. Twenty-five generations or five minutes – it's all the same to England. You should not linger here and breathe her air, unless you want to carry her contagion.'

Mo takes a bite and chews thoughtfully. 'Some begrudge it, as though nationality is a kind of cloth and they'll have no trousers if it's shared out. But I speak the truth. And drink it too. I have drunk with the good lads and lasses in Eastcheap. They call drinking deep *dyeing-scarlet*. I've drunk with the good lads and lasses of Tower Hamlets and St Paul's, Moss Side and Meadow Well. Your Williams and Kates, your Divyas and Muhammads, Jacksons and Andrzejs, your Sharmaines and Ranjeevs and Mashas. Such times I've had in their company.'

'You will not redeem it, the time?' John asks hopefully.

'Time cannot be redeemed.' There is a note to Mo's voice, as though he wishes it were otherwise. 'It is not Tesco Clubcard points.'

Before he can go on, light breaks over the hills and they hear the sound of engines. The growers are coming.

John thrusts his pie back into his pocket and retreats among the trees. Gal and Mo go back to the house. When Mo closes the door behind them, Gal's heart skitters in their chest. They wonder if they look as afraid and miserable as Hung.

Mo takes Hung in his arms and kisses him resoundingly, once upon each cheek. In return, Hung buries his face in Mo's shirt front. When he draws back, he looks him full in the face and nods rapidly. Gal wonders what Mo's been texting him. Clearly Hung trusts him with his life, whereas Gal trusts him as far as they can throw him. Yet here they are.

In the room with the mattress, a hide has been built for them from bags of soil and stacks of empty pots. Over it, Hung has thrown a sheet as though to dry. There is space enough behind it for the two of them if they crouch and press together. Between the pots, through the sheet and open door, they can see only the wall and a portion of the small room opposite with the harvested weed.

From outside, there is the sound of car doors slamming. The noise from the engines dies away. Hung's footsteps retreat into the other room and then, in the quiet, Gal hears a beep, then a lock drawing back, and the door swinging open.

Footsteps and voices. Vietnamese and English. Vietnamese-accented English. London English.

'Fucking hot,' someone says. 'Stinks like Snoop Dogg's crotch.'

A ripple of laughter. Another voice shouting in Vietnamese. Beneath it, Gal can just make out Hung's subdued replies. The shouter switches to English and his tone becomes sleek and salesman-like. 'You look it over.'

How many of them are there? Four? Seven? Nine? They come closer. Then closer still. Outside the room opposite, they stop. The Londoner inspects the harvest and asks the shouter a few questions about the set-up. Through a hole in the sheet, Gal counts eight ghostly legs.

As they turn their attention on the room in which Gal is hiding with Mo, Gal closes his eyes and shrinks back into Mo's arms. A powerful lassitude takes them. Mo brings his cheek to Gal's and lets out a long, slow breath.

'Hardly a palace,' the Londoner says. It sounds like he's standing right over them.

'Hung's cheap. A few packets of noodles. Sometimes some meat. Little vegetables.'

'He speak English?'

'You teach him, he'll learn. But it doesn't matter. Maybe better not.'

The voices move away again, back into the main room. Laughter. More talk. Gal hears the word 'passport'. Something heavy is dropped on to the floor which causes the conversation to stop.

In the silence, Hung says something in Vietnamese.

The shouter translates, 'He says you want to see upstairs?'

'Why not?'

Gal tries to count them as they go up, but it's impossible. Mo straightens and inches out from behind the pots. Just then, a deep cough comes from the main room. Someone has stayed behind, someone is blocking their way out.

Mo freezes. He turns back to Gal and mouths the word *fuck*. His eyes say, *What now?* And Gal's eyes reply, *Not a fucking clue!*

Mo looks about the room as though the answer is to be found about them. An idea arrives. Gal watches it born behind Mo's eyes. He draws one of Hung's T-shirts from the back of the chair and takes a lighter from his pocket. He beckons Gal and then indicates the room with the harvest in it. Then he hands them both lighter and shirt.

They look at one another for a long moment and it occurs to Gal that Mo's lips are objectively perfect. Mo brings them to Gal's ear, bang up against the whorls of cartilage, and whispers, 'Time to make the grand gesture.'

The man in the next room shuffles his feet. Overhead the floorboards creak as Hung shows the visitors round upstairs. They will be down soon. If it's to be done, it's to be done now.

Gal flicks the lighter and holds the T-shirt over the flame. How swiftly it takes hold! The flame running in a lick up the side towards their hand, so that they almost drop it, release all but a corner before taking two quick steps and flinging it next door.

It falls flaring on to the bags of weed. The plastic wrinkles, twists, dissolves. A small plume of smoke goes up.

Gal steps back to Mo's side. The man on the other side of the wall coughs again. The footsteps are now directly above them.

The plume becomes a pillar. The pillar sheds itself and falls to carpet the floor. Half a minute passes, then half a minute more. The smoke begins to snake out of the room, reaching for them where they stand, drifting, rising. The fire is taking hold, beginning to talk in spits and crackles.

Mo and Gal press with their backs against the wall next to the door. The air thickens. The house is becoming one giant hotbox. Seven years of sobriety, Gal thinks, and now this. How absurd it is. In a way funny, really . . .

Oh no. Oh no!

It begins in the knees, just a touch at first, just a stroke. They feel Mo tense beside them as though against an invisible force. For a second, Gal thinks they're going to be OK, but mirth takes them both like a fatal cramp.

They cling to one another, shaking with silent laughter.

'No, no, no, no,' Gal whispers. 'You mustn't.'

But Mo is writhing with it now, convulsing in its grip. Their thoughts scatter, chased by their careening senses; tears pour from Gal's eyes. When they wipe them away, they see Mo's face is suddenly deadly serious.

'Tell me about *Wasteland*. What is it?'

Gal leans in, talks right into Mo's mouth, their lips almost touching. 'I made a plague!' And then braces for another gale of laughter, because after all, it is the funniest thing ever, but then, simultaneously, two things happen.

The footsteps overhead start moving back towards the stairs and, in the main room, the remaining man coughs twice, says, 'What the fuck—' and strides to the burning room where he lets out a yell of alarm.

Mo jumps out, pushes him with two hands in the centre of his back in among the burning weed and slams shut the door. 'Come on,' he cries and, with Gal at his heels, he dashes into the main room, stopping to snatch up a navy-blue sports bag from the floor. He takes two steps, turns back, rifles the table until he locates Hung's passport, clocks the men at the top of the stairs, and makes a run for the exit.

Out, out they go, into the cool, inky night, blundering, blind until their eyes adjust to the darkness.

A man in a white shirt looms out of the black.

'Oi, you—' he begins, but they knock him down. Somewhere behind him, there's a whooshing sound and a sheet of blue flame leaps up as though to touch the moon. It's the cars, two 4x4s, now burning merrily.

Gal's body is behaving remarkably efficiently for the vast quantity of weed smoke they've inhaled. Legs scissoring. Arms pumping. They fall over a root or some such but get back up in a flash, tearing in among the trees to where the horses are waiting.

John shoots towards them like a crack-raddled badger. He stinks of petrol. He's singed his beard.

'Help me to my horse, Mo,' he pants.

'Am I your ostler?' Mo says, but he brings Nedward alongside a stump from which John manages to haul himself on to the cob's back.

'Take this.' Mo hands Gal the sports bag. He pulls Boxer's reins free and mounts the grey. 'I'm going to get Hung. Be ready to ride,' he says. 'Give Nell her head. Don't try to hold her. Stay on.' And with that, he turns Boxer, claps his knees to his sides and takes off back in the direction of the house.

Gal stumbles after him. What they wouldn't give for an ice-cold Coke and a family pack of pickled onion Monster Munch.

From behind a tree trunk, they peer out trying to make sense of the scene.

There are the burning cars. There is the house. There is the door opening and a handful of people spilling out.

Smoke billows around them, so much smoke it reminds Gal of shows on TV where the performers come out onstage veiled in dry ice. Is this a show? Are they about to start dancing in unison or performing a cover of K-pop band BTS?

One of the men has Hung by the neck and is shaking him. Gal has the awful feeling this is about to become one of those violent films they don't watch because they find them upsetting.

The whole thing needs recoding, but Gal may need to pee first. Or perhaps they're peeing already? Have they always been peeing? Or do they mean praying? Every time they pee, which is always, are they also praying?

As Gal tries to follow the rollercoastering thoughts, a huge grey horse charges on to the stage, Mo upon its back. The man holding Hung's neck lets go, seeking to evade the mighty hooves. At the same time, Mo extends a hand to Hung, wheeling Boxer so that Hung's feet leave the floor and he climbs through the air, right up, as though on wings, to land behind Mo on the grey's broad back.

Hung locks his arms around Mo's waist and Mo digs his heels into Boxer's sides, just as another of the men – large, wearing a leather jacket – tries to take hold of the grey's bridle. He has something in his other hand. Something black . . . Oh Christ, it's a gun! Boxer rears, up, up, up, like the unicorn on a fifty-pence piece, and then leaps forward, slamming back to earth, driving the man to the ground and then springing clear.

Mo spots Gal beside the tree. 'Get on the fucking mare!'

Gal staggers back to Nell as a shot rings out, struggles to get a foot in the stirrup as she's dancing and trembling with excitement. Finally, they pull themself up, just as Boxer thunders past and Nell takes off in pursuit.

Up the hill they go, through the trees. More shots from behind. A branch lashes at the sports bag around Gal's shoulders but they hold on tight, bending over Nell's neck, fingers laced in her mane. In their ringing ears, they hear John roaring with delight.

As soon as they get out of the wood and reach the better ground, the mare lets rip.

All Gal can do is hold on. They are so high, perhaps higher than they have ever been, and now faster too. Boxer and the cob are way behind them; only the moon can keep up.

On the mare races with Gal clinging to her. Around them the night is alive and full of squirming shapes: violet on black on lime, snakes and dragons and mythical beasts. Scales and wings and talons.

Beneath the beating hooves and the wind that tears at Gal's ears they hear, from deep within the hillside, from within chambers in the chalk, the downs themselves are singing.

Nine

—

Right Here, Right Now

39

Hurry Up, It's Time

——

May the first is a Saturday, so the bank holiday falls on the Monday. A long weekend, the forecast fine, the hedgerows bridal, the motorways jammed.

On the green, the maypole is dusted off and set up. Wayne watches as the kids – the boys in white shorts and tops, the girls in white dresses – practise their routine. Something goes wrong; the ribbons get in a tangle and they have to walk backwards through their paces and start again. If only life were like that.

Lou came back yesterday, slipping in an hour before closing. She gave Wayne's shoulder a squeeze and then stepped into Vern's arms, who enfolded her, dropping his lips down to the crown of her head. Half turning in the embrace, she said, 'I'm tired, Wayne. We're going up. Can you lock up by yourself?'

After she had taken the stairs, Wayne waited, not sure what he was hoping for. An invite? Or for Vern not to go, to stay below with Wayne? Vern put down the glass he'd been polishing. 'I'll say goodnight then, Wayne.'

Then he put the glass in its rack, folded the cloth, and followed on.

Wayne gets it now. What they've been trying to teach him. Seek out the good, the kind, the joyous. When the time comes, make sure you have the right gifts to pass along. The understanding makes his next task even less agreeable.

'You here to kick me out, Wayne?'

In her annexe room, Morgan's sitting on the edge of the bed. Her suitcase stands upright by the door. The look she gives him is so fierce, he remembers where he saw her before.

'You were in an airport. Qatar. You were having words with Aidey.'

'A friend of yours?'

'No.' Then, 'We served together, but I'm not like Aidey.' He hopes. He hopes. 'What did he want with you?'

'What Aidey always wanted, to get his boot on your neck. To share his misery. I knew him once. Here in Abury. Before your time.'

'What were you doing over there?'

When she speaks again, he recognises the bitterness. 'There was a lot of funding for projects. I thought I might be able to serve too. Who was the more naive, do you think? You with your gun or me with my project-implementation plan?'

'Lose some illusions?' Wayne hurries on before she can reply, the words spilling. 'I lost a part of my skull, and Gareth, and nothing—' He takes a hold of himself. 'They should seal them off, let them murder each other—'

'Reality did not conform to your fantasy of heroism and you react like a child. A racist, ignorant child. They failed to play the role of grateful rescuees, so now you will blame and damn them and never once on the whole journey will you encounter them.' Morgan looks down at her hands. 'Or so a woman once said to me.'

When she looks up, her eyes are so full of sorrow, the retort dies on his lips.

'What happened to you there?'

'I became over-involved, over-invested. I lost my judgement. So I left. I ran away.'

'You're better off out of it, you know. Out of Abury. This place will drive you mad.' Wayne finds himself wanting to tell her about the dreams. More urgent than ever now. Carly in her pink dress, with her torn throat, never far away. Even when he's awake, he's always expecting to find her in the next room.

'Is this about your and landlord's matching bruises?'

'It wasn't a fight. We have . . . an agreement.'

'Maybe it's time to renegotiate.'

'It's not what you think. It's complicated.'

'My advice? Make it simpler. It can be hard, though, can't it? To let things be simple when, deep down, you don't think you're allowed what you want, to have what you want. Hard to win a war, when the enemy is in your head.'

Her gaze is cool and clear.

'Sometimes I look at the kids,' Wayne says. 'You know, they come in here, with their unicorns and their rainbows and their pansexuality and I think, *Christ, you have no idea, no fucking idea . . .*'

'Would you want them to?'

After a moment, he shakes his head, then he says, 'The woman, the one whose name you wrote on the cenotaph. Did you love her? Did she die? Is it vengeance you want for her?'

'I have memories of her. I remember sitting at a table with her. She was working on her laptop. I was working on my laptop. I held her back from me. I kept her away for as long as I could. I want to burst into that room. I want to scream at myself for wasting time . . . but I'll take vengeance if I can get it. Or just some kind of accounting, some attempt at something approaching justice.'

'Where will you go? Will you give up?'

'No. I don't know.' But Morgan looks defeated. 'What can I do for you, Wayne? What needs to be done?'

'What do you mean?'

'There's something you need.'

His mouth is dry.

'I don't know how to ask it.'

'Ask it anyway.'

He crosses the room and sits down not quite beside her, but within reach.

'Touch my face. Put your hand over my heart and tell me you love me. Tell me you love me and you want to be free.'

'This about your agreement?'

Wayne nods.

'All right, then.'

Her hands are smaller and her touch lighter than he expected. She repeats his words back to him without faltering. When she lifts her fingers from his cheek, he closes his eyes.

'I'll be seeing you, Wayne.'

Soon he hears the wheels of her suitcase retreating over the cobbles and, as though a thread has been cut, he collapses on to the coverlet. There is a slight residual warmth. He presses his cheek where she touched him to the pillow, imagines going into the room where Gareth lies sleeping.

'I love you.'

Without hesitation, Gareth replies, 'Love you too, mate.'

'I want to be with you.'

What would he say? Wayne feels the reception flicker, like a radio frequency blurring into static.

While he waits, another scenario presents itself. Gareth lies in the bed, Wayne stands in the doorway. 'I'm not in love with you any more.'

'That's all right, Wayne.' In the bed, Gareth turns over to look out the window. There's some kind of tent below in a meadow, all decked out in scarlet and gold. 'And, Wayne?'

'Yes.'

'Will you do something for me?'

'Anything.'

'When she calls you, take a knife.'

Wayne opens his eyes. A red hair, like a thread of fire, dissects the pillow. As a child he would imagine his sheets were great open fields, making mountains with his knees, creating earthquakes at will. The red hair glints in the light and he imagines it a crack in the earth, then a stream of fire. He walks two fingers up to it, lets them prance like hooves to the melody of the William Tell Overture.

'Time to jump. Time to jump.'

When Vern comes to find him, he's still there, head on the pillow.

'How did it go?'

Wayne sits up.

'Come sit by me,' he says. 'There's something I have to give you. One last thing.'

40

Do I Have Your Blessing?

———

Where do you go when you have nowhere to go? Morgan pulls her luggage over the cobbles, swearing under her breath.

Where had Morgan gone – as a teenager – on the days where she could not bear to stay at home, to be anywhere near her parents, when she had neither the funds nor the heart to trail around the shops? It was two buses to the cinema and going alone made you a target; if anyone from school saw you, you were a no-mates, and then there were the odd men, the older men who might come and sit by you in the dark, moving ever closer, who if challenged would tell you they were just being friendly, that it was a free country.

These days, teenagers had Internet access, Netflix and social media accounts. Had Morgan been able to go online, she might have found kindred souls, some semblance of community, at least the language to recognise what was happening to her. There would have been relief from the boredom that hammered her, the four channels of TV that existed almost solely to insult her intelligence, the only decent programmes showing late at night when her father commandeered the remote to sit glued in front of the darts. But just as inevitably, Morgan suspects, it would also have meant a total absence of respite: from bullying and from the culture that manifested in the bullying. Device in hand, you could be reached anywhere.

Where could you go? Where was it safe? Very often her answer had been the library, where it was warm and dry and largely quiet. It's where her feet are taking her now.

Not that it had been entirely quiet as there were often small children, and the elderly who came in to borrow the large-print books and initiate interminable conversations with the librarians, but it was safe among the stacks. Books were abundant. Rain ran down the windowpanes. The sun cast sheets of blonde light on to the turquoise industrial carpet.

In the library, Morgan has discovered another world, her third. The first was the everyday world, the world you saw when you opened your eyes, the world of school and dinners, or tying laces and putting on your clothes the right way round. Then there was the world that she entered at night, the world that hid behind her eyelids. It was the world of dreams, where she was multitudinous, in which the familiar mingled with the uncanny, the banal and the bizarre.

The world of the unconscious, the world of dreams – you did not even have to sleep to travel there. In the right mood, you could simply drift off, floating on synaptic waves over a seabed where mysterious objects lay half buried in the sand. The unconscious was a sea of darting creatures where bubbles rose glistening, where reefs foamed, and among whose hidden passageways the tides seeped and poured.

Books, the new world Morgan discovered in the library, were portals; portals that could take you anywhere they wished, that might reproduce in perfect detail the experience of moving through the everyday world, or any world; might take the reader to ice palaces a million years old where jagged chandeliers the size of blue whales hung over vast, silent auditoriums or to 1950s truck-stops in California – everything constructed via marks on a page, or rather offered in blueprint, since reading demanded participation.

Each of the three realms was connected to the others, and each realm was shared. Even the unconscious world was not entirely discrete: secret currents fed from it into a deeper body of water, an oceanic mind, somewhere far off, or near and yet very deep. Which was why you occasionally found in a work of art your most private unarticulated thoughts, met them there with a jolt of recognition.

Now there was the Internet, an almost perfect simulacra of the collective mind, containing every teeming thought anyone had ever had, lust-filled and perverse, murderous and virtuous, absurd and banal and clamouring, its operating systems and software largely devised by young men on the West Coast of America, and now the Internet was in the library.

Morgan walks through the doors and surveys the half-dozen or so monitors that line the back wall. Not much else has changed: a silver-haired librarian sits behind a desk, a noticeboard bears news of the WI market, the children's corner has its beanbags and stuffed animals, and then there are the rows of bookshelves. The air smells as she remembers: paper, warm plastic, an indefinable element.

The luggage trolley glides over the carpet, past the large-print section, past the sign announcing the library's eBook and audio catalogue, towards the remotest corner, where shielded from view on all sides, Morgan plucks from the shelves a hardback she vaguely recognises and, opening a page at random, steps back into a story that fifteen-year-old Morgan left half-read. The same story, but not the same reader . . .

The kynge stablysshed all his knyghtes, and gaff them that rychesse and londys, and charged them never to do outrageousity nor murder, and allwayes to flee treson; also, to gyff mercy unto him that asketh mercy, and allwayes to do ladyes, damesels, and jantilwomen succor upon payne of death . . .

A dimming of the light as a cloud moves westwards. But what about, Morgan wonders, the women who were neither ladies, nor damsels, nor gentlewomen? And whose lands were the knights given?

It's how Carly's mum, Shirley, finds her. Nose deep in a book, bum perched on her suitcase.

'Faye Morgan!' Shirley, panting, two decades older but with exactly the same hair, is in pursuit of something. 'Did you see a rotten little beast?'

'Can't say I have.'

'They must hate us here. I took the two youngest ones so Linnet could have some me-time while everyone's watching the game.' Shirley fans herself with one hand. 'I had them at the play-park this morning. Then we went home for lunch and I set them up with the iPads. Angelo wanted to watch Lego videos on YouTube. I came back with the sandwiches, and one of the figures, he's saying, *Take that, you German bastard!* and they've got him, don't know how, urinating over a corpse.'

'A Lego figure?'

'Yes. He cried when I took it away. Sobbed his little heart out. So I brought them here and he's run amok.'

Morgan closes the book. 'I'm sorry if putting Carly's name on the cenotaph upset you. It was a shock, finding out.' For a second she wonders if she's done something unforgivable in saying Carly's name. 'Arthur said—'

'Arthur can take himself off to the North Pole!' Shirley takes a quick sidestep and grabs a wrist, pulling a wriggling youngster into view. 'Come on. We can talk at the house.'

The girl, Lily, is like Linnet to look at, or Linnet as she once was. Angelo has no front teeth and the scabs on his knee are picked pink. On the way home, he hurls one of his library books in the hedge and it's not till Shirley threatens to tell his mum that he retrieves it. A bit further on, they meet a woman with a puppy and he falls to his knees to pet it, cooing. Lily bends forward and slowly puts out a hand. Almost immediately, she takes a sharp step back.

'He tried to kiss my fingers!'

Once inside, Shirley packs them off upstairs.

'They'll be going home soon,' she says brightly and puts the kettle on. 'You dieting, Morgan? You did ever so well that time, remember? I've got some magazines if you want them. Can't get into it myself. I keep thinking I must have a go, but I don't know. It's kind of a hopeful thing to diet, isn't it? I used to have this image of myself in the future, slim and smiling. It inspired me. I can't see it now.'

'How did it make you feel, the image?'

'Light. But I can't imagine ever feeling light now.'

'She was a beautiful girl.' Immediately, she hates herself for saying *beautiful*. Like it mattered.

'You were all beautiful to us. Because you were ours.'

'That's the sort of thing my mum would have said.'

'I heard she passed.'

'She did. I lost someone else too. I lost . . . I lost my girlfriend.

Violent death. I don't mean to add to what you've gone through. I don't . . . Why did you say Arthur could go to the North Pole?'

Shirley unwraps a packet of biscuits, slides half a dozen gingers on to a saucer.

'Arthur was very sorry and I don't disbelieve him. But he runs everything here. Everyone owes him something. At the time, I was in shock. Everyone was. Living is grief enough, but with Carly it was like the cutting of an artery. I wasn't well for a long time. No one wanted to think it had anything to do with one of us, someone who lived here in Abury, but as time went by, I thought to myself someone knew something. Someone saw something. They must have. Why didn't Arthur put the pressure on? Offer a reward. When the police packed up, why didn't he pay investigators?'

Shirley turns away to pour out the tea.

'You think he's here?'

'The police came to see me a couple of days ago. There's new evidence. They're going to reopen the case.'

'Maybe they'll catch him this time.'

The hand lifting the pot is steady, but Shirley's back stiffens.

When she turns, the motherly warmth is gone. Her face is cold and her voice bears an ancient sorrow.

'I don't want him caught, Morgan. I want him dead.'

*

They've barely touched their cups when there's a thud overhead and someone upstairs starts howling. Shirley hauls herself from her chair and pounds up the stairs leaving Morgan alone.

Was it not just yesterday she was here, piling through the door with Carly dumping their school bags down? Was it not just five minutes ago, Carly was ransacking the cupboards for snacks while gushing over some new paramour?

He looked so fresh in his trainers with the curtains and hoodie. He's a really good dancer. He made me laugh in Home Economics. Did you see his eyelashes? The way he carries his bag?

'All they needed was a heartbeat, Carly,' Morgan whispers. 'You thought it was them. But it was you. You were so fresh. You danced so well. It was your light shining, Carly. It was you all along.'

When she hears Shirley coming down the stairs, Morgan wipes the tears from her cheeks and downs what's left in her cup. Shirley's on the phone. She pulls the handset away from her ear.

'Just a mo. It's Linnet.' When she hangs up, she's bright with the pleasure of a morsel of gossip. 'She wants me to hang on to Lily and Angelo for a few hours. There have been developments!'

Once Shirley's dished the latest news, Morgan asks her if she minds looking after her suitcase for a bit and takes down the address.

On the doorstep, she realises the empty mug's still in her hand. On the side, it says: *Nothing tastes as great as thin feels!*

The forecast was wrong. It's started raining, a proper shower, cold and penetrating from out of a blank, blue sky. Morgan hands back the cup, tapping a finger against the motto.

'Freedom does, Shirley. The blood of our enemies. Vengeance. Justice. Victory.'

41

Week Three

———

She has slipped a key into the lock of his heart and it swings open, on its rotted hinges. And what's that there, cowering in the darkness?

Now Lance spends all his nights in the other room and when she asks him if he slept well, he tells her politely that he did and smiles a ghastly corpse smile. A couple of times she jerks awake in the night with a rabbit-heart, ears straining. Nothing moves, it's always quiet, but like in the moment breath is drawn before the scream.

'And how did you sleep?' Lance asks.

'Fine,' Gwen says and they spend the day circling one another, lying, and all that was liquid and natural between them is lumpen and artificial. Their teeth clash, she hands him a cup of tea and, startled, he dashes it from her hand. Sometimes, his words come out oddly and she can't follow what he's saying.

At the sink, rinsing the breakfast plates, Gwen blinks and sees the photographer's terror-stricken eyes as the waters close over his face.

Lance wanders in, unshaven, naked to the waist in tracksuit bottoms. In her head, Gwen hears Tamara say, *He looks like a road mender, dear.* In her childhood, you were allowed to say anything about the Irish. The targets change but the hate remains the same.

'How's it going? You know . . .'

She lets him dangle.

Finally, he manages, 'In the front area?'

It doesn't hurt any more but it's still a bit off. 'Much better, thank you!'

Hard to keep the snappishness from her voice. Particularly hard today since both are aware how, under different circumstances, they'd be spending it. This afternoon, it's the big game, England versus Germany at Wembley. Kick-off at three.

Under different circumstances, they would have watched it together, with Arthur and Arthur's men. Perhaps at the pub, but more likely up at the house, in the big room with the cinema screen and all the sofas. Gwen would have walked among them, ferrying round beers, maybe hot dogs at half-time. She'd have lowered her eyes when they looked at her, ribbed them gently – *thirsty today, aren't you?* – felt the special warmth in their voices when they thanked her, when they told her that she, Gwen, was an absolute star.

Maybe, afterwards, she and Lance would have contrived a few moments alone, on the stairs, or in the room where they collected the recycling. Lance helpfully carrying in the empty bottles, Lance helpfully pressing her up against the wall, lips against her ear, erection pressing into her belly.

When England lost – inevitably, inventively – she'd make herself scarce as the mood soured, as the men grumbled about the Krauts, started humming the music from *The Dambusters* and otherwise referencing the wars of their grandfathers and great-grandfathers, the wars they held so close, but knew only through films.

Meanwhile, the one actual soldier among them sipped his soda quietly or offered up a few words here and there. It's only now, up close, she sees the energy it takes, the effort, what it costs him.

I got him back wrecked. That's what one of the women had written in the chatroom. Gwen's been lurking on PTSD forums, scrolling down threads where the wives and mothers and sisters of veterans share their woes, their desperation, outstretch their hands to one another. In the UK, if PTSD's not reported within six months, they're not entitled to help from the services.

The war on terror cost six trillion, but we live with terror every day and there's nothing.

I just want help for him. Proper help.

The kids are frightened of him. The dog is frightened of him.

When Gwen has had her fill there, she goes on Instagram. In the living room, with a cup of tea steaming gently on the side, she checks out her notifications. She hasn't posted anything since before Arthur's birthday party, but there are hundreds. More comments than likes. More hate than love. More contempt. More disgust. More ridicule.

Gwen has always known her followers' regard, like that of Arthur's men, was conditional. But it was an easy thing to forget.

She goes back to her Insta feed and scrolls at speed as though to put a great distance between herself and what she's just seen. There are holiday homes and plates of food, pets and adverts for beauty products, and every now and again, a female face upturned to the camera, lips slightly pouted. Usually the selfie-women are young, but there are older ones too. The messages they are designed to convey differ, but the effect is one of supplication as though the women are asking for mercy.

Well, they're not going to get it from Gwen. Not today, not with what she's just breathed in. *Why do I hate you all so much?* Gwen wonders. *Why do I hate your eyebrows?*

'What are you looking at?' Lance asks.

Gwen glances up from the sofa, unknits her brow.

'Just some rubbish or other.'

'I'm going out now. I'll have a bit of a run. You'll be all right?'

'I will.'

'If someone rings the doorbell, maybe just don't answer it.'

'I said I'll be all right. You go. It'll do you good.'

He bends down to kiss her, and she experiences him all in a rush, the dark bending head, the smell of him, his warm, soft lips on hers, and she's flooded with the hope that everything can be good again between them.

But once the door clicks shut, she's ambushed by panic as though it's been waiting for him to go in order to strike. Gwen paces from room to room, puts the chain on the door and peeps out the front window. The state of the bathroom sink is enough to bring her to tears. The light in the kitchen is ghoulish. Why is the bin so sinister? Like it's trying to suck her in face first. What's so wrong here?

Her mum calls but she can't bear to speak to her. The phone falls skittering from her hand into the sink and she waits, eyeing it, till it's gone silent before picking it back up.

'My mother enjoys my misfortune,' Gwen whispers to no one and goes to sit on the edge of the bed.

In her mind, she hears a great tearing, as though a veil is being rent. She finds herself shivering. A memory comes – or rather, since the memory is of something that has happened many times, perhaps it is more of a vision, a compounded memory? *Gwen bends down to undo the horse's girth and pulls first the saddle and then the blanket free, and the horse quivers, shakes its skin, a reflex to being unburdened, a reflex in response to being free.*

There is the hovering sense that this is how freedom would feel.

But freedom is not free, a small voice tells her. It comes at a cost. You must give up the toxic dream, the dream that is weakening you every moment, like an incubus crouching over your sleeping figure. Who will you be when you give up your illusions?

Old, Gwen thinks. *I will be old. Because you are young, and then you are not.* And what does that mean? Why does her heart pang so at the thought? Youth was no use and now it's gone; its last drips drop from her fingertips. Her hands are dry. The gift is going.

The phone rattles again in her hand. It's a DM from Linnet. *U ok? Can u come here? Just u. They're all out. It's really important. Gwennie, I need to see u.*

Gwen ransacks the house for a scrap of paper and a pen to scribble down a note for Lance, only the pen's run out, and then she's distracted because on the way to look for another pen she realises her shoes aren't by the door where she left them, and then she can't find the trucker cap.

Eventually, she locates both shoes and hat and thrusts herself out the house before she can lose her nerve, slamming the door behind her, and forgetting all about the note to Lance.

42

England vs Germany I

———

There will be three guests at the party, although since all come uninvited you can hardly call them guests. Gwen arrives first on Lance's mountain bike. The ride's done her good; the fresh air, the sense of agency. After she's spent an hour with Linnet, she'll start sorting things out, get replacement bank cards for the ones that burned, a hire car, take Lance away for a few days, even a few weeks if that's what he wants. Her legs pump the pedals to get her up a hill. Doctors. A therapist. Specialists.

There's a car, a black Mercedes, parked up in the lay-by near the turning into Linnet's and Gwen gives it a wide berth lest the driver, a dim shadow inside, suddenly open the door.

She leaves the bike on the front lawn next to a heap of kids' toys, hops up the steps and rings the bell. As she waits, she notices that, as usual, Linnet and Kay are doing their bit for global warming by leaving all the windows open and the heat on.

Linnet comes to the door wearing a powder-pink tracksuit from her range. Her hair's up in a towel and there's a faint curving scar that follows her hairline.

'Gwen!' she says. Then, 'Well, come on in.'

Inside there are thick grey wall-to-wall carpets. Velvety curtains, a plush sofa the size of a limo. There are Ribena stains on everything. Wherever you look, your eyes meet family portraits, all of which are dominated by Linnet's jutting bosom.

'You'll want a drink, then. Angelo and Lily are at Shirley's. They're due back in an hour. Let me see if I can put them off.' Linnet picks up her phone from the table and disappears off towards the kitchen. When she comes back, she's bearing a tray with glasses, ice, a bottle of vodka, a bottle of Baileys and an open carton of milk. She pours herself out a concoction and indicates Gwen do the same. The milk settles on the top, surrounds the bobbing ice.

Linnet takes a slug and reclines in her seat. 'You're not going back to him, then? Not going to say it was madness? I mean Lance saved your life twice. That's a syndrome right there.'

'It started long before that.'

'Yes, but you could say—' Seeing Gwen's face, Linnet stops. 'So it's over between you and Arthur?' Her eyes widen.

'After the miscarriages, it wasn't the same. And it's not like I was just a little bit . . . unfaithful. Not once. Not with a random.'

'Who keeps all the promises they make when they wed? Who has the perfect marriage? Of the promises I made Kay, I keep most, most days. All some days. At school everything over fifty per cent was a pass. I give it a C-plus.'

'And if you'd married Gareth. What would you have given it then?' The words slip out before she can stop them.

Linnet swirls her glass. 'I'd have given us an F for rowing. That's for sure. Not bickering but rowing. It hurt too much. The doctors say I've a high pain threshold, but not with Gareth. It was like I wanted us to be one person. Like I wanted for him to become me and me him, and for us to be in perfect accord. It drove me mad.' She tops up her glass with vodka. 'If you can't row with someone properly, you do damage. Listen, do you mind if I put the telly on, just for a sec.' She aims the remote at the screen on the wall and it leaps to life.

One of Britain's most famous commentators stands in a box above a luscious green pitch. Linnet mutes the sound.

'He's a dirty dog. A friend of mine told me a story. Well, it'd put you right off your dinner.' She smiles conspiratorially. The screen cuts to a montage of historic footballing moments between the two countries about to play, goals and misses, controversial sendings-off and disallowed goals, and then, and this was always going to be the destination, the penalty shootouts.

Cometh the hour, cometh the footage of Stuart Pearce missing a penalty against West Germany in 1990 and then of him scoring one in '96, the cords of his neck standing out like cables as he screams at the crowd.

'I always feel better after I've seen that,' Linnet says. 'I remember watching it at the time. His wife said he spent months in a darkened room watching himself miss the first one on replay. Then he had that chance to make it right. The whole country held its breath. I was a kid and I literally held my breath for him.' She casts a sidelong glance at Gwen. 'I can't imagine an occasion where the same would happen for a woman. Not in all my days. Why don't you add some more milk to the top, won't hurt your stomach then.'

On the screen the players are lining up to sing their national anthems. 'Aren't they handsome? Aren't they fine?' Linnet sighs and touches her lip gingerly with a forefinger. 'I just wish that just once, rather than play football, they'd have a big old orgy right on the pitch. I think we'd all feel a lot better for it.'

Gwen's on her second top-up when Linnet asks her how Lance is. She tries to tell her as best she can.

'No. I mean how is Lance today?'

'Today? You mean because it's my wedding anniversary? I don't think Lance knows. I mean, it's not like Arthur could ever remember it.' Suddenly, Gwen puts it together all in a rush – the absent kids, the scarce husband – today is also the anniversary of Gareth's death.

After another drink, Linnet shows her where they sucked the fat out of her arse, then where they injected it between the skin and muscle of her top lip.

'Not all of it, of course.'

'What do they do with the rest of it? Did you donate it to the poor? Sell it on your website?'

'Not a clue, Gwennie.'

'Sometimes I think you're leaving us bit by bit, smuggling yourself out in pieces. Sometimes I think you're cleverer than all of us.'

At that, Linnet gives her an appraising look, touches her quickly and gently on the back of the hand.

'Why did you send the message? What was the important thing you needed to talk about?' Gwen says.

'What message?' Linnet says but, before Gwen can answer, the doorbell rings, sounding a long electric note, a heraldic trumpet call that reverberates through the house.

*

'Oh,' says Gwen when Linnet walks back into the living room with Morgan at her heels. 'What's she doing here?'

'Good question,' Linnet says. She's slurring a bit. Morgan looks from the table with the bottles on it to Linnet. Is it the booze or the lip?

'Bring me a glass and I'll tell you.'

Linnet skips off to the kitchen. 'All right, but don't you start without me.'

From the sofa, Gwen gazes up at her. She's wearing jeans, a sweatshirt several sizes too big and a cap from which her golden hair springs free. She is older than she looks in the photos in the newspaper, simultaneously more and less beautiful, and crucially, all herself.

Linnet hands Morgan a glass and collapses down on to the sofa, all but clapping her hands. She digs the remote out from under her, inadvertently changing the channel. Instead of the football, the screen cuts to a man standing on a dirt road outside a concrete building.

'For now, girls will continue to be able to come to school here,' he says into the microphone, 'but for just how long, no one knows. This is me, Sikander Shah, for BBC News.'

For a moment, all three women watch in silence.

'Do you think they'd want us at their whim if they could?' Linnet says. 'Here, I mean. They get so quiet, don't they? You wonder what they're thinking. What's in their hearts. If they could, would they turn back the clocks to a hundred years ago, when we couldn't vote and they had all the good jobs, and no matter what your marriage was like, you couldn't get divorced?' She looks from Gwen to Morgan. 'Sorry, sorry,' she says. 'Don't let me hold you back.' And she waves with her hand, as if to say *play on*, presses the mute button and changes the channel back to the game.

Morgan walks over to the vodka bottle, pours herself a double, and knocks it back. She wavers for a moment and then gets down on her knees on the grey shagpile carpet.

'Gwen,' Morgan says, 'I need your help. I've come to ask for your help in holding Arthur to account. For the love we once had for one another, I ask your mercy and for your assistance. My heart's broken and if I don't get some justice, if I can't get some tiny measure of it for her, the poison's going to take me and I will go under.'

When she's done, Gwen can hear her own heart thudding in her chest. She has a clifftop feeling, even though it's only Morgan. Morgan with her freckles and red hair – a bit faded now, she sees. Morgan, whose skin has lost its dewiness and grown a touch slack around the jaw. Morgan, whose eyes are lined from laughing at jokes Gwen did not get a chance to hear. Morgan who is still Morgan, but also a stranger, who has been gone so long and who never came when Gwen needed her.

Even now, she's here about Arthur.

Morgan hates you, Arthur had written. And why not? Everyone else does. And even if she doesn't now, she will.

Gwen's heart shudders. She feels it leap up as if to say *No, don't*— as she narrows her eyes and says, 'He told me you tried to blackmail him. Why don't you go after the men who actually killed her, or gave the orders? Because you can't, so you come here and have a go at Arthur.'

Morgan climbs to her feet, her face stricken. Nods a couple of times. 'I suppose I should have known better than to come to you.'

Both women clutch their hands to their chests and everything between them feels impossibly black and hard and old, like a stone hewn from granite thousands of years ago.

Tears in Morgan's eyes. Tears in Gwen's. Because what can dissolve it? What can they do when it will not budge an inch? When it weighs so many thousands of tonnes? What are the magic words they can utter?

And just then, the doorbell goes again . . .

43

Proof

———

'Just so you know, I'm non-binary, not asexual.'

'Is that so?'

Mo lies stretched out on Gal's sofa, eyes closed. Everyone else is watching the football. Gal returns to clattering at the keyboard in front of them. After a moment, they say, 'Why did you go out to the house the first time again?'

'I told you. I met an archaeologist and asked her to show me the long barrow.'

The clattering pauses. 'Where did you meet her?'

Mo sits up. 'Oh, out on the downs. I was sitting on a stone playing the flute one morning and up she popped—'

'You do not play the flute.'

'I do!'

A pause.

'You're right. It's a lie. I met her in the pub. I persuaded her to take me out to see it.'

More tapping. 'What was she like? Did you fancy her?'

'Yes. I did.' Mo scratches his head. 'It got out of hand. I think she was married with a kid. I wasn't intending to . . . I just wanted to see the barrow. Once we were inside . . . It was like being possessed. Hot but . . . really weird. It was a bit careless.'

Gal's mouth becomes a tight line.

'That night at the grow house. One of those men had a gun. You could have been killed. Or me, or John, or Hung. That was careless too. Do you actually care about anything, Mo?'

'Why don't you ask Arthur that question? Your great hero.'

'What are you going to do with your life? Sit around criticising your dad while living off his money.'

Mo springs up off the sofa and walks over to the glass doors.

'I'll tell you what, Gal, I'm not going to spend it staring down the infinity hole of a screen while everything that truly matters is sucked into it. I watched Arthur do that. I think you might, though. That's what carelessness looks like, if you ask me.'

In the forest, the trees are decked in all their finery, as though May Day is the party they've been waiting for all year long.

'Hung wants to go home,' Mo says. 'See his gran, spread some of the money around. I might go too. Maybe you should come.'

Gal wants to die. They can't believe they're being such an arse.

'Do you fancy Hung?'

For half a minute, maybe longer, nothing happens. Mo taps his fingers against the glass and then turns and comes over to sit beside them in front of the monitors.

'I thought you were all about things being open-source.' Then, seeing the miserable set of Gal's shoulders, Mo says quietly, 'I am not interested in Hung, not in that way. I like you, Gal. I care about you.'

He takes their hand in his, lacing the fingers tight. Gal pushes off the desk and the chair rolls over the floor, till their lips bump into Mo's.

A couple of seconds later, Gal is once again staring fixedly at the screens, snow-white cheeks blooming rose-red.

'We could go for a ride later,' Mo ventures. 'Take the horses out. I'll bring my flute. We could—'

'Fuck!'

Mo blinks. 'Well—'

'No!' Gal rises from the chair, taps at the monitor right in front of them. 'Look, Mo. Look at that.'

Mo takes in the page of code. 'You'll have to help me. What exactly am I supposed to be seeing?'

'Proof,' Gal says. 'Oh God, I knew it. I knew it wasn't Bors.'

315

44

Black Chapel

———

At the lake, Lance has an awful feeling and immediately wishes he could see Gwen, then remembers he can, that she's at his house right now. He imagines calling Arthur: *Will you take her back and dole her out in spoonfuls?*

She's not a cure, just a drug, a temporary painkiller.

'Oh God, I'm sorry,' he says to no one. 'I'm sorry.' He loves her truly, and deeply wishes she would go away. Because he can't hold on to himself and perform personhood all the time.

The sky's inexplicable splendour is replicated upon the reservoir. A damp gust of wind carries with it a snatch of music – kids having a party in the woods, perhaps. Lance has seen their spots: the black smoking rings from their campfires, the crushed silver cans, the streamers, the flattened turf where they have held their revels. He always imagines Gareth among them.

A man is fishing on a rowing boat in the middle of the lake, line sunk beneath the water. As Lance hurries on, he feels the fisherman's attention on him, alert, as though waiting for Lance to ask him something, perhaps an important question with an important answer. But Lance doesn't know what it is.

Everything is a failed test.

By the time he's halfway round, the need to see her again is so bad, he runs home at a sprint. He's not put a foot inside before he knows she's gone. *Taken her chance when he was out. Must have been planning it ...*

Still, he roams from room to room, looking behind doors and even in the wardrobe.

He should have his breath back by now, but it's getting worse. In and out. In and out. He sounds like a fucking donkey. He blunders out and skirts round the house just to check.

Back inside, a part of him says ruefully, *You could have left me my bike, Gwen,* as he slides to the kitchen floor and lays a cheek against the filthy lino.

An oven chip, a baked bean and a teaspoon lurk under the fridge right in his eyeline.

'So, lads, what are we hiding out from?'

'A psychotic break, I expect,' the teaspoon says. 'You know, like those other couple of times. Hallucinations, delusions, odd behaviour.'

'Ah right, I see.'

After a while, his breath gets back to normal and something else takes over, brisk and commanding. The kind of internal force that announces itself when there's a natural disaster or you set the chip pan on fire. *Right,* it seems to say, *now's our chance.* Lance listens, nods, puts the requested items in a backpack and heads out again.

*

At times, in winter, Lance has looked at the trees, and thought about how they had lost everything – how appalled they were, taken back to the bone, all their joy and laughter gone – and he could not imagine they would wish to ever do it again: to bud to leaf to blossom, to green and grow glorious. How can they? Or is it that they have no choice?

Among the hills, the grass is weeping. Once or twice he reaches down and touches his hands to the track, to the earth and stones along the Ridgeway, and through his hands he hears the ox driver's song. An old boy had sung a snatch for him once, claiming to have learned it from his grandfather. Oxen wouldn't work without singing. But no one sings to the animals on the big farms any more, no one remembers the songs.

At Snap, he makes his way through the trees and between the tumbled graves to the chapel. Within its empty, lichen-painted walls, Lance feels a brief cessation of pain. He sits upon a stone and gazes at the ivy, at the nests among the rafters. A dry bone lies at his feet, brought in by a fox perhaps, most likely from a lamb. What's left is a joint with an empty socket. Idly, he picks it up with his injured hand and sticks his finger inside.

Behind meaning is so much meaninglessness. Meaning is a whisper. No meaning is the roar, the roar so loud, so loud, you couldn't hear meaning any more. And the sound of no meaning is frightening. To be frightened by something no one else seems to hear. He can't shout above it. He can't make himself heard.

Lance's finger moves the joint one way and then the other, one way and then the other, and when he looks up, it is no longer day and the chapel is not the same chapel as before.

In the windows are panes of coloured glass through which a shimmer of moonlight falls. Before him, across an expanse of paving slabs, within the chapel's nave, is an altar, and upon the altar lies a body beneath a white shroud. It is the body of a knight and at the head burns a single bright candle.

Lance puts down the bone and gets to his feet. Even at such a distance, he can feel the warmth of the candle's flame. There is a curtain behind the altar, a tapestry of some kind. The body does not stir within its winding sheet.

Nearing, Lance cannot believe the size of the knight. Alive he would have stood nearly eight feet tall. At his side is a sword in a scabbard and there, behind the knight's head, something glints in the shadows.

Lance takes a step closer and reaches for it. All at once there comes a savage, ringing laugh and from the curtain emerges a black hand that puts out the candle.

45

England vs Germany II

———

The men. The beers. The game still in the early stages. England one up and playing well – the team not quite the team of old: younger, sunnier, more jubilant. The men lean forward as though catching a whiff of victory.

Nice one, my son. Nice one, my son . . .

Arthur sits in his chair at the back, ashen-faced. Last night, he stayed up and read everything Rashida Taher had ever written that was available in English on the Internet. Papers and blogs and tweets. Once the supply was exhausted, he thought he'd be done with it. Instead, what he'd read gave birth to rankling questions, and this led to him imagining what Rashida's answers might be, and then she was walking and talking and making jokes in his head, because she was funny, that came across right away, witty and passionate, furious and likeable.

In the small hours, he called his mentor on the East Coast, where it was earlier, hoping for some words of reassurance. Only, when he finally got through, something was off. As they spoke, Arthur imagined him, the great man, standing on the terrace looking out over Lake Washington, the evening sun glinting off the famous glasses.

His voice sounded hoarse, like he had a cold.

'—there's going to be some bad press. It dates back . . . well, it dates back to many years ago. The lawyers are working on straightening it out, but there's going to be some press. Try not ... well, try not to think badly of me, Arthur. It was a different time.'

And his mentor had hung up.

What had Morgan said? *Something's rotten in Abury, Arthur. Something stinks to high heaven.* What will he find if he follows the smell back to its source?

For some reason, the idea paralyses him. He looks up at the game. If England win today, if England win ... maybe everything will be made better. It's an encouraging thought. England will win and everything will be as it should be.

Gal enters the room at a pace, Mo and Hung at his heels. They stop in front of the giant TV screen, working out how to pick a way through to Arthur.

'Arthur, we need to talk. I've been looking at the code, at the logs, and something's not right—'

But Gal's voice is drowned out by shouts to get out of the way as one of the young forwards – the one with the tattoo of the Jamaican flag, the one whose cars interest certain newspapers so much – streams down the pitch towards Germany's goalkeeper, until a German defender brings him down with a sliding tackle that misses the ball completely and crashes into the player's ankle.

Cries of *foul* give way to roars of approval as the referee awards a penalty.

'Hey. Hey. Hey. Move out the way, you big girl.'

Gal tries not to cringe. Their hair is tucked behind their ears, their baggy black T-shirt carries a neon scrawl that reads, *Not my circus, not my monkeys.*

'Dad, you're going to want to hear this,' Mo says. 'It wasn't Bors. Gal says it can't have been. They went through the laptop they found at Bors's house and the log on his work computer. None of it corresponds. Bors was in online meetings, writing emails, at one point on a fucking plane, when the laptop shows the hacker was active. Which means they're still out there. I've been trying to call Mum but she's not answering. We went over there but no one's home. Maybe they just popped out but—'

Is Arthur even listening? His eyes seem to be focused on the big screen behind Mo, where the player, barely out of his teens, lines up to take the shot. He takes a short run-up, hesitates and lamps it straight over the bar.

'That stupid black bastard!'

Mo stops very still and the room falls quiet. Who spoke? Who said it? The men look around. Kay thinks it might have been Garlon but Garlon, he now realises, is nowhere to be seen.

'Very unfortunate,' the commentator says. 'He'll be kicking himself over that one.'

In the doorway, Hung looks confused. What has happened? Why has the energy in the room suddenly changed?

Gal takes a step towards Mo and touches his arm.

'As a father of daughters—' Kay begins and trails off.

Everyone looks to Arthur, who is looking down at his hands. Finally, he sighs and says, 'Listen, can we not do this today? Can we all . . . just not?'

46

The Invisible Knight

———

'. . . it's not a great time, Garlon. He says they're in his den and could I show you? Christ, if he wants his photos, he should fucking well fetch them! Jesus, all right, all right, and then you take them all and piss off because we are in the middle of something here.'

And Linnet leads Garlon down the staircase into Kay's basement room, into his den where he keeps all his expensive toys, his luxurious skulking hole, the teenage bedroom of his dreams, and where on special occasions he and Linnet come to play certain games.

'I didn't know you had a dog,' Garlon says, looking at the dog bed in the corner.

'We don't.' Linnet bends and pulls out a big plastic box from beneath the desk. 'Actually,' she says, straightening, 'I'm sorry but I'm not sure I want you digging through these, if you know what I mean. Tell him he'll have to come and get them himself.'

Garlon has wandered over to the wall where a cricket bat is lined up next to a fishing rod, a surfboard and a Fender Stratocaster. He picks up the bat and positions himself against an invisible bowler.

'If I tell you something, you won't tell Kay, will you?'

'What's that, then?'

'He was unbelievably shit at cricket.'

Linnet sighs, turns back towards the stairs and takes the bat full in the teeth.

'Did you hear that sound?'

'Like a stack of books falling over?'

'More like, I don't know, a sack being thrown down a well.'

Morgan runs her tongue over her teeth. 'What's in the sack, you think?'

Linnet has to come back soon so they can start fighting properly. While she's been gone, they've both held off, Morgan working her way around the room inspecting the family portraits, Gwen mixing herself another drink then thinking better of it.

'Who was it? At the door?' Morgan asks.

'Not sure. Couldn't hear what they were saying. What are you thinking?'

'What do you mean?'

'I mean when you look at those photos, you're kind of smiling to yourself.'

'I'm not—'

'On the inside.'

Morgan purses her lips as though to say, *And what would you know about my insides after all these years* . . .

'What was she like, then, this Rasha of yours?'

'Everyone loved her – apart from those who hated her, of course.'

'Not one of those.'

'It was awful. Absolutely awful,' Morgan says. Strange that Gwen should know exactly what she meant.

'How did your mum take you having . . .'

'A female companion? With more grace that I could have expected. You forget, don't you, that they love you, among all the things they want you to be.'

And perhaps it is the mention of her two other loves, Rasha and her mother, that shifts the stone a fraction. She hears her mum's voice in her head: *It won't kill you to say sorry, Morgan.* Then why does it feel like it? Why does it feel like baring your neck to the executioner's axe? The bit on the carpet before, the kneeling, it hadn't meant anything. It had been for display.

'Gwen . . .'

'Morgan, I—'

'I'm sorry, Gwen. For hurting you. I'm sorry for Aidey. I am sorry for the things I said to you. I'm sorry I turned on you. And I'm sorry I didn't come back and try to repair things. I did miss you. I missed you so much—' Only by saying the words does Morgan learn how true they are, how deeply felt. 'I am here because of you. It's not just about Arthur. I came here to Abury for you too. I just didn't know it.'

'Stop, Morgan. Please just . . . shut up.'

'Why?'

Gwen shakes her head. A wall of emotion is coming, a giant wall of emotion bearing down on her.

From somewhere, they hear another thud. Gwen looks down at her hands and then thrusts herself up off the sofa to her feet.

'You know what? I'm going to go see where she's got to.'

47

Mortal Wound

———

The men watch Mo turn and stumble away.

'Art,' Kay says, 'aren't you going to say something? Do something?'

But Arthur shakes his head wearing a face Kay last saw just before a computer was chucked out a window. The men turn back to the game, but quieter now, more self-conscious. Gal moves between them to tug at Arthur's sleeve.

'What are you doing, Arthur? How could you? This is important. It can't wait. It wasn't Bors. It wasn't Bors who hacked the car. Gwen could be in danger.'

'I'm sure Lance is looking after her, Gal.'

'Really? That's what you have to say? You have to call the police. They listen to you!'

Mo's back. He goes over to the TV, rips the plug from the wall and the screen turns black. The sports bag is slung over his shoulder. Inside is his portion of the loot. The zip makes a tearing noise as he pulls it open.

'How much, Arthur?' Mo says.

'How much what?'

'My debt to you.'

'There is no debt.'

'I think there is.' From inside the bag, Mo extracts a banded wad of notes, which he hurls at Arthur, followed by a second and then a third.

Kay catches one. They're fifties. Each bundle must add up to five grand. 'Where did you get this?'

'You know what? Have the lot. It's paid. It's all paid.' And Mo turns the bag upside down and a torrent of money thuds in a heap to the floor.

Arthur notices there is a tear on Mo's cheek. Just one. He can't remember the last time he saw Mo cry. Maybe it's the light.

'You sit here, surrounded by your paid men, by your fools. You win and they love you. But never enough to tell you the truth.' The jester persona is quite gone; only the despair that gave birth to it remains.

Arthur grips the arms of his chair. A mask has slipped from his face too. The affability and warmth have vanished and, in their place, sit cold kingship and haughty displeasure.

'I don't remember asking for your opinion, Mo.'

'They don't love you, Arthur! Your company doesn't love you either. Gwen loves you. Once I trusted you enough to get in that car with you. I let you change my whole life. Now you must listen to me—'

'Oh, so I'm the one lacking in gratitude?'

Something snaps in Mo then, like the strings of a guitar going all at once. Everyone in the room sees it happen, the moment he gives up believing Arthur will hear him. He looks down.

'The trouble with you,' Mo says, then he swallows and lowers his voice to keep it steady, 'the trouble with you is you don't pay attention. You won't see what you don't want to see. You won't listen, you've never listened. Not when it's inconvenient to you. You can't blame her for going. First you deputised me to look after her, then Lance. You just . . .' his voice rises, cracks '. . . you just gave us away!'

And he throws the empty bag down on the pile of money and strides from the room. Hung follows him. For a moment, Gal wavers.

'This can't be what you want.'

'Don't tell me what I want, Gal.'

So Gal goes too, and this time Arthur hears the front door slam.

'Shall I put it back on?' someone says. 'The game, I mean.'

One, two . . . total loss of control.

'Get out, all of you!' Arthur shouts. 'Get out! Get out! Get out! Right now!'

326

48

Astral Plane

———

A bat watches Lance from where it hangs, upside down on the chapel's stone wall. Head first, it creeps a little lower. Black eyes and a wizened canine face, tiny tongue that tastes the air.

Moonlight pooling beyond the open door. A hare darts into the circle of silver light and then hops into the chapel.

Lance, never bested, sits with his back against cold stone. His bones are powder. His flesh paste. All night long he fought what he could not see, wrestling in darkness, the fiend's breath hot in his face. He fought dismemberment and violation, and the obliterating of selfhood, and he has prevailed. The enemy lies slain among his armour on the altar steps.

A victory on the astral plane is a victory for all.

The hare hops closer, nose twitching, and bends its head to the black greaves. The suit of armour falls from the step and crashes with an empty clatter to the flagstones. The hare flees, a grey ribbon flowing from the chapel out into the ruins beyond.

The enemy is gone. The dead knight is gone. The glinting cup in the shadows gone.

A breath of wind reaches him. What had she said?

The wind bloweth where it listeth . . .

His spirit is on its own journey and he may not understand it.

In the ruined chapel at Snap – and also not – Lance takes off his armour, strips himself until he is naked. He will not fight again. Here or anywhere else.

The night is violet. In his chest, his heart is filled with blood. He imagines it a cup and the blood love.

I wish you well.

Those already departed and those departing.

I wish you well.

Gwen, Arthur, Elaine, Wayne and Gareth, his mother, his father, Aidey, the men in the tower, Galahad and Mo.

I beg your mercy. I wish you well.

Is there anyone he has forgotten?

An afterthought: *And you too, Lance.*

No more fighting. His bag is at his side. In the quiet, he makes out the sound of the zip opening. Something within the bag moves. Then he hears the rasp of dry skin, the sound of scale upon stone.

The snake slides up the wall and casts a loose coil around his throat.

It whispers in his ear, *It is time. Are you ready?*

Lance, finding himself without words, nods once and then again.

49

What We Desyren of Men
Above All Manner Thyngs

———

Morgan waits for five minutes and then a couple more. On the screen, the game of football continues. She looks out the window and then makes a round of the family portraits.

A split is taking place.

There is her everyday self, noting with a certain glee that while in one photo Kay's hair is receding, in another more recent photo, it's not.

And then, as though standing beside her, is another Morgan. One she last saw in a mirror in a dream. The one who already knows. Who already knows . . .

The last photo on the shelf is in a pretty glass frame not much bigger than a postcard. It's a picture of Carly, wearing a pink satin dress, smiling fit to break her face. *Put it in your pocket*, the voice from the mirror says, and Morgan does as she's told, humming the bars of a tune she picked up somewhere.

A couple more minutes and she's had enough.

'Where've you both got to?' Her voice comes out shriller than she intended. There's no response. It's like the house has swallowed them up.

They're not in the downstairs loo. They're not in the dining room or playroom or study. They're not in the cloakroom with the coats. They're not in the conservatory or the kitchen.

Morgan pushes the door to the larder open, half expecting Linnet and Gwen to jump out, delighted to have lured her into a game of hide and seek. But there's just a load of cereal in boxes and Walkers multipacks.

She calls again. Nothing. Maybe they've gone outside with whoever rang the bell.

At the front door, through the pane of glass, Morgan sees a big black car is parked in the driveway. So someone is here. Somewhere in the house.

Her hand is reaching for the handle when she stops – because hasn't she just walked past a set of stairs going down, presumably to some kind of basement? And couldn't it be that the thump from earlier came from below?

Her phone's in her hand, she's ready to run. *I'll just have a quick look*, she thinks, and follows the curving staircase down and round to a dark, cluttered landing at the top of a short flight of stairs.

What game is this? What can they be playing at?

Below, Gwen sits cross-legged on the dark blue carpet, modelling a gag with her hands tied behind her back. Next to her, Linnet lies rag-dolled face down.

From Gwen's eyes, fear springs across the room to land directly in Morgan's chest, just as someone steps forward behind her, out from the shadows. Morgan receives a kick in the back and falls all the way down the remaining stairs, and the sound is just like a sack thrown down a well.

*

Garlon, so it seems, has a lot to get off his mind.

'Equality please! But you don't mean digging the roads or cleaning the sewers. Look around you. Everything you see, we built it. Every single fucking thing of value. We invented it, designed it, built it. Paid for it in blood. Fought for it. Women want equal rights, equal respect. You don't deserve respect!'

Garlon pauses as though to see what effect his speech is having on his audience: the two bound and gagged women, the third dead to the world, or possibly just dead. He frowns and attempts to pull Linnet up by her hair, wrestling her into a seated position against the wall. When he lets her go, she slumps sideways. The lower half of her face is a mess, swollen and bloody. The chips of stone that litter the carpet, Morgan realises, are her porcelain veneers. Her own collarbone is broken on the left from where she landed on her shoulder and there's a sharp pain in her side.

As Garlon lifts his hand, a hank of glossy hair comes away from Linnet's head.

'Now, that's just nasty. What he sees in you, I don't know. Now, your cousin . . .' Garlon clicks his fingers in front of Linnet's face. 'Shame. I quite wanted her to hear this. Carly, I once thought highly of. She was nice, wasn't she? Not like you three bitches. Nice. Warm. Made an effort with herself. You always felt a bit more special after talking to Carly.

'No one knew, but we were together. Secretly, like. She had a few ciders one night and fell into my arms, and I mean that literally. She was absolutely staggering. I took her home. One thing led to another. After that, we'd meet on the sly, up on the downs or in the woods.

'She was anxious, you know, in case Dan found out. But like I told her, she should have thought of that before. Sometimes, I'd make her swear to break up with him and she'd go all quiet. She didn't want to hurt his feelings, she said. But what about mine? Sometimes I wasn't very nice to her. But she always forgave me. I used to make her say it.

'Then at your wedding, Gwen, Bors gets plastered, absolutely shit-faced, and he starts crying, I mean actually crying. Tears. Snot. The works. "Garlon," he says, "I'm in love with Carly and I kissed her but there's someone else." And I was like, "Yes, Dan, her fiancé." And he was like, "No, no, she's trying to break it off with Dan, there's someone else." And I was like . . . *Oh is there, now?* Thinking *uh oh, uh oh,* because although I'd threatened to tell everyone, I didn't really want it to get out.

'And then Bors said, "Yes, there's this soldier up at Tidworth." And there was me, all cut up inside over Gwen marrying Arthur, and at the same time finding out that I wasn't special to Carly at all. It was just taking the piss and I wasn't having it.'

Garlon pokes Linnet with his toe. Still nothing. 'No one's coming to help, you know. They're all watching the footie round Arthur's.

Speaking of which . . .' And he takes his phone out his pocket to check the score. 'Nice one, nice one, two–one up! Two world wars and one world cup!'

A thought seems to occur to him. 'Where's Lance, Gwen? Did you tell him you were coming here? Sorry. Sorry. Am I silencing you?' And he pulls the gag from her mouth. 'Does Lance know where you are? Yes, or no?' From his back pocket, Garlon withdraws a knife and unfolds the blade. 'Tell me quick, before I take your old friend's eyes out.'

'Yes.'

Garlon nods. 'Suppose I better hurry up, then.'

'No. I meant no.'

'Now, Gwennie, I gave you a lot of rope. This one' – Garlon points with the knife at Morgan – 'she thought she was special. She thought she was magic. But you were the real deal. From the first time, I saw you, I was bewitched. The way you moved. The way you spoke and smiled. Your hair. Which reminds me . . .'

Garlon crouches down and brings his eyes level with Gwen's. Morgan makes a *no, no, no* noise through her gag as Garlon brings the knife to Gwen's neck, but in the event he uses it to saw through Gwen's ponytail, just above the band. When he stands up, the golden braid dangles from his fist. For a second, he looks a touch embarrassed. 'I honestly don't know what I'm going to do with it, but I do want it.

'Look, Gwen, I understood when you married Arthur. I wasn't happy but there was something right about it. He was the best of us. And it wasn't like I didn't get to see you. And then, you know, when the tech had come on a bit, I got to see a lot of you. Listen to your messages and read your texts and watch you on the security cameras. Like my own private show.

'The thing about anti-virus software, you see, is it makes excellent spyware. It really does. That's why Arthur's on such good terms with all the surveillance agencies. I think they cottoned on about *Black Prince* pretty sharpish. Promised to keep it under their hats if he let them use his software to snoop about. Expect they gave him a hand here and there too.'

Garlon swishes the severed ponytail through the air, then stuffs it into his back pocket. His face hardens.

'When people started whispering about you and that Irish fucker, I didn't believe it. Not Gwen, I said to myself. What a fool you made of me, and for years and years! There was that time, at the party, after the christening, when I nearly had a word with you. You were out of line but I let it go, put it down to all those kids you lost. Far too soft on you, I was.

'Anyway, with Carly it was simple. I just told her to meet me, spiked the whole team with GHB – not quite enough of it, it turns out – and went and did it. I got lucky with the rain and the cows and all that. Much more planning and preparation this time round. Unfortunately, it seems like I made a bit of a mistake, hiding Carly's knife round Bors's place while I was lacing his cornflakes. Well, the milk if we're being specific. Bors has it delivered to the step as it's better for the environment. Oh Bors! Was there ever a bigger twat than Bors? The little grimaces when we were having a laugh. That supercilious look. Anyway, Kay tells me he's got some photos that will put old Bors in the clear. Even if I destroy them, he'll say something. The police are reopening the case. Whichever way I look at it, Galahad or Arthur will work it out in the end. If you hadn't run off with Lance, the poor sod already would have, so thanks for that.

'Anyway, so where I'm going with this is, I've got to be off. Now, I got myself a fake passport off the dark web, used Bors's powers as CFO to tidy away a nice chunk of change for myself, and sorted myself a place to hide out till things calm down. Then I'm going to fly off somewhere sunny and take a leaf out of Linnet's book. A few nips and tucks and things will be sweet.'

Garlon's voice softens. 'But I couldn't very well leave without saying goodbye to my Gwen, could I? Couldn't let you get away with it.

'Which is why I got them all round Arthur's, why I sent you that message from Linnet's phone, and why I've got a boot full of petrol. Bit of a surprise Morgan here turning up. Made me think twice for a moment, but then I decided to look on it as a bonus.'

Once again, Garlon checks his phone. 'By my reckoning, we've got thirty-five minutes of play left to enjoy ourselves, unless it goes to extra time and penalties.' He bends down and cuts Gwen's bonds. 'Get up.'

Morgan groans.

'Sorry, Morgan, that not to your liking? You know, you're looking a bit peaky.' He takes out her gag. 'Anything you'd like to say?'

Her face is wet with sweat, and her side is wet too. Something is sticking into her. 'A curse on you, on all like you!'

'Who made us this way? Who, if not you? If not our mothers?'

Gwen crawls over to her. 'Oh Crumb, I'm sorry. Sorry for everything.' To Garlon, she says, 'I'm just going to have a look, all right? I'll just take a quick look.' And she lifts Morgan's shirt and there's a big wound there in her side, all colours of red and pink and oozing blood.

'Christ,' Garlon says and looks away and maybe Morgan whispers something to Gwen, maybe she doesn't.

'Leave her. Get up. Now. Get up!'

Slowly, Gwen climbs to her feet.

'Right, what I want you to do is go stand over there – you know, pretend that's the door. And you're going to walk through the door and you're going to see me, and you're going to hurry over and then you're going to kiss me, really kiss me, like you mean it, and you're going to do that thing with your leg like the girls do in films.'

'I'm not your dolly. I'm not your thing.'

'I beg to differ.'

So she goes and stands in the corner and pretends there's a door and hurries through it, and then speeds over to Garlon.

Grimacing only slightly, Gwen lifts her face to his. He holds her to him, the knife gripped in one hand.

'What is it, Gwen? What is it you want?' Garlon whispers.

And now, finally, right at the end, she knows. It's not Arthur, or Lance, it's not a person. It's nothing anyone can give her. It's not a thing at all.

And she takes the curved shard of glass – the one from the photo frame, the one she pulled from Morgan's side – and stabs it into Garlon's neck with all her strength and tells him what it is.

'The sovereignty,' Gwen says.

Garlon flails at her, lashing out with the knife, and Gwen goes over backwards, hand clutched to her face where the blade has caught her. Garlon falls too. He drops the knife and presses at his neck with both hands to stem the flow of blood.

A noise behind him and he turns. Linnet is on her feet. Linnet is looming over him, face smeared in blood, her teeth filed to points.

'You killed my cousin,' she says and raises the cricket bat over her head.

50

Green Chapel

——

After the day Wayne's had, you'd think he'd sleep deeply. The exchange with Morgan and then the scene with Vern. The footie, initially watched by an assortment of regulars, and then stormed by a horde of Arthur's men around the half-time mark, snorting, rancorous and at odds with one another, kicked out the big house for some infraction no one would name. Another phone call from the woman wanting Mo's number. This time, something in her voice kept him on the line.

'I do know him. I was staying with you a couple of months ago.'

'I can't give it out. But, you know, he's always in here. You could just come by.'

The second half had passed in a blur of pint-pouring – John, flush with cash, fat as a flea and waving fifties; Kay thundering nonsense; the whole pub roaring. It had gone to extra time and then to penalties. Germany scored, England scored. Germany missed, England missed, and so it had gone on. Finally, it went to sudden death and the English keeper got a hand to it and tipped it over the bar. The next one was for the match. The young striker who'd missed the earlier penalty came out.

As he lined up, Wayne fancied he could hear the whole country falling silent. In that moment, he'd had an unexpected thought. *Fuck them*, he thought. *Walk away. They don't deserve it.*

But the young man in the white kit had taken a short run-up and then placed the ball effortlessly in the top-right corner of the net, the German goalkeeper falling like scythed wheat to the left. In the ensuing bedlam, no one had noticed the sound of the sirens, not until they were right outside the window, the convoy of police cars and ambulances tearing through the market square, deafening them all. And then, when they'd passed by, in the moment of quiet, Kay's phone ringing . . .

But Wayne does not sleep well, because the girl in the pink dress comes back.

'Thick,' she says. 'Fit but thick. Gentle knight—'

Wayne pulls the bedsheet over his face. 'I know, I know, avenge your most cruel murder.'

Carly snorts, 'Job done.'

Wayne lowers the sheet a few inches and peeps out. She looks different, he realises. Her wounds are gone. At the foot of his bed, she stands pale in the darkness. 'Come,' she says, extending a slender arm, 'come and see.'

Wayne feels about the floor, slipping on yesterday's clothes. When he hesitates, she stamps a soundless foot. 'There is no more time, do you understand?'

Wayne follows her, through the pitch-black pub, and then out into the street. The girl goes ahead, returning to pluck with vaporous fingers at his sleeve when he slows.

Past the cenotaph, up past the church, and on to the downs. The air is fresh and clean. The moon is falling towards the horizon where the blue night sky bleeds into green. Were it not for the girl, he would swear he was broad awake.

Further on, they come to a stile that leads into a great verdant pasture. In the east, dawn breaks as the earth rolls towards the sun. Below, lies the hamlet of Snap.

'Run,' she whispers, 'or you will be too late.'

So he runs, boots pounding through the long whispering grass, dew soaking his legs. Among the ruins, the birds are waking.

The girl is waiting for him at a dark doorway between the trees, insubstantial now as mist.

'So, knight, how will you avenge yourself upon the world?'

From inside comes the sound of something heavy falling.

*

In the ruined chapel at Snap, Wayne takes first the knife from his pocket and then his revenge, climbing up among what's left of the rafters and then out on to the beam from which Lance hangs. Spread out along the creaking timber, Wayne saws at the rope, jaw clenched, teeth gritted.

In the chapel, as the last star spies in through the broken slates, Wayne revenges himself on all that has sought to make him brutal and unfeeling, all that would have him numb and indifferent.

His heart is in his throat. 'Don't go,' he hears himself say, 'don't go yet.'

He's halfway through when the rope severs and Lance falls to the ground with an almighty crash. Wayne slips down from the beam and kneels over him, tearing the rope from his neck. He tilts back Lance's chin to clear his airway and puts an ear to his chest, thinking he hears a faint thud.

A wheezing noise comes from between Lance's lips and Wayne wishes he had some water to give him. There's only the dew on the grass. He slips outside for a moment to a patch of dock leaves and collects the drops from each on to one broad leaf. Inside, he takes Lance's head upon his knees and trickles the dew on to his tongue.

Later, Wayne dresses Lance as though he were his own child. 'Go on, put your foot through there, well done' and 'arms up, that's right'.

Blood vessels have burst in Lance's eyes and there's no hiding the marks around his throat. There's a wound to one of his palms, but it looks like an older injury.

'Do you think you can walk?' Wayne asks.

In response, Lance makes a guttural noise and climbs on to his hands and knees and then unsteadily to his feet. He seems stunned although he walks well enough. As they near the stile, Wayne turns and sees the girl waving at the edge of the trees, transparent as the morning moon.

Coming down from the church, they meet John.

He takes one look at them. 'Big night, lads? I'm sorry I missed it.'

'Bit early for you, isn't it?' Wayne says.

'You're not the only ones who know carousing.'

'Is that so?'

John touches a finger to one side of his nose, and then leans in to whisper.

'I followed them. I found them out!'

'Who, John? What are you talking about?'

'The doggers! The doggers, Wayne! Did you not see them up there? Did you not hear their airs? A man might die happy. To have partaken in their ancient rites is to be immortal!'

Ten

—

Outro

51

Wasteland III

———

In the three weeks that follow Garlon paying the girls a visit, Arthur makes an island for himself. He overrides the security gates so no one can open them, turns the horses out into the paddock and padlocks the perimeter, Cavall keeping close at his side.

The women in the hospital refused to see him. Mo won't see him. Bors, once again a free man, hangs out every single item of dirty company laundry for all to look at. *Black Prince*, Rashida Taher, Lisa Gomez – all dwarfed by Bors's claim that Arthur's been in cahoots with the secret services since Day One, that his software has been a window for anyone with an interest to look through, and that in return a blind eye has been turned to a raft of company activities not limited to the wholesale harvesting and onward sale of personal data.

And then there are the women who come forward. First one, and then when she's given a fair hearing, another, and then another, until a tipping point is reached.

Kelly Banks, formerly a junior Customer Service Agent, waives her right to anonymity and describes her ordeal at Garlon's hands – a campaign of harassment, her drink spiked, sexual assault, photos stolen from her phone; and then her ordeal at the company – the shunning after she reported what had happened, the cold-shouldering, the attacks on her character, the eventual pay-off.

On her eponymous breakfast show, Lorraine asks if Arthur knew. Kelly looks down at the floor. 'I never met Arthur personally. He wasn't around very often but when he was, he was always lovely – so I don't want to think so. But, in the end, does it really matter? If he didn't, it was because he made sure of it.'

Arthur no longer the nation's golden boy. Arthur the bad man. Arrogant and untrustworthy, greedy and despicable. Clearly not much of a father or a husband. Arthur who wasn't protecting them all at all.

And no, just as Morgan predicted, Arthur doesn't like it.

Wrong . . . Stop it . . . Duty . . .

Arthur sits in his study staring at the screen while the sun rises and sets and the moon sails over his head.

Wasteland. The virus is a thing of perfection. Arthur could not have made it, could not have come close to making it. *Wasteland,* like a melody, as immaculate as birdsong. Gal's one-time answer to an unmanageable, unjust, pain-riddled world. A teenager's response to their own pain that they couldn't imagine ever ending.

Arthur in the chair, hair growing, nails lengthening, like a stone gathering moss. Should a perfect thing not fulfil its function?

Gal, unable to access the vault in which the virus is kept secure, messages Arthur on their private network: *Don't do it, Arthur. Please. I should never have made it. We don't have the right—*

But Arthur cuts them off.

Arthur did not create the Internet, but he has been one of its masters. A seer. A king. An enchanter. An architect. A wanderer of its endless corridors and secret passageways. With *Wasteland,* he will renounce it, will make himself obsolete.

Once released, the virus will spread like a whisper, like a breath of wind. Permeating cloud, databank, server farm. Infecting systems, software, application, program, website. Hitching rides with hackers, exploiting holes, overcoming firewalls, travelling with the traffic wherever it goes, via data packets through deep-sea cables, bouncing between satellites, seeding itself in hardware, hopping from computer to phone to tablet. Pervading vehicles, watches, fridges, talking teddy bears, motorised robot-vacuums. Settling, replicating, spreading. Invisible, indiscriminate and undetected.

Within a week it would be in the government systems – in Washington and Moscow, Beijing and Brussels. It would be in supermarket, aviation tower, power station, space programme, logistic hub. It would be in ports and it would be in factories and it would be in schools.

Then, when it was everywhere, it would wake up and kill everything. Corrupting both device and network like an affliction that could lay waste both to the organs of speech – lungs, voice box, tongue – and language itself.

Isolated networks would survive. Technology could be rebuilt and replaced – although with great difficulty since the systems that controlled manufacturing would be inoperable.

Arthur imagines the computer in front of him becoming nothing more than a shiny empty box. Imagines everyone waking to find their phones and tablets and TVs inanimate.

What about the planes in the skies? a small voice asks. What about hospital incubators? But the clarity passes, the fog returns.

Unmanageable world, failed experiment . . .

On YouTube, Rashida Taher blows out the candles on her birthday cake and makes a wish. Arthur's finger falls on the space bar and he watches her frozen face in its expression of mirth until the screensaver comes on.

Duty . . . Button . . . Push it.

The house is dark around him. Cavall lies in a furry heap at his feet. Arthur stands, stretches and turns to the window.

He will do it. In an hour, more or less.

Above, in a clear sky, the heavenly circuitry lies exposed. Among the stars there shines a bright and steady light, red-hued – Mars, perhaps.

Right now, Arthur understands why other billionaires want to go into space; the only thing he doesn't get is why they want to come back.

*

'He's not my father!'

'Then why you . . .' Hung consults the translation engine '. . . behave like son?'

The argument continues as they pile out of the car in front of the towering metal gates. Hung's English is at the maddening stage, improved enough that he can understand a reasonable portion of

345

what's said, but with his ability to express himself lagging so far behind that it feels like he's trying to play a game of *đá cầu* using only his tongue.

Gal and Mo unload the ladders from the car's roof while Morgan stands to one side. Frankly, she'd been of a mind to let Arthur reap what he's sown but over the past few days Gal's panic has seeped into them all.

'Take Morgan,' Gwen said.

'Why me?'

'Because I don't want to see him.' And she pushed back her chair and went outside. She was wearing a pirate patch. The doctors still don't know if they can save her eye.

The night is black, a cavernous vault hanging over them. Hung types furiously into the phone, composing what reads like the world's saddest haiku:

My parents split up
I was six Father vanished.
Mother in Hanoi?

He holds the screen up to Mo's face.

'I came, didn't I?' Mo says.

Gal gets the first ladder up against the gates and scales it. Sitting astride the top, they take the second ladder from Mo and lower it down the other side. The moon sits on their shoulder like a slipped halo.

Once over, Gal bangs the metal. 'Ready to go!'

Hung goes up next, waiting at the top to help Morgan while Gal and Mo hold the ladders steady.

'You going to be all right? How's the collarbone? Not going to rip your stitches, are you?' Mo says.

'Well, I guess we'll find out,' Morgan mutters and starts climbing the rungs.

*

Cavall, the traitor, gives Arthur no warning of their approach; no, he lies there like he's dead until they're upon him – Mo flicking on the big overhead light so Arthur has to put his hands over his eyes – and only then does Cavall get to his paws and trot over to have a sniff at everyone's shoes.

'You can't do it, Arthur,' Gal says.

'It was your idea. You made it. You wanted it out there.'

'But I don't now.'

'Why not? What's changed?'

Gal frowns. 'All annihilation begins with the wish to start afresh. We have to love the world as it is. Besides, who's to say there is more bad than good, more pain than joy? No one can measure that.'

'Come on,' Mo says. 'Step away from the keyboard. What are you going to do, Arthur? Get yourself some Oompa Loompas? Go the full Willy Wonka?'

Arthur growls. He puts his head in his hands so his hair sticks up through his fingers in spikes. The noise comes through his closed lips and gritted teeth, alarming Cavall who dances at his side and tries to get his face to Arthur's.

Morgan steps out from behind Mo and into the room. She's wearing a baby-blue tracksuit, one from Linnet's range, and her hair is loose about her shoulders. On her cheek, there is a yellow smudge, the last traces of a bruise.

Arthur raises his head. 'Everything's ruined,' he says.

'It's always been ruined. You're only noticing now.'

'You wanted me to take responsibility. Isn't this it?' His hands twitch towards the keys and he mumbles something, something that sounds like *dutystopit*.

Mo and Gal exchange looks. What now? Are they going to have to wrestle him to the floor? Chase him screaming through the house?

And Morgan, if ever there was a chance to be the knife, is this not it? Isn't this what she wanted? Now, in the pinch, she must admit Arthur was right. What she wants is justice, but while Justice wields a sword, she also carries a set of scales.

When she speaks again, her voice is measured. 'You have lost, and you are not used to losing. It is not so bad, Arthur, or at least it gets better. People lose their jobs all the time. Their partners dump them. They get mugged and they crash their cars. They find lumps. Their friends stab them in the back . . .'

'And what do they do, Morgan?' There are stains on Arthur's

top. Beneath the wispy beard, his cheeks are hollow. She wonders when he last slept.

'They spend days in bed, or drink too much or aimlessly wander round public parks or canal towpaths. They worry. They weep. Sometimes they have a regrettable outburst. Sometimes they are sick with shame for all their failings, for all their weaknesses. They go to their friends and hope for kindness.'

'And then?'

'Then? There's a break in the weather. Or a bit of mercy. Or they try and make up for it. Or they get over it and move on. Every day there is a little more distance between you and it, and the dread lessens.'

Arthur's doing that thing men do when they're stopping themselves from crying, hunching over, heavy with it.

He brushes his keyboard and the screensaver disperses to reveal Rasha's face frozen in the act of blowing out the candles on a cake. It's a still from the video of her birthday party, the one uploaded to YouTube, the last one Rasha would ever have.

'What was her wish?' Arthur says.

'Not this,' Morgan replies and she reaches out and takes up Arthur's hand. Her fingers weave through his and she squeezes gently. 'We'll help you put right what can be put right.'

At her touch, Arthur starts juddering. His chest heaves. He gets out, 'Mo, I'm so sorry. Oh Mo—'

Mo lays his hand on Arthur's shoulder. 'Come on, Dad, there are people in the middle of streaming series. They want to know what the end is. Come back to earth, come back to earth and be human.'

52

Comeuppance I & II

————

I

What did they do to Garlon? The blonde, the redhead, the brunette.

Of course, the newspapers tell a version of the story, from the inquest, from the witness statements. But the women don't say a word – not Gwen, not Morgan, not even Linnet. Not to anyone.

What really happened? In the basement? During the at-home Punch and Judy show, the private mummers' play?

The coroner is explicit – blood loss, blunt-force trauma, multiple blows. He shows an X-ray of Garlon's skull, or what's left of it.

No charges are brought, considering the women's injuries. Considering what was found at Garlon's house, on Garlon's computer.

To Shirley, the police return Carly's bracelet, the one with the charm of a heart on it, the one she always wore.

Into the silence, whispered speculation, wild stories. At night, the inhabitants of Abury have odd dreams that they keep to themselves:

Garlon poisoned and laid in a glass coffin . . .

Garlon forced to spin straw into gold on pain of death . . .

Garlon promised by his mother to a beast-woman in a castle . . .

In their waking hours, it niggles at them, like an itch between the shoulder blades. For is there not a lag, is there not time unaccounted for? A small pocket.

The sirens were not heard until the game was over, and the game had gone to extra time, and then penalties, and then sudden death, and even if you allow for the distance the police cars and ambulances had to travel, isn't there a blank spot?

Enclosed, like an egg inside its shell, silent and smooth, its contents expunged from any record. Expunged. The more to frighten, the more to warn, the more to keep Garlon's brothers awake at night and pondering.

An Easter egg, then, like the ones Arthur hid among his code, one that if cracked open would reveal not words, but music, the sound of girls on a school bus sometime towards the end of the twentieth century, laughing at a joke told just beyond hearing.

II

Gwen comes to the meeting with the divorce lawyers on horseback wearing a black patch over her left eye. Her hair is buzzed to a half inch. In the hospital, she made Mo bring the clippers in and do it on a patch of grass out the back of the urology department.

The plastic surgeon has said that within a year or two the scar will be imperceptible. But only time can tell if she will lose the eye.

Locks of golden hair falling to the ground, blowing into the flower beds and over the car park. Mo's hands gentle on her scalp.

Afterwards they went back to the private ward where Linnet and Morgan were waiting, bickering over which films to watch. For a woman with her jaw wired shut, Linnet was making a strong case.

'All right,' Morgan had cried, '*Ghost*, *Point Break* then *Dirty Dancing* it is!'

The nurses drifted in as they finished their shifts, the room taking on the air of a sleepover. Hands creeping into giant bags of Maltesers, shoes slipped off. Later on, Gal and Hung popped in. In the corner, Morgan and Gwen whispered and snickered, until the whole room turned and shushed them as one.

On the screen, Patrick beckoned to Jennifer and she ran towards him for the big lift and this time he held her aloft, a girl exalted, a girl in flight.

And the women sighed, happy for Baby, sorrowful for reasons they prefer not to name.

In the pub garden of the Green Knight, Gwen loops Boxer's reins around a picnic bench and he lowers his old head to crop the grass.

The meeting is in a back room on neutral ground. Arthur's lawyer wanted it to be in London, but Gwen's not getting in another car anytime soon. She'll walk or go by horse or not go. There's no reasoning with her.

After the hospital, they all went to Linnet's. Now they're at the big house where Gwen can be close to the horses. Mo, Hung and Gal come and go. Three of the nurses are staying. One of Linnet's salon girls came by yesterday. She has a cousin who needs a place for a few weeks. Gwen says yes to all of them in the same way she says no to cars, her decisions steered by a presence at her elbow, just beyond vision. Female. Resolute. A guardian who stands at the door while she sleeps.

Arthur's over at Kay's, or she presumes he is.

When she pushes open the door to the pub, Wayne looks up from the till and nods. A woman Gwen thinks she recognises, although from where she's not sure, sits at one of the stools tearing a beer mat to shreds. Spotting Gwen, she seems to sink down till her chin is nearly touching the bar.

In the back room, the lawyer lays out what she calls a very generous offer. The company is not what it was. Since the revelations, since Arthur stepped down and nominated Gal as his successor, its valuation is a tenth of prior estimations. Still, the lawyer says, Gwen will get property, including the house, a modest stake in the company, a lump sum, an income for life.

'Of course, it comes with an NDA.' She looks to Arthur for confirmation, but he's just staring at Gwen, at her hair, at the eyepatch, at the pink line that runs from her brow beneath the patch and over her cheekbone.

'I don't think so,' Gwen says. 'I don't think silence is very healthy for a family.'

'Nonetheless, our offer is dependent upon—'

'Scrap it. She can say what she likes.'

The lawyer clears her throat. 'As my client, Arthur, I must advise you that I believe you are at a psychological disadvantage. It would be highly inadvisable to continue negotiations and any settlement you agree upon today will not be bind—'

'Get out.' Gwen doesn't raise her voice.

'I beg your pardon!'

'I won't ask you again.'

The lawyer looks to Arthur. 'It might be for the best—' he begins.

At the other end of the long wooden table, Gwen is climbing up, out of her chair and on to the polished oak. On her hands and knees, she begins crawling towards the lawyer and Arthur.

By the time she's halfway down, the lawyer's stuffed her papers into her briefcase and is out the door.

'What, then?' Arthur says as she looms over him. The skintight jodhpurs and grubby T-shirt; the hot-pink nails Linnet did for her on the ward, now chipped to fuck. The smell of her and the horse. In his body, desire and fear wrestle for precedence. 'What is it you want?'

'I'm not sure,' Gwen says, running her tongue over her teeth, reaching for the end of Arthur's tie. 'Maybe everything.'

*

Half an hour later, Gwen and Arthur re-enter the bar just as Mo breezes in. He's in his usual black, the single pearl trembles from his left ear. Between his jeans and trainers, an inch of rainbow sock peeps out.

'Your dad wants to talk to you, Mo.'

'I do,' Arthur says. 'Can we go somewhere and talk? I want . . . I mean, I am—'

'Excuse me.' It's the woman who was sitting at the bar earlier. Dark hair scraped back, early thirties? mid thirties? curvy like a cello. Where has Gwen seen her before?

Mo turns. 'Oh,' he says, 'hello!'

'Hello, Mo,' the woman says. She looks like she's about to have a heart attack. 'Jude, in case you—'

'Course I remember.' Mo gestures to Gwen and Arthur. 'Jude here is an archaeologist. She very kindly gave me a private tour of a long barrow.' His smile twinkles. 'It gave me all the chills. I said, this is home to one bad motherfucker.'

'I'm sure she was,' Jude says.

'She?'

'Yes. The remains in the grave were female. From the grave goods, she was of high rank, a warrior, although some of my colleagues prefer to think the weapons may have been ceremonial in purpose . . .' She swallows hard, takes a breath.

'Thing is, Arthur and I are due a heart to heart, so if it's all right with you—'

'No.'

'Sorry—'

'No.'

And Gwen sees before either Mo or Arthur what's coming next.

'I am pregnant with your child. With your daughter, to be precise.'

There you go!

How staggered Mo is, how shocked. He looks from Gwen, to Arthur, to Jude, as though expecting a punchline.

Jude continues, the words coming out in a rush, 'I thought maybe I should have a secret abortion. So no one would ever find out. You'd be surprised how many women have secrets like that. The messes they clean up alone. Never tell anyone about. The pains they take so as not to disrupt anything, not make anyone feel uncomfortable. To be good. Nodding and smiling. That was the choice, give up the baby or give up being good.'

She clears her throat. 'And then I remembered a story my mother told me once, about a girl she went to school with back in the seventies, whose married boss got her pregnant when she was seventeen, and how she had to give the baby up. Only she went back and sneaked into the hospital and stole the baby and took it home and tried to hide it in her bedroom, in a drawer. Imagine! Trying to hide your baby in a drawer . . . You ask any of our mothers and grandmothers, they can tell you stories like that.

'I've told my husband. I said sorry. I meant it. But I'm a grown-up. I know sorry might not be enough. We're trying to work it out. I want us to stay together but I know he might leave me. It's not like we can pretend the baby's his. Anyway, I wanted you to know . . .'

Jude places a hand upon her belly, just a quick tap. 'I've been so ashamed but then, after a bit, there was another feeling. It took me a long time to work out what it was. Boredom. Boredom with shame. Isn't it boring? Isn't there an alternative?'

'What happened to the baby, the one in the drawer?' Gwen asks.

'They took it away from her,' Jude says, and something passes between the two women.

'A daughter?' Mo says, his voice rising. 'My daughter?'

Gwen steps forward, and for a second the archaeologist quails, thinking, *Is she going to belt me one?*

Instead, Gwen says, 'Welcome to the family,' and takes Jude in her arms and plants a smacker on first one cheek and then the other. 'I've got somewhere to be now but come over to the house. We can talk properly. Mo, put the champagne on ice.' Then she nods at Arthur. 'See you at the fete.'

53

Be Ye of Good Cheer

———

'I did love you, Gwen.'

'Why don't you just take my other eye?'

Lance groans. 'I'm not a well man. I will be a burden to you. And I can't do it. I can't actually do it, be with another person. Moving towards it, nearing it, but being inside it . . .'

'I don't want to be inside it either!' Gwen covers her face with her hands and then lets them drop. 'So, what,' she says, 'you're going to the monks? You're going to get old running round after those miserable old fuckers? You're choosing silence and loneliness.' A flash of knowledge: 'It's a fantasy, Lance, like I was a fantasy. You think it's going to be footsteps on stone and the sound of the sea, and then one day you'll wake up and be a new man.'

'If I became a well person, I could come back,' Lance says slyly.

'So while you're there, you'll dream of being here?'

Let him go. He will come back or he won't, a voice says in her ear. *Given time, you might not want him back. What kind of love is it, when it feels like your heart's being squeezed in a fist?*

'It feels like dying,' she chokes out.

'Gwen,' he says, 'Gwen.'

And the bodies, having had enough of the stupid minds, lunge for one another.

When it's over, he holds her close and with the gentlest touch kisses her around her scar and her bad eye.

'Will you have to get a false one?'

'Maybe.'

'And you'll take it out and hide it places to scare the children?'

'I might.'

She stands, yanks on her clothes, briefly unable to locate her knickers so that she turns to face him dressed only from the waist up.

'You know, I will be all right without you. And in the end, it's cheering, it's cheering because it means we've not broken one another, that we didn't do that. But, Lance, you have to know, if, as I was once taught in a dusty maths classroom decades ago, our choices can be drawn as trees, splitting forever into infinite leaves, and each of these leaves is a life, and only one of these leaves is a life with you in it, that is the leaf I choose, Lance, even after everything.'

As she's talking, she finds the red slip of cotton and hops about till she's got first her pants and then her trousers on.

Then, she stands there looking lost for a second before grabbing up her eyepatch from the side and putting that on too. She waits, a moment more, and then another, and then she nods once to herself, as though at a job done, if not well, then servingly, and then she goes.

Lance gets up as he hears the front door close and goes into the living room, over to the curtain, pulling it back to watch her stick her foot in the stirrup and spring up on to Boxer's back. At the gate she turns in the saddle and raises a hand to him.

The grey heads off down the lane towards the cycle path.

That is the last time I will see her, he thinks.

And then, *If she turns to wave one more time, just once, then I will see her again . . .*

And then, *And even if she doesn't . . .*

54

Look to It, Uncle

——

The conference room is packed with those that remain after the bloodbath of sackings, after all the walkouts and resignations. It's been quite the meeting, what with Mo announcing that he will be joining Gal in taking over the company reins.

'Our aim,' Gal says, 'is to make the business compostable. Can we return to our former strength? I believe so. But no empire is immortal. We will rebuild, making our legacy central to everything we do. We will show the world what an ethical, sustainable company looks like, or perish in the attempt.'

Gal pauses, eyes moving over the upturned faces, gaze lingering here and there. Finally, they bring the silence to an end.

'Now, I'm going to outline some changes you can expect ahead.' Very quickly the non-technical staff become lost. They watch the faces of those who are keeping up. Is the news good? Is it bad? Did that intake of breath denote horror or excitement? Are they on a sinking ship or one that's going places?

On balance, it seems like the latter.

While Gal talks, Mo makes a few online orders: a personalised number plate that says DADDY, an earring that says DADDY, a fat gold chain that says GRANNY, and then, because an encompassing flood of love lifts him like a wave, one more that says GRANDPA.

'Mo?' Gal turns to him.

'Right, yes.' He pops his phone down on the table, gets to his feet, and lists the latest quarterly figures, the divestments they'll be making, an acquisition he and Gal pulled off over jackfruit tacos.

If meat be the price of love, he'll willingly pay it.

When he's done, he looks around the table, channelling young and fun and absolutely not to be fucked with.

'And we're hiring so spread the word. No psychopaths, mind you.'

When they're all filing out, Kay storms in, so full of poison, he knows he has to get it out or it'll burst within him and he'll die of it.

'You're going to run it into the ground, everything we built.'

'I hope you're not going to be a fanatic about this,' Gal says.

'Have some dignity, Kay,' Mo adds.

'You pair of little snowflakes!'

'That's Boss Nephew Snowflake to you, Uncle Kay!' And Mo slaps him on the shoulder before turning and moonwalking from the room. 'See you at the fete.'

55

Avalon

———

There would be the tombola and there would be the coconut shy. Over there is the lucky dip and there is the cake stall. There, you can guess the number of sweeties in an enormous jar, and over there you can hook a plastic duck from a paddling pool with a long stick. A queue of children line up to ride Nedward around the field, a five-minute go for a pound.

Don't kick him now, don't kick him or he'll bite . . .

Over at the town hall you can rifle through the jumble or buy a yellowing paperback: a bodice ripper or an unsolved murder. Something to pass a few hours.

Taking the twenty- and fifty-pence pieces are the old, the white of hair and pink of skin. In trousers or skirts with flesh-coloured tights, shirts or blouses. A cardigan, a blazer, a windcheater over the back of a chair – old flesh feels the cold and it could come on to rain. You can't be too careful.

See the comb marks in what's left of the men's hair, the shine on their shoes, the pocket squares. See the old ladies' short curly perms, the gold wedding rings stuck behind swollen knuckles. They too came here as children. They too had their turn at the lucky dip, their go on Nedward.

In the marquee, there's tea, coffee or Pimm's, fresh strawberries with cream, a slice of Victoria sponge. Later on the vicar's wife will judge the roses.

'It makes me want to puke, Arthur,' Morgan says. Then, 'Do you have sixty p? They've got coconut ice. I haven't had coconut ice in sheer time.'

On the whole, Arthur is ignored. He minds less and less.

'How's Gwen?' he asks.

'I think it's fair to say that Gwen is in a giving mood,' Morgan says.

'Like . . . money?'

'Yes . . .' Morgan hesitates. 'But not only that. For starters, she's filling up the house with women. Anyone who needs or wants a place to stay. Yesterday, a group of Bulgarian lady fruit-pickers turned up after an argument with a farmer. Now they're camping on the lawn, Arthur.' In the small field next to the church, men are taking off their shirts and eyeing up a young Wiltshire Horn. It's an Abury tradition; in the old days, after haymaking, a sheep would be set loose in the meadow and the mower who caught it kept it. These days the winner takes half the pot of entry fees and the farmer gets his sheep back.

Above, in the June sky, larks are singing. Over by some bales of hay, a bold barefoot girl demands to be allowed a go. The farmer prevaricates but, in the end, he takes her money. In their heart of hearts, who doesn't want to see her run? The catchers spread out around the fence and the farmer launches his sheep into the field. The girl, long hair swinging, is off. How fast she is, how fleet, darting between the men while her friends whoop and cheer.

Just as she's about to get a hand to the woolly coat, the girl slips and the sheep is gone, bleating and zigging-and-zagging until it's cornered and then rugby-tackled by one of the younger players from the football team.

'Who won last year?'

'Lance. Lance always won it,' Arthur says. He has not seen Lance. It is harder to forgive a friend than a lover. The standards are higher, as is the institution.

The girl has climbed back over the fence and is being consoled by her mates. A boy thrusts a can of beer at her. She bends to kiss the mouth of a round girl with plaits and Morgan feels a pang.

'Do you remember Hocktide?' Arthur says.

'Of course.' At Hocktide, the girls chase the boys and capture them. They have to pay a penny to be freed which the girls must give to the church.

'I don't want to be let go,' Arthur says. They walk a little further. 'I mean, Mo can run the company, up the hill or into the ground or wherever he wants. Apple called, you know. Once they heard. Did you know they have an island? They've invited me there, to lick my wounds and think about my future, but I don't know. I thought I might be of use. To you, I mean. You're not going to stop, are you? I want to . . . I want to atone. I'm not unskilled.'

'We'll see,' Morgan says and Arthur's heart leaps up, joyous as Cavall when he spots a rabbit.

If there is no forgiveness, who will be willing to be held accountable?

On the market square, the bunting is out, and in the garden of the Green Knight, Wayne stands behind a barbecue cooking sausages and burgers. Smoke blows over the picnic tables.

'I hear you're moving on,' Arthur says.

Wayne nods.

'Where are you off to?'

'I have to find something. I have to hope I'll know it when I see it.'

Morgan fetches pints. Lou's behind the bar, teeth glistening, beehive slightly askew.

'I'm not saying they don't exist, John. I'm just not sure I believe you saw them.'

In the garden, the sun warms old stone. Linnet comes by with the kids and Mo pushes Angelo on the swings until he shrieks.

Vern emerges to bring in the empties and whispers something in Wayne's ear, cheek to cheek, his arm around Wayne's shoulder.

Gal and Hung hunch over Hung's phone typing into the translation engine.

'Press play. Yes, that one,' Gal says.

You're all fucking crazy, the phone says. Hung repeats the phrase, savouring it. 'You're all fucking crazy.' Yesterday he called his grandmother and told her he had a plane ticket to Hanoi. Her joy was tempered with worry. There have been people looking for him, people asking questions.

Mo comes and sits beside him. 'I've been thinking, seeing as I'm going to stick around here, maybe you should take Wayne with you.' He points Wayne out to Hung. 'He's a handy man in a tight spot and he fancies a wander.'

Kay trails Linnet about, Lily asleep over his shoulder. 'I just want you to come back to the house, Linnet. I'm begging you.'

'Should have thought of that before you asked that monster to be her godfather!'

The day fades, the fairy lights are turned on. No one wants to go home. Not just yet. Just a little bit longer.

Music starts up some distance off. The silver band are playing on the market square. When they're done, they come by to wet their whistles and Vern promises them a free tab for the night if they'll play a few songs to please the crowd. The band leader says they will, after a break.

At dusk, Jude arrives with a daughter in a pushchair and a tense-looking husband.

'Mo,' she says softly, 'I'd like you to meet Mattie and Ben.'

Gal takes Mo's hand and squeezes it and Mo shuffles to his feet. 'I promise,' he says, 'I promise—'

But what he promises can only be heard by those closest as the band start tuning up over at the stone trough.

Eight bars in and the courtyard has filled with dancers. Dancers graceful and clumsy, shy and exuberant. The drunk and the sober. Little Lily swinging from John's hand.

Meeting each other in the crowd, Morgan steps into Gwen's arms and they hold fast to one another, cheek pressed against cheek, swaying from side to side, fast song or slow song regardless. How light they feel on their feet, almost as though they are girls again.

Night beckons. Shadows slip among the dancers. The band play on until, at last, they lower their instruments.

'One more,' the crowd call out, 'just one more!'

They stamp their feet. They whistle. They beg. *A little more music. A little more time.* And eventually the band concede. One last song, just one more.

The band leader whispers something to the players and they nod.

The crowd fall silent. What will it be?

It begins softly and the listeners are still, waiting for the moment of recognition.

It is an old song, played differently. *I don't know this one*, they think. And then, *Or maybe I do . . .*

A song heard in childhood, or in youth, a melody from the soundtrack to a film, something heard on the radio when you were half asleep. A song you dreamed up or heard at a party. A song belonging to a warrior queen five thousand years dead.

One you don't know and have always known.

Finally, the band bring it to an end. The musicians lower their instruments. The dancers step apart. The band leader wipes the sweat from her brow, turns to the gathered people and smiles.

'That's the way we do it, folks. If you don't like it, you can sing it your own way!'

Author's Note

Early on in the writing of this novel, on my way from my home in Berlin to a writing residency in Scotland, I became marooned in Wiltshire. In those very strange days of spring 2020, as the world got its first taste of lockdown, I spent a lot of time looking out of my parents' living-room window at Liddington Castle, a Bronze Age hillfort rumoured to be the site of Arthur Pendragon's penultimate battle.

The roads and skies, emptied of traffic, grew quiet. Out walking along the Ridgeway, something nagged at me. Reality was echoing a book I had read more than thirty years before. With the Internet's help, I was able to identify it as *The Weathermonger* by Peter Dickinson, in which Merlin, newly awoken from a thousand-year sleep, casts a spell causing Britain to turn against technology and return to the Dark Ages. Among the ruins at Snap (yes, a real place!), the land itself seemed to reverberate with hoofbeats and the chink of armour.

Bliss & Blunder too is full of echoes. I would like to acknowledge as sources first Sir Thomas Malory's immortal *Morte d'Arthur*, and then the works of Chrétien de Troyes, the twelfth-century French poet whose works Malory himself plundered; Tennyson's *Idylls of the King*; T. S. Eliot's *The Wasteland*; Simon Armitage's translation of *Sir Gawain and the Green Knight*; and the fascinating, transporting anthology, *Anglo-Saxon Poetry*, edited by S. A. J. Bradley were also greatly inspirational.

When I set out on my first draft, I had no intention of dragging Shakespeare into it. But then John Falstaff turned up at the Green Knight and it's fair to say that in Chapter 38, I mercilessly pillaged *Henry IV Part I*. No doubt John would approve.

In writing about the British Army and Afghanistan, *Dead Men Risen* by Toby Harden and *The Changing of the Guard* by Simon Akram were particularly illuminating. For anyone wanting further insight into Arthur's business, *The Boy Kings* by Katherine Losse, *There's a War Going On But No One Can See It* by Huib Modderkolk and *The Age of Surveillance Capitalism* by Shoshana Zuboff are brilliant, unnerving reads.

Of course, there are other books that contributed to this one, far too many to list here. Besides, I cannot remember all their names. They were among the hundreds I borrowed as a child from the Wroughton Library – *Et in Arcadia ego*.

Victoria Gosling
Wiltshire, 2023

Acknowledgements

——

This book is dedicated to Abbie, the sister I acquired at birth – inspiration and pace-setter! And to the memory of Sophie Raphaeline, the sister I acquired at Another Country, Berlin, one of the greatest bookshops the world has ever seen. Sophie ran Another Country for a quarter of a century and her hospitality, generosity, and support for readers, writers and the LGBTQ+ community is the stuff of legend. We miss you, Sophie!

Many thanks to everyone at Serpent's Tail: to director Rebecca Gray, who believed in my writing enough to buy this book before I knew anything about it; to my fantastic editor, Leonora Craig Cohen, whose tireless support, enthusiasm and excellence in all fields have kept me afloat; to Anna-Marie Fitzgerald, Emily Frisella, publicist Rebecca Gray, Hannah Westland and Sarah-Jane Forder.

My sincerest gratitude to my agent, the wonderful Judith Murray of Greene & Heaton, who planted the seed for *Bliss & Blunder*. I'm thankful to Jane Flett, Tom Pugh and Divya Ghelani for their invaluable feedback on early drafts, and to Lucy Carson of the Friedrich Agency for her sharp eyes and general brilliance. Also my cousin, Ian Knight, family techie, who looked the manuscript over for me.

During the writing of this book, I was lucky enough to undertake two residencies. I offer heartfelt thanks to Foundation OBRAS – Ludger, Carolien, Flor – a truly wonderful organisation in Portugal that offers peace, space and refuge to writers and artists. Also to Hawthornden Castle and its benevolent guardians, Hamish, Mary, Debbie and Ruth, and to my jolly good fellow fellows, Miranda Doyle, Georgie Cod and Holly. I'm deeply indebted to the Berlin Senate for Culture and Europe for the generous research stipend awarded me in 2021.

As always, infinite gratitude to my family for their boundless kindness and support, and to Gijs for his good company and for helping me come back down to earth.

Finally, much, much love to my maiden-knights: all the girls who shared teenage kicks with me – especially Sian, Anna, Emily, Rachel, Kerry, Emma N, Lou, Rosie, Bridget, Emma G, Kirsty, Ellie, Liz, Leila, Inga, Sinead, Kirsten, Ana and Jen.